Arundel: Legacy of Duncan

Arundel: Legacy of Duncan

◆

Book One: Demise of the Black Paladin

A Novel

Thomas D. McAleese

iUniverse, Inc.

New York Lincoln Shanghai

Arundel: Legacy of Duncan
Book One: Demise of the Black Paladin

iUniverse books may be ordered through booksellers or by contacting:

iUniverse
2021 Pine Lake Road, Suite 100
Lincoln, NE 68512
www.iuniverse.com
1-800-Authors (1-800-288-4677)

Because of the dynamic nature of the Internet, any Web addresses or links contained in this book may have changed since publication and may no longer be valid.

This is a work of fiction. All of the characters, names, incidents, organizations, and dialogue in this novel are either the products of the author's imagination or are used fictitiously.

ISBN: 978-0-595-46057-1 (pbk)
ISBN: 978-0-595-90356-6 (ebk)

Printed in the United States of America

To my parents for giving me the ability to write this book and my beautiful wife for her encouragement and endless typing, thank-you

For my much loved cats, Patches and Big Cat, gone for so long now but never forgotten, you are immortalized in print for everyone to marvel over. You were always larger than life and the best companions anyone could ever wish for.

A special thank-you to Nancy Haggith and her 2006 Grade 10 English class at Valley Heights Secondary School for being my first test audience.

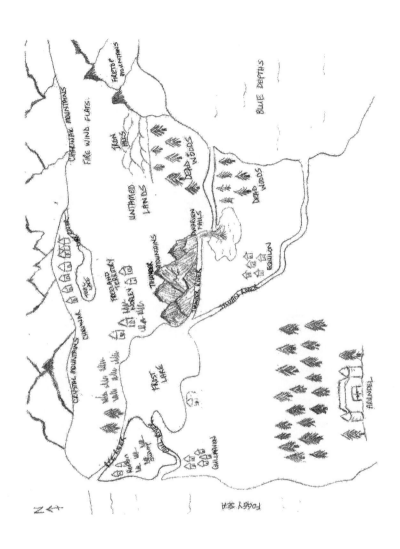

Chapter One

Nearly four feet tall at the shoulder, fur white as snow, the winter-wolves were in pursuit of their prey. With breath that could freeze a man, they were formidable opponents and that is why their master sent them. Streamers of ice cold mist trailed from their snouts and their earsplitting howls rent the stormy night air.

They had been running forever it seemed, and the young prince was tired and scared. Just a few short hours ago, he had seen his mother and father, the king and queen of the realm, killed right before his eyes by the evil Draskene. Duncan's whole world had been taken away from him and now he and the last two of his father's Royal Knights were running for their lives.

The trio crashed through the undergrowth of the old forest and hid behind the bole of a large tree. The moonless night and cloudy sky made the darkness of the forest all but impenetrable. Martyl, the younger of the two knights, peered around the massive trunk, looking for any signs of pursuit.

"I don't see anyone behind us, Connor," he panted, his large chest rising and falling with each gulp of air.

"They follow, fear not," replied the older knight wearily. "The Black Paladin will not rest until he has destroyed all that remains of King Aramid's court, even though it is only two knights and a boy prince."

As if punctuating his statement, the ground shook as thunder tore across the night sky and flashes of lightning illuminated the thick clouds. Wolf howls followed the thunder and the baying drew ever nearer.

"Hurry. We must continue on!" urged Connor. "The Black Paladin has winter-wolves in his employ and I fear that is what we just heard."

Grabbing the young prince by the hand, Connor set off at the fastest pace Duncan could maintain on his short legs. It was difficult to see every obstacle that lay before them in the darkness and several times they stumbled and fell or were struck by low hanging branches.

Although he was a prince and taught to be brave, Duncan was not yet even ten years old and had already seen his parents murdered and was now running for his very life. His breath was coming in gasps now as he struggled to keep up the relentless pace the two knights set. The howls of the winter-wolves drew closer and his pulse quickened.

Suddenly, a dark figure exploded out of the thick brush to their right and hurtled into Martyl who was in the lead. Both knights recognized what it was even in the dim light. Man-sized but covered in a scaly hide and thick tufts of hair, it was a demon, summoned from the netherworld by the Black Paladin. Its eyes shined bright red and slimy ichor oozed from its skin.

Connor released Duncan's hand and leapt forward at the demon, drawing a silvery dagger with a ten-inch blade from his belt. He was anxious to keep the beast where it was, away from the prince.

"Foolish mortal," it hissed between fanged teeth. "Your weapons cannot harm me!"

"Back fiend," warned Connor in a low growl of a voice. "This is no ordinary dagger. It is Sliver, forged long ago from part of a falling star. It has enough magic to send you back to your hell where you belong."

He lunged, the star-silver blade glinting magically, even in the shadowed darkness of the forest. The demon's sureness of its invulnerability seemed somewhat daunted as the blade's name registered in its mind. It had no desire to be killed, yet it dare not let its master, the Black Paladin, see it afraid of a mere mortal. He feinted to the left of Connor's lunge and tried to circle to his side but the Man at Arms, the King's combat trainer for all the knights, was much too quick, even for this unnatural creature.

Connor dropped to one knee and as the demon leapt he raised his left arm to push the demon away as they rolled on the leaf littered ground. The demon was tearing at Connor's leather tunic with its vicious claws as he brought his right hand around, plunging Sliver's blade deep into the demon's side. It was a killing blow but Connor twisted the blade ninety degrees then wrenched it free, just to be sure.

"Are you all right?" asked a distraught Martyl. He was visibly shaken by what had just occurred and was trying his best to compose himself. In all his twenty-five years he had never seen a demon before. They had been the stuff of legend that old knights told young squires to frighten them around banquet tables. But now he had seen one, all scales and tufts of coarse hair, reeking of rotted meat and stale air. He brushed at his leather armour where it had touched him, checking for any unseen damage.

"I'm fine," replied Connor, a little shaken himself. "I did not think that the Black Paladin's power was great enough to summon demons from other planes of existence but it seems his power has grown. We must hasten away. You will have to carry Duncan from here on."

Without another word, Connor set off at a run and Martyl, carrying Duncan, followed closely behind. The sounds of pursuit began to fade as they evaded their followers, Connor's knowledge of the countryside surrounding the castle proving its worth.

Eventually they made their way to the free city-state of Gullhaven and set sail to the west, not knowing exactly where they would go. Ancient legends told of a lost kingdom known as the Misty Isles. It was here that Connor hoped he, Duncan and Martyl could seek sanctuary until the time came to return to Arundel and avenge their fallen King.

After three weeks at sea they came upon an impenetrable fog to which no end could be seen. They sailed blindly on for another two days before the mists parted and a most beautiful sight was seen.

A large island loomed before them, with long sandy beaches peopled with swimmers. Behind the beaches were rolling hills, full of long, soft, green grass. Birds circled and called overhead to announce their arrival and a peculiar singing could be heard faintly above the crash of the waves.

The people on the beaches stood and watched them come ashore, a mixed look of surprise and distrust on their faces as they saw this was not one of their ships. Still, there were three tired and weary souls on board who needed assistance.

Their ship lurched to a grinding halt on the pebbly beach and the singing stopped. All watched in awe as Connor jumped into the warm water, knee deep and waded ashore, his legs weak with fatigue and wobbly from time spent at sea.

"In the name of the King of Arundel, I demand sanctuary."

From on the deck, Duncan and Martyl heard the singing again and began to feel even more tired. The last thing Duncan remembered before crashing into the deck was seeing Connor fall below the water.

When he awoke next, Duncan found himself in a small room with a cot, upon which he lay, and a table and a chair. On the table was a wash basin, full of warm water, and a towel. He rose and walked to the door which was closed but not locked. He opened the door and looked out.

"Ah, you're awake young sir," said the man at the door.

Duncan looked at him and noticed how deep green his eyes were and how fair his hair was, almost white. When he saw his hands, however, he gasped and stepped back.

"Ah, my hands frighten you, do they?" he queried.

Duncan nodded, but couldn't take his eyes off the webbing between the man's fingers.

"Wash up," he said. "I'll get your friends."

Duncan went back into his room and washed his face, his young mind still trying to comprehend what he had seen when Connor and Martyl walked in.

"Duncan, lad, I'm glad to see you up and about," said Connor cheerfully. "I have much to tell you about what has happened. Clean up, for we are about to meet with the King of this fair island."

As Duncan washed, Connor and Martyl related to him the events that had transpired while he slept for the past day, recovering from the arduous journey they underwent.

They found the Misty Isles of legend, and they were inhabited by Sirens, people who spent nearly as much time in the water as they did on land. The singing they heard was the Sirens, and they used their songs to lull strangers to sleep if they approached within sight of their kingdom. Then they would set them adrift at sea again, their memory of the islands forgotten, to remain unknown. Somehow, they had penetrated the mists and reached the shore without succumbing to the songs. The Kings of the Misty Isles, after hearing of their plight, wanted to meet them.

Duncan finished washing and the three were escorted to the King's chambers. Along the way, the trio noticed the artwork was very different from that of their people. Great frescoes and murals depicted scenes of men and women swimming with dolphins in waters as clear blue as the sky.

Other pictures showed what appeared to be royalty, a King and Queen perhaps, upon their thrones and at the side of each a large cat. All the Sirens they saw, men and women, in the flesh or in the paintings were very fair with liquid green eyes, the colour of the deep sea.

As they approached the King's chambers their eyes grew wide at the sight before them.

Sitting on their hunches, one with each of the guards at the door, were two cats. No ordinary cats, however, for these looked like domestic cats except for their immense size—standing about two feet high at the shoulder and about four feet long from head to tail when they stood to meet the trio's approach.

"Wait here, I will inform the King of your arrival," ordered one of the Sirens in their escort.

Being just a boy and not knowing the danger of large animals, not to mention being a cat lover, Duncan reached out to pet the great cats before anyone realized what he was doing.

"Caution, young one," scolded one of the guards. "These cats do not take kindly to strangers."

However, to everyone's surprise, especially the Sirens, the cats began to purr and rub themselves against Duncan who only smiled and replied innocently, "Cats love me."

The doors opened and the trio was ushered in, the doors closing behind them. They stood in a room, about two hundred square feet with a large pool in the centre, about fifty feet wide by one hundred feet long, and a channel running from the east side of the pool across the room and under the wall to the outside somewhere. Presumably, thought Connor, to the ocean as they must've been close to hear the crashing of the waves.

In the pool, a dolphin swam about, coming over to a man at the pool's edge to be petted then swimming away.

"Hello," he called out. "I am King Kestewan. And you are the strangers from Arundel. How do you do?" He rose and began to stride across the room to them and from the far corner of the room behind came two more of the great cats, bounding to his side.

"Do not be alarmed," he said, raising a webbed palm to them in greeting. "These cats are very well trained. They won't attack unless provoked."

"You are a very trusting man, King Kestewan," interrupted Connor, "to leave yourself unguarded in a room with three strangers."

"Should I fear you?" replied the King. "Besides, I am more than amply protected by these cats. Do not let the fact that they look like overgrown pets fool you. They are very formidable adversaries."

He was now facing the trio, only a few feet away. Like all the other Sirens they had seen to this date, he had liquid green eyes and very fair hair, almost white. He wore light blue shorts and a loose fitting shirt of a blue colour also. Very odd clothing indeed, they thought, for a King.

"I have heard a little of your journey," continued Kestewan. "Please, fill me in on the rest. And who is your King, in whose name do you demand sanctuary?"

"This is our King," replied Connor, pointing to Duncan at his side.

"He is but a child," remarked Kestewan.

"I am almost ten," remarked Duncan in as deep a voice he could muster. Connor couldn't help but smile and thought, "I could almost see King Aramid standing beside me when he said that."

"May we sit, King Kestewan?" asked Connor. "We have a long tale to relate."

"Certainly. Come with me." With that he led them to the poolside where they sat on benches and Connor began to relate their tale. Martyl, amazed with the dolphin, watched it splash and swim about in the water, its graceful, fluent movement helping bring a calm peace to his tumultuous thoughts.

Duncan, to the King's amazement, had completely won over the two big cats' confidence and was busy playing with them. A funny sight, he thought, to see a child playing so fearlessly with two animals his own size, animals that were used to kill and protect against strangers.

When Connor finished his retelling of the events leading up to their escape, Kestewan commented.

"A very intriguing story, I grieve deeply for your loss. We are a peaceful people and have had no wars for over four hundred years. That is why we have kept our whereabouts secret. We do not wish outside interference. Those ships that do find their way here, as you've already been told, are sent back to sea, their crews' memories erased of the event by our songs.

"You, however, and your two comrades, were allowed to stay because of the extenuating circumstances. I must have your word, though, that if you leave here, you will say nothing of our location."

"As a Knight of the Kingdom of Arundel, you have my solemn word that I will not betray your trust, your highness," pledged Connor, then Martyl, both on one knee, head down, to the King of the Misty Isles.

"And you have my word, as the King of Arundel," stated Duncan, his eyes meeting those of Kestewan's.

Kestewan smiled and replied, "Thank you, young King."

As the years passed, Duncan grew into a strong young man, almost a mirror image of his father. He didn't have quite his height, standing only 5'10" but he had a broad, well defined build. His thick, wavy brown hair gave him a young, boyish look and his worry free life left him no unseemly age marks.

Everyday Connor and Martyl would train Duncan in the arts of combat, with and without weapons, so that he would be prepared when the day came to reclaim his father's throne for his own from the Black Paladin.

Other things interested Duncan as well, and he sought recreation of the mind and spirit to help him keep things in perspective. He found himself particularly drawn to the large cats on the island. He learned from the Sirens that in their past, when they were a warrior people, they used them as animals of war. Being cats, they were naturally much more vicious than dogs as well as being instinctively better trackers and hunters, not to mention more intelligent. It just took a more intelligent person, or in this case Siren, to co-exist with them.

It was also found that these cats had an inherent, although limited psychic ability in that they would bond emotionally with their chosen Siren. They could feel empathically their thoughts, sensing when they were in danger, hurt or distressed.

Over time, though, as the Sirens became civilized, the need for the great cats as war animals was eliminated and they were bred to become smaller. They were still larger than anything Duncan had seen, standing almost two feet at the shoulder, four feet in length and weighing about thirty pounds!

The other thing that interested Duncan, as he grew older was Salena, King Kestewan's daughter. She was a few years his junior and the most beautiful thing he had ever seen in his life. Like all her people she had webbing between her toes and fingers to aid in swimming but her green eyes and long fair hair held his gaze captive whenever he looked upon her.

Salena was just as captivated with Duncan's rugged good looks and strong body as well as his warrior training which both intrigued and excited her. They grew up together, never far from one another's sides. Salena would sit and patiently watch Duncan as he trained with Connor and Martyl daily. Then, when he was finished, the two would go for walks in the forests and along the beaches, Salena explaining this or that that caught Duncan's attention.

She told him the history of her people, how they turned from a warrior people to a peaceful race. They kept their cats now mainly as pets, but some were still used for guard duty. As they evolved emotionally and philosophically, they also evolved physically. The Sirens began spending more time in the sea as they had mastered their islands. Eventually they became so adapted to the water they grew webbing to aid in swimming and learned the use of their sleep song from the dolphins who populated these waters.

The use of the song was very important to Connor and he tried to learn it and to get Duncan or Martyl to learn but to their dismay it could only be used by the Sirens. It also only worked in close proximity to the water. This frustrated them as they realized its value in combatting their enemy, the Black Paladin.

As the years passed, Duncan and Salena were inseparable and their hearts became entwined together. Duncan knew that she was the one he would spend the rest of his life with but only one thing stood in the way.

Salena's father, King Kestewan, would not let her marry anyone less than royalty and until he reclaimed his father's throne, he would not recognize Duncan as true royalty. Still, his life on the Misty Isles was pleasant and he and Salena were always allowed to be together and King Kestewan treated him with respect.

After fifteen years on the Isles, though, Duncan's life took another bitter turn. He and Salena were out walking on the beach one day when Martyl, now a middle-aged man, came running down to them, calling to Duncan.

"What is it, Martyl?" he asked.

"It's Connor," Martyl replied, breathless. "He has taken ill and wishes to see you, urgently."

Without another word, the two raced off, leaving Salena to wonder alone what had happened.

"Duncan, lad, come here so I can see you. You know my eyesight is failing," said Connor as Duncan and Martyl reached his room.

Duncan's face showed his sorrow and fear for his friend despite his best efforts to hide it. He had known Connor was ailing for several months now but he never could admit he may actually lose him one day. On the bed before him lay Connor, the strongest, bravest man he had known in his life, his father's Man at Arms for an entire army, stricken with old age and sickness. He knelt at Connor's side, taking his hand in his, squeezing tight, as if he might impart some of his strength and youth to his old mentor.

"I am dying, lad. I am an old man taken ill. I do not have much life left in my old body. Hopefully I have taught you all you will need to know to regain what is yours. My only regret is that I will not be at your side when you do so."

"You'll be alright soon, Connor," said Duncan emotionally.

"No, Duncan," replied Connor. "I have been ill for some time and I fear my time is now up. King Kestewan's physicians have done their best to help me but my time has come. Do not grieve for me Duncan. I have lived a long productive life and I hope the same for you. You are a fine boy and I would be proud to call you my son. You have been through a great deal in your short life already. Not many people would grow as straight and true as you after losing their mother and father right before their eyes. They would be very proud of you now, Duncan. I know they would. Take Sliver. It is all I have left to give you." With that, Connor lay silent and returned Duncan's grip on his hand.

Duncan sat at Connor's side all night, never releasing his hold on Connor, even through his fitful sleep. When Salena came in at dawn to wake him, Connor was already gone. Duncan rose, a lump in his throat so large he thought he would choke but he refused to shed a tear, trying to show he was strong.

"I must return to my homeland and take what is rightfully mine," he said, his voice like stones on slate. "I have tarried too long already."

The next couple of days were spent getting ready for the voyage. Duncan was silent and moody, keeping to himself until it was time to leave. He met with King Kestewan one final time. Not a meeting of King to young man but a meeting of equals.

"I wish you the best of luck, Duncan," said King Kestewan. "I have a couple of 'items' to send with you," he finished with a smile.

Duncan looked at him quizzically until a door in the King's chamber opened and out bounded Big Cat and Patches, the King's personal guard cats. They ran past the King to Duncan's side where they began purring.

"Yes. You may take them with you. I don't think I could stop them anyway. They seem to be quite taken by you. Amazing, really, even though these cats are loyal to their master by nature they have shown more attachment to you than they ever have to me."

"Thank you, your highness," Duncan replied, a slight lift in his voice. "But your people seem to have missed the fact that we are not their masters, only their friends."

"Maybe that is why they are so taken to you," replied the King with a chuckle in his voice.

From out of the shadows stepped Salena, tears in her eyes. She stopped at her father's side, staring Duncan in the eye.

"Please, don't leave," she sobbed.

"I must," Duncan replied, stepping forward to hold her in his arms, his own heart breaking for the second time in a week. His emotions tore at his heart like vicious demons. Anger and commitment to his vow of revenge tearing at one side while love and sorrow for leaving Salena tearing at the other.

"I will return for you, my love," he finished. Duncan gave her a kiss that seemed to last an eternity yet was over before it had begun for them.

He turned and stalked out of the chamber to his waiting ship, not looking back for fear of crying, his heart breaking all the way. The two cats followed solemnly beside him, not looking back either.

Chapter Two

Dawn broke over the horizon, the sun sending its brilliant streamers of light through the tree branches of the small camp. Duncan rose, not very refreshed from his first sleep on the mainland. Memories of his past life in the Misty Isles still lingered in the corners of his mind, wispy shadows with no substance, just out of reach of his conscious mind.

The two great cats rose, stretching and yawning silently. Although not bothered by dreams or unpleasant memories, they did feel Duncan's uneasiness and went to him to comfort him, rubbing their large heads against his side, purring away.

Too distracted by his thoughts, Duncan paid them no heed at first until their rubbing into became more insistent, almost knocking him over with their great size.

"Okay, okay," chuckled Duncan, a little more cheerful. The cats always had that effect on him. "Let's eat, then we'll be on our way."

The young man and his two cats sat down to a quick breakfast of cheese, bread and berries, dried meat for the cats, washed down with some water from a stoppered flask.

He had only been on the mainland for one day and already the memories of his boyhood escape came flooding back. Duncan had hoped he would be spared those unpleasant thoughts but he was mistaken. It was just the fact that he was home for the first time in fifteen years, he told himself, that he was feeling uneasy. He wouldn't let his father and mother down, no matter what.

Still, he had no idea how he would reclaim his father's kingdom or even where it was, for that matter. He was just a boy when he left and now to return, fifteen years later, he was a stranger to this land. Duncan also didn't know how he would defeat the Black Paladin. Draskene had the ability to summon demons and other otherworldly creatures. All he had was Sliver and there wasn't enough magic left in the dagger to kill such a powerful opponent.

Doubt and despair began to creep into his mind. The task before him seemed hopeless. He had such an easy life back on the Misty Isles. And Salena. She was alone without him. How he wanted to return!

No! part of his mind shouted, sweeping away the doubt and despair like dust on the floor. He had to go on, he had to succeed. Martyl and Connor believed in him, he had to do it. Duncan rose quickly and hurriedly packed up his few belongings into his pack and after calling the cats to his side, set off south to Gullhaven.

Although he was essentially a stranger to his homeland, Duncan knew that Gullhaven was only three days march south from where Kestewan's ship had left him. They had sailed past it on the coast to drop him off in a secluded spot. What he didn't realize, though, that the path he had chosen to follow led directly into the heart of a swamp. This was terrain that he was not used to. Growing up with Connor and Martyl, he never did much exploring as most young boys would have and therefore didn't experience the hazards of swamp travel. His time had been spent training with weapons and learning how to kill.

Duncan and his two great cats trudged along through the swamp, trying to avoid the quicksand and large snakes that lived in it. Patches led the way, his large grey and white body moving lithely through the creepers, vines and shrubs that grew in the fetid swamp. Duncan followed, picking his way gingerly through the growth, not quite as agile as the cats, to be sure not to fall in any quicksand.

Bringing up the rear was Big Cat, her orange and black bulk sashaying along. Despite her somewhat larger size and girth than

Patches, she was still extremely agile and quite good at jumping and leaping.

As the day wore on, the three became increasingly agitated. The cats' tails beat a steady tattoo as they swatted at the flying insects milling about them. The incessant buzzing began to wear on Duncan. His booted feet scuffed along, no longer lifting for each step. The blue pants he wore were now brown with dried, caked on mud. To ward off the insects, Duncan had his heavy cloak pulled tight about him, hood up and sleeves down. He was sweating heavily, his brow dripping into his eyes, stinging and blurring his vision. At least, he thought, I'm not getting bitten anymore.

The cats also were fatigued, their heavy fur kept the insects off them but the heat bore down on them worse than Duncan. Their fur was matted with clumps of dried earth and they smelled horrible.

They ambled on a little further when Duncan called a halt. The cats looked at him, almost thankful, he thought, as he looked at their dirtied faces. A smile came to his face and for the first time in over two weeks, he laughed. Slowly at first, then uncontrollably as his tension and fears let loose. He felt bad for laughing at the cats but they just looked so funny like that. Duncan would not let himself cry but he could laugh. Strange, he thought, to show one emotion but not another. But he promised his father when he was a boy he wouldn't cry, that he would be a man.

The three sat down on a half submerged log, the remains of a tree long ago fallen. Vines and creepers hung about them, casting eerie shadows as the sun began to set. Crickets began to chirp and frogs croaked, finally sounds other than the buzzing insects to fill their thoughts.

Other, more ominous sounds reached them as well, though. Moans and shrieks could be heard, some cut off short in mid-scream. Duncan shivered, images of what was causing the shrieks running through his already tortured mind. He did feel comforted in the fact that he had his two cats with him. The two largest and strongest of all the great cats from the Misty Isles, once the King's own personal guard cats, now his. However, one disturbing thought kept running through his mind—these cats aren't native to this land. What if there are creatures here even more formidable?

Duncan refused to dwell on such dreadful thoughts. Patches mmrowed to him and both cats rubbed their heads in his palms to be petted, a look on their faces as if saying "Don't worry about us. We can handle it."

Once again he smiled, realizing just how lucky he was to have such great cats. Opening his pack, Duncan gave each cat about half a pound of dried meat and himself some cheese and bread, washed down with a few mouthfuls of water.

"I hope we reach the end of this swamp soon because at the rate you cats eat, we'll be out of food in another two days," Duncan said to the cats matter-of-factly.

Laying his pack down for a pillow on the spongy earth, Duncan curled up in his cloak to sleep. He knew that even though he was alone, with no-one to keep watch, he could sleep peacefully knowing the cats would be awake long before any danger approached.

Tired from the day's long journey, Duncan fell into a deep, dreamless sleep. He was awakened though, halfway through the night by the cats' growling. Sitting bolt upright, Duncan peered about in the gloom. Fog and mist shrouded almost everything from his view except for Patches and Big Cat, hair standing on end, ears back and fangs barred. They were standing between Duncan and the way they came, growling at the mist. Although he couldn't see anything, Duncan could hear something large crashing through the undergrowth, coming their way, perhaps only a quarter mile away.

"Easy guys," soothed Duncan. He slung his pack over his back quickly and said, "C'mon. Let's get going. I don't like the sounds of whatever is out there."

Big Cat backed up slowly to Duncan's side them turned to lead the way. Duncan followed, but Patches, not one to run from anything, stood his guard.

"Patches, come on. Now!"

The cat turned, looking at Duncan as if to say, "Alright, this time."

Their second day in the swamp was even less enjoyable than the first. They were now almost exhausted from running all night and early this day but Duncan feared to stop, lest whatever was following them gained ground.

The lack of sleep and food, along with fear began to make him think he was hallucinating. Every once in a while he could swear he heard someone calling his name. The cats heard it too, he thought, or maybe they just stopped to listen because he did. Who could be calling him, he wondered. No one knew him here. Finally he let the thoughts slip from his mind, sure it was only the swamp's sounds playing tricks on his mind.

On they ran, the day passing into late afternoon. The fog and mist began to settle. First about their feet then it grew thicker and deeper, rising to their knees. Patches led the way, nimble and surefooted as always. Duncan, only a man, was not so surefooted and finally, from fatigue and all the stress, tripped on some creepers and fell, face first into the mud. Both cats stopped immediately, Patches checking to make sure he was alright.

Duncan picked himself up and sat down on a dry piece of ground. "Let's eat. I can't go on like you two without a rest."

He fed the cats some more of the dried meat and himself cheese, berries and bread, all beginning to taste exceptionally dry. The three finished off the last of their water, Duncan pouring it slowly into each cats' mouth so they could drink from the flask.

"Well, my friends, I hope we come across some fresh water soon."

The cats looked up at him, a look of understanding on their feline faces. Then he heard it again, someone calling his name. The cats looked too, back the way they had come, rising up and trotting a few paces back in the direction of the sound.

"I'm not going mad," Duncan cried exuberantly to the cats. "You hear it too!"

Still, he was cautious. What if it was a trap. But again, who knew he was here, except those on the Misty Isles. Could it be ... No, it couldn't he finished the thought. Don't be foolish he scolded himself. Dusk was now settling down on them. The fog had risen, like the night before, to waist level, leaving only the cats' heads peering above the fog, giving the illusion they were disembodied and floating of their own accord. The cats looked back at Duncan, wondering what to do. They seemed drawn to the voice, like they knew it, he thought. It did sound like—No, he told himself, it can't be.

He stood, debating if he should backtrack to check out the voice when he heard the crashing again. This time though, he heard shouting with it. A man's shout, and a shriek. What if it really is them, thought Duncan. His mind made up, he took off at a run in the direction of the commotion, both cats following on his heels.

After a five minute, headlong run through the swamp, Duncan and his cats crashed through the undergrowth to a most horrifying sight. Before them was a lizard-like creature, with four legs, standing about twelve feet high. The tail was about eight feet long and ended in a sharp, barbed point. Atop its body, where its head should be were eight snake-like heads, all lashing out, biting and spitting at none other than Martyl and Salena.

Duncan couldn't believe his eyes. His two friends, whom he left behind on the Misty Isles were here before him, battling this abomination.

"Duncan," cried Martyl, "Beware of the heads on this beast. They can attack all around it, in any direction."

"What is it?" he called in reply, already removing Sliver from its sheath at his side and stepping up to do battle.

"It's a swamp hydra," replied Martyl, his sword neatly chopping off one of the snake heads with his sword.

Duncan leapt into the fray, followed by Big Cat and Patches.

"Salena, get back," he called. "Big Cat, stay with her!" The cat mmrowed her response, running over to stand between Salena and the battle.

The Swamp hydra, despite its immense size, was deceptively quick. It swung its barbed tail to the left where Duncan stood. He jumped, just missing being hit and landed on his feet, too far away to get a jab in with his dagger.

Patches growled, puffing up his fur, making him look almost twice as large as he normally was. The swamp hydra was unimpressed and four of its heads lashed out at the cat. Patches was too quick and dodged each head, although spittle from several of the mouths did wet his fur, irritating him somewhat.

Martyl, a middle-aged man now, was not slow by any means. He swung his sword deftly, hacking away as he went. Two more heads were severed as the beast began to back away from his onslaught.

Duncan tried to rush in from the side again, and again the huge tail swung at him. This time, he wasn't so quick and was sent flying about ten feet by the force of the impact. He rolled across the ground, tangling himself in creepers and vines. Salena screamed and ran towards him, stopping just short when she realized where Duncan had come to rest.

"Don't move," she yelled. "You'll only sink quicker." Duncan looked about and realized he had come to rest in a quicksand pit, which was quickly pulling him under, his knees already below ground. He looked about frantically for something to hold onto but there was nothing. Furthermore, he had dropped Sliver in his tumble. Trying to remain calm while he sank and Martyl and Patches battled the swamp hydra, Duncan waited for Salena and Big Cat to help him.

Martyl was becoming tired now, the battle against the swamp hydra turning against him as it renewed its attack on him now that it had one less opponent. All he could do was parry the creature's attacks, no longer able to lift his sword to swing it, he was so tired.

Patches, however, being quicker than either man or beast, had an advantage. He leapt onto the creature's back, biting and clawing relentlessly. The swamp hydra had a thick, scaly skin but the cat had massive two inch fangs that easily bit through. The swamp hydra reared and bucked but could not shake the wily cat. Three of its five heads were now busy trying to bite the cat on its back. Patches clawed at them, batting them away while trying to keep his balance on the beast's back.

This gave Martyl the chance he needed and he renewed his attack, severing the two heads attacking him. He rushed forward, jamming his sword into the scaly body, blood squirting all over him, soaking the ground beneath them The creature writhed in pain, thrashing its tail wildly about. Martyl plunged his sword in again, twisting it about in the creature's chest. Finally its movements became slower and it crashed to the ground, Patches jumping clear.

The man and cat both ran to where Duncan lay in the quicksand, now up to his chest. Salena was trying to throw a rope of vines out to him but he couldn't reach it, his arms barely sticking above the surface.

"Please, Duncan," she cried, "take hold of the vines!"

"I can't," he replied. Both cats paced nervously about the quicksand, unable to help.

"Here," yelled Martyl, sheathing his long sword and laying down at the edge of the pit. He handed the sword's pommel out to Duncan. "Grab hold. I'll pull you out. Salena, hold my feet."

Duncan grabbed the sword's pommel and Martyl pulled. At first nothing happened, but after a moment a suctioning noise could be heard as Duncan began to pull free, slowly. Patches and Big Cat, needing to help, bit into Martyl's cloak and pulled on it, helping pull Duncan free.

He was almost out, only his knees below the surface when the sword's sheath pulled off, right in Martyl's hands. With no load holding Duncan, Salena and the two cats tumbled over and Martyl slid forward on the ground. Instinctively, Martyl dug his feet into the soft earth and let go of the sword's sheath, quickly and thoughtlessly grasping the sword's razor sharp blade. The edges bit into his hands, cutting deep grooves in his palms and he cried out in pain, refusing to let Duncan and the sword go.

With a final effort, Duncan reached forward grasping Martyl's wrist. Martyl released his sword and as best he could, clasped his hands about Duncan's wrist, pulling him free, the quicksand letting out a final gurgle as he was released. He dragged Martyl's sword with him in his other hand.

Free now, and out of danger, Duncan stood there, staring dumbfounded at his companions.

"What are you doing here? How did you follow me?"

"I couldn't let you go alone, I'm sworn to be your protector, so King Kestewan allowed me to sail after you. Salena had been quite persuasive in getting her father's permission to go, also not wanting to let you go alone. She steadfastly refused to stay so I was forced to bring her along," replied Martyl. "We set sail the day after you left, not wanting to lose any more time. And as for how we managed to find you, well, I think you need to take a few lessons in stealthiness from your pets here."

Duncan just smiled and Salena handed him Sliver after retrieving it.

"I am actually quite grateful to have company along after all. Let's see to your wounds and be on our way out of this dreadful place."

Together Duncan and Salena bound up Martyl's wounded hands and the three rested for the night.

The next morning, they emerged from the swamp and in the distance, over the plains, they could see the port city of Gullhaven.

"One thing before we continue," said Martyl. "I suggest, sire, that we dispense of all titles and refer to one another by name so as not to announce ourselves of who we are."

"Agreed," replied Duncan and Salena in unison.

Chapter Three

As they stepped clear of the swamp, for the first time in two days they could see the sun, feel the warmth of its rays on their skin, and hear the singing of the birds in the sky. It was early summer and the day was getting hot, so after an hour's walk they stopped to rest, thankful to be on dry, solid ground.

Both cats flopped to the ground, laying on their sides, the tips of their tails gently flicking to the sound of an imaginary beat. Martyl, Duncan and Salena sat down, in a sort of semi-circle, watching the cats with mild amusement while having a late breakfast of cheese and berries, the cats getting the last of the dried meat.

"This is such a beautiful land," remarked Salena. "I understand now why you were so eager to return."

"I don't remember that much of it myself," replied Duncan. "I only saw the castle and grounds about. A few times I journeyed into the villages with my father but that was all I ever saw."

His mood grew sullen then, a far off look in his eyes as he remembered his past life …

"Tell us about this land Martyl. You must've travelled far as one of the King's Knights," asked Salena, trying to break the silence that had befallen them.

"Very well, my young lady. About a half a day's march to our south lies the city-state Gullhaven. It is a free city, ruled by a governing council. It straddles both sides of the Gull River. This is where we must go first to get supplied for our journey ahead. Hopefully we may have some allies there as well. I have an old friend who lives in the city. I just hope Draskene did not discover I had friends there."

Martyl paused for a second, as if reflecting on something, then continued.

"Further south is Duncan's Kingdom, Arundel. It stretches from the ocean in the west to the Sylvan River in the east. To the north it is bounded by Gullhaven and Frost Lake.

"Frost Lake is a beautiful body of water, from which flows the Gull River to the west, the Ree River to the northwest and the Thunder and Sylvan Rivers to the southeast. North of Frost Lake and the Thunder River lies the Freeland Territory. There live all the rabble and dregs of society. Slavers and bandits run those parts but there are a few honest men and towns there as well, though few and far between. Finally, to the far east, lie the Untamed Lands. Not many people have ventured there and ever returned. Stories of Wraulls, winter-wolves and other vicious creatures abound there."

"What are Wraulls and winter-wolves?" queried Salena. Duncan also had perked up, his curiosity whetted by the very name "Untamed Lands."

"Wraulls," continued Martyl, "are a most foul creature. They walk upright and have bodies similar to men only they are covered in hair, smell badly and have a head between that of a man's and a wolf's. The winter-wolves are savage, monstrous, frosty-white in colour and are said to be able to freeze a man with their breath."

"Have you ever seen either?" came Salena's next question.

"Yes. Long ago, when I was younger, I went on a mission for the King and I encountered some Wraulls in the Freeland Territory. As for the winter-wolves, Duncan and I both heard them our last time in Arundel, although luckily we did not see them at that time."

All were silent at that last recollection and their collective thoughts turned to more pleasant things as they gazed quietly at the drifting clouds for an hour or so when Martyl rose, saying, "I will head into the city now, alone. I want to check it out before we all proceed. The two of you wait at the edge of those trees over there."

He pointed to his left, at a stand of trees about a half mile off. "I will return by morning and we will decide on our next plan of action from there."

"Take one of the cats with you," suggested Duncan. "For protection. We can't be too careful right now."

"Very well. Patches, come on." The great cat dutifully rose, although somewhat unhappy at finishing its sunning so early.

It was late afternoon when Martyl and Patches were within sight of the free-city Gullhaven. The sun beat down on the plain before them, the air in front of them shimmering as they gazed on the dismal sight before them.

Martyl stared in disbelief at the city. The walls around it, once a dull grey, were blackened by soot and full of holes from decay and abuse. All about were gathered the poor, decrepit and deformed, begging for scraps of food or whatever else a passerby might give them. The sight saddened him and brought him down even more.

As he approached the gates, the rabble began to throng about him, begging for whatever he could offer. At the sight of the great cat though, they drew back, frightened by its size.

"Easy big fella," Martyl reassured the cat, growling and hissing as the crowd milled about them.

"Hold there," shouted a burly guard over the crowd. He was dressed in black trousers and shirt and over his heart was an insignia—a black horse reared up on its hind legs, snorting red flames from its flared nostrils.

Martyl's thoughts raced, trying to remember if he had ever seen this insignia before in his travels for the King but he couldn't. He now feared that the free-city had been conquered, and he could just imagine by who.

"What is your business in this city? And what manner of creature is that?" the guard asked, right hand on his sword pommel and left hand pointing at Patches. His three companion guards, dressed the same, stepped out and to either side of Martyl and Patches, hands on sword pommels. The crowd had now dispersed away from the gates and this potential confrontation.

Martyl thought through his options quickly. A fight was out of the question if he wanted to learn anything but he was gone too long from these parts to know what kind of story would pass. Stroking Patches' fur to keep him calm, he replied with the safest lie he could think of. "I'm a trapper, come here for supplies. This is my pet mountain cat. He is still a kitten. I found him abandoned in the wilderness."

He hoped this lie would fool them. His muddied clothes and cut hands helped support his story and Patches did have the size of a half grown mountain cat, although his fur colour was a little off. As long as they didn't realize that mountain cats weren't grey and white very often, he thought they might make the story stick.

The guard studied him a moment longer then said, "Very well. Be warned. There is a curfew at nightfall and anyone caught out one hour past nightfall will be put in the stockade. Understood?"

"Yes sir," Martyl replied with forced cheerfulness, stepping past the guards, looking straight ahead, Patches following at his side.

"Hey, trapper," the guard called out. Martyl's heart began to beat a little faster and he thought of running, thinking the guard had seen through his lie. He decided against it, though, and turned as calmly as he could.

"Keep that cat of yours under control. We wouldn't want to have to destroy such a beautiful animal if it were to attack someone!" The guards broke out into laughter and Martyl waved, smiling a fake smile and disappearing as fast as he could into an alley before they heard Patches' growled response to their jibe.

As the two travelled through the city, Martyl couldn't help but notice the despair in the faces of those who passed them. He thought for sure they would have shown some surprise at the size of the cat beside him, but their thoughts were only on day to day survival. Packs of mongrel dogs roamed the back streets and alleys, chasing the sick and weary, fighting for scraps of food. Yet despite their numbers, they quickly ran from Patches whenever a low growl was issued. Even in packs, the dogs didn't have the courage to attack the protective cat.

Martyl also noticed the armed patrols, dressed the same as the guards at the city gate. They passed in groups of four, about one patrol every half hour. Everyone on the street scurried away from them as they marched by, sinister scowls on their faces.

What happened while I was gone, thought Martyl. This used to be a thriving, pleasant city. Now it was burned and blackened, everyone keeping to themselves. Did Draskene attack and conquer Gullhaven as well? He didn't recognize the uniform insignia of a black horse, rearing up, snorting flames, but it was possible it was Draskene's design.

Who else could have done it, he mused. He defeated Aramid and conquered Arundel. The memory of that night, stirred alive again, gnawed at the pit of his stomach like some horrible parasite.

"I must find Bartok," Martyl said aloud to himself and Patches. "Maybe he can supply me with the answers and help I need."

Martyl finished his thoughts when he reached the centre of town. A few more blocks south, towards the river that split the city into two halves, was the Nag's Tale, a tavern owned by his old friend Bartok. Martyl and Patches covered the last few blocks in a matter of minutes. The sun was now beginning to set in the west and it would be dark before long.

"Wait here, my friend." Martyl whispered to Patches. The large cat just looked at him, as if saying—Where would I go?—and sat himself down at the side of the tavern, legs tucked beneath him and tail curled around his side. He closed his eyes for a catnap but his ears followed every sound around him.

Martyl checked the sign above the door one last time—a picture of an old horse and woman, seated at a table talking. The word's above, for those that could read, said "The Nag's Tale."

This place used to be one of his favourite haunts while out on expeditions or crusades for the King, but now looked like the rest of the town, run down and beaten. Martyl took a breath, pushed open the swinging doors and stepped inside. The only patrons present were more on the armed men wearing the black uniforms with the horse insignia.

This could be trouble, thought Martyl.

"What do you want, peasant?" spat out one of the men. Out of the corner of his trained eye, Martyl saw the barkeep slip into the back-room—either to get more guards or just to avoid any bloodshed. Probably the latter he concluded as the speaker rose from his chair at the table.

Martyl, somewhat rankled at being called a peasant, bit his tongue and replied civilly, "I'm looking for a friend, but I see he's not here. Sorry. I'll be on my way." He didn't want any trouble and didn't want to give up Bartok's name, especially when it didn't look like he ran the place anymore.

The guard, however, had different ideas and stepping forward toward Martyl said, "Who would you be looking for in here, peasant? This tavern is for the Prime Guard only. Surely one of us would not be your friend."

You got that right, *friend*, thought Martyl to himself.

The Prime Guard's five friends, sitting about the table, broke into wide grins and started laughing, apparently enjoying their comrade's harassment of Martyl. Martyl turned to leave, trying to ignore their mocking, even though it burned him, a Royal Knight, to have to do so. It won't help our cause to get upset, he told himself.

"Whoa, now friend," the guard said, grabbing hold of Martyl's left arm. "I didn't say you could leave yet."

Having turned every cheek he could, Martyl wheeled about, twisting the guard's arm behind his back and gave him a boot in the rear, sending him crashing into his friends' table. The table crashed beneath him, spilling ale all over him.

"*I* said I was leaving," Martyl stated defiantly, resting his hand on his sword's pommel.

"Renegade!" shouted the guards. They all rose, drawing their swords, and rushed Martyl.

He cut down the first man in the wink of an eye, his skills no match for theirs, even though he was a good ten to twenty years older than they. Martyl backed through the door as the other four pressed in on him, parrying their blows as he went.

His hands, sore and bleeding again as his wounds reopened, could not grip his sword much longer. From his right, a white and grey blur flashed in front of him and Patches took down the foremost of his attackers, biting and scratching for all he was worth. The guard was screaming for only a few seconds before his throat was cut by a well placed blow by a massive paw.

The guards were startled for a second by this, and Martyl used that to his advantage. He lunged ahead, spearing another with his sword and disembowelling a second with a broad swipe. Only one guard still stood and he now began to look rather pale as he realized this was no mere peasant they had been harassing. Four of his cohorts lay dead and another unconscious inside the tavern.

He tried to defend himself against Martyl's attack but found he was retreating further, back into the tavern, when shouts could be heard down the street. Martyl dared not look during battle but he could tell by Patches' growl that it wasn't help for them. The barkeep called for help after-all, he thought to himself.

With a final grunt, he shoved the guard back through the doors into the tavern as they locked swords. Turning, Martyl bounded down the street, Patches in tow as more guards, at least a dozen he guessed from a quick glance, chased after them.

Martyl, unfamiliar with the city after being absent for fifteen years, ran blindly down every side street and alley he could find, not knowing where to go. The word renegade kept running through his mind, and he wondered why the guards had called him that when they saw he could fight and had a weapon.

It was now dusk and the shadows began to thicken and grow, dancing before him as he ran, causing his eyes to play games on him. The guards were still on their tails and gaining fast. Martyl and Patches were growing tired but the guards were replaced with new ones, almost every other block they ran into a new squad. They came out of a narrow alley and into an intersection in the street. To the east and west on the intersecting street, more guards approached as they heard the commotion. To their south, directly ahead, their street ended at the bridge that crossed the Gull River and joined both halves of the city.

The streets were beginning to become deserted as everyone went inside for the curfew, leaving no crowds to get lost in. Their only choice, thought Martyl, was to cross the bridge. Hopefully guards had not been alerted on the other side. Looking to make sure the cat was still with him, Martyl raced for the bridge, ignoring the shouts to halt coming from behind.

They were half way across when Martyl's worst fears were realized. There were four guards on the other side and they were alerted by the commotion. Too tired to fight, the man and cat stopped, breathless. Patches' ears were flat against his head, ready to fight as best he could, definitely not one to back down in the face of a hostile encounter!

Martyl looked to both ends of the bridge as the guards approached, swords drawn.

"I hope you can swim, pal," he said to Patches as he picked him up and threw him over the railing of the bridge before the startled cat knew what happened. The guards, knowing what was coming next, rushed Martyl, but he was too quick and plunged into the river below, following the cat.

Duncan and Salena sat down and rested just inside the copse of trees. Big Cat lay at their feet, head resting on her paws. They shared a small meal of cheese and water, the cat readily devouring the cheese. They watched the sun set behind a bank of clouds, its rays turning the early night sky a brilliant crimson red with purple fringes. Salena laid her head on Duncan's shoulder and waited for him to pay her some attention for he seemed increasingly distant lately. When she could bear the silence no longer, she asked, "Are you displeased with my being here?"

Duncan turned to face her, replying, "No. I just have things on my mind."

"What? Talk to me, maybe I can help."

"It's just this whole journey. There are so many things I don't know yet, even where to start. I also fear for your safety and that of Martyl's."

"Don't worry about us," she cut him off sternly. "We both came on our own free will and besides, Martyl spent a long time here before he left. His help will be invaluable to you. Everything will work out fine. Talk to us. That's why we're here."

Duncan was silent a moment, mulling Salena's words over before he replied.

"You're right. I'm sorry. We'd better get some rest. Martyl should be back by morning with our supplies and maybe some information on the Black Paladin or what we can use to fight him."

They laid out their bedrolls and soon fell asleep, Big Cat at their feet, keeping vigil over them, determined nothing would happen to her humans.

Patches hit the water with a splash and a few seconds later Martyl hit too. They both fought their way to the surface, gasping for breath.

"There they are!" came a shout from above and a hail of arrows rained down on them. Patches was already cat-paddling his way to the far side of the river bank, Martyl following close behind, wondering how long it would take for an arrow to hit one of them.

The river was much too strong, however, for either one of them to make the other side and they were soon swept downstream, away from the bridge and the Prime Guard. Orders were shouted and guards on either side of the river began running after them but the current was too fast and they soon outdistanced their pursuers.

Martyl did not know though if this was to their benefit or not as he realized that if they didn't reach shore soon, they'd be swept out to sea by the river current. He and the cat struggled valiantly to fight the current and reach either bank but to no avail. After about fifteen minutes of this, their strength began to fail them, already nearly exhausted from their battles and subsequent flight from the guards.

Energy spent now, Martyl was just trying to keep afloat, his clothes and sword weighing heavily on him. Patches was fairing a little better, having only wet fur to weigh him down, but he too was tiring. Martyl debated dropping his sword but without it, he couldn't defend himself and decided to hold out as long as he could.

He could hear voices now, calling out to him, or was it his imagination. No, there were people on the south bank, he was sure. One of them was tossing a rope to him. He reached for it, missed. Once more the man with the rope tossed it out, again he missed. A third time the man tossed out the rope while the others around him looked about nervously.

This time Martyl caught it, or rather Patches did in his jaws, and Martyl caught hold of the cat then the rope, as they were hauled in. They didn't look like the guards chasing them before he thought, but even if they were he and Patches couldn't hold out much longer in the river.

Martyl and Patches reached the river bank, lying on their stomachs, soaking wet and exhausted. Martyl looked up at his rescuers and saw the man holding the rope. It was the barkeep from the Nag's Tale, the one who alerted the extra guards.

He reached for his sword, barely able to stand, Patches at his side, his ears back, fur puffed up in wet clumps and teeth barred when he was struck from behind. The last thing he remembered seeing before falling was Patches taking a dart in his side.

Chapter Four

He walked the castle battlements, clothed all in black, a black cloak drawn about him, hood up over his head. The night seemed to part before him as he walked up, his form blacker than the deep of night. Clouds blotted out the stars and moon and he revelled in the blackness, drawing on it to sustain and replenish himself.

Something did not feel right, these past three days, a disturbance in the air, maybe. It was not quite tangible, the explanation slipping from his fingertips as he tried to grasp it. Draskene thought of the possibility that maybe Aramid's son, Duncan, was returning to exact his vengeance. It had been fifteen years now and never had he found Duncan, Martyl or Connor.

But still, something did not feel quite right. The feeling gnawed away at the back of his mind. Could Duncan and the others have escaped all his man hunts and executions over the years to return now? But where would they have hidden all these years? Surely in over fifteen years, if they still lived, they would have been discovered.

Besides, he thought, what weapon could they have that would harm him, the Black Paladin? Connor's dagger was not a threat to him, having insufficient magic to overcome his formidable defences. It may be able to kill his summoned demons but it could not harm Draskene himself.

Even if Duncan had somehow survived this long to grow to adulthood, he would be ready for him, thought Draskene. How he would love to subvert the last member of the house of Arundel to his dark uses. It would be a shame that King Aramid couldn't be alive to see it happen! The thought pleased him to no end.

His train of thought became distracted as he sensed Bin, his personal messenger hastening through the castle to the battlements where Draskene paced.

"What is it, Bin?" he asked without turning to face him as Bin reached the battlements.

How it made his skin crawl, Bin thought, that his master knew it was him. He pushed his uneasiness aside and replied, "There was a Renegade spotted in Gullhaven, my Lord, tonight."

"Renegade?" repeated Draskene, whirling about, glaring from beneath his bond at Bin. "I thought they had all been executed years ago."

"Apparently not, my Lord. And this was no mere Renegade. He defeated six of the Prime Guard on his own, singlehandedly!"

"What?! One man defeated six of my Prime Guards on his own?"

"He was also accompanied by a giant cat, maybe weighing forty pounds and over four feet long by eye witness accounts. They managed to elude capture and disappeared in the Gull River."

Bin shrank a little, fearing Draskene's outburst at this last piece of information.

"Send out the word. I want this man taken—ALIVE, along with this so called 'giant' cat."

Bin knew he was dismissed when Draskene again turned his back to stare out into the night.

There were only two people Draskene knew of that could perform the feat he was just told. Connor or Martyl. They were the only two who had the training and experience to do such a thing. It had to be Martyl, he thought, for Connor, if still alive, would be an old man by now. He would enjoy killing whichever one it was after he learned Duncan's whereabouts from them, and the location of more of these giant cats! They would make excellent weapons of war! He just hoped that their size was not an exaggeration on the part of the Prime

Guards involved to lessen their fault in their loss, otherwise they would pay dearly!

Draskene smiled then. A thin, rakish smile, that seemed to distort his features. How he was going to enjoy this, he thought to himself.

Salena awoke by early morning to find Big Cat sitting at her feet where she lay, keeping a silent vigil on her. It was warm already at this early hour and most of the morning dew had evaporated off the bright green grass.

She looked to her right and saw Duncan preparing them a breakfast of berries he'd just picked.

"Good morning," he called to her cheerfully but she thought she could detect a little worry in his voice.

"Is Martyl back yet?" she asked, rising to join him, her body already sounding its request for food.

Big Cat rose too, padding off into the woods, presumably to hunt for her breakfast as they had no more dried meat for her.

"Not yet," replied Duncan, feasting on the small supply he'd found. "Eat up. We'll wait here until he arrives."

"And what if he doesn't make it back today?"

"I don't know. We'll wait here until tomorrow morning at least. If he's not back then, we'll have to go in search of him ourselves."

"What if he's in trouble now? He said he'd be back by morning. It's now late morning and there's no sign of him. Aren't you the least bit worried something might have happened? We should go now!"

"Calm down," Duncan said sternly. "We can't rush into anything. Maybe it took him longer to find his old friend than he thought. It's been fifteen years." Feeling bad about his outburst, he added, "I'm worried too. We've got to give him time though. He knows this area better than you or I and he's a veteran Royal Knight. He'll be okay. Besides, he's got Patches with him."

Salena smiled, a little spritely smile and finished eating. Maybe it was too early to worry, she thought to herself. She knew of nothing that could harm Patches, the most ferocious of her people's cats, so they must be safe. After all, she had seen him singlehandedly chase off a pack of wolves when she and Duncan were much younger and got lost while exploring.

"Come on," said Duncan with a smile when they finished eating. "Let's go for a swim. I found a nice stream back up the woods. It'll be refreshing, especially after that swamp." The two rose and, after calling to Big Cat, who came slinking back out of the woods, headed off to the stream.

As they walked through the woods, Duncan and Salena couldn't help but laugh quietly at the cat as she looked this way and that, her head following every sound she heard. Birds twittered and squawked, carrying on some undecipherable conversation between themselves. Squirrels and rabbits bounded out of logs and brush, scurrying here and there as the trio approached. Big Cat made a few feints but never had a chance at catching them, her humans making too much noise for her to sneak up on anything.

As they walked the few hundred feet to the stream, Duncan couldn't help but wonder if Martyl was in some kind of danger. But then again, he was only a few hours late and it had been, like he said, fifteen years since he'd last been here.

He pushed his thoughts aside, sweeping them from his mind like clearing cobwebs from a forgotten corner. He would relax today, giving Martyl the benefit of the doubt, and if he wasn't back by tomorrow morning, he'd go after him.

Martyl awoke, and found himself lying on a small cot in what looked like a cell. Great, he thought, his mind still fuzzy, I've been caught by the guards. He lay motionless and took in the surroundings.

It was a small room, or cell, with no windows or furnishings, only the cot he lay on and a table with a wash basin and an oil lamp, which was lit, giving off a hazy light. A door was set in the far wall.

He swung his legs over the side of the cot and sat up. He wasn't dizzy so he didn't think the blow he took could be too bad. Feeling the back of his head, Martyl felt a fair sized bump but that was all. It throbbed mildly, but was tolerable. He rose to his feet and found at the foot of his bed, to his surprise, Patches, snoring away.

That's odd, he thought. I have no weapons but Patches is still with me. He was relieved no harm had come to the cat as he would hate to have to tell Duncan if something had. Martyl walked slowly to the door and listened. He could hear voices outside it, muffled and hushed, but couldn't make out much.

Turning back to the cat, he tried to rouse him, shaking him gently, then splashed some of the water on him. With a sudden jerk, the big cat awoke, rising to his legs unsteadily, snarling.

"Easy boy," Martyl cooed reassuringly.

Patches looked at him questionably, as if asking for an explanation of what just happened. Suddenly, Patches leapt past Martyl towards the door.

Martyl looked, just in time to see the great cat pounce on someone entering the room.

"Get this thing off me!" cried the man.

Martyl grabbed Patches' fur at the scuff of his neck, trying to pull him off. The cat eased up, snarling at the stranger.

"I don't think he takes kindly to being drugged and locked up. Nor do I. Mind telling me what is going on here? Where am I? What happened on the river bank, what happened to this city?"

"It's a long story, friend. Come with me and meet the others. We have a lot to talk about."

"Yes, we do," replied Martyl flatly. The man turned and led them out the door, Martyl following Patches at his side, watching warily.

They stepped into a large, dimly lit room, populated with old crates and broken boards. Martyl's trained eye picked out four armed men, standing off in a far corner by a door. Probably guarding the way out, he thought. In the centre of the room were a knot of eight people, talking amongst themselves.

Martyl noticed all wore long knives and laying off to the side were clubs and other odd shaped pieces of wood. Without a sword, he thought, he didn't stand much of a chance if things turned nasty. As they approached the group, they stopped talking and a man came forth, glaring at Martyl.

It was the barkeep from the Nag's Tale. His heart almost skipped a beat as it began racing. Patches growled, flattening his ears. They were done now, was all Martyl could think. But why let him live this long? What was going on here? What did these people want with them? He had the idea that he was about to find out soon.

The barkeep stepped forward, the look on his face almost as mean as that of the cat's. It was all Martyl could do to hold Patches back.

"Who are you?" he asked. "And don't tell me you're a hunter come into town for supplies. That story is all over the city. No mere hunter could've done what you did back there and this sure doesn't look like any baby mountain cat I've ever seen," he finished, pointing at Patches, yet keeping his hand well back of the angry cat.

"Maybe you can tell me why you left when the fight began," spat Martyl, his temper rising. "To alert more of those guards, perhaps. And why did you knock me unconscious at the river bank?"

By this time everyone else in the room had gathered round, except the four guards who stood watch at the door, and were watching Martyl and the cat intently.

The other's scowl softened somewhat and he continued, "It's obvious neither of us trusts the other. But, need I remind you, you are in no position to make any demands. However, to show you some trust on my side, I will answer your question. I slipped into the back to keep my cover. I didn't know who you were or what you wanted, and once the battle commenced, I left to get help—for you. We have to keep our location secret and we still weren't sure of your intentions so we rendered you unconscious before bringing you here. We know nothing about you but anyone who could defeat six of the Prime Guard singlehandedly would be a great ally."

He looked Martyl straight in the eye, neither man's eyes wavering, sizing each other up. Martyl knew that sooner or later he would have to reveal his identity and after a moment's thought, he replied, "I am the last of King Aramid's Royal Knights. I have been in hiding for the past fifteen years and have returned to defeat the Black Paladin. This cat is Patches, and he comes from the land I had sanctuary in. It's location, however, I must keep secret."

Everyone in the room stood there silent, mouths gaping. A Royal Knight, they thought, come back to reclaim the King's throne. And come back from a secret kingdom no less!

"That explains your fighting prowess, then," said the barkeep breaking the silence. He grasped Martyl's hand in his, holding it firmly and said, "My name is Bron."

"I am Martyl. Maybe now you could answer some more of my questions? Where are we? What has happened to this city? Who are 'Renegades' and the 'Prime Guard' and what happened to Bartok, the owner of the Nag's Tale? He was a friend of mine and that's why I went there in the first place."

"Come sit with me over here and I will explain your questions. First, have a drink and some food. Ren, bring this knight his weapon."

One of the guards at the door brought Martyl his sword and handed it to him gingerly, as if it were a baby. He then followed Bron to a large crate in the corner away from everyone else and he and Patches had some water and dried meat.

When they finished, Bron recounted the events of the past fifteen years in a quick summary for Martyl while everyone else made themselves busy fashioning weapons from the chunks of wood he'd seen earlier.

"The Black Paladin," he continued, "did not end his conquest with Arundel alone. He subverted the people of the surrounding area. Those with weak willing minds became directly controlled by him and are used as his shock troops. Those with stronger minds and bodies were recruited and trained to be the Prime Guard. These are the most feared and hated and best trained warriors there are. Never before have we seen anyone stand up to them as you did."

Bron grinned from ear to ear, obviously pleased by this fact.

Martyl just nodded, his face carved in stone.

"We merely call them the Black Guard because of their uniforms. It was less than a year after Arundel fell that the Black Paladin took Gullhaven. Many people died, including your friend Bartok. He was one of us, the Renegades. That is the name given to those who opposed the Black Paladin's domination of the free lands. They took his tavern from him and killed him when he was discovered to be a Renegade. I have, up until now, kept myself undercover. However, you represented the hope we were looking for and I grabbed onto this branch of action. You can understand our need for secrecy. This is one of our few hideouts still undiscovered. They believe the last of us to have been killed years ago but last night's events will change that."

Martyl sat quiet for a moment, digesting the information then asked, "How far does his power extend now?"

"He controls all of Arundel, Gullhaven and all the land in between. He has not yet stretched his black hand past the Sylvan River but he is amassing an army on its shores near Barlon. It is assumed he plans an assault on the Dwarven stronghold in the Thunder Mountains. They are few now, having been plagued with sickness and battles with Wraulls from the Untamed Lands. The Wraulls' numbers have grown immensely and they have an alliance with the Black Paladin."

Martyl muttered a curse under his breath and asked, "How many of you Renegades are there? Enough to do battle? We will attack the Black Paladin himself!"

"I'm afraid not, mighty warrior. We are few, all of a few hundred. The Black Paladin's troops number in the thousands. And there are the Wraulls, and worse." Bron fell silent then, his eyes seeming to stare off at nothing in particular.

"What else is there?"

Bron remained silent, withdrawn. Martyl reached across the crate and grabbed him by the shoulders, shaking him and shouting, "Come on, man. What is it? Snap out of it."

Everyone in the room stopped what they were doing and stared. A few of the bolder ones started towards Martyl, unsure of what he was doing to their leader. Patches was on his feet between Martyl and the others before they could think twice and they stopped in their tracks, even more unsure of the massive growling cat.

"It's okay," assured Bron. The others slowly and quietly went back to their business, occasionally casting a furtive glance in their direction.

"It's a bad memory," he continued. "There are giant winter-wolves and even worse things—demons. I saw one once. It killed over twenty people in a killing rampage before the Black Paladin stopped it. That was to be a lesson to anyone who considered joining the Renegades." He went silent again, the vivid memory etched forever in his mind, burning like a red hot coal.

It was Martyl's turn to reflect inward for a moment before he replied. "I too saw one of his demons. It attacked myself and a fellow knight. But they are not invincible. They can be killed with magic weapons."

"Yes, maybe. But we have none. And even if we did, it would require a very powerful magical weapon to destroy the Black Paladin. His magic is strong and protects him well."

Both men fell silent then, thinking about the possibilities they may have. After a few moments, Martyl finally broke the silence.

"There are legends from long ago, during the Black Magic Wars, of powerful weapons forged with magic by the old Dwarves. Perhaps the Dwarves in the Thunder Mountains can tell us more, possibly the whereabouts of one of these weapons. Maybe that too is the reason for Draskene's impending battle with them."

"Maybe. Maybe he just wants to conquer more land and people. He is an evil man, that one."

He wasn't always that way, remembered Martyl. Once he was King Aramid's most trusted and loyal knight, a paladin of great honour. Then he was overcome by the very evil he swore to destroy.

But to these people, that was of no consequence. He was only seen as the Black Paladin, destroyer of their homes and lives.

"With your leave," said Martyl as he rose to his feet, extending his hand in friendship. "I must be on my way. There are others waiting for me."

"Good luck to you," replied Bron, grasping Martyl's proffered hand firmly in his two. "I will see you to the edge of the city personally. I know of many secret passages and alleys so as not to be discovered. The Prime Guard will be looking very earnestly for you. Come."

The two men left the room with Patches in tow. Everyone in the room gave their best wishes and even a few hearty pats on the back. Martyl promised to return when he had some information so they could join forces in their battle. Bron gave him the street where he could find a safe house upon his return if he needed a place to hide. He also supplied him with new clothes and provisions.

They entered into a back alley, dark and dank with rats scurrying for cover everywhere. Bron led Martyl and Patches quickly across the adjoining street and down another alley. This one was crowded with old wooden crates and other refuse. A small group of people, a family by the looks of it, were huddled together amid it all.

Martyl felt a pang of sorrow and pity for these people, especially the children. Before the Black Paladin, this city was prosperous and no one was left to live like this.

Bron saw his look and said dismally, "I'm afraid it's like this all over the city, my friend. It has been so for fifteen years now."

As they passed down the alley, the parents clutched their children and tried to shield them, fearing Martyl and Bron. Martyl shook his head in dismay and followed Bron, Patches at his side. Every alley and back street they entered repeated the same scene. Martyl found himself feeling sick with sorrow and felt extremely relieved when Bron led them past the city wall and into the open. His resolve to defeat Draskene and set things back to rights was strengthened more.

"Farewell and good luck, my new friend," whispered Bron as Martyl and Patches took off across the fields outside the town wall. He watched them quickly disappear into the shadows, blending in like the night itself.

Chapter Five

Martyl and Patches travelled through the night and on into the morning. Dawn's early rays of light split through night's inky blackness with fingers of crimson. Dew sparkled in the new light and the clicking of insects gave way to the chirps of birds. As they travelled, quickly in case of pursuit, Martyl mused through his memory of all the old legends he knew about the Black Magic Wars.

Many stories were told of great warriors who fought for their clans against evil wizards and their minions. The Dwarves of old had forged great swords and other weapons for the warriors to use against the evil wizards. These weapons became lost, so the legends went, after the wars. If the Dwarves of the Thunder Mountains knew of any of these weapons they may have a chance against Draskene and his demons.

By early afternoon, he came across the camp where Duncan and Salena had stayed. He followed their noises and found the two of them splashing about in the river, Big Cat lazing a good distance back so as not to get wet.

"You two make enough noise to attract an army here!" he shouted.

Duncan and Salena stopped their activities and stared, startled by Martyl. He began to smile and said, "Come on out. I've got new clothes and some food. Then we must be on our way. While you eat and dress, I'll tell you what I've learned."

Martyl unpacked the provisions given to him. There were new boots and forest cloaks for all of them. The boots were soft, supple leather, about half way up to their knees. The forest cloaks were made from a canvas-like material and covered them from neck to ankle.

They had sleeves and straps to tie them tight about their legs. Both the boots and cloaks were a dirty brown colour to camouflage them in the woods and plains in the surrounding area as well as providing a good deal of weather resistance.

They also had new shirts and trousers of a nondescript nature, function being preferable to style at the moment. Salena ducked behind a large oak to change into her new clothes while Duncan simply changed where he stood. When finished, the three sat down to a quick meal, happy to have some more meat in their diets. The two cats disappeared into the small woods, presumably hunting.

"Well, what did you find out?" asked Salena excitedly around a mouthful of food.

"Yes," added Duncan, "when will we face the Black Paladin and reclaim what is mine?"

"I'm afraid I don't have very encouraging news," started Martyl. "It seems the Black Paladin's magic and power have grown. He has taken over the city of Gullhaven and all of the land south of the Sylvan River. His power has grown so much that we need strong magic of our own to combat him. He is even now, as we speak, planning to conquer what remains of the Dwarven people in the Thunder Mountains. However, it is not as black as it seems. I met a rebel force, known as Renegades, who wish the Black Paladin defeated as well. Their people may join us when the time comes to do battle. We must hurry now, though, to the Thunder Mountains and help the Dwarves. They may have information in their legends of old about their lost magical weapons."

Martyl rose and began packing up their supplies while Duncan called his cats. Salena, unfamiliar with Dwarves, asked what they were.

"They are a strong, stout people," replied Martyl. "They have lived in mountains from the dawn of time, mining the depths for precious metals. They are older than man and have great knowledge of magic, old magic, from the heart of the earth. Sadly, though, over the years their numbers have decreased through war and sickness and now only the Dwarves of the Thunder Mountains remain."

Martyl fell silent then, continuing to pack their belongings as Salena gave him a hand, a look of wonder on her face at the thought of seeing a new race. Within minutes they finished and the three of them, with the cats following beside, headed out.

It was late afternoon as they headed across the plain between them and the Ree River. The sun was high overhead in a blue, cloudless sky, sending down its heat. It was so hot the ground shimmered in a haze before them, mirages scattering as they approached like flocks of birds winging away.

They marched for several hours, stopping only briefly every now and again for drinks. No one had much of an appetite, the heat overcoming the feeling of hunger. As the afternoon progressed, they became increasingly tired, not yet used to the heat and exertion of their march. Martyl made them continue on, anxious to put as much distance as possible between them and Gullhaven, lest any would-be pursuers gain on them.

Finally, as dusk approached, they reached the bank of the Ree River. It's fast moving water bubbled and gurgled quietly beneath a pink and lavender cloud filled sky. The last of the sun's rays shimmered on the water's surface, glistening like thousands of tiny stars.

"It's beautiful," sighed Salena as she sat down at the water's edge, washing the sweat and dirt off her sunburned face and arms. All three had earlier in the day shed all but the most necessary of clothing, causing their exposed skin to burn in the intense sun.

Duncan and Martyl sat down and washed too. The two cats knelt at the water and after taking a few drinks, laid down and began to groom themselves, seemingly oblivious to all else at the moment.

"Shall we cross the river tonight?" asked Duncan around a mouthful of bread and cheese. "Or wait until morning?"

"We will cross after eating and a short rest," replied Martyl. "There is a ford not far from here. We must put as much distance between us and Gullhaven as possible. News of our arrival will travel fast and I'm sure Draskene will waste no time trying to find us."

"How long will it take us to get to the Dwarves and the Thunder Mountains?" asked Salena, a gleam in her eyes at the thought of meeting Dwarves for the first time.

"Barring any unforseen occurrences along the way, about two days if we travel by river, six if we must travel on land," came Martyl's reply.

When they finished eating, the trio packed up their belongings, lit torches and headed upstream to find the ford. The two cats lumbered along behind, enjoying the fact that it was now a little cooler.

Night fell and the stars were shining high in the sky when they reached the river ford. In the faint light they could make out the edges of the swamp on the far bank of the river. There also appeared to be a camp fire and loud, boisterous voices floated across on the wind to them.

"Quickly, dowse your torches," ordered Martyl.

"Have we been discovered already?" asked Duncan.

"I think not. They are most likely slavers, on their way to the city to sell something, or someone," Martyl replied in disgust. "Still, we cannot cross safely without knowing if it is an ambush. Even if it is slavers, they won't be too friendly to strangers. If only there were another way across nearby. This is the only safe place to cross in the dark."

"I think I can help."

Duncan and Martyl both turned to stare at Salena, their faces betraying what they thought of what she was going to say.

"I am an excellent swimmer," she continued, splaying her hands out to display the webbing between her fingers, "as are all my people. I could swim across downstream, sneak up on them and see who they are and how many."

"It's too dangerous," interrupted Duncan. "You can't do it. We'll find another way."

Selena shot him a look that told him better than any retort what she thought of that remark.

Martyl broke the silence with a soft, almost silent, "Do it."

Duncan just stared incredulously and said, "What? You can't be serious!"

"It's our only choice right now Duncan. I'm sorry but we've all got to make sacrifices if we're to see this journey through."

"Let me go too, then."

"You can't. The current is too strong for you or I. She's as adept in the water as on land. You grew up with her and you know that. You've got to stay level headed if you want to live to see yourself returned to the throne."

Duncan stopped his protesting as the reality of their situation sunk in. He gave Salena a big hug and wished her luck.

"Be careful," he whispered to her.

"Good luck," added Martyl.

Salena made her way carefully downstream, her path lit only by the stars and the faint light of a crescent moon. After about fifteen minutes, she stopped and slowly made her way down the embankment to the water. She shed all but her underclothes and dove in. It was cool but refreshing after the intense heat of the day.

How nice it was to be back in the water for a swim, she thought. With the webbing between her fingers and toes splayed out, she made her way across the river with ease. The current carried her a little further downstream than she anticipated so she swam back the way she came, keeping close to the bank.

With her heart beating fast now, Salena climbed out of the water, careful not to make too much noise. The light from the campfire was very bright at this point, no more than fifty feet away. There were several voices, loud and gruff. Still, Salena could not tell if they were soldiers or slavers and tried to inch closer for a better look.

There seemed to be a cage-like structure behind the men, of whom she could see four. In the cage there was someone else, but it was too dark to see who.

"Jal," one of the men by the fire shouted, "Quit playin' with it and get back here. It's time to feed your pet freak!"

Slaver's, she decided in disgust. And whoever was in the cage must be their current sale. She looked around one last time wondering where this 'Jal' might be. She couldn't risk being caught alone, unarmed.

I learned what we needed, she concluded to herself, it's best I get going. Salena turned to go back down the bank to the river when a voice froze her dead in her tracks.

"Well, lookee here," said a man, in a gravelly voice. "Ain't you pretty."

Salena didn't even turn to face the voice but ran for the bank's edge, preparing to dive into the river, to safety.

"Not so fast, pretty thing," the stranger said and she was grabbed by the back of her head and hauled to the ground by her hair.

Draskene had just received the latest status report on the hunt for the man and cat who had killed four of his Prime Guard and wounded two after a bar brawl. He was furious at his forces' inability to find this man and mysterious giant cat. It was Martyl, it had to be, he thought. But where did he come from, and more importantly, was Duncan with him?

Draskene did not believe that either one of them could pose any threat to him, but all the same he wanted anyone with any kind of power under his control, or dead.

"Bin," he called and the door to his chamber, the King's Chamber, opened and in walked his personal attendant.

"Yes, my Lord?"

"I have some important business to attend to. I am not to be disturbed until I call for you again. Call off the search for the fugitive. Tell our men to listen for any tales, no matter how strange, from people entering the city and report to you. Now leave me."

Draskene turned his back and looked out the large open window in his chamber until he heard the door close behind Bin, who knew better than to question his master's motives. After sensing the magic wards on the door activate, Draskene opened a secret door in the wall beside the window and headed down a concealed stairwell.

He had no need to light a torch, instead casting a ball of light, which hovered just in front, illuminating the way. Draskene approached the secret passageway in the old castle. He made frequent use of all of them, travelling to and from his conjuring room and other areas of the castle.

Never would he have found them all, though, were it not for his magic, using it to locate hidden doors and tunnels. And now he would use his magic to give him something to find the man or possibly men, that eluded him. After a couple of minutes, the descent stopped and Draskene passed through the door.

"Light," he said and the torches in the small room he now occupied lit themselves. The room was square, about ten feet by ten feet and on the floor in its centre was a summoning glyph, drawn out years ago in blood. The blood was his own, used so that whatever was summoned into this room through the glyph would be bound to do his bidding, and no one else's.

The room was bare of anything else. Draskene closed the door and again waited until the wards took effect. When they did, he sat at the top point of the glyph and began to meditate. After about four minutes passed, he began to levitate, still sitting cross-legged. His eyes snapped open, glowing red and his skin, normally pale, whitened even more.

"Insaed Ezrach. Soid Ezrach. In the names of the Dark Ones of old, I call upon the Demon Lords to send me one of their kindred. Mastraed Insaech!"

The air in the small room grew hot and smelled of sulfur and the torches flickered in an unseen wind. Soon the walls began to reverberate and with a flash of blinding white light, a figure appeared in the centre of the glyph.

It was tall and broad with dark skin that had the look of tanned leather. Sharp barbs protruded through the skin and the yellow teeth were like fangs. The demon's hair was long and wild, falling about it's shoulders in loose, ragged clumps.

"Who has sent for me?" it asked, its voice echoing off the small room's walls.

"I, Draskene, the Black Paladin have called you forth to this plane, that of the living, to do my bidding. Serve me well and I well reward you grandly."

The demon's black, depth less eyes stared at Draskene and it seemed to ponder his words before answering.

"I am bound by your powers, Great One. Your name is known among us. How may I assist you?" the words again echoing off the chamber walls.

Duncan and Martyl sat quietly in the dark by the river's edge, listening and watching intently for any sign of Salena's return. The two cats lay lazily at their feet, seemingly paying no attention to their humans' dilemma.

"This is taking too long. What if something's happened?" worried Duncan, jumping to his feet and trying to peer across the river in the darkness to the campsite on the opposite bank.

"Sit down and be quiet," ordered Martyl tersely, "before something does."

Duncan sat down with a huff and stared glumly through the inky blackness of the night across the river. Patches got up and nuzzled his massive head into Duncan's side, nearly knocking him over. He looked up at him with his wide yellow cat-eyes as if to say, 'it's OK'. Duncan rubbed the cat's head, scratched behind his ears and said, "I know."

The four sat there quietly for a few minutes longer when suddenly shouting erupted on the far side.

"Hey guys, look what I found! And she's all mine!"

"Shut up, you drunken fool," came the reply.

Duncan was on his feet and running for the ford at this point, both cats bounding after him. Martyl, though a good fifteen years older than Duncan was quicker yet and tackled him to the ground.

"What are you doing!" shouted Duncan.

Both cats stopped and looked puzzled by the situation but when they saw their human pinned beneath Martyl, old friend or not, and sensing Duncan's distress, their ears flattened and their teeth bared. Low growls escaped them and they inched closer, hoping to threaten Martyl off rather than actually attack him, one of their party.

Out of the corner of his eye, Martyl saw the cats moving. He grabbed Duncan and hauled him to his feet, gripping him firmly by the shoulders.

"Stop and think, man!" he said sternly. "You go rushing off headstrong like that and not only will you get yourself killed but Salena too." He let go of Duncan and the cats stopped, ears still back, just watching.

"We can't just sit here," pleaded Duncan. "You know that was Salena they were talking about!"

"I know, but we've got to stay calm. There's only two of us and unknown numbers of them. We've got to be careful. Now follow me."

Martyl led the way to the ford and began crossing the river. Duncan followed closely behind and the two cats followed after. The water was slow moving, only about waist deep on the two men, but the cats were completely immersed, only their heads above water. Still, they made their way quickly and effortlessly to the far side, but not nearly quick enough for Duncan as all the way across he could hear the shouts and screams from the slavers and Salena.

Images of her being attacked and beaten continually ran through his mind making the few minutes in the water seem like a few hours. Finally they reached the opposite bank. The two men and the cats clambered part way up and rested.

"What now?" asked Duncan, as Patches and Big Cat began to shake themselves dry.

"Let me go over the top of the bank alone to see how many and where they are. Then I'll decide what to do."

Martyl inched his way slowly up the river bank and peered over the top. Immediately he knew they were dealing with slavers. The complete disarray of their camp, broken clay bottles, presumable once full of ale, littered the ground and there was the unmistakable slave cage, apparently occupied.

More to his concern was the welfare of Salena. Off to his left, by the campfire, were four slavers, in a circle and they were pushing Salena back and forth between them, grabbing and kissing her. With his left hand, he waved for Duncan to follow him up with the cats while drawing his sword with his right.

"There's no cover between us and them so the best thing to do is rush them quickly and take them by surprise."

Duncan nodded his agreement, a look of pure anger chiselled into his boyish features. On Martyl's command, the two men leapt up and ran the fifteen yards between them and the slavers as fast and quietly as possible. Halfway there, they were spotted. Salena was knocked to the ground and kicked in the stomach, rendering her breathless.

"Unleash the dogs, Jal!" shouted one of the slavers as they rushed forward, short swords drawn.

Martyl met two of the slavers head on, swords clashing and clanging while Duncan engaged with the third. Jal released the dogs, three great mastiffs who bounded out to join the fray. Patches and Big Cat, with what seemed like smiles on their faces, leapt between the men and dogs, teeth barred, and ears back. Although only two thirds the size of the dogs, they were more than their match, despite being outnumbered.

Big Cat swatted her dog three times with her immense clawed paw, tearing out the dog's left eye and half its cheek. The dog, unable to see effectively, had its throat removed with a well placed bite by the cat.

Patches, being quicker and more aggressive went for the throat of his dog immediately, severing its jugular. The third dog fared better than its comrades and managed to bite Patches in the left side while he was engaged with the other dog. Patches let out a terrible howl and whirled about, the mastiff's vice-like jaws still clamped about his side. He clawed and hissed furiously, tearing at the mastiff's face and neck but to no avail, as it wasn't letting go.

Martyl, by this time, had already dispatched one slaver and was giving the second the fight of his life. Duncan, although well trained in the art of combat, had never had any actual life or death confrontations with another man. He and the slaver battled back and forth, neither able to gain the advantage, until he heard his cat's hair-raising scream. Spurred on by the thought of losing his feline companions, he began attacking with renewed vigour.

He slashed repeatedly at the slaver, driving him back further and further until he found an opening in his defences, plunging his sword through his opponent's chest. The slaver's makeshift camp was now a shambles. Two slavers lay dead, along with two of their mastiffs. Blood flowed like water and the ground became muddy and slick beneath it.

Duncan looked about frantically, not knowing what to do next. He saw Salena lying on the ground, moaning softly, to his right. To his left, Martyl was still fighting a slaver and in front of him he saw his two cats, tearing at the last mastiff as Big Cat moved in to help the wounded Patches.

In an instant he realized the last slaver, Jal was nowhere to be seen. He ran towards Martyl to help him when he heard something whiz past him. With a yelp of surprise, he saw Big Cat drop to the ground, a crossbow bolt sticking out of her bloodied side. As Duncan turned to face the sniper, Martyl fell to the ground, a bolt sticking out of his back.

Acting out of pure instinct, Duncan hit the ground, rolling toward Martyl. Sensing Duncan's distress and seeing Big Cat felled before him, Patches went berserk, slashing viciously with his razor sharp claws. The mastiff was sliced to pieces in seconds and the big cat wasted no time in aiding his human companions. With blinding speed and no heed paid to his wounded side, Patches leapt at Martyl's attacker, knocking him to the ground. The slaver and cat rolled about for only a few moments before there was a muffled scream and Patches sank his large fangs into the unlucky man's throat.

With no immediate cover, Duncan knew he was in serious trouble against this sniper, presumably the slaver Jal. The fire from the camp gave off too much light so there weren't even any shadows to hide in. Duncan came out of his roll in a crouch, facing his opponent, whom he could now see as he approached, crossbow at the ready.

"Come to rescue the pretty girl, did you boy?" he taunted, fingering the bow's trigger. "I'm afraid you failed. But you did save me the trouble of splitting my find with these miserable beggars. For that, I'll let you live. Drop your sword and that fancy knife at your side and I'll sell you at Gullhaven, along with that cat there and the girl, after I take my share of her."

Jal laughed, hoarse and bitter sounding and his eyes gleamed in the fire light at the prospect of his plans. Patches growled and hunkered down into a springing position, next to the slaver he had just killed.

"Easy, fella," warned Duncan softly.

"That's right, boy," replied Jal. "I already took out one of these big cats. I wouldn't want to loose this one. But I'm sure they're still worth money dead."

His voice was cold and deadly serious. Duncan began to wonder if maybe he should let Patches jump on him and then he could rush him but it seemed cowardly to loose the cat that way.

"Drop your weapon NOW, boy!" Jal was losing patience fast.

Duncan was becoming more irritated by the moment at being called a boy and almost snapped back when a shadow flickered behind Jal.

With a loud thump, Salena cracked him over the head with a piece of firewood and down crashed the last slaver, fiery embers from the log dancing like stars around his head.

Chapter Six

"Are you all right, Salena?" asked Duncan as he rushed to her side.

"Yes, I'm fine. But what about Martyl and Big Cat?"

"We'd better check. First, tie this pathetic wretch with whatever you can find. Patches, you stay here and watch him."

The cat meowed his affirmative and sat down only inches from the prone Jal, eyes fixed intently on him, just waiting for any movement. With a cursory glance Duncan could tell that the dog bite to Patches was nothing more than a surface wound, the blood barely flowing at all. He was still concerned for his cat but he had more immediate concerns. Duncan turned to Martyl and inspected him for any signs of life, his heart leaden at the thought of losing his last friend.

"Is he alive?" called Salena while tying up the slaver.

"Of course I am," came Martyl's weak reply.

"He's alive!" shouted Duncan joyously. After calming down he asked, "Can you move?"

"Not very far. This bolt has to be removed from my back before I get infected. Do you know what to do?"

"Yes," he replied solemnly.

"Good. Now check on Big Cat while Salena gets things ready."

With Selena making the preparations, Duncan turned to his cat, his mood already darkening at the prospect of operating on Martyl. When he got to the great cat, his chest tightened and he held his breath. Big Cat lay there in a pool of blood, her fur matted and caked with dried and fresh blood and dirt. He knew it was too much to expect his cat to live through this, yet when he approached and touched her head to pet her, Big Cat raised her head and meowed softly, her large yellow eyes staring up at him, full of life, and pain.

He fought back the tears biting at him as he looked at his cat who nearly gave her life for him. They had been lucky this day, he thought. When would it run out? The reality of the events of the night began to sink in now as the adrenaline faded from his system.

He had just killed a man who would have killed him had he not. Martyl and Big Cat had almost been killed and Salena had almost been sold into slavery. His mind began to swim in the uncertainties surrounding his thoughts until Salena called to him, snapping his mind back into focus.

"Duncan, come here!"

"What is it," he called back.

There was no reply. All was silent except for the anguished moans of Martyl and Big Cat. Duncan's mind began to race with fear until he saw Salena alone, staring at a man-size cage, apparently with something in it. In moments he was at her side and the sight before him was unlike anything he'd ever seen before.

"I need you to lead my army of Wraulls in their siege of the Dwarves of the Thunder Mountains," began Draskene. "They are strong in numbers but weak in morale and intelligence. The Dwarves are the last race yet to fall under my power, but I will have them and their riches."

The demon stared at him blankly, the torchlight glinting off his black, glassy eyes.

"Is that to be my only purpose, my Lord?" asked the demon, a hint of annoyance in its voice.

Draskene seemed unaffected by this and answered solemnly, "I believe that King Aramid's son has returned to avenge his family. He has very little hope in that endeavour on his own but if he gains help or weapons from the Dwarves he could be difficult to stop. I want you to search for him while on your journey to the Thunder Mountains.

If found, he is to be brought to me, *unharmed*. Anyone else with him is expendable."

Draskene looked the demon in the eye and with a voice harder than stone added, "Do you understand?"

The demon knew better than to act smart in the face of that tone of voice and replied, somewhat subdued, "Yes, master."

With a wave of his hand, the wards imprisoning the demon vanished and he left the glyph to follow Draskene into the outside world.

Duncan and Salena both stared dumbfounded at the sight before them. In the cage lay a man with a set of feathered wings growing from his back, between his shoulder blades. The bird-man lay motionless except for his shallow breathing. He was heavily muscled, especially his arms, back and chest. His skin was a deep bronze colour all over his body. He was clad only in a fur loincloth and a leather harness that crisscrossed his chest. Blood stained his left side.

"What is he?" asked Salena, still unable to tear her eyes off the sight before her.

"I don't know," was all Duncan managed to reply, still captivated as well.

"It looks like he's hurt," continued Salena. "See the blood on his side?"

"Yes. We'd better get him out of this cage and see to his wound after Martyl and Big Cat."

"What about him? How do we know he won't die in the meantime?" asked Salena, her voice filled with worry.

"We don't know who or what he is," replied Duncan tersely. "He's lived this long, he'll live another hour. Martyl needs help now."

Salena made no reply, feeling bad for forgetting Martyl and Big Cat and waited while Duncan smashed the lock with his sword pommel. The two carefully carried the bird-man out of the cage and were surprised to find that he was quite tall, about six feet, when stretched out.

They placed him on his back, surprised that his wings folded flat so easily. They placed him on a blanket on the ground near the fire to keep him warm then returned to Martyl and Big Cat. The man and cat were both nearing unconsciousness as shock began to set in. A makeshift table was set up consisting of a few benches lying about the camp.

Duncan and Salena laid Martyl face down and began to remove the crossbow bolt from his back. Although he was a brave and strong knight, Martyl was still human and his screams and cries of pain brought tears to Salena's eyes. Duncan cringed as their makeshift bandages and rags became soaked in blood.

Finally, they cut out the last of the bolt and Duncan cauterized the wound with a flaming stick from the fire. With a final cry, Martyl lapsed into unconsciousness, the pain overwhelming him. Duncan sat down, his blood stained hands shaking and his mind filling with thoughts of rage and hatred toward the still unconscious slaver lying near the fire's edge.

"Duncan," called Salena. "We've got to help Big Cat."

His head snapped up, his smouldering eyes betraying his thoughts.

He got up solemnly and walked toward his cat, who was still trying her best, despite her pain and suffering and weakened condition to clean herself up.

Duncan and Salena knelt down to inspect the brave cat's wound and were surprised to discover that she and Patches had somehow removed the crossbow bolt themselves and had cleaned most of the wound.

"Mmrow," sounded the cat quietly.

"It's okay. You'll be all right," Duncan replied to the cat reassuringly. He stroked the cat's head softly until she began to purr.

"Good girl, Big Cat," added Salena. "You two are amazing. There's not much for us to do except seal the wound. Do you want me to do it?"

"She's my cat. I'll do it."

Duncan grabbed another stick from the fire and brought it over. Salena knelt down and held the cat's head in her lap, stroking it gently. Before his eyes clouded up any worse, Duncan plunged the hot end into Big Cat's side. The acrid smell of burning flesh and hair assaulted his nostrils again and with a final agonized meow the cat too succumbed to her injuries and passed out.

Patches meowed for his friend and his humans, showing his pain as well. Duncan and Salena both gave him a hug and a few strokes while calming themselves before the next inevitable question came up.

"What about the bird-man?" asked Salena.

"Let's have a look," replied Duncan, his voice unsteady and emotion filled. "But be careful."

They strode silently up to where the sleeping bird-man lay, still motionless. Patches padded soundlessly alongside, giving a quick glance at the unconscious slaver as he twitched once.

"It looks like he's been shot too," stated Salena grimly. "Look at the hole in his wing." She pointed at his left wing, near the spot where it joined his back. Blood was dried and caked on his side and his wing and a large spot was cleared of feathers.

"Looks like it happened awhile ago," added Duncan. "The blood is dried up and the wound is beginning to heal over. The crossbow bolt must've gone right through his wing."

"I'll clean the wound and dress it. You check on the slaver."

"Just be careful. We don't know anything about this man or bird or whatever he is," cautioned Duncan.

He got up then and went over to the slaver. A couple of prods with his boot in the ribs told him everything he needed to know. The slaver would be out for awhile yet. Salena must've really hit him, Duncan thought to himself and smiled. Looking through the fire, he watched Salena dress the bird-man's wounds.

What an odd creature, he thought. He tried to search the back corners of his memory for the ancient legends he was told as a young boy by his father. Were there any about these strange bird-men? He couldn't recall any clear enough to be sure. Maybe Martyl knew who or what this amazing creature was. He'd have to wait until later to ask him, though.

How he hoped Martyl and Big Cat were okay. His best friends, both feline and human, struck down in one night by stray bolts.

Fear and doubt began to eat away at his self-confidence again. Here he was back in his homeland after being away for fifteen years. He was a virtual stranger here and without Martyl's guidance he would be completely lost. I can't let myself think like that he thought to himself. Martyl is strong. He'll survive. Besides, no matter what, I must avenge my family and reclaim what is rightfully mine.

A loud growl brought Duncan's attention back to the moment at hand. Instinctively his hand fell to his sword pommel, still at his side. He looked around quickly while dropping to a crouch beside the prone slaver.

Across the fire from where he was, Patches was in a low crouch, ready to spring. His ears were back in warning and his large teeth barred. Another loud growl escaped his throat and he inched his lowered body forward every so slowly in the bright firelight.

Duncan trained his eyes in the direction Patches was watching and felt his heart race frantically. The bird-man had apparently awakened and surprised Salena, taking her unawares. He mentally scolded himself for leaving her alone. He should've known better! Now she was being held hostage by another unknown foe for a second time in one night! His feelings of failure and ineptness threatened to drown him now as he stared.

She was held about the throat by the bird-man with his right arm while his left arm had her left arm pinned behind her back. Her mouth was covered by his right hand but her wide eyes more than expressed her fear. Duncan hoped he hadn't been spotted yet as he made his way around the large fire, trying to sneak up behind them.

"You! Behind the fire. Get out here now and get this cat before I break her neck!"

Duncan's heart sunk as he realized he'd been seen. Probably got spotted while I was just standing there with my back to them, he thought, scolding himself again. Some knight I'm making he finished, as he stood up and came around the fire to Patches' side.

The angry cat was growling ferociously and for even a large creature like the bird-man, the fear in his eyes was quite evident when faced with such a formidable foe.

"Calm that cat and get my bow. No one is going to take me as a slave. Do as I say or I kill the girl."

"It's okay," stated Duncan, hoping he made a better negotiator than guard. The bird-man's accent was peculiar, almost halting on 'r' sounds. "We're not slavers. We just stumbled across their camp and fought them in self defence. We're the ones who let you out of the cage. She was trying to dress your wound just now."

The bird-man looked at him, a little puzzled, but he seemed to consider the information he was just told, noticing the dead slavers on the ground about them.

Holding on to the back of Patches' neck in a vain attempt to restrain the large cat, Duncan continued, "Why would we leave you untied out of that cage if we were going to sell you? Look around here. You can see all the slavers are dead except for one, who we subdued. There is also an injured man in our party and another of these cats. We wish you no harm. Let her go unharmed and you can stay or go as you wish. You have my word. Harm her, and I swear I will kill you."

The tone of his voice at the end was ice cold and all sounds in the clearing seemed to stop, everything hanging on the last words spoken.

The bird-man stared at Duncan, sizing him up and judging the actual danger of the threat from this seemingly young man and large cat. Yet there was something in the tone of his voice and they way he carried himself that spoke of some hidden, underlying strength that his youthful countenance denied. He appeared no older, than himself but spoke with authority and intelligence, unlike a slaver, he thought.

After a short pause, he replied, "That is a brave gesture, but you will find me to be a great adversary. Besides, what is your word to me? Who are you to be believed?"

Duncan was about to declare himself and his title when suddenly his mind raced with a new thought. What if this bird-man was a demon, sent by the Black Paladin to destroy him? He only wrestled with that thought for a moment before realizing that the Black Paladin did not know where they were yet and even if he did and this was a demon, he might as well face it now instead of running and being cornered by even more later.

Drawing himself up to his full height, even thought he was several inches shorter than his adversary, he proclaimed regally, "I am Duncan of Arundel, come to reclaim my kingdom. Unhand her now or face my wrath."

With that he released the hold on Patches and stood, sword drawn and ready, staring the bird-man directly in the eye.

The bird-man watched him carefully for a moment, judging his character and intent.

"I am Ar'ye of the people Rey'ak," replied the bird-man at last, releasing Salena and striding forward to clasp Duncan's hand in friendship.

The silence of the night air all about Arundel was rent apart by an inhuman screech. A shadow darker than the night sped through the small forests and glades, making its way toward the Gull River.

Stealth was of no concern here as the demon Raydon feared nothing other than its master and summoner, Draskene. It left behind a trail of destruction as it went, rending branches from trees, destroying vegetation and fouling water. Even demons must feed and rest occasionally, even one as powerful as Raydon. He feasted on several deer unlucky enough not to escape him, gorging himself on their blood and fear.

The fear was sweet, he thought, but not as sweet as human fear. How he longed for the taste of human fear. It gave him power and energy. Soon, he promised himself. Soon he would have human prey to feast on, to savour and enjoy. Raydon looked up at the stars in the sky, fresh blood running down his chin, dripping to the ground at his feet, forming little puddles and howled another blood-curdling scream.

His face twisted into a vicious grin, his razor sharp teeth shining in the moonlit darkness. He would find this would-be reclaimer to the throne and his party and enjoy himself before returning to the Black Paladin.

Duncan took his would-be foe's hand with a somewhat surprised look on his face then asked Salena if she was all right.

"I'm fine," she replied while giving Ar'ye a cold stare.

"I'm sorry, my dear lady. I only meant to escape from the slavers. I had no idea you were with the returning king. I never would have harmed you. It was merely a bluff." Ar'ye bowed his head to Salena, his face flushed with embarrassment.

At last she replied, "I forgive you."

She walked past him and Duncan and began tending to Martyl and Big Cat after throwing a blanket about herself. Now that the excitement had died down, she felt a little uncomfortable at being nearly naked in front of everyone.

"It seems," continued Ar'ye to Duncan, "that I owe you and your friend my life, or at least my freedom, which to my people is more important than life without it. I am at your service." Again he bowed his head, this time to Duncan, until he spoke.

"I am grateful for your pledge. But first, tell me where you came from, why these slavers had you and how you know of me."

"I am still weak. Sit with me by the fire and I will tell you all I know as it pertains to this."

The two sat cross legged, side by side in front of the fire. Duncan looked over to see Salena applying cold water on rags to both Martyl and Big Cat to keep down any fever they may contract from their wounds. He turned back and stared into the fire, watching it dance and jump about, slowly dying as it burned the last of the wood.

With a deep breath, Ar'ye began telling his tale and Duncan listened in earnest.

"My people live beyond what are known as the Fire Top Mountains. It is a beautiful land of forests and meadows and we wish to keep it that way. That is why we have stayed hidden from your kind for so long. We fear you and your ways. We can be a warrior race also, but never against our own kind. We have occasional battles with Wraull tribes that cross the mountains, never to return, but in the last generation they have been amassing a great army and we fear they may be planning an attack on us. We also know of the Black Paladin, his allegiance with the Wraulls and his subversion and conquering of your lands."

"How do your people know so much about us yet we know nothing of you?" asked Duncan, more than a little puzzled.

Duncan watched Ar'ye's features for any signs of evasiveness as Ar'ye paused a moment before answering. The firelight cast different patterns of light and shadow across Ar'ye's finely chiselled features, making his face hard to read, but Duncan thought he spotted something, a painful look.

"We have ... spied on the lands west of the Fire Top Mountains for several generations now." A look of surprise flashed across Duncan's face but Ar'ye continued quickly. "Only in the name of peace. We hoped to find the proper time to announce ourselves. We wanted friends and allies against the Wraulls and other, worse things of the Untamed Lands. An emissary of friendship was sent out years ago, to your father."

Duncan looked absolutely stunned at that last confession. He didn't know what to think, questions tumbled over themselves in his mind in their haste to be asked. Before he could arrange his thoughts to ask coherent questions, Ar'ye began again.

"Our emissary did not make it, however. He arrived after the Black Paladin had killed your father, of which I am very sorry."

Duncan nodded, then asked, "How did your people know what happened to my father?"

"When our emissary did not return, we sent out more spies, cautiously. Over the years we learned what happened. We are now afraid that an invasion is inevitable, given his history and the Wraull forces amassing on our border.

"That is how I was captured. I was on a scouting patrol when I was spotted by these slavers and shot about a month ago, over those swamps." He pointed off to the east, to the Slave Swamps.

"Return with me to my people. Together we will convince them to join your forces and defeat this evil."

Ar'ye's face grew stern and sullen and seemed to age a decade before Duncan's eyes as he finished, "For I have seen this evil and its atrocities. It must be stopped."

"Thank you for your support. But I am afraid that my forces are just what you see here." Duncan stretched his arm out to indicate Salena, Martyl, and his two cats.

"You truly are brave," smiled Ar'ye for the first time. "Still, come with me to my people. I will see that they help you."

"I must go to the Dwarves of the Thunder Mountains first. My friend is in need of their medicines for his wound and he seeks information from them. You could go on without us and return for help."

"Alas, my new friend. My injury has robbed me of my ability to fly, for sometime I fear. I would not get through the Untamed Lands alone without being able to fly. I will stay with you and your friends, if that is all right."

"Your presence would be most honoured," replied Duncan with a smile. "I must return across the river to pick up our supplies then in the morning we will get underway."

With that, the two rose and Ar'ye followed Duncan over to Salena while he informed her of his talk with Ar'ye and their subsequent plans.

Dawn broke over the horizon that morning and the small group got ready to head out. Two travois were made, one for Martyl and one for Big Cat. The slaver Jal had come to during the early hours of the morning and begged for his releases, promising never again to deal in slavery.

Despite the great contempt Duncan held for him, and all slavers, he couldn't kill a defenceless man, but he couldn't let him go, either, in case he informed others of their whereabouts. Ar'ye was more than willing to kill him, the look of pure hatred and disgust for the slaver more than evident on his face. In the end, it was decided they would leave him tied up where he was. It wouldn't take long for someone to find him this close to Gullhaven and they could decide his fate.

So, they began to head down the Ree River towards Frost Lake with Salena towing Big Cat in the lead, followed by Duncan and Martyl. Patches and Ar'ye, now armed with his hunting knife and long bow, brought up the rear.

Chapter Seven

The small party made their way south, following the Ree River as it wended its way towards its junction with the Gull River. Their progress was slow, having to carry along an injured man and cat who lapsed in and out of consciousness repeatedly as the day wore on.

Not only that, but the terrain itself hindered them as well. There was not much solid ground to walk between the river's edge and the Slave Swamp. The dank, rotting smell only reminded Duncan and Salena all too well of their previous experience in the local swamps.

"Do you know where to go from here?" Salena asked Duncan. "I don't think Martyl will be much help now. He needs help, more than we can give him. He and Big Cat both." She grew silent then, trudging along glumly in light of their circumstances.

"We'll get help as soon as we get to the Dwarves," Duncan replied. "We'll just follow this river, I guess. What about you Ar'ye? Do you have any idea how to reach the Thunder Mountains?"

"I have only been near them once, and that was to north of them in the Freeland Territory. That was over a month ago before I was captured."

Ar'ye too looked downcast at his inability to provide any useful information.

Duncan could feel a wave of despair and hopelessness building up inside him. Here he was in a virtually unknown land with three injured comrades and not much more than a vague idea of where he was headed. Added to the fact that two of the injured required serious aid and even if they found the Dwarves in time, there was no guarantee that they could be of any help to him.

It was enough to make him want to just drop everything and run and hide in the Misty Isles, away from all these troubles and dangers. But then another part of his mind began to take hold. What would Salena think of him if he turned and ran? What would his parents think if they were alive? He owed them vengeance. He had an obligation as heir to the throne to all who lived in his father's kingdom to free them. It was time he became a man and took charge.

Like a horse unburdened from its plow, he pulled himself up straight and shook off his self-doubts. He would no longer fear all the uncertainties that lay ahead on their journey. He was determined to see his new journey through, despite the trials he would face.

"We'll follow this river to Frost Lake," Duncan said, with a hint of authority in his voice. "From there we'll try to get a boat to cross the lake to cut down our time. Martyl said it was two days by water. Now let's have a rest and something to eat."

The others agreed readily as the midday sun was at its zenith, shining down on them with a fierceness that burned their already reddened skin to a deeper red.

No other sound except the soft hum of the insects in the swamp could be heard. The air was still and humid, close to the swamp and river. The swamp smell became stronger as the heat rose, its rotting smell taking away any pleasure they may have derived from their meal. Patches, his sense of smell the keenest, was bothered the most. He constantly tried to cover his nose with his paw to mask the smell.

They ate in silence, with Duncan and Salena trying to give water to the injured cat and knight, still lying on their travois.

"I'd better change their bandages," Salena said softly. Duncan nodded his head and went to get some clean cloth from his backpack.

After cleaning and dressing Martyl's and Big Cat's wounds, Salena turned to Ar'ye for the first time in nearly a day and spoke to him.

"Just to show there are no hard feelings, would you like me dress your wound?"

"I would be honoured, Lady Salena," he replied with a bow. "Again, I am truly sorry about that incident. It was a cowardly act, unbecoming of myself and my people, but I feared you we're more slavers." He did not look at her now, too ashamed of himself.

"Apology accepted," Salena said with a smile and she began to tend his wounded wing.

As he watched, Ar'ye noticed the webbing between Salena's fingers and caught himself staring. Finally, he asked, "Whatever happened to your hands?"

Salena laughed and replied, "I guess you've never seen a Siren before, have you?" She continued to smile, a warm friendly smile that made Ar'ye feel a little more comfortable with these strangers.

"No, I haven't. I assume then that there are more like yourself?"

Salena stopped then, realizing that she was about to reveal the presence of her heretofore unknown homeland. She looked to Duncan and he shrugged his shoulders where he sat by Patches.

"I think its okay to tell him. He told us of his people who remain hidden."

Salena turned to Ar'ye and continued, now straight-faced. "I come from a place called the Misty Isles, across the sea. My father is the King there. That is where Duncan has been in exile until now. I returned with him and Martyl, along with these cats to help him in his quest."

Ar'ye nodded his head and replied, "You have my vow of secrecy, Lady Salena." He bowed his head to her in a gesture of compliance with her wishes.

"I think its time we get moving," Duncan broke in, trying his best to sound sure of himself. "We've got a lot of travelling to do yet."

They picked up their packs and the two travois and continued on their slow march south to where the Ree and Gull Rivers met. As the afternoon wore on, the sun gave no respite from its intense rays, burning away all clouds, leaving a blue, empty sky above.

Duncan and Salena both found themselves longing for the cool shady forests of the Misty Isles. Both of them could picture in their mind's eye sitting along side a nice, slow brook, listening to the birds and forest animals with Patches and Big Cat sitting at their feet. Anything would be preferable to the intense heat and fetid swamps they had seen so far.

Ar'ye's thoughts drifted too, trying to distract his attention from the unpleasant surroundings. He too thought of his homeland and wished he could be soaring in and out of the rocky crags of the Fire Top Mountains. He could almost hear the eagles and hawks beckoning him to fly with them, rising up higher than the clouds, drifting lazily on the wind currents, going wherever his heart desired.

His life, and that of all his people had been relatively carefree. He missed that and appreciated it even more after spending nearly one month captive with slavers. Thinking of that began to make him angry again, at himself for being caught and at the slavers for damaging his wing and his subsequent capture.

Now he couldn't fly and there was no telling when or if he would return to his home. Or if his home would even be there when he returned, whispered another, darker thought from some back corner of his mind.

There was still the Wraull army on their border, preparing for an eventual attack on his people, the Rey'ak. The mere thought of such vile creatures marching into his people's lands frightened and angered him immensely.

They were barbaric and uncivilized and even though his people were superior warriors and had the advantage of flight, they were outnumbered by at least fifteen to one at last estimate.

Yet they had hope, he told himself.

The rightful heir to Arundel, the strongest kingdom in the land had returned. If he could reclaim his armies, maybe together their peoples could be victorious. There were a lot of uncertainties in his thoughts but he couldn't give up hope. It was all that they had. He had to believe in Duncan himself if he hoped to convince the rest of his people.

Soon a new sound reached their ears, bringing all to alert attention. The roar of water could now be heard and the insect buzzing had stopped. The group quickened their pace instinctively as a collective unit, anxious to be rid of the oppressive swamp.

The swamp finally gave way, opening up to rocky terrain and small clusters of trees, mostly green broadleaf trees. Here the Gull and Ree Rivers met in a snarling, churning mass of water that frothed and spit like a frightened cornered animal. The Ree River ran straight into the Gull river here and ended in a nasty set of rapids. From here the Gull River continued on for a short distance to Frost Lake which they could just begin to see on the eastern horizon.

"Let's have a short meal here," said Duncan as they reached a flat spot on the rocks. With a barely repressed gasp, they all sat down, weary from the day's march. The splashing mist was welcomed for its cooling effect and even Patches didn't seem to mind the water this time. Duncan took water to Martyl and Big Cat and tried to get them to drink something.

"Where are we now?" Martyl asked weakly. This was the first time he'd spoken in nearly a day and Duncan's fears lightened at the sound of his friend's voice.

"At a rapids at the junction of two rivers, most likely the Ree and Gull, although I don't know for sure. We've been headed south for a day now," replied Duncan, kneeling next to Martyl's travois. He hoped his face wouldn't betray the fear and helplessness he felt. He needed Martyl to think everything was under control. He didn't want to upset him in his condition.

"Good. Now listen carefully," Martyl began before he winced in pain and paused for a second before continuing. "Continue east across Frost Lake until you come to the far side. There a river heads south. That is the Sylvan River. Follow it until it breaks off east. That is the Thunder River and will lead you to the Thunder Mountains."

Again Martyl stopped, only this time he began coughing violently and his eyes glazed over and seemed to be focussing on something in the distance.

"We don't have a boat," Duncan stated, hoping Martyl could still hear and answer him.

Martyl was silent a few more moments before his eyes seemed to refocus on Duncan then he answered, almost in a whisper, "Across the river. There," he pointed south across the Gull River, "is a small fishing village across this river. They will have a boat."

Martyl then grabbed Duncan's arm with enough force in his weakened condition to surprise the younger man and said, his voice even lower but still commanding, "Don't hesitate to leave me if you need to. I will only hinder you, weakened as I am."

"Never," replied Duncan sternly and he rose to his feet. "Now rest. We'll get a boat and get to the Dwarves." With that he turned and walked back to Salena and Ar'ye who were feeding and petting Patches, trying to distract themselves from Duncan and Martyl.

"How is he?" asked Salena.

"Alright, I guess," replied Duncan. "Considering the circumstances."

"Did you tell him about Ar'ye?" she continued, hoping to raise Duncan's spirits by keeping him talking.

"No. There was no point. He barely had enough strength to give me directions to the Thunder Mountains. I don't want to put him under any more stress than necessary. How is Big Cat?" He reached out and stroked his cat's head. Patches mewed softly, offering his condolences.

"Better," replied Salena. "These cats were bred for their stamina and strength, as well as intelligence."

"A truly remarkable animal," added Ar'ye as he too petted Big Cat. She purred weakly to show her appreciation and to ease the pain. A few moments of silence passed before Salena finally asked, "Well, are you going to tell us where we're headed now?"

Duncan sat up straight and looked at her squarely before replying, "We need a boat to sail across Frost Lake. There is a fishing village across this river but we have no money or anything to trade with."

Now he began to look dejected and lowered his gaze from hers before continuing, "You are the only one who can swim across but I can't ask you to steal a boat. It's too dangerous." Besides, he told himself, what kind of king will I make if I must always look to others' to solve my problems.

Salena began to grin which caused Duncan no small amount of discomfort and confusion. Before he could react further she said, "Is that what's bothering you?" and her grin broke out into an all out smile, from ear to ear. Duncan was completely nonplussed at this point, feeling angry and bewildered at once. Reaching into her pants' pockets Salena pulled out a small leather bag, the size of her fist.

"I borrowed this from our slaver friends the other night before we left," she said with a small laugh. "I don't think they'll need it." With that she opened the bag and emptied its contents, twelve gold coins.

"Terrific," exclaimed Duncan, his face brightening already. "You should go now, before it gets dark. We still have a few hours of light. But be careful."

Salena rose to her feet, followed by Duncan and Ar'ye, and replied, "You worry too much." She gave him a wink and then turned to hurry down the riverbank. When she passed the rapids, she jumped in, fully clothed, and made a beeline for the opposite shore.

Duncan watched her leave, an uneasy feeling gnawing at his stomach. Ar'ye watched her with complete fascination, mesmerized by the way her supple body cut the swift moving current like a razor sharp blade. It reminded him of how his people soared on the air currents and again his heart longed for home.

"We may as well get comfortable," said Duncan, breaking the reverie. "She may be a while."

The two men sat down next to Martyl and the two cats and tended their wounds once more.

Salena rejoiced at being in the cool water again. It was a welcome relief from the stagnant, stale air of the swampy river bed. She felt all the grime and grit washing off her beneath her clothes and smiled.

The water reminded her so much of home. She'd been so pumped up on adrenaline until now she didn't realize just how much she missed the Misty Isles. Everything was new here and so dangerous. In the past few days she had seen more than her entire life at home on the Misty Isles. Sadly, she thought, most of what she'd encountered had been death and misery.

Poor Big Cat, she thought. And Martyl. She'd grown up with them almost her entire life and now they may die soon if they didn't get medical help fast. Salena began to grow sad at these thoughts but then strengthened her resolve with the thought that she was the one getting the boat for them. She was the one upon whom they depended. This gave her a definite purpose to accomplish. She would succeed so that her friends could live.

Faster she swam, quickening her pace. Her webbed fingers and toes propelled her through the quick moving water. She paid no heed to the fact that her clothing clung to her limbs, causing her to exert more energy, or the gradual ebb of pain into her muscles.

She would get a boat if it was the last thing she did. Any maybe some healing salves from a healer in the village. On she swam, drawing on her body's energy reserves to keep going.

After about fifteen minutes, Salena reached the far shore of the Gull River and climbed out of the water, her hair and clothes matted to her body, giving her the look of a drowned rat. Looking about, she tried to locate the fishing village. Her heart sank when all she saw were a few blackened huts and a dozen or more charred skeletons about fifty yards from where she stood.

Taking a deep breath, she steadied herself and approached the remains of the village. Broken arrows and spears littered the ground, many protruding from the burned skeletons. The stench of burnt flesh and smouldering wood permeated the air. The village had been massacred and not a building was left standing. Salena felt her hopes and those of their group smashed, like a wave upon the rocks in a storming sea.

"What happened?" she said aloud to herself, just wanting to hear her own voice to dispel the uneasiness she felt in the quiet.

Salena looked around through the piles of rubble, hoping to find something to give her a clue as to what happened. Her heart nearly stopped and a shiver ran down her spine when she found a piece of cloth, presumably off an uniform, with a black horse rearing up, snorting flames.

The Prime Guard, she thought, remembering what Martyl had told them after his encounter with them in Gullhaven. Time to leave, she figured and headed quickly for the dock by the river bank. She broke out into a run, afraid more guards would be about and reached the dock in seconds, unaware of the two men seated at the side of the dock, beside a small river skiff.

The sun was now deep in the western sky, setting on the ocean, turning the dark blue waters a crimson blood colour as its rays reflected off the rolling waves. Raydon rose from his place of concealment just outside the city of Gullhaven. Even demons must eat and sleep when summoned into service on this plane and now fully awake he began his search for food.

The scent of human fear and suffering from the nearby city was strong and very alluring. Raydon was very tempted to remain and feed in the human cesspool that was once a thriving city but his master had other plans for him. To disobey them would mean incurring his wrath and even demons knew better than to anger their summoners.

He was covering ground very quickly with his unnatural speed and raced towards the Ree River. He had picked up a strange scent the previous day outside the city and was now following it. In the growing twilight he did not bother to conceal himself anymore, although even if he was spotted there were very few creatures that could challenge him.

Nearing the river, Raydon picked up the smell of human fear and anger, fresh and strong. He reared his head back and grinned a murderous smile, fangs barred, howling in a blood-lust. He would feast on human fear yet tonight, he told himself.

Jal had waited until all sounds of the departing party had faded away into the distance before he made any attempts at freeing himself. He was furious over what happened and promised himself he would have revenge. He was not too distraught over the loss of his cohorts, in fact he was actually thankful for that as he wouldn't have to split his haul, but he was extremely upset over having lost the bird-man and being tied up and left to rot. If this is how it felt to be a slave awaiting sale, he didn't care to find out. If others of his kind found him like this he knew that's how he would wind up.

Plans of revenge and repayment danced through his thoughts like minstrels in a parade as he spent the better part of the day freeing himself from his bonds. Eventually, after hours of painstaking effort, he managed to cut the ropes binding him by rubbing them on a large rock he had rolled to. Now free at last, he began picking through what was left of his camp, arming himself with his crossbow.

He had been terribly afraid earlier while he was tied up, fearing fellow slavers may come by and sell him, finding him already tied up. That fear was still with him now, although not as bad now that he was armed and able to defend himself. But he wasn't about to let his guard down as rival slave gangs would think very little of disposing of him either as a slave or just killing him for sport.

As the afternoon gave way to early evening, Jal started up a fire and began roasting a small quail he managed to shoot. His stomach growled in anticipation as the smells of fresh bird reached his nose. He had expended more energy than he thought trying to free himself. When he finally sat down to eat, it was now twilight and he hurriedly ate his meal, hoping to begin tracking his escaped adversaries that night and catch them unawares.

Suddenly a vicious howl ripped through the still silence, sending a shiver straight down his spine. Jal was an experienced outdoors man but had never heard a sound like that before. Then again, he thought to himself, he had never seen anything like the bird-man or large cats, either. Things were definitely changing and becoming stranger all the time.

Deciding against leaving right away, Jal waited to see if whatever made the noise would show itself soon. He hoped maybe it would be some other strange creature he could capture and sell to help repay his losses here. Sitting behind the fire in a crouch, his crossbow at the ready, he hoped to have the advantage of surprise.

Within minutes he saw a dark shadow cross the river at the ford, with amazing and unnatural speed. In another couple of minutes the creature was over the riverbank on his side and rapidly approaching. Jal froze when the firelight shone on the most hideous sight he'd ever seen.

Standing before him at over seven feet tall was a dark-skinned, man-shaped creature with long hair hanging in clumps all over its body. Barbs protruded from its body at different angles and when it snarled, staring right at him, fangs as long and sharp as daggers gleamed in the moonlit darkness.

Jal panicked and fired a bolt, directly into the beast before him. The bolt hit it square in the chest, but what would've killed an ordinary man only served to anger this thing. Never having seen a demon before, Jal had no idea that ordinary weapons could not harm them. He only reloaded and fired again, missing completely this time as he shook with fear.

Raydon shrieked his fury at being attacked and rushed Jal in a blood-lust as he smelled fresh human fear, strong and pungent. Jal panicked and ran, throwing his crossbow in a fit of fear. He was not fast enough and Raydon had him, grabbing him with one claw and spinning him about with the other, ripping through his clothing and flesh easier than a sword slicing thin air.

Jal shrieked in agonizing pain and fear, his eyes as wide as saucers. Blood ran down his arms in streams, dripping from his fingers to pool as his feet. Raydon revelled in Jal's fear, drinking it in and gaining strength from it. It was like a narcotic to him and he wanted more.

He wanted to feast on this pitiful human and then seek out others until his craving was sated. His clawed hands dug in deeper, eliciting long, drawn out shrieks of pain from Jal, feasting on the fear and pain emanating from him when an old memory crept into his mind.

The ones his master is seeking were on this trail. That's what led him here. Easing his grip on Jal, Raydon asked in a voice that sounded like steal on slate, "I seek others that passed by here. One is a knight or warrior. Did you see them?"

Again he smiled, that hideous fanged smile. Jal was delirious with pain and fear, Raydon's claws having ripped through the muscle of his arms and into the bone. Yet his pain addled mind did focus on the possibility that this could be his one chance for survival, sell this information for his life. It took the last of his strength to answer, and his voice came out in a sharp hiss, almost unrecognizable to himself.

"Let me go and I'll tell you how many and where they went. I can even help you track them." He hoped it would work.

Raydon became infuriated and shook Jal viciously, causing him to scream even louder, his voice echoing in the now dark sky.

"Tell me where they are headed," he shrieked. He had no need of a tracker as he was better than any human and he could tell by the different scents how many were present. He just wanted to know where they were headed to arrive before them and intercept them.

Jal had no answer and within moments his body took the last of the punishment it was going to as Raydon literally shook him to pieces, his knife-like claws easily slicing through the bone of Jal's upper arms and severing them from his body.

By the time Salena saw the two Prime Guards sitting near the dock, it was too late. They had already seen her and were rising to their feet, sword hands at the ready. She nearly panicked then, remembering what had happened the last time she snuck into an unknown camp. And besides, these were no slavers, they were members of the Prime Guard, as shown by the rearing horse insignia on their black uniforms.

"Halt. State your business here," called out one of the guards.

They were both marching toward her now, hands on sword pommels. Salena was not about to let herself fall into the same trap as before, especially with the situation their party was in now. It was nearing dark now, the sun already deep in the western sky and she found herself again remembering home and the beautiful ocean sunsets. Suddenly, an idea came to her, glaring in her mind as bright as the setting sun itself.

If only I'm close enough to the water, she thought. Both guards were now only twenty feet away and had drawn their swords, having not received an answer from her yet.

"Who are you?" called out the larger of the two Prime Guards, a very intense look on his face. His tone left no doubt that they were indeed very serious about determining who she was.

With her stomach doing cartwheels, Salena began to sing. At first, the two guards just stared dumbfounded, having never encountered something as odd as this before. Then, slowly, as Salena continued to sing, they no longer saw a slim, still dripping wet young lady in front of them. Instead, their minds were filled with visions and sounds of waves gently lapping against a strange beach. They began to sway a little on their feet then dropped to their knees after a few minutes.

Suddenly a distant scream rent the air and snapped the guards back from their trances as Salena was startled from her song. Before they could rise fully sober, Salena picked up a piece of broken wood laying nearby and clobbered each of them over the head, leaving them in a deeper sleep than her song would have. Without looking back, she ran for the skiff tied to the dock and pushed off, heading across the river back to her party.

Chapter Eight

As Salena began to pilot the small skiff back across the river, she found herself wondering how well they'd fare on board it when they got to Frost Lake. She was having a hard time controlling it now on the river and just hoped the lake was calm while they were on it. A few good waves would smash the skiff into driftwood. If only there had been a small boat there, she thought, our chances would be much better.

Still, as she surveyed her newly acquired transportation she was somewhat inwardly pleased at herself.

The skiff had a flat bottom and was about ten feet long by four feet wide. It had sides about one foot high, just high enough to protect supplies on the bottom from spray, and a large rudder at the back, where she was currently stationed, steering the skiff downstream to Duncan and the others. Two paddles lay on the bottom of the skiff, a good measure in case there was no current.

Salena allowed herself a little pride, knowing that she had now contributed a very important part to the party's journey. She could also put herself at ease a little more knowing that help was now only two days away for Martyl and Big Cat, instead of nearly a week.

As the skiff followed the river current, Salena began to ponder her newest encounter. The two guards did not fall asleep as quickly or deeply as they should have, she thought. Not only had they not fully succumbed to her song when they should have but they were awakened by the scream from up the river where she and the others had come from.

I wasn't too far from the water, she continued thinking, so why did they not fall asleep? Maybe I'm too far from my home waters. That final thought hung suspended in her mind, twisting like a leaf in the wind until she forced it out with a new thought, knowing there was nothing she could do about that now. Moving on to other thoughts, she wondered about the scream that shattered the dusk. What was that scream? It sounded like no animal she'd ever heard, almost like a man, but in incredible agony.

That really frightened her and she wondered if Duncan and the others were okay. She reminded herself that she was in a strange land and there were bound to be noises she didn't understand.

It was now completely dark, the sun having sunk in the western sky and the black blanket of night now covered all. A few stars began shining, giving off a faint light. Finally Salena spotted a small fire on the opposite bank of the river and steered the skiff to it. She was overwhelmed with relief when she saw Duncan and Ar'ye seated about the fire with Martyl and Patches between them.

Steering the skiff towards them, Salena beached it on a low spot of the bank and bounded out, running to meet her waiting friends.

"We must leave now," she said in a worried tone. "We can't waste any time."

"What's wrong?" asked Duncan.

"I encountered two of the Prime Guard in the fishing village. It was destroyed and I think they did it."

Ar'ye noticed the look of surprise on Duncan's face and nodded his head in acknowledgement before adding, "I feared as much. Their evil has already spread over much of the land. This is why my people fear the Black Paladin so much. His troops will destroy for no reason other than to instill fear and obedience."

"I got away by using my Siren Song," Salena continued. "But I fear its losing its effectiveness. It didn't take effect as quickly as it should, nor last."

She paused for a second, catching her breath, then finished, "Now please. Leave now. I heard a terrible scream from off in this direction and it really scared me. I'm afraid something terrible is coming."

Salena lowered her gaze from Duncan and Ar'ye, feeling ashamed for admitting her fears in front of them.

Duncan replied, "It's okay. We heard it too. It was more than a little disconcerting."

He hated to lie to her but he wasn't about to admit it scared him more than he cared to think about. The trio set to work quickly, placing Martyl and Big Cat on the bottom of the skiff, lying down, and packed their supplies about them to keep them from being tossed about.

Patches meanwhile kept staring back through the small trees and darkness of night at the swamp they'd just left. His ears were pointed straight ahead, straining to hear some sound not yet noticeable to the others.

When they were ready to leave a short while later, Ar'ye and Salena boarded the skiff, with Salena at the rudder. Duncan turned from the bank to call for Patches. The large cat didn't acknowledge him, his attention focussed on something only he could see or hear. His tail was puffed up and swaying back and forth.

Duncan called him again and as he approached Patches, the cat flattened himself to the ground, his rear legs working up for a pounce and a low growl escaped his open, large fanged mouth.

"What's wrong?" he asked in a low voice, crouching beside the cat.

Patches made no response other than a louder grow and flattened himself even more, if at all possible. Now all his fur was standing on end, making him look twice as big as his already formidable size.

"Duncan, come on. Now!" called Salena in a worried voice. "Something's coming! Look at Patches. He detects it already."

Duncan could tell by the anxiety in her voice that she was truly worried. With a deep breath, he reached down to pick up the cat when a thunderous crashing noise was heard at the far edge of the small stand of trees. Patches' low growl turned to a snarl of warning as Duncan tried to lift him up.

Just as he rose to his feet with a spitting, snarling overlarge cat in his arms, the creature that had occupied the cat's attention for so long broke through the small trees in front of them. Duncan froze in his tracks, his eyes wide with disbelief and fear as he finally realized what was before him. He had seen only one once before, and that was fifteen years ago as a young boy, but there was no mistaking what was in front of him now, even in the dim starlight.

It was a demon and it was heading for him fast.

The simultaneous screams of Ar'ye and Salena alerted Duncan to the fact that he'd better move quick, but before he could turn to run, Patches leapt from his arms with an earsplitting growl, knocking Duncan to the ground with the force of his escape.

The cat hit the demon with such force and speed it took it by complete surprise. His claws and teeth ripped through even the demon's tough hide, drawing black, shiny ooze that passed for blood from the wounds.

Ar'ye and Salena were out of the skiff seconds later, running to Duncan. Ar'ye had his bow out and an arrow already notched, aimed at the demon, now rolling on the ground with Patches.

"Get in the boat!" shrieked Salena, shaking with fear as she helped Duncan to his feet.

"I've got to help Patches," he protested, drawing his sword.

Ar'ye let loose his arrow, striking the demon in the leg and watched, seemingly unaffected by the struggle in front of him. The demon didn't even flinch as the arrow struck. Patches and Raydon rolled about, snarling and growling at one another. The cat would pounce, swatting his massive paws and then leap away as the demon tried to retaliate.

Raydon screamed in fury, causing the others watching to shrink back in fear. He was infuriated more than he believed possible at not being able to kill his smaller attacker. Never before had any natural creature stood up to him this long or harmed him this much. With another shriek he leapt at the cat as it coiled up to pounce and landed on top of it, crushing it to the ground.

"It's over," shouted Ar'ye. "Get in the boat!"

He and Salena grabbed Duncan as he began to protest and ushered him to the skiff. All three stumbled in and Ar'ye pushed off with a long branch. Duncan yelled out to Patches who was nowhere to be seen beneath the demon. He continued to struggle with Salena and Ar'ye, furious at them for leaving his cat behind.

Raydon heard the yell as he prepared to strike his first blow at the downed cat and realized his intended prey was about to escape. He rose with amazing fluidity and speed for something of such great size and bulk and sped for the river bank and departing skiff.

Patches rose also, his wind returned and fur matted with the black slime that was demon blood and leapt again at the demon. His teeth sank into Raydon's lower leg and neatly removed half of his calf, severing tendons and muscles alike, reaching bone. Raydon toppled over with an anguished and surprised gurgle of pain. Seeing the skiff and his friends heading down the river, Patches listened to their desperate cries to him. Ignoring any discomfort he might feel, he plunged into the water and swam after them.

For an animal that was supposed to hate water, Patches reached the skiff quickly and was hauled aboard by Duncan and Ar'ye. With a meow of thanks, the soaked cat shook himself off and set about cleaning his fur. Remarkably, Duncan could find no wounds on his cat and found himself smiling again at both cats.

When he turned to face Salena and Ar'ye, his smile was gone, replaced by his usual facade of non-emotion. Before he could speak, Ar'ye cut him off, knowing what Duncan wanted to say.

"You must understand that we couldn't kill the demon."

"I saw one killed before," Duncan replied icily.

"They can only be killed by magic weapons. You saw my arrow go right through his leg. It had no effect at all. Your cat is not of this land either. That is why he had a chance, but only a small one. He obviously has some magic about him."

Duncan was silent for a moment as the reality of the situation sunk in, then replied, "I have a dagger, given to me by old friend. It is magic. If this demon returns, I'll be prepared."

"I hope the magic is strong enough, my friend," finished Ar'ye as he went back to rowing.

"How are Martyl and Big Cat?" asked Salena from her position at the rudder, hoping to change the subject before it escalated further.

"Still in deep sleep. Hard to believe after that ruckus," replied Duncan as he too picked up an oar to row.

Even with current going their way, the trio were taking no chances in letting the demon catch up to them and rowed as hard as possible. Their tired bodies were refuelled by the adrenaline now coursing through their veins.

After a few hours, the Gull River emptied into Frost Lake, a large body of water that spanned farther than they could see in the bright moonlight. The moon was high overhead, giving off its bright light and the trio could now see how the lake got its name. The dark, impenetrable surface of the water shimmered in the moonlight with silvery-white colour, much like early morning frost on the grass.

Salena sighed at its beauty and found herself feeling strangely at home for the first time since leaving the Misty Isles.

"Isn't it beautiful," Salena said out loud.

"Yes, very," replied Ar'ye.

Duncan remained silent, seated with his oar, still rowing. Ar'ye and Salena exchanged knowing glances and returned to their rowing and steering of the skiff. Soon the excitement wore off and the day's long hours and exertion began to take their toll. Duncan fell asleep first, followed quickly by Salena and Ar'ye.

Draskene sat in his chambers in the dark, seated at a small table, staring intently at a fist-sized black crystal. As he slipped into a trance, the scrying crystal began to appear as a black hole on the table. In his trance-induced state, Draskene could use the scrying crystal as a window with which to view others.

Even someone with powers as great as his was not omniscient and he needed to know the whereabouts of his demon familiar. The scrying crystal would give him the ability to see through his familiar's eyes and read its thoughts and memories.

There were limitations to this power as well, Draskene reminded himself, as with many of his abilities. The further the demon got from the crystal, the harder it was to see its thoughts. Also, demons were prone to "blood-lust"—killing just for the sport of it, feeding off the fear and blood of their victims. This troubled Draskene as he did not want Duncan dead—yet.

The scrying crystal's light had now become a natural colour and Draskene awakened from his trance, his cold black eyes shining from the light of the crystal reflecting off them. Focussing his gaze on the crystal, he let his thoughts channel into the crystal, weaving their way through its essence, making its magical structure become part of his own consciousness. He could feel its powers snaking out like gauzy tendrils, seeking creatures from other planes like himself, honing in on their otherworldly emanations.

There was danger in using the crystal and Draskene knew it, as the crystal itself would try to overcome the user. His own arrogance however, would not allow him to believe he could be overcome. Mental barriers, like iron doors slamming shut blocked the crystal from penetrating Draskene's thoughts. Yet like light creeping through the chinks in a wall, his consciousness passed through the barriers and into the crystal.

He roamed its ethereal pathways like a moth in the wind, floating along at breakneck speed until he saw what he was seeking, Raydon.

From up above he looked down on the demon and saw him lying in a pool of his own black, oozing blood. Raydon's left leg had an arrow in it, protruding out at either end, directly through his skin and muscle.

That did not bother Draskene so much as wounds from non-magical weapons would heal very quickly. What did trouble him was the almost total absence of a calf muscle on his left leg and the constant flow of blood from the wound. It was not a clean wound from a weapon, either, but more like a bite. The fact that the blood flow had not stopped told him that the attacker was capable of harming a demon. That made the attacker powerful indeed, thought Draskene. He did not like powerful people or creatures running around his lands unless they were doing his bidding.

Draskene needed to know what kind of creature did this to the demon and prepared to enter Raydon's consciousness. Again, he needed to be careful lest the scrying crystal overcome and trap him. The danger was even greater now as he would be controlling the crystal and Raydon at the same time, but the need to know what happened overcame the caution.

Like a blast of warm air, Draskene's consciousness swept into the demon's body, entering at the base of the spine and spreading out through his entire body. He could feel Raydon's pain lance through his being and winced inwardly at its strength. It was a good sign, however, that he still lived.

When their minds met, there was a struggle for supremacy over the body and Draskene could also feel the crystal's power trying to wash over him. His unconscious mind steeled itself against both assaults, from demon and crystal, counterattacking on behalf of his conscious mind. The struggle only lasted a few seconds until Draskene's mental wards took effect, protecting him from being overcome.

With that out of the way, he began to sift through Raydon's recent memories, recounting the recent events. He learned of the attack on the slaver and the tracking and subsequent encounter with a very strange group of individuals. Draskene saw a young woman, a man-like creature with large wings, a young man and a large grey and white cat.

The woman was of no concern to him and the bird-man appeared to be another of the people called the Rey'ak of which he was already familiar. But the young man. That was another matter. He looked like the spitting image of a young Aramid. It could only be Duncan, he thought, come back for his revenge. Draskene smiled inwardly at that thought as he continued sifting through the demon's memory.

What he saw next he found very disturbing. The overgrown cat and Raydon were locked in mortal combat. The cat, although not inflicting any serious wounds, appeared to have the upper hand with its superior speed and agility. The bird-man launched an arrow into his leg with futility and fled. He watched as the battle played out before him until it stopped with the cat biting off nearly half of Raydon's lower leg.

It will heal, Draskene thought to himself. He could already sense the demon's supernatural healing system at work, stopping the blood flow and regenerating lost muscle and skin. Learning all he could for the time being, Draskene left Raydon to himself, his consciousness returning to his own body, knocking him back into his chair with enough force to almost topple it over backwards.

He sat upright slowly, taking shallow breaths of air, remaining in the darkness of the room. Duncan was back. Grown into a young man, the same likeness as his father, Aramid. But where were Martyl and Connor? Had they died or become separated over the years? Who was the girl and how did they come across one of the Rey'ak?

Maybe Duncan and the others discovered the Rey'ak in their flight fifteen years ago. That would explain a lot, he thought. But where did the large cat come from, he wondered. It could not be from these lands, not wounding Raydon like it did. Shortly before he could come up with any answers, sleep easily overcame Draskene. It was something even he could not defend against, especially after a night of scrying.

Duncan woke with a start, his mind cloudy and uneasy with unremembered bad dreams from the previous night. He looked out into the early morning light and realized he and the others were still on Frost Lake. The early morning sky was a brilliant red colour, the rising sun causing both the scattered clouds and the water below to glow with amazing brilliancy.

Even this beautiful sight could not alleviate the bad feeling still with Duncan and he rose carefully in the small skiff, scanning all about for any sign of the demon. All he could see in any direction was water. Endless amounts of water.

"Don't worry, my friend," whispered Ar'ye quietly to Duncan. "The demon is far behind us now."

Duncan turned to face his new friend, replying, "I didn't mean to wake you."

"I sleep lightly. It is a trait of my people."

"He's out there. Waiting for us. I can feel it." Duncan said it so bluntly and cold that Ar'ye felt a shiver run down his spine.

Averting Duncan's gaze, he said, just as bluntly, "We must get to shore soon. I've seen these skies before. It's going to storm."

Salena and Patches had risen by this time now and made their way from the rear of the skiff to the front. They were careful to avoiding disturbing Martyl and Big Cat.

"Good morning," she hoped rather than felt. Salena could tell by Duncan's face that he had slept no better than her that night.

"Ar'ye tells me a storm may be on the way. We'd better eat and then get to shore."

Salena nodded in acknowledgement, her own training in the ways of the sea reminding her of the flimsiness of their craft.

Duncan quickly set about getting their breakfast, dried meat, cheese and water, from one of the packs. When they finished, Salena went to change Martyl's and Big Cat's bandages. Ar'ye, his wing beginning to get better, was able to tend to his own dressings.

"How are they?" asked Duncan, more than a little worry showing in his voice.

Salena swallowed hard, trying to steady her voice before replying, "Worse, I'm afraid. If we don't get help soon, I don't think they'll make it. They're both out now and their breathing is very shallow."

"Let's get going then. Steer us east."

With that, Duncan sat down and began rowing in earnest. He didn't want anyone to see the redness in his eyes or hear the lump in his throat if he spoke. He felt he had to stay strong in front of the others to give them all the strength to carry on.

As they rowed through the morning hours, the sky darkened instead of growing lighter. Ar'ye's forecast was beginning to look as if it would come to be. The winds began to pick up speed, causing the waters of the lake to churn and froth, tossing the occupants of the skiff about with impunity. Duncan and Ar'ye fought the waves with their small paddles as Salena tried desperately to hold them on course.

A course to where, she was not sure of. During the night while they all slept, exhausted, the skiff had floated about freely, following whatever current it encountered. Salena hoped they were still travelling in a south-easterly direction to where the lake ended at the Sylvan River. Her people had inherent directional abilities, but like her Siren song, it seemed somewhat diluted in this new land.

Again she pondered this new fact. Anything, she thought, to keep her mind off the aching pain in her muscles. It had been a long time since she last piloted a small boat, and she could feel it.

The only explanation she could come up with for her failing abilities was the fact that she was so far away from her homeland. The islands and water surrounding them were what gave her people their special abilities. Here she was surrounded by land and fresh water, not salt.

Even so, she still found this to be disconcerting. After all, these were attributes she was born with and had all her life, only to fade away now when she needed them most. Becoming frustrated, Salena concentrated sharply to ascertain their bearing. She was convinced after a few moments that they were indeed headed in the right direction. I've still got it, she thought to herself and smiled.

The spray from the waves was becoming stronger and soon everyone on the skiff was soaked. Duncan and Salena faired best with only the hair on their heads to get wet but Ar'ye's wings were a great burden when weighed down by the water. Patches was absolutely beside himself in self-pity as his beautiful grey and white coat of fur became a dull colour when fully drenched by water. Martyl and Big Cat were a little better off as they were lying down, covered by a tarpaulin Ar'ye had placed over them.

Duncan got up and retrieved their forest cloaks from their packs. "Here," he called to Salena. "Put this on. They're supposed to be waterproof."

He and Salena quickly pulled them on, fastening the leg straps. Already they felt better with the warmth provided by the sleeved cloaks.

"Would you like Martyl's cloak?" Duncan asked Ar'ye. "He's covered already. It'll be alright." He found himself beginning to shout now as the wind picked up even more in the nearly black early afternoon sky.

"No. It wouldn't fit over my wings. Besides, my people aren't very good swimmers and it would only hinder me more should we capsize."

Duncan only nodded as the reality began to sink in that they may be literally in over their heads. Turning back to sit down, a large wave crashed into the skiff with such vehemence that Duncan was thrown clear over the side of the skiff. Gone, in the blink of an eye.

"Where is he!" screamed Salena, not daring to leave her place at the rudder even though her heart was tearing apart at that very instant.

"I don't know yet!" came Ar'ye's shouted reply over the wind and waves as he shuffled to the other side of the skiff to peer over the edge on his knees. Both he and Salena scanned the choppy waters but the whitecaps and dim light did little to help their search. The little skiff was now being tossed about like a child's toy and Ar'ye began to wonder if he would ever reach land again.

"Take the rudder!" shouted Salena.

"What?" came Ar'ye puzzled reply.

"Take the rudder. I'm going in after him."

She had already removed her sleeved-cloak and was removing her shirt and pants when she saw his puzzled look.

"Just hold us steady. I can swim in this. It's Duncan's only hope. Do you understand?"

Ar'ye nodded yes as he crawled back to the rudder, careful not to get tossed out himself. He found himself admiring Salena's strength and courage as she dove into the torrid waters, clad only in her undergarments.

Patches was silent and anxious with all the excitement going on about him and his tail flicked back and forth as his eyes easily followed Salena in the dark. Repeatedly, as he watched Salena carried up high on the crest of a wave and then disappear in the trough that followed, he would crouch down, his back feet working up as if to spring.

Ar'ye followed the cat's gaze but even though his eyes were sharper than those of mere men, they were still no match for those of a cat. He gave up trying to pinpoint Salena's whereabouts and just focussed on keeping the skiff from capsizing.

He marvelled at the courage and bravery these strangers and their animals had and felt that with inner strength such as they had, maybe they could accomplish the task they had before them.

Realizing this, Ar'ye summoned up what strength he had left and turned the skiff into the waves. "Lead on, Patches," he called out to the ever fearless cat.

Maybe he couldn't swim but he did possess the strength to still paddle and steer this skiff after Salena. He just hoped Patches' eyesight didn't let them all down. With his massive arms and back, Ar'ye knifed the paddles through the water, spray soaking him even further. He noticed that the bottom of the skiff was now covered in several inches of water and Martyl and Big Cat were now completely drenched. The water was already becoming bloodied from washing out their bandages and wounds.

Wave after wave pounded into the bow of the skiff, tossing the four remaining passengers about like rag dolls. Ar'ye fought with all his strength to keep the tiny skiff from capsizing while at the same time trying to paddle in the direction Patches was indicating.

Several times he thought he spotted someone—Duncan or Salena, he couldn't tell, on the crest of the waves. But just as his eyes began to focus on whatever it was, another wave would crash over, washing everything away.

It had been several minutes now since Salena had leapt overboard after Duncan and Ar'ye began fearing if he would find either of his new friends again. Suddenly Patches sprang from his perch in the bow and flew through the air, landing with a splash about ten feet in front of the skiff.

Ar'ye was startled for a moment until he heard Salena call out from somewhere in front of the skiff. Faster now, he began paddling with renewed zest, following the large cat as he cat-paddled his way through the ever roughening waters to his human companions.

After a few more tense minutes of battling the white water, Ar'ye reached Salena and Patches, both towing Duncan along on his back through the water. Reaching over the side, Ar'ye grabbed Duncan by his forest cloak, the muscles in his arms knotted like steel cords, and pulled him in. As the skiff continued to get pounded relentlessly by the waves, Ar'ye quickly hauled Salena and Patches on board.

All four sat down exhausted, unable to fight the raging waters any longer, their muscles and lungs aching with exertion. Patches was too tired to even shake himself dry or preen his fur. Instead he just nuzzled his large head into Duncan's side and purred.

"Thank you," was all Duncan could manage to say in his breathless state. "I thought I'd be drowned out there."

"We're not in the clear yet," replied Ar'ye. "We'd better bail out some of this water before Martyl and Big Cat drown."

Only then did Duncan realize he was sitting in a few inches of water. He was half-drowned himself and didn't notice all the water in the skiff. Immediately he and Ar'ye, their tired and weary bodies already beginning to slow noticeably, began scooping water out of the skiff with cupped hands.

Salena, not bothering to waste any time dressing, merely donned her forest cloak and again manned the rudder. Her arms felt like lead and her chest was still heaving, her lungs trying in vain to get enough air to feed her exhausted muscles.

On top of the physical strain was the added fear that if they didn't reach shore soon, they wouldn't ever. Salena pointed the waterlogged skiff in the direction she felt was closest to shore, relying on her instincts to guide her.

The winds and rain were worsening now, pummelling the river skiff with unrelenting assaults. The sky was growing ever darker as afternoon gave way to evening and their eyesight became virtually useless as Duncan and Salena could barely see each other at opposite ends of the skiff. Ar'ye however, had eyes keener than theirs and scanned the horizon, or what he could see of it over the waves, for land between handfuls of water.

If only I could fly again, he thought to himself. I would be able to guide Salena with a better view. A surge of anger toward the slavers shot through him as he thought about his wounded condition. To his people, the loss of flight was considered a fate far worse than death and he hoped his wing would heal properly. He did not want to consider what would happen if he were to remain flightless. These past few weeks had been bad enough and he knew he couldn't bear a lifetime like that.

A large wave splashed over the skiff, drenching him and Duncan even more, if at all possible, bringing his attention back to the matter at hand.

"Mmrow," called Patches from the bow with a sense of urgency in his voice.

"What is it?" asked Duncan, looking at his cat without stopping his bailing.

"Land!" shouted Ar'ye over the crashing waves and howling wind. "He sees land. I can just make out the outline myself! Dead ahead, Salena!"

Ar'ye and Duncan both stopped bailing, which had been almost useless with the waves washing over the sides and began rowing with the oars as fast as their weary bodies would allow them. Patches sat up tall in the bow, ignoring the water splashing his saturated fur and pointed the way, his yellow cat eyes like beacons in the night. Salena steered the battered skiff in the direction Patches was looking and within a few harrowing moments the shore was in sight for all to see.

"There!" cried Ar'ye, pointing straight ahead when he could see the beach. He and Duncan both renewed their efforts and with the help of the waves now at their backside, beached the skiff on the shore.

"Get Martyl and Big Cat away from the water, quickly," ordered Salena.

Carefully, Duncan and Ar'ye lifted Martyl's travois out with him on it and carried it away from the crashing waves. Patches leapt off the skiff then and sat guard over Martyl while Duncan and Ar'ye returned for Big Cat. Salena tied the skiff to a small tree after hauling it out of the water.

The trio, exhausted beyond their bodies' endurance, collapsed next to Martyl and Big Cat.

"We made it," muttered Duncan as they all collapsed on the wet beach, completely exhausted from over exertion.

Chapter Nine

Draskene rose from his bed, a beautiful mahogany four posted canopy bed and crossed the room to his boudoir, lighting a candle in the darkness with a snap of his fingers. The furnishings in his room, the former royal couple's personal chambers, had been completely replaced immediately following his ascension to the throne.

I deserve these trappings he thought to himself as he washed up, pouring water from a golden decanter into a matching gold wash basin. After all, I worked hard for them. He chuckled ruefully to himself as he dried himself off with a cloth.

He was well rested now after his journey into the scrying crystal. Those ethereal journeys were always trying and they left him with such a reassuring need to be surrounded by his personal gains. Draskene looked about the room, drinking in the beauty of the lavish tapestries hung from the high rafters. From his boudoir he donned a black silk shirt and matching black trousers made of deerskin. To his left side he attached a silver scabbard which housed King Aramid's old sword.

He crossed to the window and threw open the shutters he closed the previous night while using the crystal. The late afternoon sun streamed through the open window, causing Draskene to squint as its intensity. Peering out, he noticed a storm was working its way south towards them, darkening the sky as it progressed. A nice night for a ride, he thought to himself. First, something to eat.

He turned to leave his quarters while at the same time sending a mental message to the castle cook to prepare his meal. With any luck, it would be ready for him at the stable when he arrived. Lucky for the cook, he finished silently.

It took him nearly a quarter of an hour to traverse the castle courtyard after exiting his chambers. On the courtyard's far side were the stables, home to his army's steeds, all of them midnight black war horses, standing sixteen to seventeen hands each. Truly magnificent beasts, he thought, but his personal horse had its own private stable, housed in a large structure beside the others. That was where his one passion lay.

Draskene approached the outer doors to the stable and with a wave of his hand removed the protective wards surrounding them. With his left hand extended, he pulled it towards himself and the doors swung open, allowing him to enter.

"Hello Night," said Draskene, a touch of happiness in his voice as he approached his steed. He stood over seventeen hands and his eyes glowed red in the darkness of their own accord. Steam rose from his nostrils every time he snorted. His coat was darker than the night and he seemed almost invisible in the blackness of his windowless stable.

From his stall, Night whinnied and snorted, knowing that his master was here to take him out for a ride in the approaching storm. He enjoyed that, as did his master. Draskene grabbed his bridle and led Night out of his stall, tying him to a post. Before he began to saddle his unearthly horse, he sensed a presence, someone approaching.

Ah, my meal, he thought. Then he realized it was his messenger, Bin, and two others. He could feel their fear and nervousness as they drew near. So did Night and he began dancing about his rope, looking like a shadow flitting in and out of a darkened corridor.

"What is it, Bin?" Draskene asked with more than a hint of annoyance in his voice, upset at being interrupted.

"These two men have some information I thought you would find useful, my Lord," replied Bin hurriedly as he stepped into the doorway of the darkened stables.

"Come forward and speak," Draskene commanded.

The two men, members of the Prime Guard, stepped forward to face their master, their faces flushed and stomachs churning. Bin couldn't help staring at Night, noticing how much the insignia on the Guards' uniforms resembled the frightening horse before him.

"My Lord," the braver of the two stammered. "We travelled all night and day from the old fishing village on the Gull River. Yesterday afternoon we were attacked by a woman who tried to lull us to sleep with her voice."

His face, and that of his companion were nearly as red as Night's eyes as he continued, "She nearly succeeded except her concentration was broken. In our weakened state she clubbed us over the head and escaped on a river skiff. We feared she may be some kind of sorceress and came to tell you right away."

Draskene digested this information for a moment, considering who it was his Prime Guard may have encountered. It was most likely she was the girl Raydon encountered with Duncan. But what would she be doing trying to sing his Prime Guards to sleep? This sounded utterly bizarre to him and he wondered if that part of the story was concocted by the guards to save their lives at their ineptness. In the end, it came down to the fact that he knew of no sorceresses and his men had been defeated by a woman. He could not tolerate this. This was the second time his elite force had been beaten by some unknown person. He was going to make an example of these men.

"Thank you for your concern," Draskene answered as he began untying Night, "But you know I don't tolerate defeat of my Prime Guard, by a woman or anyone else."

The two men stared open mouthed for a second then began to stammer an excuse. Before they could cajole their thoughts Draskene released Night's reins. The massive Hell Horse rushed forward to the doorway, rising up on its hind legs. Down came his front hooves, each one splitting the skull of the man beneath like an eggshell. Blood squirted from each man, spraying Bin as they fell to the ground. Night trampled their lifeless bodies into the ground beneath him. When he was satisfied they were dead he lowered his massive, squared head and ripped their hearts from their chests with his sharp, demon-like teeth, swallowing them whole.

"Let this be a lesson to the rest of the Prime Guard. I will tolerate no more defeats," Draskene stated bluntly as he saddled Night and swung himself onto his mighty back.

Bin only nodded as he scurried away, his mind frozen in shock with the image of the demon, known as a Hell Horse, trampling to death two men right beside him. His appetite gone due to his anger, Draskene shot Bin a withering glance as Night sauntered through his open doorway.

"Ride!" he shouted to his steed as the two thundered into the darkening distance.

Ar'ye was the first to awaken, his hunter's instincts at work even in sleep. He rose to his feet slowly and quietly, both sore and cautious, wary of what might be lurking in the trees beyond. A small amount of light was given by the few stars peeking out from behind the dissipating clouds. He noted nothing in their vicinity. Patches, however, was pacing back and forth by Duncan and seemed nervous, for a cat anyways, he thought.

Striding over to Patches, Ar'ye tentatively reached out to pet him with one hand while shaking Duncan to rouse him, with the other. Startled, Duncan scrambled to his feet, back peddling away from Ar'ye fumbling for his sword. Salena sat up with a gasp, awakened by the commotion.

"Easy, easy," soothed Ar'ye, rising to his feet. "I didn't realize your people startled so easily."

"It's okay," replied Duncan. "We've all been on edge the past few days and we're all going to need time to adjust to each other. But I still can't shake the feeling that that demon isn't still after us."

"It couldn't possibly know where we are now. We don't even know where we are, do we?" asked Salena from Martyl's side, checking his wounds.

Duncan only knelt down to Big Cat to check her wounds, silently conveying his answer to Salena's questions. "It's a miracle they're still alive," he said, hoping to change the subject.

"I believe I know where we are," stated Ar'ye. "I cannot be entirely sure as I've only seen it from the air before but I think we are on the western shore of Frost Lake. The Thunder Mountains should only be two days march through those woods, given our present situation. You should see mountain tops from here in the daylight." He pointed towards the forest at the edge of the lake before continuing, a note of uneasiness seeming to creep into his voice.

"I am not sure, however that the demon won't be far behind us. Their kind are ruthless, persistent creatures that will stop at nothing to accomplish the task set before them."

"Well then, I guess we'd better get going then," stated Salena as she threw on her forest cloak. "Martyl and Big Cat aren't getting any better and I for one don't intend to wait around for that thing to return."

"You're right," replied Ar'ye as he bent down to pick up Martyl's travois. "I will lead the way. My eyes are better in the dark and I've seen these woods before." As an after thought he added, "At least from the air."

Duncan put on his forest cloak as well after quickly changing into some drier clothes in his pack. He and Salena both threw their packs on their backs and Duncan picked up Big Cat's travois.

"Let's go," Duncan said with as much enthusiasm as he could muster at this point, his body aching like never before in his life.

Ar'ye crossed the beach, Martyl in tow, and entered the woods. Duncan with Big Cat followed and Salena brought up the rear with Patches padding along silently next to her. The storm clouds had now completely blown over, leaving the sky a black blanket, dotted here and there with shining stars. The moon was out, full and round again, giving off a welcome brightness for the travellers as it filtered through the tree tops.

All three marvelled at the beauty of these woods and the cleanness of the air. They were away from the fetid swamps and insect hordes encountered earlier in their journey and it made their aches and pains seem a little less. The leaves on the trees, maple, oak and elm as well as some various pine trees, glittered like giant fireflies in the moonlight as the trees whispered to the travellers in an eerie, rustling voice.

The wind reminded Ar'ye of home and the fast, fiery winds of the Firetop Mountains. He stretched his wings tentatively, as far as he could in the confines of the trees and worked them back and forth gingerly. The pain was greatly reduced since his rescue from the slavers and the subsequent ministrations of Salena.

"How's the wing?" asked Duncan from behind.

"Better," replied Ar'ye, turning his head sideways to give Duncan a smile. "Thanks to you and Salena."

"All in a days work," Duncan said with a chuckle, pleased to have conversation to take his mind off the strain of hauling Big Cat. Thirty pounds was a heavy load after two days of rowing. Ar'ye it seemed had no difficulty at all hauling Martyl behind him. It must be all those muscles he uses to fly, thought Duncan silently.

"If you two are going to talk instead of walk, how about us eating?" chimed Salena with mock contemptuousness in her voice.

"All you had to do was ask," patronized Duncan playfully as he and Ar'ye stopped and lowered their travois.

Salena looked at Duncan, smiling in the moonlit forest and saw him again for the first time, her heart warming at his telltale smile and gleaming green eyes. He somehow seemed different now then when the journey began, maybe a little more mature, a little wiser, a bit more solemn and moody. But there was his smile and playful banter, back again as they approached their destination.

Duncan wasted no time in getting their meal, apparently quite hungry himself. The three of them and Patches sat down to the last of the cheese and dried meat in his pack and shared some water from a flask.

"What do we have left for provisions, Salena," asked Duncan when they finished.

After rummaging through her pack she replied, "There should be enough food for another two days at this rate. We have some to spare since Martyl and Big Cat aren't eating, and we have plenty of water."

Their moods darkened a little with the remembrance of Martyl and Big cat lying within reach of death's dark embrace. Rising to his feet, Duncan slung his pack over his back and said, "We'd better get moving. Help isn't going to come to us." He bent down to pick up Big Cat's travois when Patches sprang to his feet, growling.

"Do you think he hears the demon again?" asked Salena, her voice sounding more than a little worried.

"It couldn't be. Not this far away," replied Duncan, also a little nervous.

"I fear it may be," cautioned Ar'ye. "We'd best be moving on, now!" Already he was moving, pulling Martyl along behind him on the travois.

"How can you be so sure," asked Duncan as he too began moving. "We could be on the other side of that lake for all that demon knows."

"Don't be so impetuous," scolded Ar'ye as he stopped and wheeled about to stare Duncan straight in the eye.

"I've seen demons before and none we're as fearsome as this one. They have powers you couldn't begin to understand. They can see into other planes of existence and can follow the trail left by magic, like the magic in the dagger you said you have."

"Salena," Duncan called, "take Big Cat and follow Ar'ye. He'll lead you to the Dwarves. I'll catch up later."

"Where are you going," she demanded, already knowing the answer, yet she forced herself to ask it.

"If that thing is following us because of Connor's dagger then I'm going to kill it or at least hold it off until you can get to safety."

"Don't be a fool," warned Ar'ye grabbing Duncan's shoulder with his hand, as if to hold him there.

Patches had by now backed up to the trio and was growling louder, his fur standing on end down the entire length of his back, his ears back and flat on his head.

"Go now while you still can. It's the only chance for Martyl and Big Cat. You know I'm right, Ar'ye."

"You truly are brave like your father and his knights. Good luck to you." Ar'ye grasped Duncan's right arm in his in a farewell gesture and turned to grab his travois.

Turning to Salena, Duncan saw the glimmer of tears in her eyes in the bright moonlight. Under other circumstances, he thought, this could be romantic, but right now his heart was racing and his stomach churning as he gave her a hug then turned to leave before things got worse.

"Duncan," Salena began choking on her words.

"Don't," he replied, "I'll be okay." He meant it but didn't feel it. "Stay with them, Patches," were his last words before leaving. Without turning back to look at his departing friends, Duncan took off into the woods as fast as he could with only the moonlight to guide him.

Knowing that the demon could track him by sensing the magic in the dagger he carried unnerved him somewhat. He wondered how far off it was and if the dagger's magic was strong enough to kill it. It had killed a demon before, he saw it when he was a child, but that had been a demon in a human body. He presumed that would be a weaker class of demon, living in a human host. Duncan felt his skin crawl as he imagined being possessed by a demon.

Duncan approached a fallen tree and crouched, resting and listening. Where was this thing? Could Ar'ye and Patches, whose senses were better than his or Salena's, be mistaken? He didn't know about that, but he knew he was an experienced woodsman. From his childhood days at Arundel and up until just recently in the Misty Isles he spent hours upon hours each day in the forests. He learned how to track and to cover his tracks. He knew how to travel silently and quickly in dense foliage. He would be alright, he assured himself.

Peering around the trunk, a stick cracked behind him. In the silence of the forest it sounded like a clap of thunder and he wheeled about, dagger down, to find two yellow eyes staring at him in the darkness.

"Patches," he whispered, breathing a quiet sigh of relief, his heart threatening to burst from his chest it was beating so fast.

"I told you to stay with the others," scolded Duncan, yet at the same time he reached out to pet the loyal cat.

Patches, for his part, merely cocked his head to one side and purred quietly, looking at Duncan as if to say, 'You need my help.'

Duncan smiled, whispering, "I know."

Knowing Patches could sense the demon's approach sooner than he could helped relax Duncan somewhat. He watched the muscular cat as he crept up to the edge of the fallen tree and peered around it. Patches' body flattened to the ground, his tail twitching rapidly from side to side. His ears were pointed straight ahead, listening for sounds Duncan couldn't possibly hear.

As quietly as he could, Duncan crept up to where Patches lay listening and knelt beside him under cover of the foliage. Still he could hear or see nothing and wondered if maybe the big cat could be mistaken. Looking down at the dagger Sliver in his hand, glinting in the bright moonlight, Duncan wondered again if it would be enough to destroy this demon. With his left hand, he reached down and felt the pommel of his sword, still in it's scabbard at his side. He felt a little better knowing he still had it with him, even if it was supposed to be powerless against the demon.

Maybe we'd better move in deeper, thought Duncan. Beginning to rise from his crouch, he looked out again into the dense forest before completely leaving the cover of the fallen tree. From his left, out of the corner of his eye, Duncan saw Patches spring like a bolt of grey and white lightning with a howl that could have cracked stone.

The great cat cleared the fallen tree with room to spare and crashed into the demon with enough force to send both thudding into the ground. Duncan stared dumbfounded for a second, realizing that without Patches, he never would have heard or seen the attack coming. Clambering over the tree, he ran to his cat's aid.

Patches and the demon rolled about on the ground, crashing into trees and logs, eliciting howls of pain from both. Before Duncan could reach the fray, Patches leapt clear, landing in a crouch, his fur matted with leaves and dirt. His large mouth was open in a snarl, lips curled back to expose fangs nearly half the length of a man's fingers. Black demon blood, thick as tar dripped from his fangs and covered his paws as well.

Patches backed away from the demon, still keeping himself between it and Duncan, although now he was moving slower than before. As he turned to keep the raging demon in sight, Duncan saw why his cat was moving so slow. The fur above his rear left upper leg and part of his side was torn off and hanging by a flap of skin. Blood ran freely down his leg.

"Give up, boy," snarled Raydon, also bleeding, from wounds on his chest and abdomen. "Your cat is a good fighter but will not last long. My master wants you, and I will bring you to him, along with your magic, as puny as it is."

The sound of the demon's voice made the hair on the nape of Duncan's neck stand on end. He was stunned by the sight of what just happened to Patches but now anger began to take hold. There was no way he would be beaten by this abomination of nature. He was angered even further at the sight of his injured cat.

Raydon, still circling with Patches, made a lunge for Duncan. The cat leapt, sinking his fanged mouth into Raydon's forearm. Howling in pain, Raydon brought his other hand around, fist closed and hammered it into the cat. Patches hit the ground in a crumpled heap. Outraged beyond his capacity to reason, Duncan covered the six feet separating them at a run, and hit Raydon who stood nearly a foot and a half taller than himself, driving his shoulders into the Demon's midsection. Raydon staggered only a little from the blow but doubled over instantly when Duncan drove Sliver deep into his belly, wrenching it sideways as he pulled it out.

Raydon fell to the ground, burying Duncan beneath his massive bulk. Kicking and squirming about wildly, Duncan managed to roll free. He was covered in the black slime that was the demon's blood. The stench of it nearly made him wretch. Rising to his feet, he gave the demon a prod with a nearby stick to see if it was still alive. Getting no reaction he tried again. Faster than he could have believed possible, the demon grabbed the end of the stick and jerked it towards him. Being surprised, Duncan failed to let go and was pulled along with it.

Rising to his feet in a flurry of flailing arms and flying, knotted hair, Raydon caught Duncan in the chest with a backhand that sent him careening into a tree five feet away. There was no mistaking the sounds of ribs snapping like twigs.

Gasping for breath, Duncan tried to rise to his feet. Sharp pains shot through his chest and dark spots swam before his eyes. The demon was moving towards him, flashing a hideous, fanged grin. Panic surged through him as he saw Sliver glinting in the moonlight, lying in the dirt, well out of his reach.

"You are mine, boy. I shall be greatly rewarded for finding you." Raydon reached out and with a massive hand and picked Duncan up off the ground by his shoulder with seemingly no effort. Duncan winced as pain, hot as fire, shot through his chest.

"Don't worry, boy. There will be a lot more pain before I take you back. We demon's feel pain too, and you caused me a lot." Blood was flowing quite freely from Raydon's midriff and he staggered, dropping Duncan to the ground.

Duncan screamed in agony, his chest feeling like hundreds of knives were simultaneously jammed into it. Raydon dropped to his knees, his head spinning, hurt worse than he realized at first. There was more magic in the dagger than he thought. He would live from this wound, he knew, but he needed time to heal.

Duncan, through his pain clouded vision, saw the demon fall and knew he had to act fast. From his position, lying on the ground, he tried to crawl to his dagger. With each muscle movement, pain lanced out through his upper body like lightning bolts, keeping his movement to a bare minimum.

After what seemed like an eternity, Duncan was only an arm's length away from reaching his goal. He extended his right arm, reaching for the dagger when he felt a pain so terrible he forgot all about his broken ribs. The demon had grabbed hold of his left leg, putting his claws right through his calf to the bone. Duncan screamed and kicked out with his free leg but couldn't connect. The fire in his leg washed over his entire body, flooding his mind with more than he could take and blackness began to overtake him. Something deep inside refused to let him succumb, however, and he pulled himself along with what strength he had left.

Duncan's fingers brushed the handle of the dagger but he couldn't quite reach it. Then a thought raced through his numbed mind. His sword. He could still feel it as his side. Reaching back, he fumbled for the pommel of his sword and pulled it free. Duncan rolled to his back and swung the sword at the Demon's arm. With a blow that would have severed a man's arm, Raydon's skin merely broke, allowing a small flow of blood.

Raydon tightened his grip and dragged his quarry back to himself. Duncan fell back, unable to fight any longer, his sword falling from his weakened grip. Images of Salena, Martyl and Big Cat flashed before his eyes. Darkness crept in from the sides, allowing him only a tiny window of sight. He found himself hoping Ar'ye would get them to safety.

Duncan turned his head to look at Patches, wanting to see him one last time. He thought he was imagining things when he saw the great cat, bloodied and battered, rise with a snarl and dive at the Demon.

The Demon's shriek and subsequent release on Duncan's leg alerted his pain wracked mind to the fact he was free again. With a final effort, Duncan hauled himself to Sliver and rolled over to face the Demon. Patches had locked his massive jaw onto the Demon's arm and was proceeding to chew through it, having pulled him to the ground. The Demon was pounding the cat with its free arm, but with greatly reduced strength.

Duncan crawled to the ongoing battle and rose to his knees, Sliver raised high above his head. Dropping to the ground, he plunged the dagger deep into the Demon's chest. Easily, the magic blade pierced skin and bone, puncturing the Demon's black, soulless heart.

"Don't call me 'boy'," hissed Duncan with what little breath he had, "especially if you can't beat me."

Crawling to a nearby tree after retrieving his sword, Duncan slumped against it, stroking Patches.

"We'd better get you some help," he said to the cat, wincing as he looked at his torn side.

The cat paid him no attention, staring off into the woods to the east. He tried to rise to his feet, beginning to growl, but his legs were shaky, forcing him down.

"What is it?" asked Duncan, knowing all too well at this point not to question his cat's senses. He held his dagger ready in his right hand and continued stroking Patches with his other, trying to calm the cat, and himself for that matter. He too was in no condition to stand and wondered what Patches sensed.

Maybe it was just a wild animal passing nearby he thought to himself. His worst fear, however, was that the Demon had a companion. He knew that he and Patches stood no chance against another attack, so he decided their best chance was to put as much room between themselves and this spot as possible.

"Come on, Patches, we've got to go."

Duncan rose ever so cautiously to his feet, using the tree trunk for balance. Slowly, Patches rose to his feet, not quite as wobbly now, but he still favoured his left leg. Duncan spotted a low lying branch and, drawing his sword, chopped it off in one fell swoop of his sword. The effort required nearly toppled him over in the process but the tree trunk saved him as he fell into it. A stifled scream escaped his lips as the fall into the tree trunk battered his ribs even more. Slowly he bent down to retrieve the fallen branch and without much further ado other than stripping off a few offshoots, he constructed himself a crude crutch.

Tentatively he began to walk, or rather hobble back the way they had come, relying heavily on his makeshift crutch. With every step, his torn calf ached and his ribs sent stabs of pain through his chest. Patches followed behind, every bit as much in pain as Duncan.

They took no more than a few steps when a dozen figures, all camouflaged with leaves and grass, stepped out from their concealment, effectively surrounding them.

They were all short and stocky with very broad chests and shoulders, standing no more than four and a half feet tall at the most. All had long, thick beards and carried battle axes.

"Halt!" commanded the stranger closest to Duncan. "Who are you and what is your business here?"

He stood directly before Duncan now, his burly arms folded across his chest, battle axe slung over his back.

Too weary to think of any cover story, Duncan told the truth, knowing when he was beaten.

"I am Duncan, son of Aramid, come to reclaim my kingdom of Arundel."

He knew he didn't look or sound very regal at this point but he didn't care. He and Patches had just stared Hell in the face, literally, and barely survived. He held onto Patches by the back of his neck, hoping the cat didn't decide he still wanted to fight, growling as he was.

After his announcement, a quiet murmur arose among the strangers and the one who approached Duncan conferred with two others in hushed voices. A few moments later, he turned back to Duncan and said, "I am Dirn, leader of the Dwarven Patrols. Allow us to escort you to our king. I believe he may want to speak with you."

For the first time in days, Duncan was elated.

Chapter Ten

"I will return in a short while, Duncan," said Dirn, "and you can tell me how it is you came to our forest."

With that, he and eight of the Dwarves headed back to the Demon. Exhausted from his battle and subsequent wounds, Duncan was prostrate on the ground with Patches next to him while one of the Dwarves attended to his wounds and those of Patches. The two others stood off a distance in the woods as lookouts. The rest of the dwarves set about burying the Demon beneath a pile of deadwood. They cleared an area of trees around the Demon so as to not to have it ignite and then lit the deadwood on fire.

"Why are they burning the Demon?" Duncan asked the Dwarf tending to his wounds.

"The corpse must be sent back to the fires of Hell whence it came. To leave it here would only alert others of its kind to your where-abouts," came the reply, cold and stern.

The Dwarf's ministrations became more gruff, eliciting an occasional groan from Duncan as his bandages were applied. Duncan waited for Dirn to return, anxious to inform him of the others in his party. Soon the acrid smell of burning flesh began to waft through the woods and Duncan recoiled from the smell. The other Dwarves, including Dirn, came back from the fire after ensuring it would not spread.

"Dirn, I must tell you of the others with me," began Duncan as the Dwarves neared him. He tried to rise to speak one on one with the Dwarf but could not, lying back down with coughs wracking his body. His chest felt as though it were compressing his lungs until they would burst.

"Easy now," warned Dirn, crouching down next to Duncan. "What others?"

For a second, Duncan hesitated, fearing that maybe he shouldn't trust these Dwarves. They must have seen or heard this battle with the Demon yet they refrained from helping. Why would they not have helped? Could they somehow be different Dwarves than those of the Thunder Mountains, in league with Draskene? Thinking it over, he realized he had no other choice, though, as he was in no condition to argue, much less fight. Martyl had said there were only the Dwarves of the Thunder Mountains left so these had to be one and the same. Besides, Martyl and Big Cat needed help. The last thought decided the answer he would give.

"I was travelling with a young woman, another of these cats, the last of the Royal Knights and a Rey'ak. The knight and the cat are severely injured and require help immediately."

Several of the Dwarves began murmuring amongst themselves at this disclosure of information until Dirn silenced them with a sweep of his massive arms through the air.

"We encountered them earlier," stated Dirn bluntly. "Others from our party are already en route with them, as we speak, to the Thunder Mountains."

Though it was dark and he lay in the shadows of the trees, Dirn could easily see the look of anger and betrayal cross Duncan's face.

"Why didn't you tell me earlier?" spat Duncan furiously, trying to rise.

Faster than he thought possible for such a stocky creature, Dirn was kneeling on the ground next to him, pinning his shoulders to the ground. Patches growled a warning to the Dwarf who dared accost his human but was easily held back in his weakened state by another Dwarf.

"Listen to me," hissed Dirn through clenched teeth. "We had no, nor do we yet, have any proof of your or the others' identities. We do not trust men. You and your friends at least tell the same story. For that much and the fact that one of you may well be a Royal Knight, we'll give you safe passageway to the Thunder Mountains. Ask for no more." With a huff, Dirn rose to his feet.

"Are they alright?" Duncan asked defiantly.

"The girl and the Rey'ak are uninjured, if that is who you refer to. The man and the cat have been attended to as well as possible in the forest. Now we must go."

Dirn motioned over the Dwarf that had attended Duncan's wounds and took a small flask from him, adding, "Drink this. It will help you heal faster."

He proffered the flask to Duncan, who took it with some hesitation. Duncan removed the stopper and smelled it first. It had a pleasant aroma, like a fresh spring day. Raising the flask, Duncan drank slowly, feeling a warm glow spread throughout his body, relieving the pain he felt.

"The cat too," Dirn said, his voice still cold and authoritative.

Feeling a little lightheaded but much more comforted, Duncan offered Patches a drink. The cat drank what he could from the flask as Duncan poured it on his tongue. The warmth from the drink began to make both Duncan and Patches very tired. Duncan tried to rise but found his limbs incapable of responding.

Almost in a trance, Duncan watched the Dwarves milling about him prepare a stretcher for him and Patches. He tried to speak but was unable to. One of the dwarves removed his sword and dagger and he was powerless to stop him.

Slowly his vision began to fade and darkness crept in from the corners. As he was tied down to the makeshift stretcher, a calm state of euphoria descended upon him. Part of his mind tried to resist, fearful of being weaponless and powerless but soon his resolve dissipated as he fell into a peaceful sleep.

The forest was becoming thinner as they marched on in the darkness. At first, Salena thought it was just her eyes playing tricks on her, but as the sun began to break over the eastern horizon, she could see vast sections of it uprooted and burned.

Hundreds of massive trees lay on the forest floor, desecrated by whom she did not know, nor for what reason. Some were partially intact, others had sections hewn out, yet most were simply burned down. The earth was blackened and nothing grew, not even weeds. It was such a stark contrast to the beauty they had seen upon entering these woods and it saddened her to see such destruction.

"What has happened here?" Salena asked Rorn, the Dwarf leading their party.

Without turning to face her, he replied sharply, "Men did this, to supply the Black Paladin's war machine."

Salena knew from the tone of his voice not to press this subject any further. Of all the Dwarves in the patrol that found them earlier that evening, he was the only one who would speak to her or Ar'ye, and then not very pleasantly.

At first she had been alarmed and more than a little frightened when the twelve Dwarves had almost literally appeared before their very eyes. They were surly and rough in manner, and not very trusting, although considering the circumstances she could understand the latter. With Ar'ye's reassurance, and the fact that they had little choice, she and Ar'ye told the Dwarves their plight and asked them to help Duncan.

Much to their surprise, Rorn, the patrol leader, told them another patrol was already watching Duncan. Both patrols, he said, had spotted the party shortly after they entered the woods.

Salena was dumbfounded by this revelation and wanted to know why they had not been helped earlier. Before she could ask, Ar'ye motioned for her to be silent.

"Can you aid our injured?" he had asked Rorn, staying close to Salena.

"We'll do what we can then we must be moving," replied Rorn, his voice ice cold.

While the Dwarves had ministered aid to the wounded Martyl and Big Cat, Ar'ye told Salena of the Dwarves mistrust towards others and warned her not to be too inquisitive. When the Dwarves were ready to go, Salena and Ar'ye had been removed of their weapons and marched along single file with the Dwarves.

The entire night, Salena wondered if Duncan was okay and swore to herself if the Dwarves did not bring him along unharmed she would have vengeance. The one thing that did comfort her was the fact that Martyl and Big Cat were treated well.

Now that it was daybreak, she could see the tops of the Thunder Mountains looming overhead. They looked majestically serene in the early morning sun, their snow covered peaks a brilliant white against the retreating darkness of night.

Ar'ye's heart soared at the sight of the magnificent mountains, reminding him of the aeries of his beloved homeland. Unconsciously, his wings began to flex, the muscles of his back expanding and contracting with the effort. His heart raced with exhilaration and anticipation, longing to be high in the crystal blue early morning sky.

"Not thinking of leaving us, are you Rey'ak?" asked Sten, the dwarf behind Ar'ye. He grabbed hold of Ar'ye's right forearm, his grip like an iron vice.

"Alas, I'm not flying anywhere, I'm afraid," replied Ar'ye dismally. "As you can see, my wing is still injured."

Sten gave Ar'ye a disapproving glare yet Ar'ye paid him no attention, his thoughts still on his loss of flight.

"We will rest here for a short while," commanded Rorn, turning to face the marching party.

Salena and Ar'ye sat down, fatigued from the past night's forced march. They readily accepted the water, dried meat and fresh berries offered to them by the Dwarves. Everyone rested in the cover of a fallen tree, in strained silence. The Dwarves still looked sullen as usual, their bearded faces not betraying anything they may be thinking. Salena wondered why they were so forlorn and mistrusted others so much. How was it they were wronged? She only hoped they would give Duncan the help he needed and the information Martyl sought.

After a few minutes, Rorn rose and removing a piece of cloth from his pack, tore it in two. "From here to the mountains, you will be blindfolded," he said matter-of-demon to Salena and Ar'ye. "Our passageways must be kept secret to all outsiders."

He approached them, blindfolds in hand and applied Salena's first. Ar'ye with his keen hunter's eye and sharp memory scanned the rolling foothills before them and the destroyed forest currently surrounding them. He hoped, as his blindfold was put on, he could remember their location should anything unforseen happen.

Their sightless march continued on for several hours before they reached their destination. During their pilgrimage, Salena and Ar'ye were both escorted by two Dwarves each, as much for physical support as for guidance. The Dwarves' stamina seemed almost inexhaustible, marching all night into the next day without slowing. Salena and Ar'ye found themselves stumbling over the uneven and rocky terrain of the foothills, too tired to lift their feet. Near the end of the march, they were both practically carried by the Dwarves.

Finally, the march was called to a halt. Salena and Ar'ye were allowed to sit on a group of small rocks, blindfolds still on. Salena slumped into Ar'ye, too tired to hold herself erect and quickly dozed off. Ar'ye too could feel the pleasant darkness of sleep encroaching but he fought it off, listening to the Dwarves hushed talk somewhere in front of him. In his sleep deprived condition and their low voices, he could neither hear nor comprehend what they said. He did, however, hear the unmistakable sound of stone grating on stone.

A hidden entrance into their mountain stronghold, no doubt, surmised Ar'ye. No sooner had he finished that thought when he heard Rorn's unmistakable gruff voice.

"Come on, you two. It's time to enter the passage. Once inside we'll remove the blindfolds."

Ar'ye felt Salena lift off him as she was brought to her feet by the Dwarves. He rose after her, escorted along by the Dwarves. They walked about thirty feet when he noticed the ground beneath his feet was no longer stony earth but now solid rock. His heart quickened as he realized they were now beneath the Thunder Mountains. The thought of leaving the vast expanse of open space above ground for this passage beneath the mountains was more than a little unsettling.

"Stop," came Rorn's voice, echoing off the stone walls.

Once again Ar'ye heard the sound of stone grating on stone as the entrance way was sealed off behind them. From in front of him he heard one of the Dwarves approach and remove his blindfold. He blinked repeatedly, his eyes trying to adjust to the almost total darkness. A few torches were lit, emitting a little light and Ar'ye immediately scanned for Salena.

He found her after a few moments, sitting slumped against the tunnel wall. "We need to rest," said Ar'ye, his voice almost a whisper as he slumped next to Salena.

"Very well," replied Rorn scornfully. "Trin, you and the others continue on with the wounded."

Rorn motioned to four of the Dwarves and they quickly headed off into the darkness with Trin leading the way. He carried a lit torch while the other four transported Martyl and Big Cat.

While Ar'ye and Salena slept, Rorn and the other Dwarves fashioned two more stretchers from their supplies.

"Let us be underway with these two," stated Rorn to the others as they carried Salena and Ar'ye off down the tunnel. "We can't wait until their weak stamina's recuperate."

Duncan was running as fast as he could through the woods. He didn't remember how he escaped from the Dwarves or when. He was free and that was all that mattered. Something seemed amiss, though, as he ran, feeling no pain in his leg or ribs. He only gave that a moment's thought before dismissing it. The trees seemed to be getting thicker, almost as if they were closing in about him. And Patches, where was he? Duncan couldn't remember what had become of the cat, only that he wasn't with him.

Still he ran, stumbling over roots and stumps as he became increasingly more fatigued. The night air around him in the forest was dark and impenetrable, unnaturally quiet and still. No animals or owls could be heard, even his own footfalls were silent, realized Duncan.

Duncan froze in his tracks. He could hear his heart beating like thunder and his lungs gasping for air. But now something else was also audible. Before, everything was silent, but now he could hear someone, or something, following him.

Instinctively, he knew what was happening. The Demon. It was back and coming for him. This had to be some kind of spell, figured Duncan, to confuse and daze him so the Demon could take him unawares. Instantly, Duncan crouched down behind a wide tree, his right hand reaching to his side for Sliver. For the first time since he had escaped the Dwarves, Duncan realized he was weaponless.

Fighting back the rising fear and panic, Duncan rose to his feet, determined to meet this challenge like a man. He was not going to die cowering like a dog. Stepping out around the tree, Duncan peered into the darkness, listening intently. The sounds were closer now, louder. There was more than one, thought Duncan, as the sounds were now only yards away and discernable from one another.

Duncan crouched behind the tree again, grabbing a fallen branch for a club and waited in ambush. Sweat began to bead on his forehead, dripping to the ground as the anticipation began to mount. His stomach began to twist and flutter, his fear and anxiety growing stronger by the moment.

Repeatedly, Duncan fought the urge to turn and run. The fear was becoming overpowering and the waiting almost unbearable. The Demon or Demons should be here by now thought Duncan in exasperation. What is going on?

As if in answer to his thoughts, Duncan heard voices. Familiar voices, calling out to him. Salena and Ar'ye, he remembered, are still out here somewhere. What if they are in trouble? That was their voices he heard, he was sure.

Summoning up the last of his courage, Duncan stepped out again in the open and headed towards the sounds of his comrades. Club at the ready, he cautiously headed back through the woods. Again, everything was deathly quiet except now for the cries of help he heard.

"Duncan," the voices called, "Don't leave us. Help, please." It was Salena and Ar'ye, closer now.

Duncan followed the sounds but couldn't close in on their location. His fear turned to frustration and despair as he realized he was getting nowhere, having gone in circles. Forgetting any hope of surprising their captors, Duncan in act of desperation, screamed out, "Show yourselves! I'm here if you want me!"

"We're here," came the reply. Duncan wheeled about, his eyes burning with rage, all fear displaced by anger.

His anger faded immediately, however, when he saw before him the misty, obscure images of Salena, Ar'ye, Martyl and his two cats, Patches and Big Cat. All were levitating above the ground a couple of inches and had no corporal substance.

"No, not you too!" Duncan sobbed, dropping to his knees, head down.

"Get up, Duncan," they called to him.

He didn't respond, no longer caring what happened to him. He had lost everything now and if this was his time to die, so be it. He lost everything that mattered to him. What good was his kingdom without his loved ones there to share it? It was his obsession with recovering it that caused their demise. All he wanted now was to join his friends, all thoughts of revenge and retribution washed from his mind. Guilt and remorse for what befell his comrades because of his failure became too much for Duncan to withstand and he cried out, "Forgive me for my failure!"

"Get up," came the call again, louder, closer. "Get up," they called a third time, grabbing his shoulders and lifting him up.

Unable to resist their eerie summons, Duncan remained standing where they lifted him and finally raised his head to meet his fate head on. When Duncan at last opened his eyes, he saw Salena standing over him, her beautiful face smiling.

"It's okay, Duncan, you were dreaming."

Chapter Eleven

"Salena, you're okay," gasped Duncan, sitting up and giving her a hug. The sharp pain in his ribs reminded him that not everything was in his dream.

"Sit back and rest now," scorned Salena playfully. "You still have a lot of healing to do yet." She broke into a wide smile of relief at seeing Duncan up.

"Where are we?" asked Duncan, looking about the room they were in. It was furnished rather sparingly, he noticed. The only furnishings besides the cot upon which Duncan lay were a small table with a wash basin and pitcher of water and a wooden chair, upon which Salena sat. Sunlight streamed in through open windows, casting a warm glow on Salena's hair.

"We're in the Dwarven city of Calheller," replied Salena. "We've been here for two days now."

"I've been asleep for two days?"

"Off and on, yes. It was induced by the healing drink they gave you, called Tal Shar, I believe. The Dwarves said it heals the body and mind, making you face whatever fears you have, helping overcome them. When the mind is at rest, the body can heal faster. That is probably why you had the nightmare."

"What about Martyl, Patches and Big Cat?" Duncan asked anxiously, full recollection of the past few days returning. "And where is Ar'ye? Where are my weapons?" he finished with a frantic sweeping of the nearly empty room with his still sleepy eyes. He could care less at the moment about facing any hidden fears in his dreams.

"Easy, Duncan. Everything is okay. Martyl is across the hall and Patches and Big Cat are in a third room next to his. They're all okay and beginning to recover, albeit somewhat slowly."

Relief swept across Duncan's features at that news and he began to breathe easier, his mind eased of at least one burden.

"Ar'ye is out in the city, trying to learn what he can from the Dwarven people about the impending Wraull attack and the previous battle with the Black Paladin's forces."

"He's already attacked?" asked Duncan incredulously.

"The Dwarves won't tell us much. They're very secretive and not very trusting towards outsiders. We did see a massive section of the forest we were in that had been burned down and destroyed. That must be where it took place." Salena sat back in her chair, a look of sadness crossing her beautiful features.

"It was horrible, Duncan. You must understand that the Dwarves don't trust us yet, either, that is why they're holding our weapons."

Before Duncan could speak or become overly upset, Salena cut him off, continuing, "But don't worry. They treated Ar'ye and I well, giving us free roam of the city by day, under escort at night. You, Martyl and the cats have received the best treatment possible. We really have no choice."

Duncan was angered by the mistrust towards himself and his comrades by the Dwarves but he did realize Salena was right. If they were to receive aid from the Dwarves, they would just have to prove themselves. He just hoped it was as easily done as said.

"I must speak with their King," Duncan said, again trying to rise, ignoring the mounting pain in his chest.

"You're going nowhere until you're better," replied Salena sternly, easily pushing Duncan back into the cot. "Now don't make me call for help," she said smiling.

Duncan fumed at his own weakness, but accepted the situation. "What about Ar'ye?" he asked, changing the subject. "What does he know about the Dwarves?"

"As I already said, they're very mistrustful of men. Apparently this is the Black Paladin's doing as recently he and his forces attacked the Dwarves. The battle ended in the forest between the Thunder Mountains and Frost Lake, causing the destruction I saw. Thousands of Dwarves were killed, hundreds more taken as slaves. Now the Black Paladin has an army of Wraulls ready to attack from the Untamed Lands. That is all he could learn from them. He has learned very little else."

Duncan's face was shadowed with the uncertainty he felt. He wondered if the Dwarves would ever help them now. There was a noise in the hall and Duncan and Salena both looked to the door, feeling a little uneasy. When it opened and Ar'ye stepped into the room, both breathed a little easier.

"I'm glad to see you awake," said Ar'ye with a broad smile on his weathered face. "I didn't mean to startle you both."

"Did you learn anything new?" asked Salena as Ar'ye came to stand next to Duncan's bed.

"I am afraid not," he replied sullenly. "Did Salena tell you of the recent battle?" he asked Duncan.

"Yes, she did. Why didn't you tell us about it when we first met? We told you we were headed here."

"You forget, my friend, that I was north of these mountains when I flew here and was held captive by the slavers for a month. I knew nothing of this battle." Ar'ye's face grew dark at the resurgent memory.

"How do you feel?" Ar'ye asked, changing the topic of conversation.

"Better. I'm still sore all over but I should be able to get around. I want to meet with the King and ask for his help."

"You're not going anywhere until Shorn says you can," interrupted Salena.

"Who is Shorn?" asked a puzzled Duncan.

"She is the Dwarven Healer that has been attending you, Martyl and the cats. When she says you can be up and about, you can leave this bed. Until then, you're staying here."

Her voice was stern and authoritative but Duncan could see the pain and fear in her eyes that worrying about him had caused.

"I agree," added Ar'ye. "Now, tell us about your battle with the Demon. It's not every day someone does what you did!"

Within a couple more days, Duncan was well enough to leave his room on his own and was glad to do so. Patches was also out and about, and like Duncan, was walking with a limp. His leg was healed over where it had been torn open but the fur had not yet grown back.

Duncan repeatedly asked Shorn, the Dwarven healer supervising their recovery, to see Martyl and Big Cat. She refused steadfastly, saying they needed their rest to regain their strength. Unlike Duncan and Patches, their wounds were left too long and would require extra time to heal.

Although stern and somewhat gruff, as were all the Dwarves he'd met thus far, Duncan could actually sense a genuine warmth and caring beneath her projected facade. She was the only female Dwarf he'd seen so far and was surprised to find that she resembled the males very closely in appearance, being stocky and muscular with the exception of having no beard.

Ar'ye and Salena spent their time with Duncan and Patches, helping them in their recovery. They spent the daylight hours walking about the vast grounds that surrounded the Healers' Quarter. The grass was green and lush, soft as air to walk upon and the trees were tall and broad, full of singing birds and chattering squirrels. The cool, crisp mountain air was refreshing and felt as though it cleansed their bodies as they filled their lungs.

Ar'ye occasionally tried his wing, the wound now fully healed, to see if he could fly. The muscles were sore and stiff from lack of use so he worked both wings back and forth slowly, building a steady cadence. Duncan and Salena watched in stunned silence as he slowly lifted off the ground, the massive muscles of his back and chest flexing with supreme effort against gravity. Patches lay down in the soft grass, yawning in spite of the spectacle before him.

Now hovering over their heads, Ar'ye looked down at Duncan and Salena, his face alight with sheer joy.

"Please excuse me while I indulge myself," he called down to them, "It's been awhile." Smiling exuberantly, Ar'ye was off, floating on mountain winds that blew into the valley.

Duncan and Salena joined Patches on the grass, looking up to watch Ar'ye soar like some kind on enormous bird of prey. In a few more minutes, he returned from the skies and joined them on the solid ground. His face was flushed and perspiration covered his brow and chest.

"I forgot how tiring flying can be," he said breathlessly.

"It looks like fun," said Salena, "but I think I'll stick with the water." She smiled and rose to her feet, adding, "That really was something to see. Now how about showing us around the city?"

"Yes," added Duncan, getting to his feet. "I've been cooped up long enough."

His breathing returning closer to normal, Ar'ye nodded in ascension and bade them to follow. The trio started off north through the Healers' Quarters courtyard, Ar'ye and Salena making a conscious effort to keep the pace down for Duncan. Patches watched them leave from his vantage point in the grass then rose to his feet slowly. In no hurry, the cat yawned widely, barring his immense teeth. After a quick, full body stretch he set off at a light run, careful of his leg, to join his friends, staying at Duncan's side. The lush grass ended at a small copse of trees which they passed through, following a wagon path.

"You will find," stated Ar'ye as they walked, "that the Dwarves are not only a stubborn and stalwart race but also very insightful."

"That's an odd combination," chuckled Duncan sarcastically.

"Yes, but nonetheless true," continued Ar'ye, pleased to see Duncan in a jovial mood. "Take for instance these woods. They serve as a buffer zone between the city and the Healers' Quarters. It helps keep the noise out and provides a tranquil view for those requiring healing. And, in a moment, you'll see other reasons."

As the party stepped clear of the woods, Duncan and Salena stared in complete disbelief at the sight before them.

The Dwarven city of Calheller, lay stretched out before them, glinting in the afternoon sun and surrounded by the mountains like a diamond set in rough stone. Stepping clear of the woods, they entered a beautifully manicured garden of flowers and shrubs. There were flowers of all colours of the rainbow, planted in various arrangements and configurations. The shrubs were thick and green with prosperous white flowers all over their tops. They were planted in such a manner as to resemble mazes, pathways leading to and fro between them.

"I never thought I'd see another sight as beautiful as the shores of the Misty Isles," stated Salena in awe, "but this is absolutely breathtaking."

"It certainly is," added Duncan, equally spellbound.

Ar'ye led them through the garden and into the city which spread out before them. The streets were busy and bustling with Dwarves going about their daily business. Merchants hawked their goods from stands in front of their shops while stonemasons and blacksmiths plied their respective trades. Remarkably, no two buildings looked the same, even though all were made of stone, quarried from the surrounding mountains. The streets were cobble-stoned but shone with a brightness that almost hurt the eye.

"Why do the streets shine so, Ar'ye?" asked Duncan, shielding his eyes as he looked to his friend.

"The Dwarves have paved their streets in silver," he replied. "Their wealth is so great. It also illuminates the road at night when the stars or moon are out. You will get used to the brightness shortly."

Being a cat and a hunter, Patches was already fully accustomed to the extra light, his yellow eyes shining like stars, the pupils closed to narrow slits.

Continuing on, they passed through the merchants' section and entered the armouries, here the Dwarven blacksmiths forged spears, swords, maces and other weapons of war.

As they passed by, Salena whispered, "Why do none of the Dwarves give us any more than a passing glance? I've seen no other people here except Dwarves so we can't be all that common an occurrence."

"Very true, Salena," replied Ar'ye. "The Dwarves have isolated themselves from Man and the Rey'ak for many years now since the Black Paladin's rise to power, trusting no one. However, news of our arrival has spread already so most of the Dwarves were aware of our coming."

"Why are they allowing us to stay if they have such mistrust towards other races? Are they going to help us after all?"

"It is more likely they seek help from you, Duncan."

"How is that?"

"You are the son of King Aramid, come to reclaim your throne. The Dwarves will be looking to you for a plan of action."

Duncan remained silent then, realizing that it was appearing more and more that his success was going to lie on his shoulders and no one else's. He still had no idea how he was to accomplish this task.

They passed through the armouries, still heading east through the city in silence when they reached the Dwarven farms. Here the fields grew thick and tall with amber waves of wheat and rye. The valley plateau upon which they were situated was a very favourable environment for their crops. Amidst the varying browns of wheat and rye were seas of yellow and green, beautiful yellow flowers on green plants. Extensive irrigation systems ran through the fields, fed by nearby mountain rivers.

"What are those pretty flowers used for?" asked Salena, bending down to inspect the yellow flower crop. As if trying to figure out for himself, Patches was beside her, sniffing the flowers with his pink nose.

"The Dwarves make an oil from them which they use for fuelling lamps and for cooking. The flowers are called Danelo."

"Amazing," said Duncan, obviously impressed. "I guess they are a very thoughtful people after all, even if they are somewhat pernicious."

Feeling some discomfort in his leg, Duncan sat down at the edge of one of the Danelo fields. Patches sat down next to him and immediately began to nuzzle his head into Duncan's side, informing him it was time to pet him.

Salena smiled at the pair and went to sit with them, changing her mind as she saw Ar'ye staring intently at the mountains to the east.

"What is it, Ar'ye?" she asked quietly.

"Listen…. out there," he pointed to the eastern mountain ridge.

Salena followed his finger and listened. Out of the corner of her eye she could see Patches' ears erect and forward, obviously listening as well. Straining, she could detect a dull booming sound carrying through the air.

"Is that why these are called the Thunder Mountains? Because of that noise?" she asked, her interest piqued.

"No. These mountains get their name from the sounds of the waterfalls beyond these mountains." Ar'ye stopped for a moment, his features growing sullen, dark thoughts invading his mind, filling it with uncertainty and fear before he continued. "Those sounds are closer. They are the sounds of war drums."

"Whose?" asked Duncan, rising to his feet again, Patches following. "The Wraulls?"

"Yes. Their armies are just beyond those mountains. From what I've learned so far, they may attack at any time. They have been there for several weeks but appear to be waiting for something. A signal, possibly."

"And you fear they may also be marching on your home," Salena said, reading the fear and helplessness showing on Ar'ye's features.

"You are an excellent observer, dear Salena," confided Ar'ye, a hint of a smile crossing his brown face. "We must return to the Healers' Quarters now. It will soon be dark."

Duncan woke in the morning, his legs somewhat stiff from the previous day's excursion but feeling refreshed overall. Early morning light filtered in through the unshuttered windows, warming and brightening the room. Rising, Duncan looked to the foot of the bed and saw Patches sleeping tranquilly on the floor. He smiled warmly at the cat, remembering how he had saved his life only days ago. It amazed him that something so peaceful could be so deadly when provoked.

He owed Patches his life for defending him against the Demon, twice, and wondered how he could ever repay the cat.

As if in response, Patches raised his head, yellow eyes still half closed and gave Duncan a quiet, "Mmrow," as if to say, "I understand. It's okay."

Duncan smiled again and began to get dressed, the sights of the past day flooding back to his memory. What a lovely city, he thought. So much wealth and beauty, it was a shame the Dwarves had closed themselves off from the outside world. Maybe it was for the better, though. It would be terrible to see it fall into the hands of the Black Paladin or his minions.

Pulling on clean pants and a short-sleeved shirt provided by the Dwarves, Duncan looked about for his leather boots, one of the few things he owned to survive this far, when Patches ran to the door. Turning, Duncan watched the door open and stared in disbelief as for the first time in a week he saw Martyl and Big Cat standing on their own.

The two cats greeted each other by rubbing their heads together, purring so loudly it sounded like distant thunder. Martyl walked past them, picking his steps gingerly and extended his hand to Duncan. Duncan took the preferred hand in his, noticing the cuts from the swamp had healed leaving deep scars, and held it a moment before pulling Martyl closer for a friendly embrace.

"Your father would be proud of you Duncan. I know I am."

"Thank you, Martyl. That means a lot. But it wasn't all me. I had a lot of help. Sit down, please." Duncan motioned to the bed and pulled up the only chair in the room next to the bed.

Big Cat wasted no time and trotted over beside Duncan, sitting at his side to catch up on some much needed bonding.

While Duncan stroked Patches and Big Cat, one on either side of him, he recounted his tale to Martyl.

"That's absolutely amazing," was all Martyl could say at the end of the tale. He found himself staring at Duncan in almost total disbelief. The two cats, however, seemed indifferent and having had their share of attention laid their heads on their paws to sleep.

"Not only did you meet a Rey'ak, something I only heard of in legends, you destroyed a Demon too!"

For the first time he could ever remember, Duncan saw that Martyl was truly excited. Patches raised his head up to look at Martyl as if to remind him that he helped too.

"He knows Patches. I told him," Duncan soothed his cat's feelings.

Smiling, Martyl's weathered features seemed even more creased yet somehow less distraught as he said, "You really believe that they understand you, don't you," looking at the two large cats resting on the floor.

"I know they do," replied Duncan, his voice completely serious. "And I understand them."

Before he could continue to lecture Martyl about the special bond between himself and the cats, Duncan was interrupted by a knock at the door.

"Yes?" asked Duncan.

The door to the room opened and in filed Salena and Ar'ye, followed by Shorn.

"Shorn told us Martyl and Big Cat were better," said Salena, striding across the room to Duncan and Martyl. "I'm so glad to see you recovered," she added, hugging Martyl then reaching down to pet Big Cat. "You missed out on a lot of excitement."

"So I've been told," replied Martyl, rising and turning to Ar'ye. "I'm Martyl, the last of King Aramid's Royal Knights, pleased to make your acquaintance." He offered his hand to Ar'ye who shook it briefly before bowing his head.

"No, it is I who is pleased to meet you, Royal Knight. As I have told Duncan, my people are in grave danger from the Black Paladin and his army of Wraulls. The fact that the two of you have returned to defeat this evil will bring great hope to my people."

"All my life I have heard legends of your people. It would be more than an honour to meet and assist them."

"I know you have much to discuss," interrupted Shorn, her voice mockingly gruff, "but you, Martyl, Royal Knight or not, are under my care and need further recovery. I must insist you return to your room immediately."

A seasoned knight and a previous visitor of the Dwarves from long ago, Martyl did as Shorn bade, knowing full well the Dwarven Healer's reputation for looking after her charges. As he headed for the door, he turned to Duncan before leaving to say, "We'll talk later."

"Yes. When I say you can leave your room," added Shorn, her voice still gruff but with an unmistakable caring warmth in it. "The rest of you, including the two cats, may do what you wish as long as you don't bother the knight."

With that, she turned to leave the room, closing the door behind her.

Four more days passed, as uneventful as the others already gone by. Duncan and the others spent their time in the courtyard and woods surrounding the Healer's Quarters. The cats honed their hunting skills on the game in the woods while Ar'ye continued to improve his flying skills. Duncan, armed only with a broken tree branch, practised his sword-play as best he could.

Salena, having had enough of bloodshed earlier in their journey, turned her time and efforts to something she found a little more productive.

Knowing all too well how easy it was to kill, she decided to learn how to heal. When not tending Martyl, which she insisted she do alone, Shorn taught Salena what she could of the Dwarven healing arts.

Salena practised on a small rabbit that she rescued from the cats. Their first day out hunting, Patches and Big Cat had discovered an entire hutch and systematically caught each rabbit. Hearing their squeals of fear, Salena rushed into the woods in time to save one of the babies. She was saddened and sickened by the sight and scolded the cats fiercely. For their part, the cats slunk away and made sure they did any future hunting well away from her.

Salena felt silly at first, using the skills Shorn was teaching her on a rabbit but she grew attached to the animal and realized the same principals could be applied to any of them.

Shorn showed her which plants and roots growing in the wild were useful for their healing tendencies and how to prepare them for use. When not learning from Shorn, Salena spent what time she could with her new pet, figuring if Duncan could have his cats, she'd have this rabbit, which she named Chey.

On the fifth day since Martyl's temporary appearance, a group of four Dwarves, bearded and stocky and powerfully built like all the others, marched through the courtyard and into the Healers' Quarters. All were dressed in bold, bright blue uniforms, with a crest bearing a majestic mountain range with the sun rising over them. They paid Duncan and the others no heed as they marched by and Shorn whispered to them to be quiet and not interfere with the Dwarves.

Duncan hastily asked Shorn what they wanted. Her reply was gruff as usual yet held an undertone of affection. She said they were there to talk to Martyl.

After an hour of uneasy standing by, Duncan watched the Dwarven party leave and Martyl followed, stopping to discuss with the others what had recently transpired.

"We are to meet with the King tomorrow," he began. "All of us. Two hours after sunrise the King's honour guard will be here to escort us to the Conference Hall."

Martyl paused, seeing the look of confusion and betrayal that flickered across Duncan's face.

"I'm sorry Duncan, but you've got to understand the situation. I'm not trying to undermine your position. It's just that the Dwarves don't trust outsiders. I've been here before."

"I understand," replied Duncan listlessly.

"I hope you do. If it wasn't for you killing that Demon, and my being with Salena and Ar'ye, we might not be here now. This quest is as important to me as it is you. Remember that."

He hated being so stern but Martyl couldn't afford to have Duncan thinking the wrong things. Seeing that he couldn't rectify the situation, Martyl finished, "We'd better turn in for the night. Tomorrow will be a long day." He knew that Duncan would realize the truth of his words, that the Dwarves already knew him and would see him as the leader of their group regardless of any titles they possessed.

Chapter Twelve

Duncan had a fitful sleep, if it could be called sleep. He was up most of the night, his stomach doing cartwheels and his mind playing over the endless possibilities of the upcoming day. He rolled and tossed on his bed, getting up every so often to pace the room, as if that would bring the advancement of the morning that much quicker. Patches and Big Cat both managed to cat nap through most of the night although they did spend time pacing with Duncan.

Finally the sun came up, its bright yellow light scattering the darkness as it flowed through the open windows. The cats yawned and stretched, rising from their resting places at the foot of the bed. Both headed straight for the door, knowing that was where Duncan was headed.

Stretching himself, Duncan washed quickly at his wash basin and strode to the door. Patches and Big Cat were both looking back at him expectantly, as if to say, 'Hurry up. You were waiting for this. And we're waiting to be fed!'

Duncan reached down and stroked each cat for a few moments, easing his anxiety a little before opening the door. Taking a deep breath, Duncan opened the door and stepped into the hallway, followed by the cats. Almost as if on cue, the others stepped out from their rooms.

"I thought you would have been up a long time ago," chuckled Martyl as he too stepped into the hallway.

"I was," muttered Duncan, rubbing the redness in his eyes.

"Me too," added Salena, yawning as she closed her door behind her.

Ar'ye left his room and the group conveyed together.

Shorn came down the hall, calling out, "Come now. I have prepared breakfast for you. I won't let you leave my care without eating one last time."

As she walked past them leading the way to the kitchen, Duncan caught the hint of a warm smile on her face for the first time.

They were all seated at a large rectangular wooden table, the cats having their own dishes on the floor. The table was covered with fresh fruits and berries and bowls of warm stew. They were all pretty anxious of the upcoming meeting so they merely picked through their food in silence. The cats seemed oblivious to the tension around them and ate heartily.

Each person at the table was imagining what was going to transpire when they met with the King. They all ran various scenarios through their minds, trying to ease their fears, preparing themselves as for what to say, how to act, knowing they would only get one chance at this.

Finally, Martyl broke the silence. "I must inform you all when we are in conference with the King, speak only when asked. The Dwarves demand and assure respect and honour. As you know, they do not normally accept outsiders and this is a great honour for us."

The others nodded their understanding, too nervous to speak.

"I believe it is time for you to go." It was Shorn, standing in the doorway.

Behind her stood the four Dwarves from the Honour Guard. All were dressed in their bold blue uniforms with their imperious crest of a rising sun over the mountains emblazoned on the chest. Large battle-axes were slung across their backs. As usual, their bearded faces bore the same stoic look.

"I've enjoyed your stay here with me," continued Shorn. "I hope you enjoyed it as well." For the first time ever, her face bore a broad, unmistakable smile. "Since I may not see you again, I wish you luck now, wherever you journey may take you."

"Thank you," they all replied in unison, smiling in return.

As they walked past her and into the company of the Honour Guard, Shorn pulled Salena aside, giving her a brief hug.

"Remember all I taught you," she said, looking up at Salena. "You will be able to field dress and tend wounds much better now." With a warm smile she added, "And I'll look after your rabbit."

"Thank you Shorn, I will," replied Salena, smiling and returning the hug.

"We must be underway now," stated one of the Dwarves matter-of-factly.

Salena bid Shorn a final farewell and fell into place with the others. The group left the Healers' Quarters with the two of the Honour Guard leading the way. Duncan, Martyl and the others filled in the middle and the other two guards brought up the rear. They continued marching this way through the forest and park and into the city proper.

Unsurprisingly to Duncan and the others, the Dwarves of the city were already going about their daily business at this early hour. With the sun just coming up over the tops of the mountains, the city streets were not shining as brightly as on their previous visit. The Dwarves did pay them a little more attention this time as they passed by. They all stared briefly at the small party, their faces as impassive as usual.

Their march continued on in unabated silence headed north through the city. This was a new part of the city they were now seeing compared to the farmlands they saw beyond the city to the west. Here the buildings were even more skilfully and artfully designed. They stretched three or four stories into the sky and were carved out of granite. Frescoes of Dwarven warriors battling malevolent looking creatures were hewn out of the walls.

For a thoughtful and peaceful people, thought Duncan, the Dwarves sure have a mean streak in them.

Eventually the buildings gave way to a vast, open courtyard that was beautifully decorated. Here the distant rumbling of waterfalls crashing into rocks could be heard even louder. Flowers representing virtually every colour of the rainbow flourished in abundance in vast gardens. In the centre of each flower garden were two evergreen trees, entwined together, reaching into the clear blue sky as one massive tree. Progressing through the flower gardens, they could hear the songs of birds, their voices pleasant and uplifting. They reached into the depths of their souls, warming them like a hot summer breeze.

The sun was now nearly directly overhead, the trip through the city to this point having taken most of the morning. The party began to grow tired and Duncan realized it was a wise idea by the Dwarven King to postpone their meeting until they were all well. They would have been too tired to confer with the King if they weren't fully healed.

Duncan looked about at the others and saw that they too felt as he did. Even Salena, uninjured thus far, was beginning to drag her feet. The Dwarves made up for their lack of size with endurance. They had not even broken a sweat in their uniforms and weapons.

As last when he began to think that maybe they would never see the King or his Hall, Duncan and the others were ordered to halt as they rounded a corner in the garden. In silent admiration, they all stared, even Martyl who had been here once before, at the majestic sight before them.

Rising straight up from the ground, resembling the jagged back of a gigantic juggernaut, were the Thunder Mountains. The steel-gray rock face was nearly flat and featureless for about the first two hundred feet except for a single road carved out of the rock face. This made the mountain a virtual fortress, unassailable save for the single road.

From high above, on the mountain peaks, shrouded in the clouds and mist, ran streams of water. They gathered speed and noise as they snaked their way down the mountain face, crashing thunderously into large pools at the foot of the mountain.

Duncan and the others, save Martyl, were dumbfounded by the fact that with all the water cascading into the pools they didn't overflow. In fact, it seemed as if the water level remained constant.

The cats, sensing an opportunity to rest, sat down immediately. Uninterested in the sights around them, they busied themselves with grooming their fur. After all, they had marched with their people all morning and had to look good for the upcoming meeting.

"The rest of you may relax also," said one of the Dwarves to Martyl. As with the others, his voice was stern and gruff, lacking any warmth.

Without any further pleasantries, the Dwarf pulled a large horn from the belt at his side and blew into it. The sound was loud and deep, echoing off the mountain walls. From high atop the road came a reply call. From their vantage point on the ground, Duncan, Martyl and Salena could see only small dots milling about. Ar'ye, seeing better than them with his Rey'ak eyes and knowing this, informed them that a cart, drawn by four ponies was on its way down.

"What is that for?" asked Salena.

"To carry us up the mountain," replied Martyl.

"Well, it's nice to see someone has some manners around here," quipped Duncan, a slight edge in his tone.

Their Dwarven escorts, standing between them and the road either didn't hear or didn't care, paying it no heed.

Salena shot Duncan a disapproving glance then continued her questioning, turning back to Martyl.

"That was such a beautiful garden. Do you know why those trees were grown entwined together like that?"

"It is supposed to be a symbolic representation of the way all things in life are interrelated to one another. All the different coloured flowers represent the diversity in life—the different races and cultures, animals and such."

"Where does the water go from those pools?" asked Duncan, still watching the waterfalls.

"The Dwarves have an underground irrigation system. Tunnels from the pools lead to the fields to supply water for their crops."

"There is something I do not understand, Martyl," began Ar'ye. "Why did we not see this particular range of the mountains until we were right beneath them? Even to my keen eyes they seemed far off yet."

Martyl looked over his shoulder at the Dwarves behind him. They did not seem to be paying any attention so he began his answer, his voice hushed.

"This is, if you haven't already guessed, the Royal Hill. To protect its location, a spell has been cast upon this section of the range to make it appear further away than it really is. Not until you get beyond the garden can you see it."

Lowering his voice to an almost whisper, he continued, "That is another feature of the garden. It holds the spell."

"We know the secret and location now," said Duncan, "Aren't they worried about that?"

His gaze sweeping over the other three, Martyl answered, his voice hard and cold like stone. "No one leaves here alive if the Dwarves suspect their secret is not safe."

Salena felt a cold chill travel up her spine, jolting her. Duncan and Ar'ye both averted their eyes from Martyl to stare at the Dwarves behind him, wondering what chance they would stand if the Dwarves decided to kill them. They had no intention of just lying down to die but didn't think they'd fare too well unarmed, either.

"Make no mistake about your vulnerability. The Dwarves have lived here longer and more peacefully than any other race and intend to keep it that way, at all costs." Martyl's voice was still cold, the weight of his words sinking in even more.

They sat in silence now, broken only by the low purring of the cats, content to laze in the sun. A few minutes later the cart arrived and they were instructed to climb aboard. The ponies, like the Dwarves, were short and stocky but powerfully built. Their legs were thick and bulging, easily pulling the wooden cart up the mountain side in a remarkably short time. Reaching the top, everyone was ordered out of the cart and marched up to the gate.

Six armed Dwarves, each dressed in the brilliant blue uniform and bearing battle axes stood before the gate. The blazing sun over the mountains crest was covered by heavy chain-mail armour.

"These are the visitors come to see the King," stated the Dwarf currently in charge of the party and the Honour Guard.

The six armoured guards sized up Martyl, standing ahead of everyone, eyeing him cautiously. They gave the others a quick glance, Ar'ye receiving a particularly unpleasant one. Their curiosity seemingly satisfied, the armoured Dwarves stepped forward from the iron portcullis behind them, and split into two single file columns of three, one on each side of the party.

"Raise the gate," called out the Dwarf who was in charge of the Honour Guard. From somewhere in behind the rock face, Duncan and the others could hear the iron chains and gears groaning like the laboured breaths of a great beast. Slowly at first, then faster as it gained momentum, the portcullis raised up, stopping when it was about seven feet high.

"Quickly, now. Enter," demanded the Dwarf leading the Honour Guard.

As before, Duncan and the others were marched single file between the Dwarves, two in front and two in rear. When the last member of the Honour Guard was through, the portcullis lowered quickly, slamming into the stone floor of the mountain, the echoes reverberating off the cavern and making them feel sealed in. Duncan felt a cold shiver run up his spine as he realized they were now cut off completely from the outside world.

Glancing about quickly before they were marched off again, the small party was surprised to find the chamber they were in was brightly lit, despite the fact they were inside the mountain. Torches were hung in sconces on the walls about every twenty feet but none were lit. The walls themselves seemed to glitter like small stars and it took several minutes before they realized where the light was coming from. Small holes were cut into the upper reaches of the chamber walls and ceiling, leading up and out. Sunlight streamed in through the small shafts and glittered off the gem encrusted walls.

"Breathtaking," whispered Salena under her breath. "Absolutely breathtaking."

Ar'ye turned and smiled at her then motioned her to be silent. Salena blushed, not realizing she had spoken so loud, but remembered that Ar'ye had exceptional hearing. She was not the only one in awe, though, as the others, including Martyl who had been here long ago, stared in silent awe at the beauty of the Dwarves' creation.

The chamber in which they stood was hewn from the mountain itself, the walls as smooth as glass. The overall size was small, only about thirty square feet with an iron door at the opposite end of the chamber as the portcullis. The ceiling was about fifteen feet high but halfway up the walls were balconies carved out of the rock, five per side. Upon these balconies were two Dwarven soldiers each, also dressed in chain-mail armour. They all manned large black cauldrons, filled with what Duncan and Salena could only imagine.

Martyl, an aged and hardened warrior, knew all to well that what was in the cauldrons and their purposes. He had not seen boiling oil dumped on a soldier in his day, but he remembered the stories related by the older knights to know what these were and just what kind of damage they could do to man or beast.

Following the Honour Guard, they marched through the chamber to the iron door at its end. Reaching into his uniform, the lead Dwarf produced a key and proceeded to unlock the door. Opening the door, he ushered all the others through then locked the door behind him. They now stood in a hallway that led downwards at a steady but shallow incline. Like the chamber before, it was lit about as bright as a cloudy day, by sunlight channelled in through shafts reaching the surface.

As they continued down the hallway in silence, they noticed other passages heading off in different directions through the mountain. Some led up and others continued down like the one they were presently in. All had unlit torches hanging in their sconces similar to the first chamber, illuminated instead by sunlight reflecting gems.

At last they reached the bottom of the hall which Martyl silently estimated to himself to be two hundred feet below ground. Amazingly, the Dwarves managed to get sunlight in, even this far below the surface. The chamber into which the hallway ended was huge. The vaulted ceiling, carved out of the rock was over fifty feet high. The walls were lined with diamonds only, unlike all the other walls which contained gems and stones of many types. The chamber was round, not square like the first and about one hundred feet in diameter. In the centre was a pool of clear water about thirty feet by twenty feet. Growing up from the bottom were reddish stalagmites, resembling miniature mountains rising from the sea.

At the far end of the chamber, directly across from the hall they exited were a set of oak doors, bound in iron. Standing before the doors were two burly Dwarf guards. Both were covered in silver chain-mail armour that shone like the full moon itself even in the underground light. Following their Dwarf escort, the party skirted to the right of the pond and approached the doors.

Duncan swallowed hard, trying to ease his nervousness. The big moment had come and now everything he had planned to say faded from his memory like stars covered by clouds at night. Fighting back his nervousness, Duncan steeled himself for their upcoming meeting. Both cats, still at his side, rubbed their heads against his legs to offer their support, as if saying, 'We're with you.'

Salena stayed behind Duncan, every bit as nervous and fretful as he was. They had come too far and through too much to be turned back now, she told herself. They would succeed. They had to.

Ar'ye brought up the rear, his thoughts turbulent also, but for an even more personal reason. He knew the Dwarves did not like his people for not helping against the Black Paladin years ago. If this would affect his new friends' chances for help he didn't know. But, there was also the chance they would get help and in turn could help his people, the Rey'ak. For that he was willing to risk some discomfort and uneasiness.

Martyl, in the front, used his experience and training to clear his thoughts and calm his nerves. He needed to be in complete control of his faculties if they were to persuade the Dwarves to assist them.

"Halt!" commanded the two guards in unison from their position before the doors. Everyone came to a stop, including the Dwarves who were serving as armed escorts. One of the armoured guards opened the doors slightly and slipped inside, closing them behind him.

Duncan began to tire of these games the Dwarves seemed to enjoy playing at their expense. He wondered if the King was really here or not. Getting restless, he began to rock back on his heels, easing his mind of boredom and uneasiness, when Martyl reached back and grabbed hold of his wrist without even looking.

Squeezing hard, Martyl turned his head slowly and gave Duncan a glare that could have shattered stone. Blushing, Duncan stood still, looking at the floor, too embarrassed to meet Martyl's gaze. Besides, now he had the pain in his wrist to occupy his mind.

Within minutes, the guard reappeared saying, "The King will see you now. Enter."

Each guard grabbed a door and pulled it open without breaking a sweat, despite their immense size and weight. Martyl stepped into the room beyond, followed by Duncan and the cats, Salena and then Ar'ye. Behind them the doors closed and their Dwarf escort remained outside.

The room into which they entered was the Conference Hall. Like everything else beneath the mountain, it was carved out of solid rock. The walls, however, were lined with obsidian, polished smooth as glass and the party could actually see their reflections on the walls. The ceiling was high and arched, oak beams running across for support and artistry. Unlit lamps hung from the beams along with large, woven tapestries with the emblem of the sun rising over the mountains emblazoned on them.

In the centre of the rectangular room was a large table, made of black obsidian also. Rich wooden chairs lined each side of the table with one at the head. Seated about the table were several faces they recognized. On the left side of the table were seated Dirn and Rorn, leaders of the Dwarven Patrols that found Duncan and the others. Both were dressed in the now familiar blue uniforms with the Dwarven crest on the front.

Beside them were seated four other Dwarves, each dressed in long robes of various colours—red, blue, green and black. The right side of the table had six wooden chairs, all unoccupied.

At the head of the table sat a seventh Dwarf, dressed in a rich blue robe. His beard and hair were the colour of raw silver and his face lined with age and wisdom. Around his head he wore a simple band of gold, only half an inch wide with a brilliant green emerald set in the centre.

"Welcome," he said, rising to great his guests. The other seated Dwarves rose also, their steady gazes never wandering from the newcomers.

"I am King Balamir and as you already know, these are Dirn and Rorn," his voice was cold and authoritative as he continued. "These others are my chief advisors. This is Galani, my General of Defence."

Balamir pointed to the Dwarf next to Rorn, dressed in red.

"Second is Belan, my General of Offense, in the blue. Third is Deelam, my First Minister in the green and in the black is Grendle, the best of our magic-users. We shall listen to your plea and decide how to act upon it. Now be seated."

Blunt and to the point, thought Duncan. Maybe now they could get somewhere.

Balamir sat down in his chair which the others observed to be somewhat higher and more ornately decorated. Following his direction, Martyl led the way around the table and took the next seat on the end closest to Balamir. Duncan sat next to Martyl, the cats both sitting directly behind his chair, eyes wide and alert with anticipation.

Salena took the next seat, followed by Ar'ye, his wings folded neatly behind his back to allow him to sit in the backed chair.

"Now please, introduce yourselves and inform us of your plight," commanded Balamir, his voice filled with a resonance that demanded attention.

Martyl rose, taking a deep breath. He knew Balamir was testing them, to be sure their story was true and not a lie. If they were to receive any help from the Dwarves they would have to be truthful as well as tactful.

"I am Martyl," he began, his voice strong and unwavering. "The last of King Aramid's Royal Knights."

He paused for a moment, letting the weight of his announcement sink in. The Dwarves cast furtive glances back and forth amongst themselves.

Ar'ye and Salena patiently held their breath and Duncan now realized fully how important it was that Martyl, not he, begin this discourse with the Dwarves. He admired Martyl's strength and poise and wondered if he could have started half as well. Stretching his left arm out, palm splayed toward Duncan, Martyl continued.

"This is Duncan, son of Aramid and rightful heir to the throne of Arundel. Next to him is Salena, an old friend and Ar'ye, whom we rescued from slavers upon our journey. We hope his people will help us in our quest also."

"You will get little help from their cowardly race," derided Dirn in an obvious attempt to barb Ar'ye.

Ar'ye paid him no heed save a quick, cold glance. He had many retorts on the tip of his tongue, yet held them on behalf of his friends.

"That is enough, Dirn," scolded Balamir, not rising from his chair but raising his voice enough to echo off the chamber walls.

"It is quite possible that they do not know about certain past events. For them to remain hidden from the Black Paladin so long they must have been very secluded.

"I have heard of you Martyl and your exploits with the Royal Knights when you were younger. I know you were here in our kingdom many years ago and even received care from our healers then. That is the only reason I have granted your party an audience.

"Many people over the years have claimed to be the lost heir to the throne of Arundel. Naturally, they are silenced by the Black Paladin quickly. Others are his pawns, sent out to infiltrate any resistance groups so they may be destroyed."

Duncan felt the colour leave his face and noticed the others, seated beside him, also paled. All except Martyl who kept his gaze solidly fixed on the King.

"That is why we had to take such precautions with you," continued Balamir, "in case you were such. In your favour, Duncan and one of the cats defeated a Demon. There a few people who could perform such a deed, none without magic."

Reaching into his robe, Balamir pulled out a dagger, immediately recognized by Duncan as Sliver. He sat breathless, watching as Balamir continued.

"The magic in this knife is indeed strong, yet it is not powerful enough to defeat the Black Paladin. I regret to inform you that it will require much more than this if you hope to have a chance at all."

"That is why we have come to you," interjected Martyl, rising to his feet again.

In the cold silence that followed, the sound of his chair grating on the rock floor as he pushed it back was all the others heard.

Hoping to gain momentum in his speech, Martyl continued. "During my quests for the King, I heard many legends of lost artifacts and weapons from the Black Magic Wars. Most were made by your people for the men and Dwarves that fought the Demons unleashed by the evil wizards of old. I hoped you could possibly shed some light on those legends and we could find a weapon to use."

Duncan and Salena secretly held their breath, hoping for a possible answer. Ar'ye already feared the worst, rejection, and just hoped they would be allowed to leave alive. All three noticed the looks of surprise on the faces of the Dwarves, however and then the hard scowls that soon replaced them.

"What makes you think we haven't already searched for these lost weapons?" asked Grendle his face now composed.

Martyl started to answer when Balamir spoke again, saying, "Now we know your reason for seeking our help and once again you must understand our reluctance. This is exactly like one of the Black Paladin's ploys. If we were to help you find any of these lost weapons and you were in league with him, it would prove disastrous for us.

"Besides, as you yourself said, they are but legends. And even if they are real and you are who you say you are, you will still need more than your small group. Even if you manage to get the help of the Rey'ak it may not be enough to battle the Black Paladin's forces."

Unable to bear sitting in silence any longer and not liking the direction the discussion seemed to be taking, Duncan rose in his chair with such swiftness it startled both cats. Patches and Big Cat scrambled from his sides, ears back and eyes darting about, before settling back down, this time by Salena.

"What would you have us do then? Sit here in this rock, waiting patiently for the Black Paladin's armies to lay siege? Not me. I plan to reclaim my kingdom and make him pay for what he's done!"

"You make a brave noise, boy," growled Rorn rising to stare Duncan down from across the table.

"Why don't you tell us how you managed to stay hidden from the Black Paladin for fifteen years. I find it very odd that you appear just before his armies are about to lay siege on us. And to make it even more unbelievable, you show up with a cowardly Rey'ak."

Ar'ye had listened long enough too and rose to his feet, his wings spreading out to give him some flight advantage should he fight. He was not about to sit by idle, this being the second inference to his race being cowardly. Besides, Duncan was involved now and he owed him and Salena his life.

"Be seated, now!" commanded Balamir, rising from his seat, his voice reverberating off the chamber walls in anger.

Rorn sat down slowly, his eyes never leaving Duncan or Ar'ye. Duncan and Ar'ye glowered back as they resumed their seats at the table.

Martyl stared in a combination of anger and disbelief at his two companions while Salena stroked the cats' heads, hoping to keep them calm.

"Be seated, Martyl," stated Balamir, his demeanor now composed again. "As you can see, we both have distrust towards each other that must be overcome. We have much to lose if we trust too easily. Maybe if we could learn about your past, your time spent in seclusion, we may be more understanding."

Balamir, for his part was trying to be diplomatic and keep his calm despite the commotion going on around him.

"Yes," began Deelam, the First Minister. "We would be very interested in hearing how you managed to evade the Black Paladin's forces all these years."

"They stayed with my people."

All eyes were on Salena as she stood and faced Deelam. Martyl and Duncan registered shock while the Dwarves looked bewildered. Ar'ye merely stared off at the far wall, awaiting his next confrontation with the Dwarves.

"It's okay," she said to Duncan and Martyl.

"And who might your people be?" asked Deelam, a hint of sarcasm creeping into his voice.

Holding herself tall and proud, Salena locked eyes with Balamir and continued. "My people are Sirens. We are a peaceful race who live across the ocean in what we call the Misty Isles. For centuries we have remained hidden from your lands but occasionally sailors blown off course will find our shores. To keep our secret, we have a magical song which can cause others to fall into a deep sleep and forget about us. Their ships are then turned around and set into the wind. When the crews awaken, they are far away and remember nothing. Look at my hands. Do they look like the hands of people from these lands?"

She held them up to the unbelieving stares of the Dwarves so they could see the webbing between her fingers before continuing.

"When Duncan was a boy, he, Martyl and another, Connor, arrived on our shore, battered and beaten. We knew nothing about them, yet when Connor jumped from the deck of their ship onto the beach demanding sanctuary, we knew they were different and important. In trade for sanctuary in my land they promised to keep its presence a secret. That promise they have kept, even though it meant endangering their position in these talks.

"I beseech you, as Salena, daughter of the King of the Misty Isles, help these men in their quest, and just as importantly in your quest, in the defeat of the Black Paladin.

"And as for this 'cowardly' Rey'ak, he has helped us immeasurably in our journey thus far. He has kept our secret in trust and regardless of what his people have done in the past, is willing to come here for help with us."

Duncan stared in awe, unable to believe what he had just seen. He knew Salena had a fiery streak but never imagined this would happen.

Balamir rose again then, addressing all four of the newcomers.

"This explains a great deal we did not know about your past. If you will leave us now and wait in the main hall with the guards we will debate our further involvement in this matter."

With no further ado, Balamir called in the guards and had the party escorted out, oblivious to their stares of confusion.

Chapter Thirteen

"Sit down, now," commanded Martyl in a tone Duncan and Salena had never heard before. Both were startled at its harshness and quickly obeyed, averting their eyes from his. Ar'ye sat too, knowing not to cross Martyl at this point even though he hardly knew him. The cats sat next to Duncan, ears lowered.

Martyl paced back and forth in front of the others where they were seated in front of the crystal clear pool. He took a couple of deep, relaxing breaths before starting his tirade on Duncan. The last thing they needed was to cause a scene in front of the Dwarves guarding the King's Chambers.

"What was the outburst all about?" his voice was low and calm but Duncan did not mistake the tone.

"They were treating us like a band of refugees and fugitives. We gave them respect yet they gave us none. We deserve better than that." Duncan met Martyl's glare and held it, difficult as that was.

"For your information, in case you haven't already noticed, the Dwarves do not think very highly of our race. We must try to earn their respect and help, no matter how it may bruise your ego." Martyl paused, taking another calming breath before continuing.

"I must say, however, Salena, that your speech may have made up for Duncan's. I'm proud of you."

Salena blushed as Martyl complimented her diplomatic skills and noticed Duncan's face turn a brighter shade of red.

"And you, Ar'ye, maybe you'd like to give us a quick history lesson. It seems for some reason or another that the Dwarves have a grudge against your people. Is there any particular reason you didn't tell us of this problem earlier?"

Martyl now shifted his rock shattering glare from Duncan to Ar'ye, seated on Salena's left.

"I am sorry, my friends," began Ar'ye, glancing from Duncan to Salena to Martyl. "I did not tell you of this friction between the Dwarves and my people because I feared you would not help me or my people. The Dwarves are angry with my people because we did not aid them in an earlier attack by the Black Paladin. About thirteen years ago he attacked the Thunder Mountains and after a lengthy battle his forces were eventually driven back.

"My people had just made contact with the Dwarves and even though good relations were being established, we thought it prudent to keep out of the battle, not wanting to take sides." Ar'ye saw the looks on their faces and immediately answered the question before it was asked.

"Yes, even though one of our emissaries to King Aramid had been killed by the Black Paladin we did not at the time know all the details. We were, and are a peace loving race and thought it best to remain neutral. Now we have seen that is no longer a reality and are prepared to do whatever it takes to stop the Black Paladin.

"Forgive me, but it is a mistake our people are prepared to amend. Alone if need be. I truly am sorry if I have hindered your chances at all."

"It's over and done with now," stated Martyl coldly. "Are there any other secrets we need to know before we go back in? If we do."

"None Martyl. You have my word," replied Ar'ye.

Duncan and Salena both gave him a pat on the back of his wings in reassurance while Martyl nodded and resumed pacing.

"Relax, Martyl," soothed Salena. "It won't do us any good if you are all worked up too."

"I suppose you're right," he conceded. "But you two better behave yourselves next time," Martyl directed to Duncan and Ar'ye. "If there is a next time."

Sitting down next to Duncan, Martyl thought to himself for a second before adding a little reassurance to Duncan and Ar'ye.

"Don't take it too hard, guys. When I was your age I was just as impetuous. It's just that now I realize how near to death I came back then for those reasons. I don't want you to make the same mistakes."

Duncan met Martyl's gaze and nodded, understanding how foolhardy his outburst had been. Ar'ye nodded his silent agreement also. The quartet, feeling more than a little downtrodden, sat quietly by the still waters of the pond. Each entertained thoughts of what they could have or should have said, hoping that their chances to obtain help from the Dwarves were not doomed.

They waited only a short time although it felt like hours before the King himself emerged from the Conference Hall. All four jumped to their feet at once, hearts racing with anticipation. The two cats were the only ones who remained calm, lifting their heads up from a quick cat nap to see what all the commotion was about.

"My friends," stated Balamir, his voice calm and sure as ever. "Please re-enter my chamber and be seated."

Not wasting any time, Martyl followed after Balamir immediately. Salena, Duncan and Ar'ye all exchanged confused glances at the King's new, personable demeanor. Shrugging his shoulders at the other two, Duncan quickly followed after Martyl with Salena and Ar'ye picking up the rear. With wide yawns baring their two-inch fangs, the two cats followed in last, paying no heed to the widening eyes of the Dwarf Guards.

After everyone was seated, Balamir spoke again from the head of the table.

"You must forgive my people and I, Duncan, Son of Aramid and Martyl, last of the Royal Knights."

All four sat back in their chairs, completely at a loss for words with this unexpected turn-around by the Dwarves.

"We also ask forgiveness of you, Lady Salena and you, Ar'ye of the Rey'ak."

Martyl and the others were still speechless. Even Rorn and Dirn, the two most strongly opposed to the party seemed to have acquiesced.

Continuing, Balamir added, "As you know, we are very distrusting with all outsiders, in light of the events since the Black Paladin's coming to power. It is true, Duncan, that we had good relations with your father and his father and so forth. It is for that reason we granted this audience. First however, we had to be sure that you were indeed the son of Aramid. Our magic is failing. Once we were highly skilled magic-users, but now we have all but forgotten it. Only a select few can still call on the power of the earth and command it to do our bidding. As I already stated, Grendle is the best in my Kingdom."

Balamir raised his left hand to point to Grendle who rose. Removing his right hand from his robe, Grendle produced an opaque silver orb, about six-inches in diameter.

"This is a scrying crystal," began Grendle, the hard edge gone from his voice also. "With it I can see and determine many things, such as if a person is lying, possessed or protected by magic charms or wards."

Sudden realization flickered across the faces of the others and Balamir held up his left hand in a staying gesture.

"There are limitations to it, however," continued Grendle. "The Black Paladin's magic is strong and can sometimes deceive the crystal. Within the walls of this mountain, however, his magic can not yet penetrate. To be certain you were not spies sent by him in some elaborate plan I had to use the crystal in here. That is why you were all brought here. In your weakened condition upon arrival, you posed no threat to us. We removed your weapons for analysis and kept you under close observation."

"Thank you, Grendle," intervened Balamir again. Grendle sat down, the crystal deftly disappearing into his robe again.

Turning to address Martyl and the others, Balamir could see the hurt looks on their faces. He knew they were feeling betrayed and used at the way the previous proceedings went and felt obligated to explain.

"Please understand that while shortly after arriving inside the mountain we knew your identities were as you claimed, we needed to know if your convictions and loyalty to others were worthy. Personal traits that come from the heart cannot be divined by a magic crystal. They must be seen and expressed by living beings."

Slowly Balamir saw the confusion and hurt on their faces turn to recognition and understanding.

"You all showed loyalty to one another while we questioned you and you told us the truth we already knew. For that, and for the reason that we see no better opportunity to rid ourselves of the Black Paladin's coming oppression, we agree to help you in whatever way possible."

Salena let a sigh of relief and grabbed Duncan's hand in joy. Preoccupied as he was, Duncan's only thoughts were of getting out of the Thunder Mountains and on their journey, wherever it may lead next.

Ar'ye permitted himself a brief smile, hoping that this would mean help for his people as well.

Martyl rose and clasped Balamir's outstretched hand in his, saying, "Thank you. Now may I be so bold as to ask what help you have in mind for us?"

"First, let me return your possessions. Grendle, their weapons."

The Dwarven sorcerer rose and waved his left hand in front of the wall behind him. The air before the wall shimmered for a moment then part of the wall disappeared to reveal a shelf cut in the rock face. Reaching in, Grendle drew out Martyl's sword, Duncan's sword, Salena's long knife and Ar'ye's bow and knife.

When Grendle finished returning the weapons, Balamir walked around the table to Duncan and handed him his long knife, Sliver.

"This is a fine weapon, Duncan," remarked Balamir. "I meant no disrespect of it earlier. I just want you to realize the strength of the power the Black Paladin wields. Judging by your expressions when your weapons were revealed, none of you realized part of the wall was an illusion."

Duncan and the others all nodded silently in assent. Returning to his seat, Balamir motioned for Deelam, the First Minister to speak.

"The magic used here was a very simple illusion, a protection ward. The magic wielded by the Black Paladin is much stronger and much more dangerous. As you surmised, Martyl, there were indeed great weapons used many, many, generations ago. It was during the Black Magic Wars that these weapons were forged by Dwarven smiths of old, in the fires of these very mountains. The dwarves were already a mature race at this time of Darkness. So were the Demons. Man was a relatively new race but some of your kind had become quite adept at using magic and became powerful sorcerers.

"Unfortunately some of them used it for the wrong purposes and tried to subvert everything around them. They learned to control and unleash Demons on the uncooperative populace. For years the Demons and their ilk wreaked havoc on these lands and their inhabitants.

"Our magic was pitted against the black magic of the Demons and their masters for nearly ten long years. Thousands upon thousands of Dwarves, Men and Demons perished. Finally, good prevailed, and the Demons were driven from this dimension and forced into another plane of existence.

"From what we have been able to learn, the Black Paladin has discovered an ancient tome of spells from this time. Many existed then, mostly among the sympathizers of the Demons in the races of Man and Dwarf. When the Demons were vanquished, so were these individuals and the tomes destroyed. Obviously some escaped destruction and the Black Paladin discovered at least one.

"With this book, or books, he can perform much destruction. Worse, as has been seen by all of you, he can release Demons into our world."

A look of fear crossed the faces of Ar'ye, Salena and Duncan as they recalled the dreadful battles with the Demon they encountered.

Martyl lowered his gaze from all the others, painfully aware of the fact that he had been saved by one he was sworn to protect.

"All is not as dark as it may seem," continued Deelam. "The magic that vanquished the Demons is older than the magic the Black Paladin possesses and will prevent him from opening the flood gates to the Demon plane.

"His 'gates' that he can open are limited in size and duration. Furthermore, we have discovered information that may lead us to a cache of lost weapons from the Black Magic Wars. This is where you, Martyl, and the others come in."

"What is wrong with the magic in my knife?" asked Duncan, rising from his seat and holding out Sliver to Deelam for inspection. "It has dispatched two Demons already. With a strong enough army we could attack now and save precious time."

"You are indeed brave, Duncan," commented Deelam. "But I see part of our discussion has eluded you. The blade you possess, and many others like it, including your father's, were forged after the Black Magic Wars. They were given to the men who aided us in battle as a token of our appreciation."

Deelam paused, noticing the puzzled expressions on the visitors' faces. Even Martyl did not know how the old magic worked.

"You see," Deelam continued, "the Demons, evil as they were, were part of the 'magical fabric' of this world. When they were forced into exile, much of the magic left with them. The magic that was left to forge new weapons was not as strong as the old magic.

"The Black Paladin possesses a tome that was written with the old magic. That same magic is what he wields. To stop him will require a weapon forged by the old magic, something with an equal amount of power."

"What of the Demons?" asked Salena, voicing the question in everyone's mind. "They are of the 'old magic'. How come this newer weapon destroyed them? What about Patches? He fought the Demon off almost completely by himself the first time."

The grey and white cat raised his head from his paws at the mention of his name. What seemed like a smile crossed his feline features before he returned to his catnap with Big Cat.

"Very good questions, Lady Salena. What you must understand, though, it that the Demons are being brought back into a world that has lost much of its magic. Therefore, the Demons' power is reduced in this transaction. The weapons and Tomes of Magic that have survived to now were created with the old magic and still retain it about them because they never left this dimension.

"The cat, Patches, as you call him, as well as the other, are both magical creatures. Their magic is not of the old magic but of an elemental source, from nature itself. I did not think it strong enough to combat a Demon, but I suppose I was mistaken."

"How do you know that these cats are magical? My people knew not of this!" Salena asked incredulously.

"I can see it in their auras with my scrying crystal," replied Deelam matter-of-factly. "I am surprised your people did not know of this. There are many animals that have magical properties, although their numbers are diminishing with time. Cats of all kinds, as a species, are one of the most magical animals known to us.

"Now, if I may continue with my previous topic, I believe there may be good news for us all."

Duncan was scarcely aware of Deelam's speech at this point as he turned to stare at his cats. A broad smile flashed across his face as he gained even more respect for the great cats. Duncan noticed Salena was watching the cats now, trying to see with her own eyes the magical 'aura' around them.

Salena couldn't believe her people never knew of the cats' magical properties. They always thought the cats' intelligence and strength were natural. She too found herself marvelling anew at these great creatures.

"You have information then on a weapon? One that could be used against the Black Paladin?" Martyl could scarcely contain himself, wanting now to get to the heart of the matter.

"That we have," replied Deelam. "We have searched our Hall of Records and found reference to expeditions into the Untamed Lands shortly after the Black Magic Wars by Dwarves and men, including members of the house of Arundel. Our peoples were looking to expand outwards and the Iron Hills seemed like the ideal place for a new colony."

Salena and Duncan were both now staring at Deelam, completely fascinated with his tales of the past. The places and events he described were completely alien to them and they hung on every word.

Martyl and Ar'ye had both seen these areas in passing and knew all too well the dangers present. They listened intently also, yet already surmised the final outcome.

"However," continued Deelam, "it was not. Within a few months of the colony being established, it was overrun by Wraulls. I'm sure, Martyl, and Ar'ye, that both of you are aware of these vicious creatures."

"Unfortunately so," replied Ar'ye to the cold, unyielding stares of all the Dwarves except Balamir and Deelam.

"I too encountered them years ago, when King Aramid still ruled. Are the legends of their origins true?" added Martyl.

Duncan lowered his eyes from everyone for a moment as the mention of his father brought back memories of his parents he thought were long repressed.

"They are the descendants of Demons who took human females as mates. Although they possess no magic, they do have incredible strength and are intensely aggressive. After they overran the colony, we sent out an army in retaliation. It was during this battle that one of the greatest swords forged by our smiths was lost, the Brach'dir, Mountain Light in your tongue.

"Their numbers were far greater than anticipated and the people that survived were forced to retreat. The wielder of the sword, knowing they had lost, feared the sword falling into Wraull hands. Before the army was defeated, he buried the sword somewhere in the Iron Hills. Over the long years there have been many skirmishes with the Wraulls but we have never found the sword.

"It is this sword, however, we hope to find. It's power should be strong enough to combat the Black Paladin. We have sent out three small expeditions so far, but none have returned."

Deelam sat down then, his head hung low in admitting the defeat his people faced.

"This is what we come to you for," began Martyl, rising from his seat. "We will go in search of this sword in return for your aid against the Black Paladin."

"There is the matter of who will wield the sword when and if it is found," stated Belan, General of Offense.

His features were hard and cold and Martyl knew exactly what he meant. But, he had other plans and felt the Dwarves should know them before there were any misconceptions.

"I believe Duncan should carry it into battle," was Martyl's reply.

Duncan, although embarrassed by Martyl's compliment, held himself erect in his chair and met the Dwarves' hard stares.

"He is but a boy!" came Belan's straightforward reply. "It is a Dwarven relic and should be returned to the Dwarves. This evil known as the Black Paladin is Man's doing. Were it not for your people's weakness, the need to conquer and attain greater power, we wouldn't be facing this dilemma."

"You are correct, Belan. It is Man's doing, but for that reason they must be the ones to correct it." Balamir was standing, addressing everyone in the room, Dwarves and Men together.

"The time of the Dwarves is winding down. We need to entrust our world's safety with others. Duncan must take the sword into battle and reclaim his kingdom. By defeating a Demon single-handedly he has already proven his fighting prowess. Besides, the sword was forged for a king of men during the Black Magic Wars. It is only fitting the heir to Arundel carry it into battle again."

Belan stared at Duncan with a fire burning behind his eyes that threatened to burn him up. Seating himself slowly, he conceded to himself that his King was right, that it was up to this boy to defeat one of his father's own turned against them all. Still, he didn't have to like it.

Duncan met his gaze, feeling his own anger well up inside him at being called a boy in front of everyone. Soothing the anger was the fact that King Balamir had sided against his own general in choosing him to carry the sword.

"We thank you for this honour, King Balamir," said Martyl trying to ease the tension as diplomatically as possible.

The Dwarves stared at him and Duncan coldly, yet they would follow their King's wishes.

"There is not much time left to us now," began Balamir again. "So it would now be best if you set out first thing in the morning."

Relief flooded across the faces of Duncan and Ar'ye, both anxious to leave the sullen Dwarves as soon as possible.

"However," he continued, "you will not be sent alone or without provisions. Rorn and Dirn will accompany you as their knowledge of the Untamed Lands is among the best of our people."

Duncan and Ar'ye both looked across the table to find the two Dwarves staring right back at them, eyes as hard as granite. Salena actually felt relief that someone would be accompanying them who had any knowledge of this strange land.

"Thank you for your generosity, King Balamir," said Martyl with a bow.

"No thanks is required, Royal Knight. We must all work together to vanquish the darkness that has befallen our peoples."

Balamir and Martyl both surveyed the room and saw the stern, angry expressions on everyone's faces, Man, Dwarf and Rey'ak alike, redden in embarrassment.

"First thing in the morning, you shall leave by river boat on the Thunder River, following it through the Dead Woods and to the Iron Hills. When you reach the Iron Hills it will be up to you to find the sword. The colony where it last was used was, to the best of our knowledge, is located three leagues north of the river.

"Should you be successful, the mere possession of the sword will not ensure victory. Troops will be needed to get you past the amassed armies of the Black Paladin. The Dwarven armies are not large enough alone. Can you convince your people to help us, Ar'ye?"

All eyes were now on Ar'ye, but instead of feeling uneasy, he stood up and addressed Balamir and the other Dwarves with the utmost of confidence.

"My people wish to make amends with both the race of Man and Dwarf. We see our error now in watching idly as others fought against the evil about us. We now face that same evil and will help in whatever way we can. That is why I was this far west. Many others of my people will be following if they haven't already left to seek help where we can find it. For what it is worth to you, you have my word."

"I too know of possible help," added Martyl. "When we first arrived from the Misty Isles I encountered a group of resistance fighters known as Renegades. Their numbers are few but they are strategically located."

"Yes, we know of them too. Their numbers are small but any help will be appreciated," added Belan.

"Very well then," concluded Balamir. "We wish you the best of luck. If you will accompany Rorn and Dirn they will take you to the boats where you may spend the night. And be careful, my friends."

At the King's dismissal, the party with their new Dwarven escorts left the King's Chambers and headed out on their new journey.

Chapter Fourteen

The trip across the Dwarven city to the east side was long and quiet, with no one saying a word during the march. Duncan and the others were nearly exhausted, having received very little sleep the previous night. Their meeting with the Dwarves this day did little to relieve their anxiety even though they were granted assistance. None of them worried the least bit what awaited them beyond the mountain walls of the Dwarven city. All they wanted now was to rest.

Dirn and Rorn led the way, marching side by side, the huge iron heads of their battle axes gleaming in the bright moonlight where they hung from their backs.

They too were silent, brooding amongst themselves at the fact that they would have to help find a relic forged by their own people and relinquish it again to a member of the race of Man. As they got closer to the eastern edge of the mountain range Duncan and Salena could hear the pounding of the Wraull war drums that Ar'ye pointed our earlier, only now it was much closer and more recognizable.

Martyl heard it too and he wondered if they would even get past the mountains, let alone into the Untamed Lands beyond.

At last, late that night, they reached the edge of the Dwarven city. They had not realized how big Calheller was until they travelled through it. The sound of water moving fast could now be heard and the party could see a large stream twinkling at them in the starlight.

"Rest tonight, for tomorrow will be a long day, and possibly our most dangerous." It was Rorn, his voice piercing the silence about them.

"We must travel by river boat down the Thunder River, past Wraull patrols and the Dwarven Falls. Many Dwarven patrols have been lost within sight of here to these dangers." Dirn's bleak statement did nothing to alleviate everyone's anxiety. In silence, the group laid out their sleeping rolls among the boats.

The weariness in their bodies and minds over the days' events soon overcame them and they drifted off to sleep, still hearing the steady tattoo of war drums. Big Cat and Patches, having slept most of the day, were not as tired and only napped occasionally. They kept a silent vigil over their friends.

Dirn and Rorn had stamina much greater than that of the others and needed less rest. They spent the next few hours quietly discussing the next few days plans and contingencies for various scenarios. Being Dwarven Patrol leaders, they were very thorough and left nothing to chance.

It was not yet dawn when Dirn and Rorn woke the others.

Martyl was the first to awaken, his field training from years before sharpening his sleep clouded mind to a state of readiness in moments.

Ar'ye followed, on his feet, fetching his bow and quiver. His years as a hunter coupled with the desire to return to his people with hopeful news had him ready to leave in no time.

Duncan and Salena were last to fully waken from the night's much needed sleep. But once awake, they were quick to gather up their things.

All six shared a quick breakfast of cheese and berries, washed down with a Dwarven drink called Trinal. It tasted pleasant, almost like honey-sweetened water, yet left a mild tingling sensation in the body for several minutes after. Dirn, in a rarely talkative mood, explained that the drink provided extra energy for the body when used sparingly. Too much, he said, could cause an adverse affect by overloading the body with stimulant and cause extreme fatigue when the drink wore off …

The cats fed themselves by the stream bed, having caught some fish on their own before the others had awoken. When they finished eating, the sun's orange rays began to funnel through the mountain peaks and lit up the darkened city streets below.

"We must leave now," said Rorn, "before the light extends west. Our best chance at getting past the Wraulls is in the twilight of dawn. Hurry."

He and Dirn were already loading the two river boats with supplies and motioned for the others to climb aboard. Wanting to keep both boats as equally loaded as possible, the Dwarves had separated everyone according to size.

Duncan couldn't help but notice how closely these 'boats' resemble the river skiff they had been on several weeks ago. He winced inwardly at those memories and stepped over the low side of the flat bottomed boat, seating himself. Ar'ye followed Duncan and sat behind him, as told by Dirn who took the till at the stern.

Having been wounded severely and unconscious for most of the previous trip, Big Cat didn't know what to think of the boat but jumped in bravely when Duncan called her. Following in the next boat were Martyl, Salena with Patches and Rorn.

"Remember," continued both Dwarves to their respective passengers, "silence is of the utmost importance if we are to get beyond the Wraulls."

Everyone picked up a paddle and began paddling as silently as possible, even though it required more effort. Going with the current, the two small river boats picked up speed and travelled along the Thunder River and through the mountains.

Like a giant trail marker, the sun lit up the river ahead of them, the water glowing a brilliant orange-red in the early morning light, almost as if the river were on fire. As the early morning wore on, the sky began to brighten even more and the mountains began to thin out. At the same time, the booming of the Wraull war drums could be heard, louder and more ominous.

"We are safe for a while longer yet," called out Rorn from the back boat. "The Wraulls have not yet penetrated our mountains, although they have tried. Even though you cannot see them, there are hundreds of Dwarves from the Dwarven patrols in these hills and they haven't let any Wraulls in. Beyond these hills is where the danger lies."

Soon the mountains gave way to tree covered hills and the river along with the land through which it travelled began to slowly descend. They had been in the river a couple of hours now and dawn had broken over the hills ahead of them. The early morning light warmed their faces in the cool morning mountain air.

Flickering in the distance, on both sides of the Thunder River were camp fires. They resembled fireflies flittering about in the early morning half-light of dawn. Without the Dwarves saying a word, everyone knew the fires were far more sinister. They were the camp fires of the Wraull armies.

So bold were they in their strength and numbers that they were camped only hours from the Dwarven city of Calheller. This was an effort to drive fear into the hearts of their enemies, as well as to further remind then of their own fearlessness.

Salena, along with the others, felt a cold chill run up her spine as the incessant beating of the war drums became louder and louder. Duncan, Ar'ye and the Dwarves steeled themselves against the fear with anger over what the Wraulls and their master, the Black Paladin had done. Martyl, even though he had not seen battle in fifteen years, was still a veteran Royal Knight and kept any fear he might have locked inside.

"We must be vigilant," warned Dirn. "For the Wraulls will be patrolling the hills along the river bank."

"And if we spot any?" asked Duncan.

"They will be in small scouting parties," answered Rorn from the rear boat, "of two to four Wraulls. It will be up to your Rey'ak to stop them from alerting others."

Ar'ye could easily detect the hidden sarcasm in the Dwarf's voice but he still permitted himself a wry smile. He was not worried about the onus being placed on him. After all, he was an excellent marksman with his bow.

Duncan too could feel the sarcasm in Rorn's remark. He did not appreciate his new friend being talked to like that yet he realized the Dwarves would be undoubtably upset given the recent circumstances regarding them all. In the end he decided it best to remain silent but given the opportunity, they were all going to sit down and sort out these differences. After all, this trip was uncomfortable enough as it was.

Shifting in his seat, Duncan stretched his legs, rubbing the cramps out as best he could. Behind him, Ar'ye stretched too, his keen eyes never leaving the wooded hills around them.

Taking the lead in front of them, Martyl and Salena decided it was time to stretch their sore legs also, shifting about as best they could in the low boat.

Both Dwarves remained motionless at the till of each boat, their compact bodies' strong physiques making them more suited for the long, cramped voyage. The cats also were unaffected, curled up at the helm of each boat, asleep.

The morning wore on, the sun climbing high into the blue, cloudless sky. Its rays beat down on the boats and their passengers, causing their efforts to be even more laboured in the midday heat.

The brightness of the water became a hazardous aspect as they couldn't scan the hills on the river ahead for dangers. Even the cats with their nictitating third eyelid had to squint in the brightness, the odd time that they woke from their frequent naps.

The lack of activity, however, did not lull them into a sense of false security. The constant thundering of the Wraull war drums reminded the river boaters all too well they were in unprotected waters.

Even the trees seemed more ominous the further east they went. The brilliant green foliage of the needle and broadleaf trees closest to the Thunder Mountains now gave way to dark green, almost black leaved trees. Their trunks were gnarled and twisted, the bark black and scabby. Large vines hung from many branches, resembling ropes for snares or large snakes waiting for prey.

Not only the flora changed as they headed east, closer to the Untamed Lands, but so did the fauna. The sweet sounds of birds chirping in the trees soon changed to squawks and screams, ear piercing and soul shattering. Dark shapes, resembling no animal forms they recognized, flitted in and out of the shadows of the almost primeval forest. Some were bold enough to venture into the light quickly for a drink from the river. They were large and covered in shaggy black fur, walking on four legs. Their heads were large and square, sporting massive fangs. With bodies the size of horses, they ambled about fearlessly in view of the boaters.

Shielding their eyes from the water's glare, everyone except the Dwarves stared in silent awe at the fearless beasts across the river.

"They are called Walusks," informed Rorn from the back boat. "One blow from their mighty paws can disembowel a Man, Dwarf or Wraull. Yet there are things in the Untamed Lands even they fear. We may stop for a short rest and some food. There will be no Wraulls here. The Walusks have insured that."

"Can they swim?" asked Salena, a little anxious as they floated past the beasts, only a dozen or so yards away.

"Yes," replied Rorn, "but they won't go out of their way to attack us in the water."

In spite of Rorn's reassurance, Salena and the others kept a silent vigil while they ate.

"Eat well," instructed Dirn as he handed out dried meat and cheese to everyone. "Before night fall we must portage the Dwarven Falls. It will be dangerous and physically demanding. Be on the lookout for Wraulls. They will surely have patrols at the portage."

"Why have we not seen any yet?" asked Duncan after washing his food down with a mouthful of Trinal.

"I must admit I find it odd myself," replied Dirn. "It is possible we got by their patrols in the pre-dawn hours. They do not see well in the dark, but don't let that fool you into thinking they are helpless at night. They have an excellent sense of smell and could sniff you out of hiding from several yards."

"We must begin paddling again." It was Rorn, his paddle breaking the still water surface before the words finished registering in Duncan's mind. "Our time is short."

The other five dipped their paddles and set the boats in motion again. The cats finished cleaning themselves after their meal and perched in the bow of their respective boats.

The midday sun was no longer directly overhead as they paddled on now, having slid westward across the sky, getting ready to begin its journey below the horizon. Paddling on, they covered a few more miles, their muscles beginning to tire and ache from nearly twelve hours of constant use.

Shifting his weight to relieve his cramping legs, Martyl heard a "plop" in the water and a light mist of water splash his hand. His instinctive training snapped his head to the left where the sound was. A second later he heard four more plops as something splashed the water about them.

"Lie down! Everyone!" shouted Martyl as the others now noticed similar sights and sounds.

"Wraull archers!" shouted Dirn to the others. "A patrol has spotted us!"

"Ar'ye!" called out Martyl, his voice surprisingly calm under the circumstances. "Can you fly up and spot them? Possibly eliminate them?"

"I'll try," came the reply, not as calm as Martyl but not showing any fear either.

The rain of arrows had stopped momentarily with no visible targets for the Wraulls but as soon as Ar'ye stood up, a new shower fell on them. Several thudded into the low sides of the boats, coming closer to their marks this time.

"Hurry!" implored Dirn. "Without us paddling, the current will drift us into the river bank where we'll be even more helpless!"

How ironic, thought Ar'ye, that the very people who detested his kind so much now looked to him for their salvation. With that thought still in his mind, he stretched his wings as he softly leapt into the air, taking flight.

More arrows flew, some at Ar'ye, the others at the boats as they drifted lazily toward the river bank. The occupants spread out in the boats now, fore and aft, leaving the centre open and less area for them to be hit.

From this vantage point, Ar'ye could see where the arrows were coming from but he could not see the archers' exact location from the excellent cover provided by the foliage. Luckily for the boaters, this same concealment made it more difficult for the arrows to get beyond the trees.

The muscles on Ar'ye's back and chest flexed and rippled with the strain of holding his body in the air. Up and northward he flew toward the river bank, screeching the Rey'ak battle cry, "Ra'ak, Ra'ak," hoping it would draw the archers' attention to him, away from his friends in the boats.

The tactic seemed to work as more arrows flew at him.

"Paddle now," commanded Martyl as he grabbed a paddle. "We've got to put some more distance between us and the Wraulls."

Following his lead, the others began paddling also, still crouching as low as possible, lest the Wraulls take aim at them again.

Drawing an arrow from his quiver, Ar'ye aimed his bow and prepared to fire, his sharp hunter's eye scanning the trees fifty feet below him for any signs of movement. An arrow pierced the canopy below him and flew just inches past him in a swish of air. Seeing his opening, Ar'ye let loose with an arrow, his perfect marksmanship sending it right through the other arrow's opening.

A shriek rang out below followed by the sound of tree branches breaking and a bone crunching thud.

Duncan and Salena both looked to their left and up to see if their friend was okay. Martyl and the Dwarves paid no heed, paddling harder now to gain some distance in the confusion.

The arrows rang out again, now in renewed fervour. Ar'ye unleashed a volley of his own in hopes that his aerial advantage would keep the Wraulls pinned down. For the time being he had them at a standoff but he was beginning to tire, his endurance not yet fully recovered after his wound.

Not only that, he had only a limited supply of arrows, of which he had only a few remaining. Realizing this, Ar'ye knew he had to act fast. From his childhood hunting, he recalled an old hunter's trick.

Turning in the air, he flew westward and put his back to the sun, keeping the Wraull's position in sight. Their arrows followed his every move until he was directly in line with the sun when suddenly they stopped. Ar'ye hovered in the sky, motionless except for the steady, almost silent beating of his wings, resembling a giant humming bird.

"What is he doing?" asked Salena out loud as she followed Ar'ye's movements, squinting into the sun, no longer able to see him.

"Becoming invisible," answered Martyl wryly.

Ar'ye floated there, effortlessly in mid-air and scanned the forest below him. All was silent and motionless, the Wraulls at a loss as to where he went.

Dark memories flashed across his mind in seconds as he waited there in the air, causing some unease. The last time he was flying he was shot down and help captive by slavers for a month. He was not about to let that happen again. And he had no illusions of what would happen to him if the Wraulls got hold of him.

He permitted himself a glance at his friends in the boats and saw they were out of harm now. I could easily fly back to them, he thought to himself, still afraid of being captured again. The Wraulls are no threat now. A wave of guilt poured over him after finishing that thought, burning his self-esteem and pride like hot coals. Never, he chastised himself. He was a Rey'ak, strong and proud. He would not give up until his friends were safe.

A glint of silvery metal caught his eye then and Ar'ye let fly another arrow, its zing through the air bringing him all the way back to reality. Moments later he heard the snapping of branches and the thud of a body below.

An arrow flew out of the forest below, the sound of leaves tearing off branches heralding its arrival long before it became visible. This one was not even close to Ar'ye, the sun at his back effectively blinding his opponent below.

Taking careful aim, his arrow stock in his quiver almost depleted, Ar'ye released another arrow, directly on target where the previous arrow came from. There was no shriek this time, the shot making a clean kill.

Ar'ye waited patiently where he was for several moments and when no more shots were taken at him, he decided it was time to head back to the boats. With very little effort, he gained speed and caught up to his companions on the river below. Reversing the movement of his wings slowed him down and he gracefully landed on the floor of the boat.

Setting himself down into a seated position, Ar'ye felt the thrill of battle slowly wash from his veins like the ocean tide leaving the beach for open water. Like the barren beach, he felt damp and exhausted.

"Excellent shooting," remarked Duncan as he turned to congratulate his friend. "Are all your people that proficient?"

"Yes," he replied, a sense of pride in his voice. "Some are even better."

"How many Wraulls did you kill back there?" It was Dirn, his voice hard as usual toward Ar'ye.

"Three," replied Ar'ye, turning to face the Dwarf. If Dirn's continual curtness towards him bothered him, Ar'ye didn't let it show.

"Were there any others?" asked Dirn, a slight earnestness in his voice.

"Not that I saw. I waited a few moments after the third kill and no more arrows were fired."

"Then it is likely there is one more yet alive, now on his way to inform other patrols of our whereabouts." Dirn's voice was taking on an accusatory tone now, not at all pleased with Ar'ye's efforts.

"What did you expect him to do?" remarked Duncan, turning to face Dirn, forgetting to paddle for a moment. "Go into the woods alone on the off chance that there may be one more Wraull waiting for him? How do you even know there was one more?"

"Because," replied Dirn, his voice stone cold and unwavering while he glanced back at Duncan and Ar'ye, "the Wraulls always travel in pairs. They are a cowardly race and run for help as soon it looks like they may face defeat. They get their strength and courage in their numbers."

"In that case, I suggest we keep moving and forget our differences."

It was Martyl, his boat now alongside the other since no one was paddling. His voice was firm and filled with the assuredness of authority that made the other three listen.

Duncan and Ar'ye turned and resumed paddling while Dirn took the till. All three sat in silence, unproductive thoughts filling their brooding minds. None, however, voiced any further comments, their backs burning from Martyl's fiery stare.

A light breeze began to blow now from the east, setting the smooth river surface in motion with tiny crests. The breeze also carried on it a cool refreshing mist, easing everyone's tired muscles.

"We are nearing the Dwarven Falls, Martyl" informed Rorn. "We must prepare to portage. It will be about one league ahead, on the north bank." Lowering his voice and careful of the tone, not to offend anyone, he added, "We must also keep an eye out for Wraulls. They will surely be present."

"Very well then," replied Martyl, his voice not betraying the uncertainty he felt in facing the unknown ahead of them.

The two river boats and their occupants began to speed down the river faster now as the current began to pick up speed. Both Dwarves strained at the tills of the boats, fighting the increasing current to hold their course. The muscles of their arms bulged, hard as stone with a network of veins rising to the surface. They looked as if they were threatening to rupture the skin in their effort to feed the straining muscles their precious blood supply.

The roar of the Dwarven Falls crescendoed now, the river rushing them to meet it in a fury of frothy white water and bone splitting rocks. The water in the river began to churn and froth, crashing against the rocks that were sprouting up in the boats' paths. The rocks were dark and slick with water and patches of moss that clung to their tops with unabated tenacity.

"Rock!" shouted Duncan as a particularly nasty one seemingly appeared out of the white frothed water before them.

"Paddle hard!" shouted Dirn from the back of the boat as he himself leaned all his weight into the till to turn the boat.

Duncan and Ar'ye began paddling as if their lives depended on it, which indeed they did. Their paddles plunged into the maelstrom of what was once a calm river, trying to divert their course. Within seconds the speed of the current carried their boat past the rock, just narrowly avoiding it after their intense efforts.

Rorn steered the second boat behind the first, Dirn's skilled navigating showing him the way.

"Paddle for the north bank now!" shouted Dirn over the water's intensifying roar. "We must get out of the water soon or be dashed upon the rocks!"

For the first time since they had left Calheller no one argued or bickered over the order that was given. With more enthusiasm than they had shown yet, the occupants of both boats worked together to battle the river and reach safety.

Duncan and Martyl kept a constant vigil while paddling for rocks and reported them to their respective tillers. Ar'ye and Salena paddled extra hard, their backs and arms beginning to strain from the effort.

With their combined efforts, the paddlers began to gain on the current, edging the boats at what seemed like a snail's pace to the north bank. The roar of the falls was all they could hear now, the sounds of water crashing into rocks far below drowning out all other sounds.

"That is where we must beach," shouted Dirn over the ever increasing noise. "The low spot on the river bank. There!" He pointed briefly so Duncan and Ar'ye would know where to paddle.

Having had their fill of river travel weeks earlier on Frost Lake, Duncan and Ar'ye were only too pleased to hear this news. Mustering the last of their energy the two friends plunged their paddles into the churning water propelling their boat faster towards the shore and safety. The river spray from the waterfall was beginning to soak through their clothes and both cats growled softly in irritation, their fur becoming increasingly wet.

Navigating past a few last treacherous rocks, Dirn beached his boat on the river bank. With a grinding of wood on the pebbly beach, the sturdy craft lurched to a halt, sending its occupants tumbling. Rising from their floor of the river boat, Duncan and Ar'ye both heard a ringing in their ears that they attributed to the crash.

Dirn called out, "Wraulls!"

Big Cat leapt from the boat landing on the beach, her fur up and growling, followed by Duncan and Ar'ye. Dirn stepped out, hefting his battle-axe into attacking position before him.

"Hold back, Rorn!" he shouted out to the other boat. "Listen to the Wraull war horns. It's an ambush." Turning to Duncan and Ar'ye he continued, "Get the boat back in the water, now!"

Shouts could now be heard as they struggled on the slick pebbly beach to push the boat back in. Duncan slipped and fell, slamming his head into the bow. Struggling to get up, blood clouded his eyes from a deep cut above them. Seconds later, arrows began to rain down on them as a patrol of ten Wraulls stepped from the trees.

"Paddle!" shouted Martyl, only twenty feet away on the river.

Before he or Salena and Rorn could resume paddling, a large coniferous tree crashed into the river only three feet from their boat. In the sudden confusion, Rorn lost control of the boat and it careened down the river, slamming into it. The boat collided into the trunk broadside, a large branch ripping right through its side.

Patches leapt immediately onto the tree, his reflexes much quicker than the others. Rorn grabbed hold of a branch and pulled himself on top of the downed tree as the current swept the back half of the destroyed river boat away.

Martyl grabbed a branch too and pulled himself out of the water, looking about frantically for Salena who did not fare as well, being thrown from the boat on impact.

"Salena!" shouted Martyl, a cold fear beginning to gnaw at his stomach.

"Wraulls!" came the reply, shouted by Rorn.

Martyl turned to look and saw a column of Wraulls, battle-axes in hand, marching out onto the downed tree in a less than friendly welcome.

"Salena is lost!" cried Martyl as he frantically scanned the churning waters about them, his eyes fixing on every floating piece of debris heading past the gigantic tree.

War horns blared on the shore, sounding the impending Wraull attack. Like the seasoned warrior he was, Martyl turned his attention from the swirling river to the new, approaching menace. It pained him terribly to leave the search for Salena but the Wraulls were a serious threat to all of them. If these Wraulls weren't dispatched quickly, it wouldn't matter where Salena was for the Wraulls would get her if she reached shore and Martyl new it.

"Bray'la!" cried Rorn at the top of his voice, the Dwarven war cry ringing out against the din and noise of marching Wraulls. The Wraulls roared their rebuttal to Rorn's Dwarven battle cry. They continued their march, chopping and smashing tree limbs out of their way. Rorn was doing the same from his end, Martyl and Patches stepping over smaller branches as they joined his side.

The tree was an ancient mountain pine, seemingly as old as the mountains themselves. From the river bank where the Wraulls felled it, it reached seventy feet out into the river to where the boat careened into it. It's massive trunk was over fifty feet around, easily large enough for three large men to walk abreast.

"We've got to reach Duncan and Dirn!" shouted Martyl. "When the river's shallow enough, jump in and head over."

Rorn was the first to enter the melee, his blood raging with a lust born of years of hatred and aggression. Raising his battle axe, he swung hard, nearly cleaving the foremost Wraull in half. The dark red blood flowed freely, running off the tree and into the river in a red foam as the Wraull fell, its body twisting into a heap on the trunk. Three other Wraulls fell, tripping over their fallen comrade in their haste. Martyl was on them immediately, his sword slashing and cutting, piercing flesh and bone. Patches leapt into the fray, a blinding flash of grey and white fur, paws the size of a man's fist, shredding flesh and gouging bone.

Screams of agony rang out from the Wraulls as the man, Dwarf and cat, trapped on a downed tree, fought for their very lives. Rorn severed the legs of a second Wraull while Patches tore the throat from another with his razor sharp teeth. Martyl pressed on deeper into the throng of Wraulls, his sword and arm covered in the reddish-black ooze of Wraull blood.

The three pressed on, gaining very little ground, managing barely to stay on the tree and out of the swirling river below. Rorn swung again, his massive arms showing no signs of tiring, despite the weight of the axe. The axe came down again, but this time the intended Wraull had time to react, the initial surprise to their adversaries' ferociousness overcome now. The Wraull raised his axe to block Rorn's blow, the axe heads clashing together, sparks shooting off them. Using his weight and size to his advantage, the Wraull leaned into Rorn, forcing him back. Rorn pushed back, his compact size belying the strength in it, trying to keep his balance.

"They're trying to surround us!" shouted Martyl, raising his sword to parry an axe blow that would've removed his head.

Rorn didn't need to look, nor could he afford to, locked in a deadly struggle with one of the Wraulls. The splashing of advancing Wraulls in the water told him what Martyl already had. Straining against the Wraull, Rorn pushed with all the strength he could muster, the axe handles sliding back and forth, wood on wood.

The Wraull pressed back, his larger size and weight beginning to wear the smaller Dwarf down when Rorn suddenly stopped pushing and pulled back. The shift in movement caught the Wraull off guard and he fell forward, completely off balance. Rorn stepped to his left as the Wraull fell but couldn't avoid being knocked off the tree trunk by the surprised Wraull. As soon as he and the Wraull hit the water, another two Wraulls moved up, effectively surrounding Martyl and Patches on three sides.

Martyl, becoming fatigued now, assumed a defensive position instead of an offensive one. Patches was backed up behind him, snarling and spitting, his fur matted with Wraull blood. Their time was limited and Martyl knew it. The only chance the two of them had was to get off the tree and he took it.

With a final pseudo-thrust at the Wraulls, Martyl turned and jumped into the raging water below. Hating the water as much as he did, Patches was not about to be left behind and leapt into the river behind Martyl.

Dirn lost sight of the other boat as a gigantic coniferous tree, nearly seventy feet long crashed into the water only feet away from where he last saw Rorn and the others. With the Wraulls on the beach here, he knew one must have escaped alive from Ar'ye's attack earlier to warn its comrades.

The sounds of arrows whistling through the air brought his attention back to a more immediate problem. Instinctively, Dirn spun about, crouching, his battle axe hefted to swing when he realized it was Ar'ye shooting now, not the Wraulls. Two of the ten now lay dead and Ar'ye was already in the air, flying towards them to distract the attack from Dirn and Duncan on the ground.

Duncan, thought Dirn, where is he? Dirn could hear Big Cat snarling and growling to his right and glanced quickly. He did not want to take his eyes off the Wraulls, even if Ar'ye had them occupied. Sitting half-propped against the bow of the river boat was Duncan, blood streaming down his face. Dirn rushed to his side, only a few strides away. Arrows followed him and he knew that Ar'ye's ploy no longer had the Wraulls surprised.

"I'm okay," murmured Duncan weakly, his head pounding as if the Wraulls were beating their war drums in it. Still, he could read the worry on the Dwarf's stony features.

"I slipped on the stones and hit my head."

The arrows came closer this time landing only inches away. A winged shadow passed over their heads followed by the sound of grunts as another Wraull hit the ground.

Dirn wasted no more time with Duncan. He would survive that wound, he surmised, so long as the Wraulls didn't get him. Rising to his feet, Dirn rushed forward, swinging his battle axe. To his surprise, he heard the Dwarven battle cry ring out before he could scream it himself. Instinctively, he knew it was Rorn, bringing him some relief in the fact that at least some of the others survived this long.

Dirn met what remained of the Wraull attack party with a blinding fury of his flailing axe. Only four remained now, Ar'ye having dispatched six already with his excellent bowman-ship. The first Wraull Dirn encountered fell immediately from a disembowelling hack from his axe. Blackish-red blood stained the sandy beach as it flowed from the open stomach wound, forming as sickening coloured mud.

The last three Wraulls, sensing their impending doom turned and fled, realizing they had a better chance for survival if they could regroup with others.

"Ar'ye!" shouted Dirn, "Don't let them escape. We can't afford another ambush!"

He didn't mean to imply that this ambush was his fault for allowing a Wraull to escape before but Ar'ye could shoot them down easier than he could chase them down.

If Ar'ye took any offense from the remark he didn't show it. Landing beside Dirn he simply replied, "I'm out of arrows."

"Fly over to the other boat and help them. I'll get Duncan in our boat and row up there as fast as I can." Dirn didn't wait for a reply as he walked back to the beached boat and Duncan as fast as his short legs would carry him.

Big Cat sat by Duncan's side, not leaving her wounded human until help arrived. Dirn marvelled at the graceful cat's raw animal power hiding under such a quiet, unimposing exterior facade. He was glad this cat, and the other, were on their side, remembering how they had defeated a Demon.

Watching Big Cat carefully with one eye, her fur just beginning to return to its natural state of flatness, Dirn bent down and easily picked up Duncan's now limp, unconscious form and laid him of the boat's floor. Without invitation, Big Cat jumped right in after him and set to work immediately cleaning the blood from Duncan's face and scalp, her raspy tongue doing an excellent job of cleansing and disinfecting the gash.

Climbing out of the boat and onto the beach, Dirn took one last look in the direction of the retreating Wraulls then pushed the river boat, Duncan and Big Cat aboard, effortlessly, back into the water.

Martyl pushed himself to the surface, kicking with his feet against the downward pull of his wet clothes and dead weight of his steel sword. Breaking the surface of the river, he gulped down a quick lung-full of air and looked about quickly.

The tree he jumped from was now several yards away and getting further away by the moment. The river current was faster than he had realized and was carrying him downstream at breakneck speed. The Wraulls shouted and hollered but did not jump in. Apparently they were not prepared to die needlessly. Instead they ran down the felled tree and back to the shore. Martyl watched in silence as they ran down the shore, between the trees and river bed to follow his course from the safety of land.

Martyl found sheathing his now useless sword a great difficulty in the rapidly moving water as it tossed him about with indignity. At last able to use both arms, he began swimming with the current, since that was his only possible course of action. Trying to remain where he was, treading water in the hopes of spotting Rorn, Patches or even Salena was fruitless as the current was too strong. The only chance they had was for him to reach Duncan and his boat, if it wasn't too late, and then search for the others.

"Martyl!" came a call, from above, he swore. Rolling on his side in the ever-quickening river, Martyl looked up to see Ar'ye, effortlessly floating in the air above him.

"We secured the portage area. Dirn is behind me in our boat and will pick you up. Where are the others?"

Continuing his swim, Martyl replied, "I don't know. The current could have taken them anywhere."

"I'll look." With that, Ar'ye sped off through the air, his feathered wings and muscular back propelling him onwards toward the downed tree.

Almost immediately, his sharp eyes caught sight of Patches, his grey and white fur now fully saturated with water. The cat was paddling along with amazing ease, despite the weight of his wet fur and the speed of the current. Not surprisingly, he was only a few yards behind Martyl.

Swooping down like a huge bird of prey, Ar'ye wheeled about in the sky and plummeted towards the water, arms outstretched. Muscles flexing, Ar'ye's wings pumped the air, straining to lift the drenched cat from the rushing water's grip. With a final jerk, Patches was lifted free of the water, the river rushing on without him.

Flying back towards the portage beach, Ar'ye passed Martyl again. It tore at his moral fibre to leave him yet he knew he was too much to lift. Patches was almost too much and his sore wing muscles told him so with every wing-beat.

To his surprise and relief, Ar'ye spotted Dirn, rowing their boat to meet him. It was slow going against the strong current but the taciturn Dwarf would not let it stand in his way. Coming down to meet the boat faster than he liked, Ar'ye dropped Patches off and informed Dirn as to Martyl's plight.

Dirn acknowledged him and continued paddling upstream, while Ar'ye headed off to look for Rorn and Salena. Within minutes, Martyl reached the boat and pulled himself on board, nearly exhausted.

"Is he alright?" asked Martyl at once upon seeing Duncan's unconscious, bleeding form.

"He hit his head," replied Dirn, his voice once again not belying any emotion he may feel. "It isn't life threatening. There is a healing salve in the healing pouch. Apply some to the wound."

Martyl rummaged through the pack and found the salve, applying it as Dirn continued to row.

"Now use the smelling salts to wake him."

Martyl put the remaining salve away then found the smelling salts. Waving them before Duncan's nose elicited the response he hoped for.

Slowly Duncan opened his eyes and moaned, his right hand automatically clutching his wounded head. His mind was still cloudy and he closed his eyes again in an attempt to sleep until it cleared.

"Relax," ordered Martyl as he held Duncan down to prevent him from moving and further injuring himself.

"Dirn," called out Ar'ye, just ahead of them. "I've got Rorn."

With Martyl paddling now too, the boat travelled a little quicker and they reached Rorn. He was half swimming, half flying as Ar'ye pulled him along the top of the water, not quite getting him in the air.

"What about Salena?" asked Dirn.

"I can't see her anywhere," replied Ar'ye dejectedly.

"She was thrown from the boat on impact," informed Martyl, his voice low and leaden.

Wasting no more time, Dirn turned the dangerously overcrowded river boat about and redoubled his paddling. Martyl paddled too with renewed effort, trying to regain the time they just lost and make it to the portage beach before the Wraulls. It would be close but they did have the quicker means of travel, by far, when with the swift current.

They hadn't paddled long when the speeding boat lurched aground for the second time that day.

"Everyone out!" ordered Dirn, already pulling the river boat further onto the shore. "We must portage the falls before dark and before the Wraulls are again upon us. Hurry, for they are not far behind!"

Dirn's warning was not needed as they saw how close the Wraulls were to the beach from the river.

"Rorn and I will carry the boat with Duncan in it as our stamina and strength is greatest. Martyl, you take the point. The path is well used and easy to follow. Ar'ye, follow on rear guard. I'm sorry about Salena but I know this river well. If Ar'ye didn't spot her from the air already, she is lost. We can waste no more time. Let's go."

Dirn was blunt and to the point yet everyone knew he was right. Martyl and Ar'ye both silently acknowledged thanks that Duncan was too weak to realize what was happening.

Patches ran to Martyl's side at the front as they headed down the path. Dirn and Rorn followed next, their arms and shoulders showing little sign of the stress they bore. Dirn's axe hung from his back as they walked, causing little extra encumbrance. Rorn's, however, lay at the bottom of the river, having been dropped so he could swim. Ar'ye ran after to catch up in the rear, Big Cat at his side. He was a little behind, having stopped to retrieve a half dozen unbroken arrows on the ground to refill his quiver.

Chapter Fifteen

"Bin," called Draskene, his voice steely edged like always.

The smaller man stopped in his tracks, a cold shiver running down his spine despite the warm summer breeze blowing across the open courtyard.

Turning quickly to reply lest he anger Draskene, Bin had a nasty mental flash of the last time Draskene had been given bad news. The image of that Demon horse trampling two members of the Prime Guard to death had greatly unnerved him. In his mind's eye he could still see the two guards' heads split like rotten melons beneath the Demon horse's hooves.

Looking at Draskene now, Bin wondered where such hatred and evil could come from. The setting sun shone in his dark eyes, giving them an unearthly glow. His clean shaven, chiselled face belied any signs of aging, appearing still to be only in his forties even though he knew him to be much older.

It was that charismatic appeal, decided Bin, along with the promise of greatness, that had seduced him from being one of King Aramid's aides. He joined the Black Paladin, as he had become known in the surrounding areas, to elevate his own status.

And it was his brutal, iron-fisted rule that kept him, and any others that doubted what they had done, from ever leaving or betraying him.

"Yes, master?" replied Bin, wondering if he had forgotten to relay any important information to Draskene.

He had just left him moments ago after informing him of Duncan's last known whereabouts. His animal familiars in the Dwarf city had reported their arrival eleven days earlier and their subsequent departure early this morning. With this information they had been able to alert the Wraull patrols along the Thunder River to be on the look-out for them. Where they were going and how many was not known. Draskene had theorized they may be looking for lost relics in the Untamed Lands. They did know, however, that it was indeed King Aramid's son Duncan and the last of his Royal Knights, Martyl, that had cost them so dearly thus far. The identity of the girl that escaped from the two Prime Guards was not fully known. Her name was Salena but where she was from was unknown. Even more puzzling was the fact that her fingers and toes were webbed! They also had a Rey'ak with them who pledged his people's help and two of the large cats that had been seen in Gullhaven.

Everything, thought Bin. I've reported everything. What could it be? Sweat began forming on his brow and his heart began to beat faster. Draskene was at least twenty feet away and unarmed yet Bin knew that if Draskene wanted to punish him for some unknown dereliction of duty, conventional methods did not have to be used.

"I almost forgot," began Draskene again. "The information your spies have provided is very interesting and thorough. Well done." His thin lips parted into an unusual and oft unseen smile that seemed ungainly on his dark features. To Bin, the smile made Draskene look like a snarling wolf.

Continuing, he added, "I have changed my mind, however, about the Wraull ambush. In light of this recent information on the girl, I believe it may be beneficial to the security of our position if we capture her alive. We must determine if she is an aberration of nature or a member of a heretofore unknown race. If the latter is true, they could be a threat."

Again he smiled that eerie smile, completely unnerving Bin. Bin knew what 'threat' this possible unknown race posed—a free thinking populace not under the Black Paladin's control. Still, it was his job to gather intelligence on their enemies and he prided himself on performing it well.

"Yes, master," replied Bin. "I will send word at once to the Wraulls along the Thunder River and the Untamed Lands that she is to be brought to you immediately upon capture."

Bin hesitated then for a moment, wondering if he should ask his next question for fear of making Draskene repeat his orders. The consequences of not asking, however, should there be a change in his thoughts on the matter as there was already one now, far outweighed his fear.

"And the others? They are still to be disposed of on sight? Except, of course, for Duncan."

Immediately the smile began to fade from Draskene's face and Bin hastily added his next thoughts to the question.

"It is possible they may have information that is valuable as well. And would you not like to take personal vengeance on them for the trouble they have caused you?"

The twisted smile returned to Draskene's face.

"You are a wise man, Bin. That is why you hold the position I gave you. If they can be brought to me safely with no hope of rescue or escape, then good. If not, everyone but Duncan and the girl are to be killed on sight. Understood?"

Bin knew the tone in the final word was the signal the conversation was ended. He was lucky that Draskene was not offended by his questioning.

"Yes, master," he replied to Draskene, already a black form melting into the twilight shadows of the courtyard.

Where Draskenen was off to now, Bin could only speculate. As for himself, he was returning to his personal stables to send word of Draskene's new demands to their Wraull troops. He had great faith in his personal messengers, trusting them more than any of Draskene's minions. That was why he was good at his job, his liegeman, or liege-animals as they were more aptly named by him, were completely loyal to him.

It was an inherent trait in all his people and Bin allowed himself an appreciative smile as he remembered the stories of his ancestors his mother had told him as a child.

His people, the Namives, lived in the flat-lands to the east of Arundel scores of generations ago, raiding the countryside as they saw fit. They worshipped the animals and had a natural rapport with them. They were able to communicate with them and used the animals as their messengers and servants in both war and peace.

Until the Kings of Arundel. That part of the legend still caused a fire to burn in the pit of his stomach. Except for a handful of elders who kept the old ways alive in secret, passing their secrets down through the ages, the Namives had lost that ability. These few were waiting, hoping, their twisted anger eating away at what was once good, turning it into a black hatred of the rulers of Arundel. And when Draskene proposed his plan, Bin and the others of his kind were only too willing to help in the downfall of Arundel.

What bothered Bin now was the fact that Duncan, a distant son of Arundel, seemed to have some of the Namives' powers. That is if the reports from the spies in the Dwarf city were accurate. He did not like the idea of a non-Namive being able to communicate with the animals, even if they were only cats. It ate at his pride, gnawing at it like a rabid rat.

Reaching his stables, Bin opened the door and entered, lighting a lamp in the doorway before closing the door behind him. Low growls rumbled from his right and Bin smiled in response. The sounds were a pleasant change from Draskene's iron bound voice.

"Ah, my wolves. I miss you too."

Reaching into one of the deep pockets of his cloak, Bin pulled out several pieces of dried meat and threw them to the wolves in the converted stable.

There were six of them, fur as white as snow, eyes as red as embers. Their razor sharp teeth gnawed viciously on the morsels Bin had brought for them. They were winter-wolves, the scourge of hunters and farmers, slaughtering man and beast alike for no reason other than sport, possibly. They were as evil as the Demons that spawned them centuries ago during the Black Magic Wars. Standing nearly four feet at the shoulder and weighing in excess of one hundred pounds, they were formidable opponents indeed.

Shrill, piercing squawks erupted from above, forcing Bin to reach into his other pocket. Withdrawing his hand, Bin threw another handful of meat, this raw and red, into the air above his head. With a rush of air that ruffled his scraggly hair like the wind, four fighting falcons dove from the rafters and snatched the meat before it fell to the ground.

"No, I didn't forget you either," Bin said to the falcons, now perched above him again in the rafters. He smiled at their perfect forms, hooked beaks deftly ripping the cold meat apart where it was held in their talons.

Moments later when they finished he continued, "Haak, Leik."

Immediately, two of the falcons flew down, one resting on each of Bin's shoulders, their heads' a good six inches above his.

"I need you to send word to the Wraull troops waiting in ambush near the Dwarven Falls. The girl is to be brought here if it can be done safely, along with Duncan. The others are expendable but if their capture is possible, do so."

The two birds squawked in reply and waited patiently for several minutes while Bin scribbled the new orders on small pieces of paper. He rolled the pieces up and attached one to each bird's leg with a metal band.

"Go," he commanded and both birds left the building through an open window into the darkening sky.

Bin hoped the birds would reach their destination before the Dwarven party did but he did not expect them to. The birds were fast and would make it before sunrise but it was most likely that the party leaving Calheller would reach the ambush this evening. Leaving the stable for his quarters, Bin hoped to himself that Draskene would not view that outcome as his fault.

Draskene closed the door to his personal library, swiftly crossing the room to a shelf full of dust-covered books, the lamps automatically lighting by preset spells.

This was one of Draskene's favourite places. Here he was surrounded by the knowledge of the ages. In the time of King Aramid and the Kings before him, it had been open to all in the kingdom in the name of freedom. The first thing Draskene did after his coup was close the library to all but himself. The old kings were right—knowledge was freedom. By denying the people knowledge, he could deny then their freedom easier.

Draskene smiled his wicked smile as he thought to himself of all he had accomplished. Much had been added to the library in the past fifteen years. He had seen to that personally, amassing any information at all that he could use to gain power. The walls were covered with thick, leather-bound volumes and tomes from various cultures. The information others would use to learn about these cultures for peaceful purposes, Draskene twisted to use it to control them. From their literature he learned of their strengths and weaknesses, fears, loves and hatreds. He permitted himself a stifled laugh as the memories of his conquests flooded back. The sound echoed in the tomb-like silence about him, sounding odd to his ears, a sound he hadn't heard in years.

Reaching the bookshelf of his search, Draskene dismissed all his other thoughts and scanned the dusty books before him. Sandwiched between two large, black spined, leather wrapped tomes was the object of his search. It was a small paper book, only a handful of pages thick, seemingly out of place amidst all the large volumes on the shelf.

Gingerly, Draskene removed the ancient book from the shelf and gently blew the dust off of it. The pages were long ago turned yellow with age and were as brittle as dried leaves.

Years ago Draskene had come across this diary of a captain of a sailing ship lost at sea for months. The diary was over one hundred years old when Draskene discovered it in an old abandoned warehouse on the waterfront in Gullhaven, locked in a chest. The story in it amused and intrigued him so he kept it. The crew perished and the captain was the sole survivor. When he returned to the port of Gull-haven, he told strange stories of an island kingdom shrouded in mist. Everyone at the time dismissed him as mad and he died soon after-wards. Now Draskene thought he may know where this girl was from. And that meant an unconquered land. Again the wicked, twisted smile crossed his thin lips as he began to read the old captain's forgot-ten tale.

The path wound its way down through the steep remains of the mountains. Spray from the cascading water drenched everyone. It car-ried on the light breeze far into the thick woods all about them. The setting sun at their backs was almost completely below the Thunder Mountains now and Martyl picked his way slowly and carefully in the thickening darkness. Less than a thousand feet below them lay the Untamed Lands and all its uncharted dangers.

Slowing their pace in time with the decreasing light, the heartbeat of everyone in the small group steadily rose with anticipation of what would await them at the base of the waterfall. They had narrowly escaped death at the hands of the Wraulls and the river and weren't in any condition to face any more obstacles at the moment.

Martyl and Ar'ye both wrestled privately with the painful fact that Duncan would have to be told soon of Salena's fate. The Dwarves marched on in silence, their faces still resembling carvings in stone. What they felt of the situation they did not let it be known to the oth-ers, keeping their thoughts and feelings to themselves.

This angered Ar'ye and he fought back the urge to confront Rorn and Dirn over it. He could not believe they would hold a grudge against his people for so many years. They had no qualms against showing their anger yet when a member of their own party was lost over the falls they showed no remorse. Ar'ye forced himself to remain calm, knowing that a show of anger right now would not help them. They still weren't out of danger yet.

Changing his train of thought back to their present situation, Ar'ye listened intently with his acute Rey'ak hearing for any signs of pursuit. Although his companions were trying their best to remain as silent as possible, their attempts lacked the training and discipline his people were schooled in. Ar'ye winced to himself as he thought of the noise they were causing.

At his side, Big Cat looked up at him in the near darkness, her orange, black and white furry head cocked to one side. Ar'ye smiled as he imagined what the cat must be thinking of his efforts to listen for pursuit and remain quiet while travelling in the dark. Although he and his people were good at this, he knew they were no match for the cats that travelled with him.

This eased Ar'ye's mind of some of his wariness, knowing that Big Cat and Patches would detect any danger long before the rest of them.

Marching on, the trail zig-zagged down the hillside, doubling back upon itself in areas. They followed the switchbacks and maneuvered over and around fallen trees in the darkness for another half hour. The Dwarves never once uttered a word or slowed their pace despite the burden of carrying Duncan in the river boat.

As they neared the steppes below the mountains, Dirn called the party to a stop. Before turning to see what the Dwarf wanted, Martyl peered through the thinning trees into the river churning beneath the falls to their right. He could detect nothing else, but he knew too well that was no guarantee another ambush wouldn't be waiting.

Martyl looked to Patches for confirmation of his observance. The cat too was peering through the edge of the woods and tentatively sniffing the air for signs of danger. He didn't react to any which made Martyl feel a little better.

Satisfied for the time being, Martyl turned to face Dirn, asking, "What do you propose now?"

"This is farther than any of our patrols have reached in years," replied Dirn, speaking effortlessly despite the burdened trek down the mountain.

Setting the boat on the ground with Rorn's help he continued, "I cannot say for certain what dangers we will encounter from here. I can only say they will be many and deadly."

As if to underscore his remark, the sounds of the Wraull drums carried down the mountains to them, their steady beat pounding out even over the roar of the falls.

"How's Duncan?" asked Martyl, more concerned with their current dilemmas than the Dwarves.

Dirn leaned into the boat, producing his smelling salts. Duncan was on the verge of unconsciousness, moaning softly where he lay in the boat. The smell of the salts snapped his eyes open almost immediately, eliciting a series of gags.

"He'll be fine," replied Dirn, his voice still emotionless. "Drink this," he said to Duncan, offering him a flask from his pack.

Memories of his last drink from Dirn flashed back to Duncan and he gave the Dwarf a cautious look while holding the flask.

"This is a denatured version of the Tal Shar you had before. It's effects are not as strong," stated Dirn, reading the expression on Duncan's face.

His eyes never leaving Dirn, Duncan slowly raised the flask to his lips and took a shallow sip. The liquid burned his throat but the pain in his head began to subside almost at once. Tipping the flask up, he drank a mouthful before returning it to Dirn.

Feeling considerably better, Duncan rose slowly to his feet and looked around to his companions.

"Where is Salena?" he asked. A feeling of dread began to settle over him as he saw the shadowed looks on his friends' faces.

.Ar'ye's gaze fell to the ground before his feet while both Dwarves stared at him with no expressions on their bearded faces.

Martyl closed his eyes and opened them again slowly, his mind racing for the words to say where there were none.

"Martyl?" he asked, stepping gingerly out of the boat towards his old friend.

"She was lost when our boat crashed," replied Martyl, his voice sullen and low. "She was thrown from the boat on impact and then the Wraulls were upon us. When we dispatched them, Ar'ye searched by air but couldn't find her. I'm sorry Duncan, but we had to leave or the rest of us would have been killed when more Wraulls arrived."

He held Duncan's gaze then, the despair and failure he felt burning his face and the pit of his stomach.

"We have to look for her!" cried Duncan. "She's a better swimmer than any of us. She might have survived."

With that Duncan began to run for the river, emotion, not reason driving him now. Rorn was the closest to him and the first to react, reaching out with a powerful arm when Duncan went by him, knocking him to the ground.

In a blur of movement, Patches and Big Cat were on Rorn, pouncing on him and pinning him to the ground. Their razor sharp teeth and claws slashed at the Dwarf's heavy leather clothing, tearing through it like paper.

Martyl knew better than to tangle with the massive cats but he tried to call them off Rorn before they injured him badly. Dirn wasn't as patient, raising his battle-axe and striding toward the cats.

He took two steps before stopping dead in his tracks, an arrow protruding from his axe handle just inches above his hands.

"The next one hits *you*, understand!?"

Dirn turned slowly and faced Ar'ye who already had another arrow drawn and ready to fire. His vision in the dark left nothing to the Dwarf's imagination and he held his ground, eyes smouldering.

"Stop it!" shouted Martyl, at last losing his patience.

He didn't care at this point about keeping everyone quiet, since they had already made enough noise to raise the dead. Everyone turned to look at Martyl, even the two cats. Duncan rose to his feet, calling Patches and Big Cat to him.

"If we don't straighten out our differences *now*, we'll do the Black Paladin's work for him." Martyl's voice was hard and authoritative and no one would meet his eyes in the darkness, not even the Dwarves.

"Duncan, you and Ar'ye take the cats and check the river for any signs of Salena. Dirn, you attend to Rorn's wounds. I'll check the area for any signs of the Wraulls."

Without waiting to hear confirmation, Martyl turned and headed down the last of the trail and out of the woods. He had been young and impetuous once but when confronted with indisputable authority, he knew when to listen. As did the others, he told himself.

And that they did. Dirn immediately set to bandaging Rorn's wounds inflicted by the cats while Duncan, Ar'ye and the two cats ran to the river bank without looking back.

Martyl scouted the edges of the woods, careful to stay in the shadows lest any unfriendly eyes spied him. He suppressed a dark smile as he searched for their enemies. This incessant bickering had to stop or they would all be dead soon, he told himself.

For a man of his size and age, Martyl moved remarkably quick through the dense underbrush and fallen trees. Years of in-the-field experience came back to him as he doggedly searched for traps, snares and ambushes. After a thorough examination of the area, Martyl was confident that they faced no immediate dangers, save their dislikes of one another. Still, he knew they couldn't tarry long. The Wraulls that ambushed them on the river bank would be along soon and they would not readily be defeated this time.

Knowing he needed to buy them time, Martyl headed back into the woods to the boat. Rummaging through their supplies, he secured a 50 foot section of rope.

"Rorn, Dirn," he called to the two Dwarves, finishing their ministrations on one another. "We must trap the trail down the hillside before the Wraulls are upon us again. There is no one around us at the moment so we must hurry while there is still time."

Without waiting for their reply, Martyl turned and headed back up the trail they had all just come down. The Dwarves picked up their battle-axes, Rorn a spare in the boat. Without saying a word they dutifully followed behind.

Under the cover of night, Martyl found it difficult to find an appropriate spot to plant his trap but at last he found it. Fifty feet up the hillside, the trail switched back on itself in a s-shaped bend before continuing on.

"We're going to set up a trap here to stall the Wraulls advance," stated Martyl. He was already measuring out lengths of rope from the fifty feet he brought.

"I want you two to gather any fallen logs you can find and chop these trees down, flush to the ground."

Rorn and Dirn looked at Martyl with puzzled looks but did as they were asked. Rorn began chopping down the two trees Martyl had indicated, his massive arms swinging his battle-axe with ease. Dirn collected all the fallen trees he could locate in the nearby vicinity, neatly chopping then into six foot lengths. All the logs were stacked into a pile on the bend in the trail.

Martyl set up a trip rope across the path, neatly hiding it beneath fallen leaves. One end was tied around the base of a tree and the other to a stake holding the logs in place. When Rorn cleared the last tree from the path of Martyl's trap, all three covered the logs with branches and foliage. The three had worked feverishly and were done in just under an hour. Their arms and backs sore from overwork, the trio meandered back down the trail in silence.

Duncan and Ar'ye searched frantically along the river bed and base of the falls for any sign of Salena. Patches and Big Cat both tracked up and down the river bed, their keen eyes and sharp noses searching for any clue to her whereabouts also.

"Salena!" called out Duncan, his hopes of finding her slowing sinking like a stone in the sea. "Salena!"

His mind clouded over with fear and dread at the thought of losing his best friend and future companion. Despair crept from the dark corners of his mind like rats leaving the shadows at dusk, gnawing at his resolve to carry on.

"Salena!" he called out again, trudging perilously close to the raging river's steep bank.

"Duncan, we must be silent lest we alert the Wraulls to our presence here." Ar'ye hovered above the foaming water in front of Duncan, his feathered wings beating softly in the still night air.

Duncan shot him a glance that said 'Don't push me now', not realizing or caring that Ar'ye's keen vision would spot it in the dark.

"I fear for her to, my friend," Ar'ye replied, ignoring Duncan's withering gaze.

He knew there was no point in telling Duncan he found no evidence of Salena so he turned and flew back downstream. He owed Salena as much as Duncan for his rescue and wouldn't stop looking for her either.

Still, he knew as well as the Dwarves that the likelihood of someone surviving the trip down the falls was slim. Even then, the Wraull patrols they left upstream and the ones ahead yet would be on to anyone trying to get out of the river. Although he didn't want to admit it, Ar'ye knew deep down that Salena's chances for survival were slim.

Duncan watched Ar'ye fly into the darkness, his large wings propelling him along, just above the surface of the water. Even though he had only known Ar'ye for a handful of weeks now, Duncan knew he could trust Ar'ye to do his best, and then some. He already regretted the look he shot Ar'ye for telling him to be silent. He was right, after all. All of them could fare much worse if the Wraulls found them.

Groping about the river weeds along the river bank in the darkness, Duncan doggedly continued his search for Salena. Realizing how limited his vision was in the darkness, he truly appreciated the help of Ar'ye and his cats who could see much better.

A splash caught Duncan's attention and he stopped dead in his tracks to listen. His heart was pounding so hard and fast it threatened to burst his chest. The warm night air was silent now except for his laboured breathing.

Scanning the river bed near him, Duncan caught sight of something moving in the reeds. He rushed forward, his hopes of finding Salena as high as the stars in the sky.

"Salena," he called out softly, remembering Ar'ye's warning. "Salena, its Duncan."

The movement in the reeds intensified as Duncan neared them. He reached out to part them, kneeling down to the water's edge. As fast as lightning and nearly invisible in the inky water, a black river snake shot out of the reeds towards Duncan.

Pure luck more than anything else saved him from the venomous bite. Startled, Duncan slipped and fell, sliding past the eight foot snake and into the water with a resounding splash. The snake shot by and bit a mouthful of air.

Duncan, his head beginning to pound again from his previous fall hours before, floundered in the deep water. He flailed about trying to grab something to keep from being swept away by the current. The river snake turned and began to slither back into the water. It was now in its own territory and wouldn't miss again.

Duncan didn't see the snake coming for him, being nearly lost in the darkness. Patches, however, had much keener eyesight and leapt to his human's rescue. With a splash almost equal to Duncan's, the massive cat hit the water, jaws open for an instant. The next instant they were closed neatly, severing the snake in half.

Without so much as missing a stroke, Patches swam over to Duncan and let him grab onto his back. Together, the two paddled back to the river bank.

The pair scrambled up the muddy riverbank, Duncan gasping for air and Patches cleaning himself off. Like a great wave, exasperation and despair finally washed over Duncan. He fell to his knees, his head in his hands, fighting back the urge to cry or scream. The realization that Salena was, in all probability lost, began to suffocate him.

His stomach twisted in knots as he sat there trying to comprehend the situation. His eyes began to sting with unshed tears. It would be so easy to break down but he couldn't, he told himself. He would be strong for Salena.

The air above Duncan stirred and he looked up to see Ar'ye hovering above him, his winged form silhouetted in the starlight.

"What happened?" he asked, his voice showing only some of the concern he felt.

Embarrassment, shame and sheer fatigue showed in Duncan's response. "I slipped in."

Big Cat was back too, circling Duncan and Patches to show her concern. Both cats rubbed heads, reaffirming that everything was alright.

Ar'ye, even in the dark, could read the pain in Duncan's face and knew not to press the matter. He was about to offer his condolences when he heard sounds coming from the woods behind them.

The cats turned too, their sharp ears picking up the sounds of people approaching. Unlike Ar'ye, their noses matched their ears and they picked up the familiar scent long before anyone came into sight. Ar'ye and Duncan both caught the cats' subtle cue that it was Martyl and the Dwarves approaching.

Landing next to Duncan with a small fluttering of his wings, Ar'ye helped him to his feet. Stepping from the trees to the riverbank was Martyl, followed by Rorn and Dirn carrying the remaining river boat. The Dwarves' faces were taciturn as usual and they kept to themselves as Martyl approached. With a glance, Martyl sized up the situation quickly. From the looks of Duncan he knew that he had fallen in the river during his search for Salena. That, and the yelling he had heard earlier.

"She's gone," mumbled Duncan pitifully, a hard lump forming in his throat. The effort of holding back his sorrow and despair was beginning to wear him down and he wouldn't look up at Martyl, even in the darkness.

Martyl didn't know what to say to console his friend. Death was something he was accustomed to as a Royal Knight but Duncan was just a young man and hadn't been battle hardened. It was events like this that could make or break a man but they didn't have the luxury of time to wait and see. Duncan had to move on now or all their lives would be in jeopardy. The only course of action he could see to take was the blunt, straightforward one and hope Duncan snapped to.

"I'm sorry, Duncan," Martyl began. "But there's nothing more we can do. We must be going now." It hurt him to say those words but Martyl knew they must be spoken.

"We haven't found her body yet," Duncan choked out.

"This river rarely relinquishes its victims." It was Dirn, his voice not betraying any hint of emotion, merely stating a fact.

Ar'ye shot him a glance that almost burned a hole through his thick leather armour. Both cats stopped their preening at the sound of his voice and turned to stare at the Dwarves, tails twitching side to side.

"That's enough," stated Martyl, his voice cold and authoritative. "We're not going through this again. If we don't move on now, we will all face the same fate."

As if to reinforce his statement, a resounding crash was heard in the forest behind them, followed by screams of pain.

"In the boat, NOW!" shouted Martyl, the need for secrecy and quiet all but gone now.

Rorn and Dirn, despite their stocky builds, moved deceptively fast and had the river boat in the water in seconds. Rorn climbed aboard, manning the till while Dirn, arms straining against the current, held it in place.

Martyl grabbed the startled Duncan by the arm and steered him towards the boat.

"Get in," he commanded, pushing Duncan forward. They had only minutes before the Wraulls extricated themselves from his make-shift trap and were upon them.

Patches and Big Cat bounded after them, jumping effortlessly into the bobbing boat. Martyl got in next, taking the lookout position in the bow. Dirn looked back for Ar'ye who waved him on. Not wasting another second, he jumped into the already overcrowded craft and the river current swept them away, with Ar'ye in flight in hot pursuit.

Chapter Sixteen

The small river boat bobbed up and down in the swift river current, its occupants precariously close to being thrown out. Patches and Big Cat flattened themselves to the bottom of the boat, claws extended, gripping the wood. Both cats growled mildly in irritation at the jostling they were taking, not to mention the water soaking their fur.

Duncan paid the cats no heed, sitting directly behind them, staring instead at the water's surface. His thoughts were completely incoherent now, his mind wrought with disbelief and despair. He just couldn't accept the fact that Salena was gone. The image of her face was still emblazoned in his mind's eye, her warm smile lighting up her face.

Within minutes though, the sorrow began to give way to pure hatred. It boiled to the surface giving Duncan something to focus on. It not only sharpened his mind, it was a survival instinct. Now he had a purpose in the immediate future—exact his revenge on any and all Wraulls he would come across.

Tired of feeling sorry for himself over Salena's demise, Duncan grabbed an oar and began to paddle. Every time he plunged the paddle into the water, the fire in his heart coursed through his veins driving the boat on.

"Easy, Duncan," warned Dirn from behind him. "Save some of that energy for later. We have a long night ahead."

Slowly, Duncan eased up on his power strokes. Even in his rage-clouded state-of-mind he knew the Dwarf was right. There would be plenty of time in the near future for revenge, he told himself.

The boat carried on in silence now, save the splashing of the water caused by the rough current. Everyone on board, including the rugged Dwarves, were feeling the events of the past day take their toll. They weren't even gone one complete day yet and already they had had two run-ins with Wraull patrols. Worst of all, to everyone involved, one of their party had already been lost.

How much more bloodshed and sorrow they would encounter, Martyl did not know. He tried to keep those thoughts from clouding his already weary mind. They all needed to remain alert and focussed if they were to survive this journey.

He and the Dwarves knew this well but Martyl feared that maybe Duncan and Salena did not realize the full gravity of the situation. Until now. It pained him greatly, as a Royal Knight and as a friend to abandon the search for Salena. But he also knew, as did the others, that more than just one life was at stake. The lives of thousands relied upon them. They had searched long enough for Salena as it was, with the Wraulls bearing down upon them. Besides, Dirn was right, this river, with the falls and creatures lurking on its banks, rarely relinquished its victims.

A soft fluttering in the air overhead brought Martyl's attention back to the matter at hand. Looking up in the darkness he could make out the faint outline of Ar'ye's winged form.

"Martyl," he stated quietly, his wings pumping the air about him as he tried to keep up to the fast moving river boat.

"I waited to see if the Wraulls escaped your trap and saw eight emerge from the woods unwounded. From their furious demeanor, I surmise they must have suffered some severe casualties."

Martyl thought for sure he could detect a happy lilt in Ar'ye's voice and permitted himself a brief smile in the darkness at his own ingenuity.

"Furthermore," continued Ar'ye, "I've scouted ahead a ways and saw no further Wraulls."

"Good," replied Martyl. "See if you can secure an appropriate landing for us where the forest ends. We need to rest tonight."

Without a word, Ar'ye was off into the night air, disappearing like a giant bat into the darkness.

Although it was dangerous to go ashore, it was even more dangerous to stay in the water. From the lack of noise behind him, save an occasional paddle breaking the water, Martyl knew the others were as sore and tired as him. If they fell asleep on this swift moving river there was no telling where they'd wake up. If they even did.

It had been over fifteen years since he was last here but Martyl remembered the Untamed Lands and its life-threatening dangers well enough. They had travelled several leagues already and much faster than the Wraulls could through the tangled forest. Within a few more leagues they would leave the forest and enter the flat steppes of the Untamed Lands. Here, he thought to himself, would be their best place to rest. Anyone approaching from the north, east or south would be doing so without cover. In this spot they would have an escape back into the forest or the river.

Turning for a brief moment, Martyl told Duncan to prepare to beach soon and to relay the message to the others. By the time Rorn, still at the till, acknowledged his orders, Ar'ye was back hovering over Martyl.

"Martyl," he half whispered. "I've found a good location to shelter in. Follow me."

"Rorn," called out Martyl, "follow Ar'ye."

The Rey'ak stayed low and close so the others wouldn't lose him in the dark. He flew across the river to the south bank and landed softly on his feet. Rorn piloted the overcrowded river boat towards Ar'ye and the river bank.

Everyone stopped paddling as they let the river do the last of the work for them, the swift moving current carrying the bow of the boat right onto the shore with Rorn's direction. With a grinding shudder, the boat lurched to a stop on a low, sandy section of the bank. Immediately the two cats leapt from their crouching positions and landed on the beach. Martyl was out next, holding the boat firm with Ar'ye.

His arms and back ached from the fighting, paddling and swimming he had done earlier but he refused to surrender to fatigue just yet.

Duncan stepped out next, grateful for the darkness to hide the pain on his face. A great deal of it was from the physical exhaustion he was facing but much worse was from the emotional strain of losing Salena.

Dirn and Rorn clambered out last, their movements a little slower and more calculated than usual. Even their rigorous constitutions had limits.

"This way, quickly," whispered Ar'ye to Martyl at his side.

Stealth and speed still of the essence, Martyl motioned for Duncan to give the two Dwarves a hand in carrying the boat. The three of them struggled with it in their fatigued state, trying to keep up to Ar'ye so Martyl joined in to give them a hand. In the starlit darkness, the two men and two Dwarves followed Ar'ye and the two cats who carried on as if it were daylight.

In a matter of minutes they left the beach and crested a small hill. The sounds of the forest carried out to them here, sending chills down every spine. The sounds of the Wraull war machine could still be faintly heard far off in the distance.

Ar'ye took them only a few more yards towards the forest when large, gray shapes loomed up from the ground before them. The four carrying the boat faltered for a moment, preparing to take a last, defensive stand against a new enemy. They feared the worst, a Walusk or group of Wraulls emerging from the woods to ambush them.

To their surprise, and then relief, Ar'ye and the cats led them on. As their eyes focussed in the darkness they realized the shapes were nothing more than rocks. They jutted up out of the grassy hill like giant beasts, weathered and beaten but a welcome relief. They would provide excellent shelter for the night.

Setting the boat down, all five men and both cats huddled into the rocks and in moments collapsed from exhaustion, their bodies refusing to do their bidding any longer.

Everything happened so quickly after she had been thrown from the boat that Salena had no time to even think of yelling for help. Besides, she told herself, if she couldn't survive these waters, none of the others would even have a chance.

It took every last bit of resolve in her strong will to just keep her head above water after being struck by the tree and subsequently thrown from the boat. Valiantly she had struggled to reach the others but to no avail, her head spinning from the impact. Her last memory of the others brought tears to her eyes as she hid in the reeds along the river bank, still in the water. She remembered seeing Rorn fall off the tree, entangled with a Wraull. Seconds after that she saw Martyl and Patches forced into the raging water.

She would have tried to reach them but she was slammed into a moss-slicked rock again, her vision and mind clouding over with excruciating pain. The water whirled her on, whisking her toward the falls as she bobbed helplessly in its grasp. Where the strength came from, Salena could only guess, but with a final effort she propelled herself through the water toward the shore. After an agonizingly long battle, she reached the reeds by the river bed. Dragging herself through them, she collapsed on the riverbank, a mixture of agony, despair and joy at just being alive overcoming her.

It was dark now when she woke and Salena thought it best to be moving on. She took stock of her condition before extricating herself from concealment. She winced in pain with every deep breath or extended movement. After checking herself thoroughly, she discovered nothing was broken, just severely bruised. So long as she moved slowly and cautiously the pain remained at a minimum.

Worse, however, was the fact that she had no provisions and no clothing or weapons except what she wore now and her long knife at her side. Deciding to worry about those problems when they arrived, Salena crawled the rest of the way up the river bank.

She shivered in the cool mountain air as her drenched clothing clung to her skin. Despite the chill, she knew that staying wet was the best way to hide from the Wraulls. She remembered what Rorn and

Dirn had said about the Wraulls having poor night vision but excellent scent capabilities.

Keeping that in mind, Salena slunk along as best she could in the dark, trying to remain silent and out of sight. Where she was going she wasn't entirely sure but she did know that they had all been heading to the Dwarven Falls originally. That would be a start, she told herself.

Cautiously, Salena continued on through the undergrowth along the river's edge. Continually her mind replayed the last images of the others she had seen; Rorn going over the tree with a Wraull and Martyl and Patches following right after.

Salena hadn't seen what happened to Ar'ye, Duncan, Dirn and Big Cat but she had heard Dirn's shout of an ambush. What happened to them she could only guess. That was the worst part. For all she knew, she might be the only one of the party left alive. To make matters worse, she was more than likely still surrounded by Wraulls with no way back to Calheller or even home!

Home, thought Salena wistfully. Why did I ever leave it for this? For Duncan, she chastised herself, and Martyl. This was their homeland and they were her friends—and more. She owed them this much, to give all the help she could. If I can just reach the portage point, Salena continued silently, maybe I can find a sign as to where they went if anyone survived.

Sloshing along in her waterlogged clothing, Salena felt as if a new ray of hope was shining down on her. So long as she was alive, she would not give up hope that the others were also alive. Finally, after almost three quarters of an hour of painstaking effort to remain silent and concealed, Salena reached the portage point.

Peering through the dense foliage, she strained in the dim moonlight to see what lay in the clearing beyond. At least a half dozen bodies lay in a tangled, bloody mess near the pebbly beach. A wave of nausea threatened to wash over Salena as she feared the worst.

Abandoning all caution, she rushed into the clearing to get a closer look. Like a gust of wind blowing away the clouds to reveal the sun, relief washed through Salena as she saw that the bodies were Wraulls, not her comrades. Quietly she searched the horrendous scene before her for any clues as to the others' whereabouts. Even though Salena was not a skilled warrior like Martyl or the Dwarves, she could tell by the broad, open wounds that most of the Wraulls had died from axe wounds.

Others had arrows protruding from their fallen, grotesque bodies while some bore the marks of animal attack, specifically that of a large cat as their throats were clearly removed. Despite the death surrounding her, Salena was elated that at least half their party survived. With any luck, she thought, they all might have.

Hurriedly Salena looked about for any signs as to where the others went from here. She may not have been an experienced tracker but it didn't take an expert to follow the trail left behind by the Wraulls. From the amount of trampling in and around the clearing leading off into the woods beside the falls, Salena had an easy trail to follow. Knowing the Wraulls were excellent trackers by smell, the reinforcements of the not so fortunate Wraulls at the ambush would be well after her friends by now.

Judging by the wake of destruction left behind by them, Salena knew there had to be a lot of them. She knew her friends were excellent warriors, possibly the best in these strange lands, yet even they had limits. If any of them were injured in the ambush or lost in the river like her, their strength would be greatly reduced. Even uninjured and at full strength, they couldn't fight these immeasurable odds forever. Sooner of later their skill and luck would run out.

Salena hoped it would be later. Carefully so as to be quiet, yet not too cautiously as to waste precious time, Salena made her way down the mountainside trail. She hoped to rendezvous with the others before they got too far ahead or met with more Wraulls.

Maybe, she thought with a rueful smile creasing her face in the dark, she could come upon the Wraulls unawares from behind and ambush them. Then she would prove her worth to the distrusting Dwarves! Determinedly she trudged on and down, the cool mountain night air and damp clothing doing little now to keep her from perspiring as her body worked itself up.

Even though there was a trail there to follow, made wider yet by the unseen advancing Wraulls, Salena still staggered and fell repeatedly. Her body was reaching exhaustion, the day's earlier adventure having robbed her of most of her strength. She hadn't eaten in over half a day now as well and her body just couldn't cope with the demands placed on it anymore.

Slowing her pace to conserve energy and strength, Salena picked her way gingerly down the slope. As she staggered and wobbled, branches slapped at her and creepers grabbed at her feet. The shadows cast by the pale moonlight flitted past her while hordes of insects, attracted by the smell of sweat, buzzed incessantly about her head.

Finally, the fatigue, pain and utter anger became too much. Tripping on the creeping vines one time too many, Salena screamed in frustration as she hit the ground. Her clothes torn, her body battered, she lay face down in the dirt and leaves and sobbed. Far from home and now utterly alone, her broken spirit yearned for a reprieve.

How Duncan managed to deal with everything she couldn't guess. His strength had carried her weeks ago to this point but now he was gone. Dead or alive, she didn't know. All she knew was that the others in her party must think she was dead. That is the only reason they would leave without her. No one could have survived that river unaided, or so they would think.

"But I did!" she exclaimed triumphantly.

Smiling wryly, Salena carried on now, picking herself up slowly and tenderly from the ground, anxious again to reach her fellow travellers. Slowing her pace now to avoid overstressing herself, Salena rounded a bend in the trail. Even in the pale light filtering in from above the canopy, it was easy to discern the carnage before her.

On the slope below her, an avalanche of logs had come to rest. Amid the logs, arms, legs and sometimes whole bodies lay in view. Cautiously, Salena made her way through the mass destruction. All the bodies she could see were Wraulls. And a great deal of them.

This brought her renewed hope in finding the others as she knew Martyl had to be alive. This was his doing. And the dwarves obviously, to perform the heavy labour. Her heart lightened considerably, Salena pressed on. Within half an hour, she reached the edge of the woods and the river bank.

Peering through the dense foliage around her, Salena tried to make out the dark shapes milling about the river bank. Her heart beat faster as she tried to determine who was out there. The pounding of her blood became so loud in her ears that she didn't even notice the hand close over her mouth before it was too late.

Futilely she tried to struggle but her unseen foe was too strong. Hot, foul smelling breath stung her eyes and nose. Loud grunts filled her ears and within seconds, large squarish shapes began to materialize out of the dark woods around her.

Wraulls, thought Salena. Fear of what was about to happen to her engulfed Salena and she began to panic, struggling even harder to escape her enemies. The effort brought her nothing but a sharp blow to the head. At least their brutality is like the stories told her by the Dwarves, Salena thought wryly. She felt the warm stickiness of blood flowing from her scalp down her face. Maybe their lack of intelligence is the same. This new thought was all she had to give herself hope as an idea took form in her tired mind.

"Let her speak," grunted the largest of the Wraulls in front of her.

Immediately the hand over her mouth was released and Salena gulped fresh air as she was thrust forward at arms length from her captor, still not fully released.

"You travel with the Dwarves and Rey'ak," grunted the Wraull in front of her. It was more a statement of fact than a question and seeing the raised, gnarled fist Salena held her tongue in check.

She replied with a curt, "Yes."

"What do you seek?" came the next question.

Anything Salena thought about the Dwarves being discourteous and gruff was quickly replaced by the realization that the Wraulls were much worse.

Fear of torture or death at the hands of the Wraulls was weighing heavily on Salena but she knew if she answered the question she would endanger Duncan and the others. Her hesitation brought her another swift blow to the head. For a moment, her vision went dark and if not for the Wraull holding her from behind, she would have fallen to the ground.

"Answer, woman," hissed the Wraull before her through clenched teeth.

Weakened by fatigue, stress and now the beating from the Wraulls, Salena wanted nothing more than to just collapse and let everything fade away, even if it meant death at the hands of her captors. But deep inside, a fire burned, locked away, an inner strength that would not allow her to surrender just yet and now it threatened to consume her. A renewed strength coursed through her body and fought through the haze that clouded her mind.

I am the princess of the Misty Isles, she told herself. I will not be defeated by these brutes. It I am to die, it will be with dignity and on my terms. With a sudden flash of insight, Salena had a plan.

"We search for a lost relic with which to combat the Black Paladin." She hoped her voice sounded despondent and desperate.

"Where," came the only reply, the brutal hand poised to strike again.

"Let me live and I will tell you," replied Salena, holding her breath.

"Show us the way. We will take you with us. If it is a trap, you will be killed. If not, you might live." The Wraull grinned wickedly, showing black, misshapen teeth that made him look even more menacing.

Salena allowed herself an inward sigh of relief. She realized that she would most likely die either way, but if her plan worked, maybe she could buy time for the others by leading the Wraulls on a wild goose chase.

"See to her wounds then bring her along. We must be leaving shortly. A relic awaits us."

Closing her eyes and steeling herself against their rough, animal behaviour and smell, Salena endured their ministrations and then was unceremoniously tied at the wrists on a long tether attached to a collar about her neck. After her bonds were checked, she was marched out into the open steppes of the Untamed Lands.

Chapter Seventeen

It was well past dawn when the beleaguered party rose. All were feeling the aftereffects of the previous day's trials. No one said a word as Martyl passed around a loaf of bread and cheese from their supplies. Everyone was lost in his own dark, secret thoughts and even the cats seemed to be mourning Salena's loss as they lay at Duncan's side, heads on their paws.

After washing his breakfast down with fresh, cold water from a nearby stream, Martyl decided it was time he got the small company on their feet and moving again. He didn't want to give them too much time to brood over things.

"How long would you say it is to the Dead Woods, Dirn?" asked Martyl. "It's been a long time since I was last in the area."

"About two days' travel down the Thunder River," replied the always grim faced Dwarf.

"Then I suggest we get started now. Duncan, get the cats and check the river bank with Ar'ye. The Dwarves and I will bring the boat."

"We can't all fit in the boat, Knight," growled Rorn, still upset over the previous night's encounter. "It's too dangerous to overcrowd it like that. The cats will have to swim and Ar'ye will have to fly." There was a definite edge to his voice when talking about the cats and Ar'ye.

"That's not acceptable," snapped Martyl, too tired yet to keep his voice neutral as usual. "We all fit in the boat last night. Why is it different now?"

"The river is swift moving and deep from here on." It was Dirn, his demeanor more subdued than Rorn's. "There are also many rapids, some more dangerous than those above the Falls. Even properly loaded and expertly guided, it will be a difficult passage. These boats are sturdy but what you require would push them beyond their designed limits."

"Then what do you propose we do, Rorn's idea not withstanding? We need to continue on as fast as possible to keep ahead of the Wraulls."

"There is one other way," spoke up Rorn, feeling the need to redeem himself in front of the Royal Knight. He still burned inwardly at the chastising they had all received from Martyl the night before.

"It is as dangerous, if not more so," he began, Martyl and Dirn both turning to listen. "There is a small community of horse breeders a day's march south of here, called Equilon."

"Yes, I remember now!" exclaimed Martyl. "It has been so long, I forgot all about the village."

"And you would do just as well to continue to forget about it, Martyl," warned Dirn, his stare berating Rorn. "It was conquered long ago by the Black Paladin. As you know, their horses were legendary and the Black Paladin wanted them for his own troops to use."

"He is right," added Rorn, shrugging, "but you wanted an alternative. There it is."

Martyl was not to be dissuaded, however and his experienced mind began racing, a new hope already taking root.

"It is our best hope," he began, trying to convince himself as much as the Dwarves. "We will lose a day's march to get there but we will gain more than triple the time lost on our return journey. Think about it. Even if we had both boats, the return journey would be upriver, against the current all the way. With horses, we could cover the distance much quicker."

"That is true," replied both Dwarves.

"But realize that there will be a least one entire garrison watching the village and surrounding lands," added Dirn. "How will we get in and out, unnoticed and alive?"

"We'll work on that," replied Martyl, a smile beginning to crease his weathered face.

"What's going on?" asked Duncan, returning from the beach with both cats and Ar'ye.

He was not overly pleased to find Martyl and the Dwarves standing about in idle conversation when there were relics to be found.

"We have a new plan," stated Martyl, filling Duncan and Ar'ye in on the next step in their adventure. "It's best we get moving now to avoid losing any more time. Everyone take enough provisions for himself for two days and leave everything else back at the boat."

Within minutes they were packed and moving, anxious to get underway.

On through the early morning hours they continued to march. The ground was barren and nearly lifeless. All that grew were scraggly clumps of brush with very few leaves of any particular colour. Large boulders littered the ground, the deposits of an ancient glacier from the Char'nak Mountains. Moraines and small ox-bow lakes appeared every now and again, the only areas to support any type of green plant life. Here, large broadleaf trees grew in small copses with strange bird and animal sounds emanating from within.

Even though their party was large and well armed, at least twenty Wraulls by Salena's wearied count, they stayed well clear of the wooded areas and valleys between the moraines and kept to the flat, open land.

Salena had withdrawn into herself and even the breathtaking beauty of the red morning sky did nothing to cheer her up. Her feet were beginning to blister and crack, the extended forced march which she had no choice but to endure was taking its toll. The Wraulls had not stopped their march eastward since capturing Salena twelve hours before. Dried blood left a red streak like a scar down her left cheek and her head still pounded from the blows she'd received the night before.

Countless times her leaden, exhausted legs faltered and buckled, causing Salena to stagger and sometimes fall. Each time she was unceremoniously yanked to her feet by an unsympathetic Wraull.

How can they keep going like this, she thought to herself through a haze of pain. Still, she forced herself to be vigilant and spot a way to escape if the opportunity arose. Eager as she was to escape, however, Salena knew she couldn't do it by force. She wondered if even Duncan could. Or Martyl. They were both strong and Martyl even had the giant size of a Wraull but doubted either of them had the stamina. Every few miles, a party of four Wraulls would break off from the group and disappear over the horizon, presumably scouting the terrain ahead for any danger. Upon their return, a new party would set off, their stamina seemingly endless.

Despite the odds, Salena would not give up hope that a rescue, either by Duncan and the others, or herself alone, would occur. Without that hope, she had nothing to keep her going.

At last, near midday, the patrol stopped its march. They rested near the shore of a small lake, or rather large pond as Salena could see to the other side easily. A small stand of trees provided a dismal amount of shade and relief from the intense sun. The four Wraulls who reported the area safe during their scouting were left on guard. Presumably to be the first attacked if they missed something, thought Salena.

Her hands still tied and tethered by a ten foot rope to the patrol leader, Henaach, she'd heard him called, Salena was allowed to sit at last and rest.

"Drink this", commanded Henaach in a tone that demanded attention.

He offered Salena a flask containing a most foul smelling liquid. Raising the flask to her lips, Salena's nose wrinkled at the rank smell. The sight of Henaach's raised fist about to strike if she disobeyed his order overcame any qualms she might of had at drinking the liquid.

Opening her mouth she took a quick swallow before the flask was snatched away again. Like liquid fire, it burned all the way down her throat and set her body on fire with its heat. Almost at once, the pain in her body began to lessen and she felt rejuvenated. This must be like the drink Tal-Shar that Duncan was given by the Dwarves, thought Salena. Only probably a great deal more bitter she finished, tasting the aftereffects still.

"That will help ease some of your pain, weak one," snapped Henaach in his rough, guttural voice, not at all sympathetic. "Enjoy this rest. We will be underway again in minutes."

He tossed her a stale loaf of bread and, like a mangy dog, tied her to a nearby tree as he turned to inspect his patrol.

Ignoring the bitter jibe and the indecency of being tied to a tree, Salena attacked the hard bread ravenously, not realizing until now how hungry she had been. In no time at all she had finished the bread, hungry for more but not expecting any.

Despite her fatigued body, ravaged feet and pounding head, Salena forced herself to remain alert and survey her current situation.

The Wraull Patrol was spread out all around her but no one was any further than fifteen feet from her at most. Too close to even try and make a run for it, she thought, even if I wasn't tied to this tree.

Staring into the water, absently assessing the damage to her face, an idea flashed through her thoughts like lightning.

The song!, a voice inside her shrieked. Use the song!

Yes, she almost shouted aloud. My Siren song. How could have I forgotten? Fatigue, yes, that's why.

From deep inside, in a part of her body where it was kept locked away for an emergency, a burst of power and energy surged through her body, into every nerve ending, tingling and burning more than the Wraull drink.

Quietly at first, then building in volume, Salena began to sing her Siren Song, hoping to lull the Wraulls into a sleep long enough to allow her to escape.

Her eyes locked shut in concentration, Salena increased the tempo and volume of her song again, putting the last of her energy into this last ditch effort to escape.

"Isn't that a lovely song," barked Henaach, tugging on Salena's rope.

Salena's eyes snapped open at the gruff sound and her heart sank, her spirit now truly broken as she realized she was too far from her home for the song to work.

"Get up, girl," he commanded. "We're leaving now."

Throughout the morning, no one said a word as the five men and two cats marched on in the blazing heat. The sun beat down relentlessly and the humidity in the air made everyone sticky and uncomfortable.

To keep his mind off the loss of Salena, Duncan's thoughts turned to the Black Paladin once again and the revenge he would exact upon him. He had to keep his pain and sorrow locked inside in order to go on. He felt that releasing it would not only show weakness to the others but that it would somehow allow the Black Paladin a measure of victory over him. And that was something Duncan was determined not to let happen.

Clenching his jaw, he walked on in an increasingly black mood. The cats too noticed and shot him distressed looks every now and again. Their empathic link with Duncan transferred all the hate he was feeling to them also. This forced them to fight their own battle against the oppressive feelings.

By mid-afternoon, Martyl called a halt, the first person to break the silence since they set out that morning.

Sitting beneath the shade of a large elm tree, everyone had a long needed meal of bread and cheese, washed down with fresh water. Both cats ate some dried meat Duncan brought along for them, not feeling like hunting just yet.

"We shall be upon the village of Equilon shortly after nightfall," stated Rorn, breaking the mid-day silence. "We are already on the rich pastures used to feed their stock." He picked a handful of the thick, rich, green-blue grass to show everyone.

Continuing, he added, "I know that when we arrive at Equilon we will all be tired but we must acquire the horses and be on our way tonight. We will need the cover of darkness to aid us as we will be vastly out-numbered."

"Why can't we rest for a while before we raid the village?" asked Ar'ye, not liking the idea of doing something this dangerous with so little preparation and time.

"There is nowhere to hide in the meantime. From here to the village, the ground is open grasslands. Without the cover of darkness under which to shelter our approach we would be seen from a mile away and an armed mounted patrol would be sent out to greet us," answered Rorn, a hint of impatience in his voice.

"I agree," stated Duncan, matter-of-factly. "Besides, we can't afford to lose any more time. We must reach the Iron Hills as soon as possible."

Martyl looked at Duncan questioningly, wondering how much of this added bravado was because Salena was gone and Duncan felt he had nothing left to lose.

He'll lose his life is what he'll lose, Martyl thought to himself. Still, he had been young and brash once too and knew that sometimes that could help. Sometimes.

Still, Martyl made a mental note to watch Duncan a little more closely the next couple of days just to be sure.

Stretching his short legs one last time, Rorn rose from his resting place beneath the tree and motioned everyone to follow. The march to Equilon was on again.

Rorn and Dirn were again in the lead, their compact bodies and short legs amazingly resilient in the stifling heat. Quietly, almost in a whisper, they discussed plans on how best to accomplish their goal of retrieving five horses.

Ar'ye, Duncan and the cats followed next, their youthful bodies giving them the energy needed to keep up to the others, their stamina and endurance not as developed.

A few paces back, Martyl brought up the rear, his sun-bronzed face completely emotionless as he steeled himself for the battle about to come. He had never personally been to Equilon before but the legends of the horses there were known throughout the lands. As a Royal Knight under King Aramid, Martyl had ridden on an Equilon steed, as had all the other Royal Knights. It came as no surprise to him that the Black Paladin had conquered these peaceful people and taken their beautiful animals.

Since it was the Black Paladin's forces that now controlled the village, Martyl had no qualms about stealing horses from them. He just hoped they could do it without losing anyone.

Martyl knew the loss of Salena would be hard on Duncan. It was on him also. But he had faced death and lost friends and loved ones many times before. Duncan had not, except his parents when he was very small. He hoped this would not interfere with their quest, that Duncan would not do something rash and get himself or someone else hurt or killed from not thinking clearly.

That was all the more reason to keep an eye on him. He was the last of the Royal Knights and he had to see the rightful heir to the throne of Arundel back on it. Even if it meant losing his own life in the process. Martyl knew that and was prepared to accept it, so long as it wasn't through foolishness.

He wanted to say something to Duncan, to console him and let him know that he hurt too but decided against it, not wanting to bring the subject up if he didn't have to.

In the end, he resolved himself to following silently behind the others, occasionally glancing back to be sure they weren't being followed. Finally, as dusk began to take its shadowy hold over the land, Rorn called a halt again.

They were standing on the top of a low rise in the grasslands and the two Dwarves motioned everyone to lie down.

"We made better time than I expected," began Rorn. "We will lie here, out of sight until complete darkness in another hour or so."

"In the meantime, I will explain our plan," whispered Dirn, causing everyone to inch closer to him before he continued.

"Before the Black Paladin, this was a free village and everyone sold or traded their own horse stock. Now, all the animals are kept corralled in one central location—a large field at the southern end of the village.

"We will have to pass through the village using back alleys to remain undetected to reach the horses. From there, we will need to dispatch whatever forces may be guarding them, steal the horses, and then escape. Simple enough?"

A wry smile crossed his face at the implied humour, hoping to alleviate some of the dread and hopelessness they were all no doubt feeling.

"Ar'ye, we will need you to fly in and scout the troops before we begin."

"I'll leave as soon as its dark, Rorn," replied Ar'ye, glad to be doing some flying at last. "Until then, I need some food. I'm famished."

Without waiting, Ar'ye was digging through his food, eating with vigour. The others followed suit, their appetites not affected by the apprehension they felt.

Little more than an hour passed and the sun had finally set in the west, the night sky dark with an ominous covering of clouds. No stars or moon shone, the clouds obscuring all light from above. A strong wind from the east had risen, the long lush grass whispering to the would-be horse thieves in the darkness. Thunder rumbled and bright shards of lightning flashed above them, casting an eerie glow on the ground each time. During these lightning flashes, Martyl observed Duncan and feared anew for his friend and charge.

Each lightning strike that illuminated the area also illuminated Duncan's face. Martyl watched the dark shadows flicker across it, as black and dangerous as the moods beneath them. He began to fear again for Duncan, watching him sitting withdrawn from the others, the cats keeping an ever vigilant watch over him.

These next few hours could prove to be their most dangerous yet, walking into an enemy town, a whole garrison strong against five with only the cover of night for protection. If Duncan weren't up to this, if he were to do something brash and dangerous in his present condition, it could prove deadly for all of them.

More than once while they lay waiting for nightfall, Martyl had considered leaving Duncan here on the back of the hilltop, out of danger, while he and the others attempted to steal the horses. Every time he weighed the alternatives, he knew in the end Duncan would be there with them. Martyl knew he would not willingly stay behind while the others risked their lives for him and that he would undoubtably follow them anyways.

Turning to the others, he whispered, "Rorn, can Ar'ye go in and scout the area for us now?"

With a final check of the night sky and a long, slow look over the hilltop, Rorn replied, "Yes. It is time. Ar'ye, you will fly over the village, checking for the best way in. Be sure to note the size and position of troop locations as well as the location of the horses. They should still be in the south of the village."

It was nearly the same speech the Dwarf had given him a few hours ago but Ar'ye didn't mind, he was anxious to begin showing the Dwarves how well his people could be counted on.

With a last glance toward his friend, Ar'ye felt a pang of sorrow for Duncan over Salena's loss. She was a friend of his too, even though only for a brief period of time, and he vowed inwardly to do the best he could to see that she didn't die in vain.

"I will be back within the hour, Martyl," stated Ar'ye as if nothing out of the ordinary were occurring.

The lightning flashed again and in the brief moment of light, the rest of the small party saw a dark shadow already streaking towards the village of Equilon below them.

They had flown for nearly an entire day now and they were beginning to reach the end of their stamina. Both wanted nothing more than to rest their weary wings and feast on fresh meat, but their master had sent them on an important errand and they would see it completed.

The two birds, Haak and Leik, both messengers of Bin, servant of the Black Paladin, were in search of Henaach, the leader of the Wraull patrol stationed to ambush the party from Calheller. Early in the morning, a few hours after dawn, they came upon the place of the ambush. The smell of rotting flesh from the dead Wraulls assailed their fine sense of smell but these birds did not eat carrion. They were better than mere vultures and they wheeled about in the bright morning sun, their exceptional eyes scanning the forest below for any sight of their quarry. They ignored the insects and animals that converged on the gruesome scene below them.

Suddenly Leik let out a screech, alerting Haak to what he had spied. Many miles to their east, a large group of Wraulls was marching towards the Dead Woods.

With a quick dive, both birds swept down, their sleek, feathered bodies gaining speed and propelling them towards their new destination.

On through the day they travelled, never stopping, only slowing their pace marginally as time wore on. Soon, however, they began to overtake the Wraulls they were following, coming to within a few miles after they stopped for a brief rest near a small lake.

Haak and Leik could afford no such luxury and on they continued, their seemingly tireless wings beating, soaring, beating, soaring as they drew ever closer. Finally, as dusk began to settle over the forbidding landscape of the Untamed Lands, the two birds reached the Wraulls. Shrieking their greeting cry, the two birds plummeted towards the Wraulls below them.

Having been a seasoned Wraull leader in the service of the Black Paladin for many years, Henaach recognized the call of the animal servants of his master. He drew his patrol to a halt, sentries already melting into the settling dark around them. Salena, grateful for another break in the forced march, immediately sat down to rest.

Henaach held out his right arm and both falcons immediately set down on the offered perch. Without saying a word, Henaach removed the banded message about each bird's leg after handing Salena's rope over to another Wraull.

Quickly he read the message, the same on each bird, written in his own tongue. He knew from experience that for Bin to send two of his falcons to deliver the message it must indeed be important. They were an expensive commodity to use without good reason.

With barely disguised surprise in his voice, Henaach turned to Salena and said, "It seems you are worth more than I thought, girl. It is unfortunate you cannot show us the whereabouts of this supposed relic you and your companions were in search of but the Black Paladin has a more immediate use for you."

Despite her weary state and the Wraull's thickly gnarled speech, Salena understood what was to become of her. Had she been able, she probably would have cried at that point but her beaten and sun burned body could not afford to relinquish the water for the tears or the air for the sobs. Dejectedly, she collapsed on the ground, not caring anymore until a shrill scream rent the night air, pure instinctive fear pulling her back to the situation at hand.

Ar'ye flew swiftly and silently towards the town of Equilon. Even with his excellent hunter's night vision he would have had trouble seeing in the near black brought about by the approaching storm if it weren't for the frequent flashes of lightning that streaked through the night air.

His wing was fully healed now and he had no problem keeping a high altitude and speed to help conceal his approach. He would be glad, however, to acquire a steed of his own. Even though his people had the ability to fly, it required enormous effort and energy. Even the strongest of the Rey'ak were not capable of more than five or six hours of continuous flight a day.

A few minutes later and Ar'ye was over the town. He realized now just how correct the Dwarves had been in insisting they wait until night fall. From the hill top to the town, it was about a mile and a half of wide open plain, covered in a lush growth of grass. Had they approached in daylight, the party would most certainly have been spotted by the dozen armoured guards on horseback at the gates to the town.

His wings held motionless in the fully outstretched position, Ar'ye glided silently over their heads, praying to himself that any one of the myriad flashes above did not give him away.

With his sharp, hawk-like vision, Ar'ye took in every detail he could. The entire town was itself like one large corral. A large, six-foot high fence covered the perimeter with only one entrance or exit, over which he just flew.

Shops and stores of all types lined the once prosperous streets but now all were abandoned, the local populace long since killed or enslaved by the Black Paladin's forces now occupying the town.

Mixed emotions of hatred and loathing, fear and despair ran through Ar'ye as he realized that this same fate awaited his people and that of the Dwarves. Both the Rey'ak and Dwarves were stronger than this small town but Ar'ye also knew that there were larger armies advancing on both peoples even now. Divided, the two peoples did not stand much of a chance, but if this quest he was on with Duncan succeeded, they may yet all survive.

Returning his attention to his survey of the town's forces, Ar'ye flew on. As he neared the southern end of the town, the buildings grew less and the area more open.

Several large forges were burning into the night and even in the thunderous skies Ar'ye could hear the ringing of the blacksmiths' hammers. The fires from the forges lit up the area to such a degree that Ar'ye was forced to climb higher into the dark night sky to escape possible detection by any would be sky watchers. Several soldiers milled about each blacksmith, waiting for their armour and weapons to be repaired.

With the increased light, however, he was able to see much greater detail below him.

Behind the forges, but still within the fence that surrounded the town, was a huge pasture, at least ten acres of open grassland and within it were the objects of their search—horses. And at least one hundred of them, thought Ar'ye excitedly. No one would miss five.

However, with the increased light, Ar'ye was also able to see the mounted patrols riding the inside and outside of the town's fence, as well as the guards' barracks stationed all around the forges and entrance to the pasture.

Circling almost one hundred feet above their heads, Ar'ye took as quick and accurate count as possible of the forces below and then streaked back to his waiting comrades.

Salena's heart beat quickened and her breathing began to become irregular with anticipation.

The Wraulls were scurrying about, taking up a defensive position where they stood. Henaach barked out orders she couldn't understand in the rough Wraull tongue. Moments earlier, immediately after the first scream, he had driven a large stake deep into the ground, about which was the leash Henaach kept her on. With her mouth gagged, hands and feet bound, Salena waited anxiously to see what would happen next.

The Wraulls were very unhappy about being caught unawares in the open and despite not knowing their language, Salena was sure she could tell a curse when she heard one.

It was dark now and Salena knew that that would put the Wraulls at a greater disadvantage. In the dim torchlight she was able to take a quick head count and found that two Wraulls were missing from the original number. That would confirm the shrieks she had heard.

Secretly she hoped that Duncan and the others had found her and this gave her new hope but she could not call out to warn them. She feared that the odds may be too great against them, each Wraull as big as or even bigger than Martyl, let alone Duncan or the Dwarves.

Still, she knew of no one who had the fighting prowess of Duncan and Martyl and she would not give up hope. She did not come this far to be given to the Black Paladin by his foul servants.

She had to help the others. She must! Struggling to free herself, Salena worker her wrists back and forth in a circular motion, completely oblivious to the commotion going on around her.

The ropes were coarse and unyielding, cutting into the soft flesh of her wrists. Still Salena would not stop and she worked feverishly against her bonds.

"Sit still, girl, or I'll slit your throat for your troubles."

It was Henaach, his rough voice and foul breath telling Salena he was behind her, leaning over her.

"Ogres are upon us. You won't fare as well with them. Pray we protect you."

With a huff he was gone again, as were Salena's hopes. From the sounds of the chaos about her, she knew the Ogres were not a threat to be taken lightly. And as for a fate worse than what she was facing now, she couldn't imagine that. She knew now that it wasn't Duncan and the others come to rescue her, her false hopes fading again.

Her wrists were raw and bleeding from a seemingly useless attempt at escape. Screams rang out all around her now, accompanied by the ringing of metal on metal and the sickly crunch of metal on bone.

Again Henaach's voice rang out above the din, his patrol gathering about him, leaving Salena in the open now. Apparently she was expendable at this point, she thought to herself.

Seeking refuge or shelter of any kind, Selena crawled about on the ground, trying to get as far away from the raging battle as possible.

Rough guttural voices, deeper than those of the Wraulls, rose in volume and strength, pressing nearer and nearer.

From high above, Salena heard the shrieks of the two falcons as they plummeted earthward, talons and beaks raking and tearing at the Ogres.

These new noises were all too close for Salena and she lay flat on the earth, trying to look as invisible as possible in the darkness. A moment later she heard a loud shriek, not like any of the others, followed by two soft thuds on the ground by her feet.

Rolling over to look, Salena saw both falcons, bodies crushed, laying in the short, bloodstained grass.

A cold shiver ran up her spine and settled in the pit of her stomach. The realization of the fact that these could very well be her last moments alive tore through Salena. With a renewed fury, she worked feverishly at her bonds yet again, panic beginning to take control of her actions.

Gone were the sounds of the battle and the screams of agony around her. Gone were the thoughts of anything except escape.

Quickly now, she told herself, quickly. I must go now!

The ropes cut deeply into her skin and the blood flowed even more freely but still she did not stop. With the determination of a terrified animal, Salena at last wrenched her hands free of her bonds, her mind totally oblivious to the white flashes of pain that coursed through her beaten body.

Not wasting precious time with her gag, Salena immediately set to work untying her legs. With a labourious, frantic effort, she was free and on her feet in a few short minutes. Stumbling on her legs that felt like leaden rubber, Salena set off at a fast walk, the best pace she could manage in her condition.

In the dark and confusion of the battle, she didn't know where to go—just away from the noise. Chancing a look over her shoulder for any signs of pursuit, Salena saw none, nor did she see the uneven ground before her.

Down she went in tangle of arms and legs, her body rolling twice before coming to a stop. Raising herself to her hands and knees, Salena greedily gulped air, her exhausted body needing the precious oxygen more than ever. With a supreme effort, she stood, only to be knocked down from behind.

"Going somewhere, girl?" growled Henaach.

Thirty minutes after he had left, Ar'ye returned to his friends on the hill top. As gently as a small bird, he landed behind them, only the cats noticing his arrival until he spoke.

"It is as you said, Rorn. The horses are in a huge corral on the south end of town. However, there are mounted patrols both inside and outside the fence around the town. There are also a dozen mounted guards at the entrance to the town."

The Dwarves just nodded stoically, already suspecting as much. They did not even say anything when Ar'ye told them of the burning blacksmiths' forges all around the entrance to the corral, taking away from the cover of darkness. At last Ar'ye finished his detailed description then got into what the Dwarves viewed as most important—tactical information.

"It would be nearly impossible for the five of us to successfully attack the dozen mounted guards and acquire their mounts. I have only three arrows left and that would still leave nine guards. I think it best if we cross the plain below giving a wide berth of the gate. We could quickly cut our way through the fence at an unprotected point to gain access to the town. From there we could use the deserted town buildings as cover until we reach the forges and the corrals."

"I still think this is too risky," muttered Rorn, shaking his head disdainfully.

Dirn stood quietly stroking his beard with one hand, thinking the possibilities over to himself.

"We have no other choice," growled Martyl, becoming irritable with the irascible Dwarf. "We've come too far to turn back now. Ar'ye's plan is as good as any. We need the horses to make up time. We must go in."

A loud burst of thunder cracked overhead and a brilliant flash of white light illuminated the near blackness for a brief moment. It did nothing to assuage Martyl's fear for Duncan when he glimpsed his forlorn features. Yet again he began wondering what would befall his young friend. He had an uneasy feeling this night but they couldn't wait. He would not let anything happen to Duncan, he tried to reassure himself. He couldn't.

Raising himself to his full height of well over six feet, Martyl towered above the others and in his most commanding tone continued, "We will go in now. Ar'ye, fly ahead of us about one quarter mile to scout any danger. If there is none to be seen, continue ahead. I will lead the four of us, Big Cat at my side for extra sensing. Duncan and Patches will follow with Rorn and Dirn bringing up the rear.

Ar'ye, lead us to the quickest and easiest way through the fence. Any questions?"

No one said a word, everyone already moving into position.

"Then let's be off."

The small group started off at a fast pace, eager to cover the open plain before they were sighted or caught in the open during the coming storm. Within moments, Ar'ye was lost from view, winging his way ahead of his friends in an effort to detect any armed patrols before they did.

Many times Martyl wanted to look back and check on Duncan but he couldn't afford to, not yet anyway. Besides, he told himself, he had Patches for protection, and that cat was more than a match for any one of them.

On they crept, slinking as low to the ground as possible while still maintaining a respectable pace. Ar'ye had not returned yet and they had been underway for almost ten minutes now.

We should be over half way there, thought Martyl. Ar'ye should be back with an entrance route soon. If he wasn't, they would march right up to the front gate of the town very soon. And that would not be good.

The wind began to pick up again, sweeping down off the hilltop behind them and driving into their backs. Several times it gusted with such force the tall blades of grass whipped against the small party, threatening to cut their exposed skin.

Another thunderous boom reverberated across the night sky and with it a deluge of rain. Everyone pulled their forest cloaks tighter about themselves, trying their best to stay dry. The cats growled softly in annoyance, not at all enjoying the weather.

With agonizing slowness they trudged on, the ground beneath their feet becoming waterlogged and soggy. The grass and lush vegetation sagged beneath each person's weight, sucking their feet in and holding on with amazing tenacity. It became an effort just to keep moving. Only the cats seemed unaffected by the muddy terrain, their broad paws easily supporting their large bodies on the weak earth.

Moments later a huge, shadowy shape could be seen looming out of the darkness ahead. Immediately Martyl called a halt and motioned everyone down into a kneeling position, already realizing where they were. A series of lightning flashes streaked across the clouds overhead and in the brief moment of illumination Martyl saw what was before them.

Ignoring the mud they were in, Martyl dove to the ground immediately, motioning for the others to follow. In complete silence, everyone followed his lead and flattened themselves as close to the ground as they could, their brown cloaks blending in perfectly with the mud. Even the cats complied, however uncomfortable they may feel in the mud.

"Equilon is before us," whispered Martyl, hoping the others could hear him over the wind. "Maybe only two hundred yards. It is hard to tell in the storm."

"Yes, I saw it too," replied Dirn in a hoarse voice that passed for a Dwarven whisper. "I also saw many armed horsemen before the gate. I hope we were not spotted."

"We cannot lay here waiting in the mud like swine waiting to be discovered," growled Rorn, obvious irritation showing in his voice. "Ar'ye must have been found or he would have been back by now. We must go."

"We've got to go forward, not back," replied Martyl, knowing that the Dwarf was implying they turn around and leave.

"I'm not losing anyone else," snapped Duncan, speaking for the first time since that morning. "I'm going in there, with or without you."

Even in the dark, Rorn could tell Duncan was staring at him, defying him to stop him or say anything else. His face flushed red with anger but he held his tongue in check. Barely out of his boyhood, Duncan along with his cats, had travelled through hundreds of mile of unknown land, slain a Demon and gained the respect of the Dwarf King Balamir. Rorn remembered this, and the ever present knight and decided he would see this foolhardy plan through, even though it went against all his common sense. Although he would admit it to no one, Rorn was beginning to feel a grudging respect to Duncan.

"Very well," growled Rorn. "We skirt to the west of the town and hope to find a section of the fence free of mounted patrols. The fence was built solely to keep horses in the town, not for defence as Equilon had no enemies until the Black Paladin. Going through it should pose no problem."

Smiling to no one but himself in the dark, Rorn patted the massive, double-headed battle axe securely strapped to his back to prove his point.

"Good," snapped Duncan, not bothering to hide the irritation in his voice.

Again Martyl fought back the feeling of impending danger towards Duncan, wishing he could trust his young charge's actions in the hours to come.

"Follow me," he whispered to the others behind him.

Lying flat on their stomachs to avoid possible detection this close to the town, the four men and two cats wriggled at a snail's pace across the muddy plain.

Everyone was soaked and irritable now, the rain coming down in sheets and saturating the ground beneath them. Mud splashed up off the ground into their mouths and eyes, the rain coming down so hard at times. Thunder continued to roll through the dark night sky, heralding its arrival with gigantic booms.

The Dwarves cringed with each one, remembering all too well the Wraull war drums booming day and night just outside their mountain home. Each successive crash of thunder only helped harden their resolve to see this mission through and return home to help their brethren.

Barely audible at first to anyone but Patches and Big Cat, a faint beating of wings travelled to the party in the mud. Following Big Cat's gaze, Martyl glanced up into the black night sky and moments later a shadow was seen heading their way in the sky from the direction of the town.

"The storm slowed me," gasped Ar'ye, setting down next to Martyl in the mud. He knelt, careful not to get mud on his feathers. "I found a spot where we can enter. The guards at the gate can't see you now and the mounted patrols are weathering out the storm. Hurry."

Not wasting any precious time, Ar'ye took to the air, flying just above their heads as the others got up and ran. The fence about the town was only fifty feet away and despite their fatigue and muddy bodies, the distance was covered in seconds.

Ar'ye flew over the fence, was gone for only a few seconds, then returned.

"No one is in sight or on the other side. Cut through now!"

Martyl nodded in affirmation and Dirn and Rorn removed their axes and set to work. The fence was remarkably strong, constructed of six foot tall wooden beams that were six inches thick, planted side by side in the ground. Planks spaced at two foot intervals in height ran the length of the fence to lend rigidity. In all, the fence's construction resembled a wall more than anything else.

Both Dwarves swung repeatedly at the wood, the broad heads of their axes hewing large chunks of the fence away. Soon a small opening, three feet high and about four feet wide was cut in it.

"That's good," Martyl half shouted above the sounds of splintering wood. "Everyone through the hole. Now!"

Ar'ye kept his aerial vigil as first Martyl, then Duncan and the cats and finally the Dwarves crawled through the opening. When Dirn, the last one through was on his feet, Ar'ye said, "Follow me. We'll head to the corral."

On his feet now, his tired wings tucked in closely to his body to stay dry, Ar'ye led the way through the maze of town before them.

They kept to the side streets and back alleys, moving quickly and silently in the darkness. Rain continued to pelt down on them from above, washing the mud off their clothes and skin.

Although not as large a town as Gullhaven or Calheller by any means, the circuitous route Ar'ye led the party on soon had everyone but Martyl confused as to what direction they were now travelling in. Only his seasoned days as a Royal Knight on errands for his King gave Martyl the tracker's skill required to keep his bearings.

Soon, Martyl realized that they were not travelling closer to the coral but further away and called a halt. Tired, wet and cold, Duncan and the Dwarves slumped against the wall of an abandoned shop, trying desperately to flatten their bodies closer to it in an effort to avoid the rain. Both cats, their fur already thoroughly soaked, went over to Duncan and tried to follow his lead and seek shelter where there was none.

"Ar'ye," whispered Martyl, keeping his voice down in case a patrol were nearby. "I think that you're lost. I've been keeping a mental note of our journey and we've been in this part of town already."

Ar'ye could see the frustration in Martyl's weathered face as the rain ran down it, following decades old, wind swept cresses in the bronzed skin. He felt embarrassed and ashamed yet he knew that all their lives depended on him at this point.

He swallowed his pride and replied, "Yes, I'm sorry, Martyl. From the air, everything looked different. And now there is the storm."

He hung his head in shame, the rain pouring down his soaked head to join the puddles already at his feet.

"It's okay," Martyl reassured Ar'ye.

He reached out and gripped the other's shoulder in a show of support. He had been careful to speak to Ar'ye apart from the others to ease him some of the pain of admitting he was lost. It also helped Ar'ye to keep the respect of the others.

An alarm call rang out then, louder than the thunder claps overhead, saving Martyl from explaining to the others their current situation. They knew what the alarm was for—someone had spotted the hole they made in the fence to gain entry to the town. Everyone sprang to attention, weapons drawn and at the ready. Heartbeats and pulses quickened, the sound of pounding blood in their ears all that they heard.

Seconds later, Martyl called out, "This way! Now!"

Off he tore, speeding down the near black alley, his booted feet splashing through the muddied ground in a desperate attempt to put some distance between them and their would-be pursuers. Close on his heals followed Ar'ye,then Duncan and the cats, and then Rorn and Dirn bringing up the rear on their short but powerful legs.

Once again, years of battle training came back to him and Martyl knew where to go. From the sound of the alarm horn and the mental notes of the journey through the town, he knew that their entry point into the town was behind them. The clarity of the alarm and its loudness told him that they were maybe a quarter of a mile away. To reach the coral, they would have to elude capture and eventually turn and head to their left, or south, through the town.

Heedless of the noise they made now, the group crashed through alleys and side streets, knocking aside old crates and debris that stood in their way.

Glancing back over his shoulder as he brought up the rear, Dirn spotted several bright lights bobbing up and down behind them. Soon they were joined by loud, angry shouts and more lights.

"We have pursuers!" shouted Dirn to the others. "There are at least a dozen torches behind us and their numbers are growing!"

"Keep moving!" Martyl shouted in return.

He took a quick left turn that was so sudden and abrupt that Ar'ye ran past the alley Martyl ducked into. Duncan slammed into Ar'ye full tilt as he too missed Martyl's turn. The cats were quicker and rounded the alley without missing a step but they stopped to check on Duncan.

"I'm okay," he reassured them, and himself, as he picked himself up.

"Come on, get moving," growled Rorn as he grabbed Duncan's arm and propelled him after Martyl.

Dirn offered the fallen and winded Ar'ye a hand, yanking his large body to its feet without any effort. Using the burly Dwarf for support, Ar'ye hobbled down the alley after the others. Within a few moments, his breath and strength returned, allowing him to keep up on his own.

In the blackness of the night the group could not tell how far the alley extended, their eyes only able to make out what was directly in front of them. The sounds of pursuit were all about them and closing from all sides. After a few more minutes of running the alley, Martyl skidded to a halt. In front of him was a stone wall, sealing off the exit of the alley. Upon closer examination of the alley he realized that the walls on either side of the alley had also been stone for quite some time. During their fear induced run in the darkness no one even saw the buildings change from wood to stone.

"Back the way we came," growled Martyl. "This is a dead end."

"It's no good," replied Dirn. "The guards are already at the mouth of the alley. Look at the torches."

Everyone glanced back down the alley. Dirn was right. Dozens of torches blazed like beacon fires in the stormy night sky. Another flash of lightning lit up the sky momentarily as if the heavens wanted them to have a last look at what they faced. Displeased as they were, the party didn't waste the opportunity they were given. Even through the sheets of rain coming down on them, everyone clearly saw the small army marching down the alley towards them.

"Ar'ye, try and hold the guards as best you can with your remaining arrows," commanded Martyl. "The rest of us will try and find a way out of here."

"That's suicide!" shouted Duncan.

"Don't worry, we're not leaving him behind," added Martyl. "We're in this together."

Stepping forward, Ar'ye fired off his last few arrows, deftly dropping three guards. The others slowed but still kept coming.

Shouts from their pursuers were growing even nearer now, only a few hundred yards away. The growing torchlight cast numerous shadows against the alley walls, making them come alive with an evil all their own.

Above the din, Ar'ye heard something else, something strange, and he mentioned this to Martyl, not wanting to leave his companions alone. The cats heard it too and began pacing back and forth by a storm drain on the east wall of the alley.

"What is it?" Martyl asked, quickly growing impatient.

Everyone followed him to the storm drain, Dirn and Rorn walking backwards, their heavy battle axes ready, eyes never leaving the confrontation marching towards them.

Shouts of, "I see them!" rang out over the crashing of thunder and the small army of guards broke towards them, a mere one hundred yards away. The alley was wide enough here for three men to run abreast, weapons drawn, and they did so.

"It's a woman, in the storm drains," replied Duncan, completely dumbfounded.

"Remove the cover and follow me to safety," she told him hurriedly. "Now!"

Chapter Eighteen

Salena lay on the ground, her face buried in the grass to mask her sobs. *I was so close!* she screamed out in her mind. *I should be free!*

Her battered and beaten body could take no more and her once proud spirit was now finally broken. Salena now understood the gravity of her situation and the utter hopelessness of trying to escape. She lay on the ground, still in the same place that Henaach had felled her from behind. She knew he was likely to kill her and she didn't care anymore. Death was a shadow that had followed her for the past several days and now she grew weary of the chase. If this was to be her end then so be it.

"Get up, girl!" shouted Henaach, his foul breath still causing her to wince, even through the sea of pain wracking her body.

Unceremoniously, he yanked Salena to her feet and began tying a rope about her waist. Salena offered no resistance, her mind, spirit and body incapable of functioning anymore. Moments later, her hands were pulled behind her and bound again. This time Salena shrieked in agony, bolts of pain lancing through her wrists to her mind with lightening speed. The rope dug deeply into the flesh of her already raw and bleeding wrists. Like a breath of air to a drowning man, the extreme pain brought Salena back to the world of the living.

Henaach grabbed the back of her head and pulled back as he gave her some more of the foul Wraull drink. This time she welcomed the feel of its fiery tingle spreading through her veins, relieving pain and fatigue, giving her a renewed sense of strength. Henaach, however, did not permit her the time to bask in her new-found relief.

"Get moving, girl," he ordered.

A flash of lightning lit up the dark night sky and Salena thought she saw fear in the hideous Wraull's eyes. Instantly she knew what happened to the other Wraulls. The Ogres had won the skirmish and would most certainly be after Henaach and herself! A chorus of booms echoed across the night sky causing Salena to jump and Henaach to glance about nervously.

Grabbing her by the elbow, Henaach began to march Salena along, eager to put as much distance between them and the Ogres as possible.

The Wraull drink was doing its work on her body, the searing pain in her wrists now just a dull ache and her legs seemed almost fine, for now. Salena wondered what the long term effects would be, knowing that her body needed time to rest and heal its wounds naturally. This drink may be alleviating her pain for now but she was afraid it would extract its toll on her in the long run. There was, however, one immediate benefit of the drink. Her wrists had stopped bleeding, leaving her hands and forearms a red, sticky mess.

Henaach smelled the blood and felt it on his hands where he gripped Salena tightly. It made his blood boil, keeping alive his ancient drive to kill. With great difficulty he fought the desire back. He knew that his master, the Black Paladin, wanted the girl and he would see to it that he received her. But first, they both had to escape the Ogres that pursued them. And the Ogres had to pay for what they did to his patrol.

Wraulls and Ogres were bitter rivals in the Untamed Lands since time immemorial. Each would attack and kill the other any time there was an opportunity. Henaach swore a Wraull oath that he would have vengeance on the Ogres for killing his patrol members. If he could just make it north of the Dead Woods he should be able to hook up with another Wraull Patrol from the Char'nak Mountains. Then he could hand over his worthless human charge and along with a new Patrol, exact his revenge.

Still seething with hatred and rage, Henaach propelled Salena along at what she could only think of as an inhuman pace. The Wraull drink was allowing her already exhausted body to fight on, overcoming fatigue and despair. Her legs did not seem to belong to her anymore, they did the bidding of the Wraull drink.

Henaach knew the frail human woman couldn't go on forever like this, her constitution no match for his. If she died before he could get her back to his Master, he would face a fate much worse than at the hands of the Ogres. With both messenger birds dead, there was a good possibility that his Master may not know that he had the girl. In that case, he was free to do with her as he pleased. Henaach didn't entertain that thought for long. He knew the Black Paladin would find out one way or another that he had the girl and it was that fear of Draskene that made him go after her in the first place, even with the Ogres in hot pursuit.

Still, Henaach knew that she must be given time to rest and heal. Stopping them both for the briefest of moments, Henaach double checked Salena's bonds for tightness, adding another rope that bound her arms to her sides. Without any sign of effort, Henaach grabbed her and, like a sack of flour, flung her over his shoulder and took off at an even faster pace than when she was walking.

On his own, he knew he could outdistance the Ogres, his kind being smaller and quicker than theirs. Henaach also prided himself, as a Wraull, as being more intelligent than the Ogres. Because of their extremely low intelligence, and secretive ways, the Black Paladin had not bothered to enlist the services of the Ogres. The Wraulls worked as troops much better. However, Henaach knew better than to under-estimate his enemy and let his guard down. Ogres could spring an attack quite easily in the vicinity of the dead woods.

The Ogres had paid dearly in lost lives for their attacks on the Wraulls in the past. The Black Paladin had been swift and efficient in dealing with them for attacking the Wraulls, his chosen minions. This, coupled with the age-old hatred between the Ogres and Wraulls, all but ensured that the Ogres would continue to track

Henaach and his human hostage. Henaach knew this but he had another advantage over the Ogres besides his intelligence. It was quite likely the Ogres did not know how many members were in Henaach's party to begin with. With any luck, he and the human girl may not even be pursued. Still he couldn't take that chance, and lumbered on.

Salena, for her part, offered no resistance. She was bound far too tightly to extricate herself. Except for the awkward position of being hoisted over the monstrous Wraull's muscular back, she almost enjoyed the fact that her weary body was allowed a chance to rest and heal. Despite the effects of the Wraull drink working through her exhausted body, Salena gradually began to drift into an uneasy, shallow sleep. Her body's own healing mechanisms along with the Wraull drink worked overtime to repair the damage of the past day's forced march on her.

A loud crack of thunder boomed across the sky, causing Henaach to drop to the ground in search of cover. Salena hit the ground on her back, knocking the air from her lungs so that only a small moan escaped, completely masking the pain she felt.

Henaach was no coward, a Wraull didn't rise to his position by being one, but he was nonetheless on edge after having his entire patrol slaughtered by Ogres. Realizing it was only thunder, he took a quick look around, using the occasional lightning flash to assist his poor night vision. As sure as he could be that there were no Ogres about, Henaach flung his human cargo over his shoulder and set off to the north again.

Within moments, the sky above opened up on them and the storm from the south finally caught up to them. Rain fell in sheets, completely soaking Henaach and Salena in minutes and turning the open plain of the Untamed Lands into a muddy quagmire. For the time being, Henaach was glad for the storm. The rain would wash away any tracks they were leaving behind. However, when the storm stopped and the sun came out the next day, the ground would dry and harden, leaving a trail for the Ogres to follow.

"Come on, now!" the woman implored them. "This is your only chance!"

Duncan stared dumbfounded at the woman in the storm drain beneath them. She was trying to push the drain cover up but from her position below it couldn't gain enough leverage.

Shouldering past him, Martyl grabbed the steel grate with both hands, and with muscles straining, heaved it up and over to the side.

"Quickly now," commanded the woman. "The guards will be on us in no time!"

"Do something!"shouted Rorn, looking at the approaching small army heading their way. They had only about two hundred feet separating them now and the shouts to attack were almost deafening.

Trusting his instincts, and knowing they had very few choices left, Martyl faced Duncan and said, "I'm going down there. If it isn't a trap, I will call for you and the others to follow."

Without waiting for an answer, Martyl dropped through the opening, sword drawn. With a splash, he landed knee deep in a swift flowing river of water rushing to where he didn't know.

Standing before him was a pretty, light haired woman of about his age, early forties. Her hair and clothes were soaked through, showing she had been down here for sometime. Waving a torch she said, "Please, we must hurry. Bring the others."

She had an imploring look on her face and a trusting look in her eye that Martyl felt compelled to follow. With no time to spare, he called to Duncan to have the others follow him.

Keeping the mysterious woman in his sight in front of him, Martyl guarded the sewer as Duncan dropped down, followed by the two cats. Rorn and Dirn dropped down next and then all hell broke loose.

Screams were heard from above and the sound of bodies crashing into the street above.

"Ar'ye!" yelled out Duncan, rushing beneath the open storm cover to peer up.

A sword pierced through the opening, narrowly missing his shoulder. Martyl reached out and pulled him back saying, "Don't be so foolish. He probably flew away. I'm sure those were Prime Guards looking for revenge on their comrades after Ar'ye put arrows in them back in the alley."

More swords were thrust down towards them through the opening, everyone now well away from it.

"I told him to meet us at the corral whenever he could," spoke up Dirn. "The guards were on us too soon for him to get in and he flew up to provide us cover. I'm sure he's safer than us."

As if to add credence to his statement, two Prime Guards quickly dropped into the storm drain, swords drawn. Much too their dismay, they found themselves in the center of the very people they were pursuing. Not hesitating a second, Martyl struck without warning, killing both in seconds before they had time to react.

More swords were thrust downward at them, but to no avail. Soon, rocks and other debris were being hurled at them in an attempt to clear a safe area for more Prime Guards to drop in after them.

"We seem to be safe for the moment," stated Martyl. "The opening in the storm cover is too small for them to come down here in force. However, I'm sure they'll find another storm cover to enter one or two streets over then find their way here. It seems we will have to follow our new friend here."

Everyone turned to look at the woman, her striking beauty out of place in the dark, dank sewers.

"I can get you to the corral if you wish. Follow me." Turning, she began to head off into the tunnels.

"What about them?" asked Rorn, pointing up above to the street. "It will only take a few minutes before they try to send another couple of guards down through there and when they do, they'll know its safe to send everyone."

"We can't just wait here for them to circle us, either," replied Martyl, a weary look crossing his features.

"Don't worry, we'll lose them," called back the woman, her patience clearly starting to wane from the tone of her voice.

"Go on. Follow her," commanded Martyl.

As the others filed past him, he moved beneath the sewer opening and thrust his sword up several times, dueling with the guards above. As the light from their rescuer's torch began to fade in the tunnel's distance, Martyl left the sewer opening and ran after then, hoping the guards would still wait a few more minutes before following them.

Reaching his comrades, Martyl shoved past the two Dwarves at the rear and next past the two big cats to reach Duncan and the mystery woman at the front.

"Who are you?" demanded Martyl, grabbing the woman by the arm and wheeling her about to face him. Even in the dim torchlight he was able to see the beauty and proud character etched in her face.

"I am Reyna," she replied matter-of-factly, "and if you wish to meet your friend at the corral, Martyl, I suggest you and your party follow me now. No more time can be wasted now on idle chatter. We are surely being pursued as we stand here wasting time talking."

Martyl and the others were speechless as the mysterious rescue woman used Martyl's name as if she knew him. Reyna, however, did not waste any more time and true to her word, she set off again, tugging her arm free of Martyl's stunned grip.

As if to accentuate her statement, the splashing of feet in the water could be heard coming from behind them. Duncan and the two Dwarves looked at Martyl, awaiting his decision on this matter.

Martyl just shrugged his shoulders in the growing darkness and said again, "Follow her."

On they sloshed through the town's sewer system, the fetid smells of rotting debris and stagnant water threatening to overcome them at times. Rats, some the size of house cats, scurried about them, gnashing their teeth and occasionally darting out at one of them to protect their territory. Big Cat and Patches, however, were more than up to the challenge and easily kept the rat problem at bay. Each cat merely had to give a quick hiss to send the rats scurrying. Any rats brave enough to venture into reach made a quick evening snack for the cats.

The only positive aspect any of the party from Calheller could see from being in these horrid tunnels was the fact that any sign of pursuit seemed to have died off long ago. Occasionally they would hear the shouts of Prime Guards somewhere in the distance as they continued their search but Reyna seemed to always lead them away.

Martyl wasn't sure what to think of this. He was somewhat distraught over the loss of being able to explain how Reyna knew his name. Any further attempts at trying to get her to talk and explain who and where she was from were met with frustrating replies of, "Silence. We can't let them hear us."

Always thinking ahead, trying to stay one step ahead of the enemy, Martyl tried to think of how this woman could possibly know him and if she were leading them into a trap. As for his name, it was possible one of the others had used it while they were first in the sewer or even above on the street. That had to be. And as for her leading them into a trap, well, she had plenty of opportunities to deliver them to the Prime Guard already if she had wanted to. It was unlikely she was working for another hostile faction. The Black Paladin's forces were the only ones in all the lands at this time, as far as he knew. Could Reyna be part of another group of Renegades like the ones in Gullhaven? Martyl hoped so. That would explain why she was helping them and even offered another explanation as to how she knew his name. Maybe the Renegades from Gullhaven sent word to their comrades here, telling them to be on the lookout for him and his party. After all, with two big cats like Patches and Big Cat, how hard would they be to miss? Having reasoned this out, Martyl felt a little more secure in their current situation. Still, ever vigilant of his young charge, he kept himself directly behind Reyna and in front of Duncan. Just in case.

The Dwarves, accustomed to living and working both above and below ground, were not as disconcerted as the two humans and cats at traversing this underground maze. They both would have preferred the clean, dry tunnels of their mountain fortress over these dank, dark sewers but they would survive. Furthermore, they used their innate Dwarven tracking skills to orientate their position below the town's streets. Conferring together, Rorn and Dirn were fairly sure they were headed, albeit in a circuitous route, to the horse corral. To ease Martyl's worries, Dirn waded up to Martyl to whisper the information to him. Martyl thanked him quietly and believed even more now that Reyna was part of an Equilon Renegade group.

Still, one thing nagged at his mind. They had been down here for about three quarters of an hour at his estimate, and still they had not run into any other people at all. Reyna couldn't possibly be the only person in the town who was free! Martyl didn't like the thought of that very much as it meant no help for their group in the way of reinforcements. However, he was beginning to develop a grudging admiration for this remarkably resilient woman.

If she was indeed alone, she would have to be a very cunning and strong individual. After all, she somehow remained undetected while they had been spotted shortly after their arrival. Albeit she didn't hack a section of the city wall to gain entrance but still she managed to evade capture on her own. Martyl continued to marvel at Reyna's remarkable skills and wanted to get to know her better as soon as circumstances permitted. She could definitely be an asset to their party if she would join them. But then again, what if she wasn't alone? Maybe she had a family to look after. What if this all were an elaborate trap? There still was no absolute proof she was really on their side. Martyl silently chastised himself for getting carried away in his thoughts about Reyna. He should know better! Setting his resolve, Martyl promised himself that as soon as they reached the corral or the nearest possible place with a defendable position, he was going to stop Reyna and demand answers to his questions before they continued on. He didn't want to do that at this very moment because their position in the tunnels was not easily defendable. He wasn't about to risk having the Prime Guard get them just to have his curiosity satisfied. So long as they were headed towards the corrals and there were no immediate signs of pursuit, Martyl was satisfied to follow Reyna.

Meanwhile, Duncan had his own concerns. Just the day before he had lost the love of his life, Salena, and now there was the chance he was about to lose his friend, Ar'ye. Duncan knew that Ar'ye was resourceful and able to look after himself, but still, he was one against scores of Prime Guard. Looking for reassurance, he approached Martyl.

"Do you think Ar'ye is okay?"

"I'm sure he is," replied Martyl, also in a whisper. "He is probably waiting at the corral for us now. At least he didn't have to trudge through these horrible sewers."

As if to make his point, a pack of sewer rats scrambled past the party, chittering and gnashing their teeth. Both cats snarled a warning and Reyna swept her torch at them to fend off any stragglers.

When the last of the rats had scampered away, Reyna stopped the party and said quietly, "We are just outside the corral now. When we enter the street above we will be in a small alley behind one of the blacksmiths' forges. We must be quiet and careful, lest we become spotted by the Prime Guard. The sewers go no further so we must exit now. The horses you seek are just beyond the blacksmiths' forges. We must grab them quickly and be on our way. The Prime Guard ride patrols through here regularly and will not take kindly to our taking of the horses, even if they do rightfully belong to my people."

Reyna had spoken more now than in the whole hour the party had known her and all were quite shocked by her authoritative and straightforward attitude. She spoke with a tone that befit a queen more than a peasant woman in the city sewers.

At least, thought Martyl, she is shedding some light on the mystery of who she is. Once again, he found himself enamored by her attitude and bearing but he had more pressing matters to attend to.

"What exactly do you mean by 'we'?" he asked Reyna. "You have no idea who we are, where we are going or what we are doing. Do not presume to be with us just because you helped up this far. You could be leading us into a trap for all we know right now. Before we go anywhere beyond here, I want some answers from you. Who are you? How did you come to find us? How many others are with you? How do you know who I am?"

Even in the dim torchlight of the sewer, no one missed the icy look that flashed across Reyna's face that moment. Her eyes held each of them, a fire burning inside them that seemed to cause the sewer to glow brighter. A shiver ran up the spine of all four men as Reyna held them in her frigid glare.

Once again, when Reyna spoke, it was in a tone the demanded attention and all four men stared transfixed as this petite, beautiful woman began her story.

"As I told you, my name is Reyna. I live in and around this city by myself. I was a young woman when the Black Paladin's forces took this city almost fifteen years ago now. At the time, my father was head of the city council. He, like all our people, was proud, and could not, in good conscience, allow the Black Paladin to take our beloved horses without a fight. Sadly, we were ill-prepared and overmatched and quickly defeated.

"However, I and many others did escape the initial slaughter. We know these plains well and were able to hide effectively in the small forests near the Sylvan River. We probably would have been safe but we have one weakness. Our lives revolve around our horses. My people love their animals and treat them as family members. We could not stay away from our homeland and so we used to make forays back to Equilon to retrieve any horses we could. Of course, this was perilous and sometimes some of us would be killed.

"Eventually, I was the last person left. It was my love of our horses that kept me going the last three years, all alone."

Everyone stared dumbfounded at Reyna. Duncan's heart immediately went out to her. He was a great animal lover and couldn't imagine being separated from his cats. They were all he had left now that his parents and Salena were gone.

Dirn and Rorn were both impressed also, amazed that a human woman would have such strength and resource.

Martyl too was impressed and now he knew why he liked this woman so much. She had all the qualities of a Royal Knight—strength, resourcefulness and leadership, yet the beauty of a queen. For someone to survive against such odds, she had to be strong indeed!

Not finished yet, Reyna continued, determined to make sure none of the party before her had any doubts.

"Despite your efforts at being stealthy, I saw the hole you cut into the city's fence. From there I entered the city as well, following from a safe distance until I could determine if you were friend or foe.

"I was taken aback when I saw the bird-man and big cats with you but many strange things have been afoot as of late. I see that the legends of the Rey'ak are true after all."

Martyl and the others offered no affirmation to her assumption and without batting an eye, Reyna continued again.

"When I saw that the Prime Guard was on to you and where you were headed, I quickly ducked down a side alley and entered the sewer. That is how I found you. As for how I know you, Martyl, do you forget that easily, Royal Knight?"

Reyna smiled, the warmth in that smile almost taking the damp chill out of Martyl's soaked body. Instead, he just stared nonplused.

"When I was but a girl, not quite into womanhood, I was on a trade mission with my father. We were headed to the village of Norlev to trade some horses for gold and supplies. Our caravan was waylaid by a band of slavers and all was nearly lost until you and another Knight, Baly, I believe his name was, came to our rescue. You were but a young knight then, barely older than I was. I never forgot that day, Martyl, and always hoped I could repay you some day."

Like a storm rushing in, Martyl's memory flooded back to him. Of course, his memory screamed out! That is why she looks familiar to me and how she knew my name. In his mind's eye, he could see Reyna, over fifteen years ago, sitting on her horse, her long golden hair blowing in the soft breeze, and blue eyes flashing in the sun. Then, as now, he was struck by her stunning beauty and strong, all business attitude.

Interrupting his happy memory was the sadness at the loss of his friend and mentor, Baly. It was less than a year later when he had been killed defending the King from Draskene's forces.

Fighting back the bitter memory and the pain associated with it, Martyl replied to Reyna, "I remember now, Lady Reyna. Please forgive me for being so rude earlier. It was just that under these circumstances and all that has happened recently ..."

"No apology necessary, Martyl. All I ask is to go with you and your party. I have lived here alone long enough. As much as it pains me to leave my home, I can hopefully perform a service somewhere else."

"We would be honored to have you with us, my Lady," Martyl said with a sweeping bow. "Now let's see about getting out of these storm sewers and onto some horses."

Chapter Nineteen

On he lumbered, the weight from the small human woman he carried on his shoulders barely registering on Henaach's mind. He had more important things to worry about, such as the possibility of Ogres following them. If they could just make it to the Dead Woods, they may be able to take refuge from the Ogres, if any were following.

Henaach couldn't be sure if the Ogres were after them or not. He knew Ogres were tenacious and unlikely to allow them to escape without a determined chase but he did manage to snatch up the human woman and disappear into the dark with her as the Ogres butchered the last of his patrol.

Anger and hatred at their loss burned in Henaach, driving him onward. He hated running from anything but he did know when to cut his losses. His entire patrol was slaughtered by the Ogre ambush, and he was barely able to escape with his life. His one consoling thought was that he managed to kill more than a few of their attackers himself. If he was able to make it to the Dead Woods he could hopefully find another Wraull Patrol to aid in his revenge.

The rain continued to pelt down on him and his human prisoner, turning the ground beneath them slick and muddy. Soon, even Henaach's superhuman strength was reaching its limits. Several times he slipped and staggered on the slippery, mud soaked grass, catching his balance at the last second. The next time, however, he wasn't so lucky.

Henaach stepped into a foot-sized depression, and went down hard, his leg sliding up to the knee in the muddy hole. Salena flew from his shoulders and hit the ground hard with a scream, jolted back to reality by the firm ground beneath her.

Henaach cursed, then ordered, "Shut up, girl. There may still be Ogres about."

In the storm induced blackness, his poor night vision was reduced to but a few feet in front of him. To top it off, his expert sense of smell was greatly hampered by all the rain and high winds.

Salena tried to stifle her moans and sobs, knowing all too well what would happen if she drew the big Wraull's anger on herself.

Henaach rose to his feet, slowly, he himself feeling the effects now of nearly two days forced march, carrying a human female and a battle with Ogres. He opened his flask and took a long hard drink of his healing liquid. Putting it back, Henaach marched over to Salena and unceremoniously yanked her to her feet. Attaching a rope between the two of them, binding them at the waist, about two feet apart, he said, "You're walking again. Stay in front of me. Let's go."

On they marched into the night, Salena trying desperately to keep pace with the larger, stronger Wraull. Her raw and blistered feet were now bleeding. The blood seeped through her worn and tattered water-logged leather boots, puddling in each footprint she left on the softening earth. Several times she fell, getting dragged behind Henaach a few steps before he would grab the rope and pull her to her feet.

Salena had been through a lot in the past few weeks, seeing and enduring a great deal of hardship. She was by no means a weak person but everyone had limits, and she now felt hers approaching. Images of Duncan, his boyish smile lighting up his face, crept across her vision. She saw him playing with Patches and Big Cat and smiled at how a complete stranger to her land could inspire the loyalty of the animals, native to her land. And, of course, steal her heart. A tear left the corner of her eye as she realized she would not see him again, at least in this lifetime. Salena did not want to give up, she was a fighter, but she didn't want to be given up to the Black Paladin, either. Besides Duncan, there was her own people to think about and their possible detection. Slowly her body began to register less and less of the pain, Salena's eyes closed, her strong spirit as last giving up. As her legs crumpled beneath her, her last breath whispered, "Good-bye Duncan. I love you."

Draskene had spent an entire day and night in his personal library, perusing all the books he could possibly think of that may contain information, no matter how minute, on a missing island kingdom. In the end, all he had was what he started with—a story, given by a half-mad, all-drunk sea captain about a lost island several weeks sail from here, inhabited with beautiful people who liked to sing.

This information was not very helpful in itself, realized Draskene. There was no mention of whether the old captain had sailed west, north or south from Gullhaven. The ocean was vast, too vast for even one with Draskene's power to scour indefinitely. If only he had more information.

Then something triggered a memory in his mind. The two Prime Guards who were defeated on the Thunder River by a woman said she tried to "sing" to them. Could this have anything to do with the old captain's tale? Draskene knew it was a stretch, but still, it was an odd coincidence, and he didn't like to believe in coincidences. All things happened in a logical sequence. You just had to figure out the sequence and why!

Then another memory came to Draskene. His spies in Calheller had reported to him in their fashion that the woman traveling with Duncan and Martyl was strikingly beautiful and had webbed fingers. The old story had mentioned the beauty of the mystery people and their love of water. Another coincidence?

Not likely, thought Draskene. It was most likely that a race of people who enjoyed the water and spent a great deal of time in it would over time adapt to life in it. Like having webbed hands, and most likely feet, to aid in swimming.

Draskene smiled to himself, pleased with his own deductive thought processes. Now it was all that much more imperative that the woman traveling in Duncan's party be brought back to him, *unharmed.*

Reaching out with his mind, Draskene's consciousness traveled the psychic link that bound his faithful servant to him like an ethereal rope.

Bin's servants should have returned by now, thought Draskene to himself, after summoning Bin. I must know if the woman has been seen or captured yet.

Draskene left his study, for the first time in over a day, and headed back to his private chambers, where Bin would be waiting for him.

Upon his arrival, Bin bowed, replying to his summons, "Master."

"Have your servants returned yet?" demanded Draskene, not wasting time on pleasantries.

"I sent my best two falcons to contact Henaach, the leader of the Wraull Patrols along the Thunder River and Untamed Lands. It has been nearly two days now and I haven't heard from them yet." He kept his eyes downcast, fearing his master's reprisal for not having his information.

"It is imperative that word is sent to the Wraulls that the woman is NOT to be harmed, and is to be brought back here at ANY cost. It that understood?!"

"Yes, master," replied Bin. "I will send out more messengers at once."

Bin headed for the door and continued on to the castle courtyard where his own private, converted stables lay. Upon entering he called for Frost, the largest of his winter-wolves to come forth.

The big wolf approached him, nuzzling its head into Bin's side, seeking his usual treat.

"None today, my friend," stated Bin, not wasting any time. "It's VERY important that you find Henaach and give him the message again. The woman is to be brought here, immediately, and unharmed."

He tucked the written version into the wolf's collar, not having to bend to reach, his neck above Bin's waist.

"Now be gone—hurry!"

With an ear-splitting howl, the huge wolf raced from the stable, a white streak in the torch-lit darkness.

Martyl looked up through the sewer cover opening into the rain streaked street above him. Surprisingly, the street was well lit, by the blacksmith forges Ar'ye had told them about after his reconnaissance flight over the town earlier.

Unfortunately, he could not see well enough from his current position to see if there were enemies near by.

"I can't get a good enough view to see if it is safe to leave here," he told the others.

"This is a dead-end street," replied Reyna. "I would not lead you to a compromising position."

Martyl looked at her in the torch-lit sewer tunnel, trying one last time to see if he could see any deception in her face. After a moment, he realized they had no other choice and called the Dwarves over to him.

"I will need a boost to get up to the cover and remove it."

Rorn dropped to one knee, his hands laced together before him and said, "Here. Be careful, Martyl. We still don't know what is up there."

His distrustful nature of the race of man made him give Reyna a last scornful look.

Stepping into Rorn's hands, Martyl was hoisted up. Dirn grabbed his free foot to provide extra support and lift. As Martyl muscled the sewer cover off from below, he marveled at the strength and the sturdiness of the two Dwarves holding him up. They were as solid and unyielding as two stone pillars!

With a stifled grunt, Martyl at last had the cover off and slid it across the street. Carefully, he poked his head out far enough to see above the street level. It was well lit by the blacksmith forges and was indeed a dead end behind him. Before him, it opened into an intersection that had three different routes, all of which appeared clear at the moment. To his left were more old, abandoned shops. To his right were the forges and over the crackle of the burning fires he could hear horses neighing and whinnying over the storm.

"It appears safe," he at last called down to the others. "Send up Reyna then Duncan. After they're up, we'll help pull you two up."

Martyl pulled himself free of the sewer, glad to at last be away from the oppressive smell and tight, dark confines. He sat in a crouch, his eyes continually watching the street ahead for any signs of their pursuers. Occasionally he glanced skyward, hoping to spot Ar'ye.

A few moments after Martyl had extricated himself from the tunnels, Reyna appeared in the sewer opening and Martyl gave her a hand in pulling herself up and out. Again he found himself marveling at her beauty as the firelight from the forges sparkled in her sharp blue eyes.

Not one to shirk his duty or responsibility, Martyl only looked for a second or two before returning to the sewer opening to aid Duncan in exiting the tunnels.

Next, Rorn and Dirn each grabbed one of the cats and lifted them up to the opening. Duncan, laying in the mud, reached down and first lifted up Big Cat then Patches. Both cats remained calm, just glad to be out of the smelling sewers.

"Keep a careful watch on that street intersection ahead," Martyl told Reyna, "while Duncan and I help the Dwarves up."

Patches and Big Cat instinctively stood guard with Reyna, one on either side of her, their golden cat's eyes never wavering from the street ahead.

Martyl knew this was the most dangerous part yet, as it would leave them vulnerable to attack, yet they had no choice. Dirn and Rorn were too short to reach to the street level from the sewer without help.

Lying flat on his stomach in the muddied rain-soaked street, Martyl lowered his body from the waist down into the sewer. Duncan sat in a crouch, holding his feet, ready to pull him back when told. Rorn was closest to Martyl and grabbed his hands in his. Duncan, sensing the extra weight, dug his heels into the muddy street and strained to pull the man and Dwarf back. Martyl pulled upwards and raised Rorn to a position where he could grasp the edge of the street himself. Using only his powerful arms, Rorn hoisted himself up the rest of the way.

No sooner was Rorn out of the sewer that he took Martyl's position, leaning half-way back into the sewer to pull his friend up. Martyl hung onto the stout Dwarf's legs while Duncan joined Reyna and the cats on guard duty.

Within moments, Dirn was free from the sewers also and the entire party regrouped in the shelter of a shop overhang, as far from the light of the forges as possible.

"Reyna," began Martyl, "I assume the horses are in a corral behind the forges, from the sounds I hear."

"Yes, they are," she replied. "And the only entrance now is through the gates at the end of that street." She pointed to the street that turned right off the one they were currently on. Continuing, she added, "It is always heavily guarded and now will most likely be doubly so since the Prime Guard know you are here."

"What will our approach be like up to the corral gates? Do they have an easily defendable position? How soon after we turn onto the street will we be noticed?"

Martyl had to know the answers to these questions before they could go on so he could devise a plan to give them the best possible chances of success. If only Ar'ye were here, he could fly overhead and give an accurate account of what lay ahead, thought Martyl. He was now beginning to wonder if he had made it away when they escaped to the tunnels. Martyl saw Duncan looking repeatedly to the night sky, searching for any sign of his friend. Placing a reassuring hand on Duncan's shoulder, Martyl said, "I'm sure he'll find us soon. Give him time."

After a moment's thought, Reyna replied to Martyl. "The corral gate is about two hundred feet past the intersection. The entire street is wide open, big enough for six horsemen to ride abreast in. It's well lit by the fires from forges, and I fear we will be spotted the moment we turn onto the street."

"This is a fine turn of events," Dirn snarled. "I didn't like this plan from the very beginning. We could have been skirting the Dead Woods by now if we didn't come here!"

Martyl didn't like their current situation any better, but he wasn't about to let his fear and anger get the better of him.

"I know the odds aren't good, but we have no other choice at this point," he replied.

"Maybe I can help some more," Reyna countered, a smile crossing her wet features.

From beneath her rain soaked tunic, she produced two small flasks, each about twice the size of her fist.

"I'm no trained warrior like you four but I have learned a few things about survival on my own. These are flasks of torch oil. I keep them handy in case of emergency, like this one."

Martyl was beginning to like Reyna even more, her resourcefulness seeming to never end! He knew exactly what she had in mind—throw the oil flasks into the forges and they would explode, killing the Prime Guard if they were close enough, or at the very least, providing a valuable distraction!

The others knew what she had in mind also and even the Dwarves began to admire Reyna a little more. She was indeed resourceful.

"Alright then," Martyl began. "We have an equalizer now. We must act quickly before any reinforcements arrive. We will approach the intersection cautiously, assess the situation and then make our final choice for a plan of action."

Everyone nodded in agreement then headed down the street. Martyl led, followed by Duncan and the cats, then Reyna and lastly the two Dwarves. Lightning flashed in the rainy night sky and thunder boomed all around them. The rain continued to pelt them mercilessly, soaking everyone right through.

After a few tense minutes of creeping in a low crouch, trying to stay as close to buildings as possible for cover, they reached the intersection. Martyl held up his hand for everyone to be still and cautiously peered around the corner of the last building. It was just as Reyna had told them—the street was wide, wider than the rest and extremely well lit by the forges. At the far end was a large gate leading into the walled-off corral. Martyl didn't like the odds but they had little choice now. Turning back to the others, he told them what he saw.

"The odds could be better," said Rorn with a wry edge in his voice, "but we will follow you Martyl. It may be suicide, but we're in this together." Turning to Duncan, Rorn added, "And I wish your friend Ar'ye was here with us now. We could really use his bow."

"I'm sure he'll be with us soon, Rorn," Duncan replied. "He wouldn't let us face this alone if he could help it."

The others knew his implied meaning behind the words and Martyl was glad to see that at last they were all getting along, as friends. It was just too bad it had to be at a time like this.

Before everyone got too sentimental, Martyl told them his plan for action.

"We will rush out into the street, spread out as much as possible and making as much noise as possible. There is no chance of a surprise attack so we will try to make them think there are more of us than there really is. Maybe that will work to our advantage. When they rush us, I will throw the oil flasks into the fires nearest them. After the explosion, we all group together in a circle, our backs together and take out the remaining guards. When we have a chance, we'll break for the gates. Ok?"

Everyone nodded in agreement, their hands tightening on their weapons.

"Reyna," Martyl began again, "I cannot ask you to put your life in further danger. Stay here until it is safe."

"You saved my life before Martyl and I saved yours earlier tonight. Let me keep the score in my favour."

With a smile, she pulled a long knife from inside her trouser leg. "Besides, I am in this all the way now."

Like any good warrior, Martyl knew when he couldn't win and smiled back.

Chapter Twenty

Now that plans were underway to capture Duncan and this unknown woman who traveled with him from an unknown land, Draskene had other matters to attend to.

It had been several months now since the defeat of his Wraull armies at the hands of the Dwarves. This was a particularly painful thorn in Draskene's side as they were all that stood between him and control of the known lands. Once they fell, he could concentrate his efforts on the races of the unknown lands, such as the Rey'ak and the mysterious race across the ocean who seemed to be in league with Duncan and Martyl.

About the only good thing to come of the battle, thought Draskene, were the capture of hundreds of Dwarves for use as slaves in his war effort. A few had been released, after being placed under a spell, to act as spies in the Dwarf city of Calheller. That was a good stroke of fortune, too, thought Draskene, as it gave him definitive proof that Duncan and Martyl were indeed in his lands, and quite possibly with the help of an unknown race!

Now that the Wraulls had amassed themselves on the Dwarven border, Draskene thought it was time to attack again. The Dwarves needed to fall, now, so he could concentrate his efforts on the Rey'ak next. He knew the two races did not exactly care for one another but his spies in Calheller told him that there was a Rey'ak and two Dwarves with Duncan now who were in search of a lost relic.

He had to conquer the Dwarves and subjugate them before they managed to convince the Rey'ak to help them. It is always easier to conquer your enemies one at a time, he thought to himself, than all together.

This time, he would not accept failure or retreat from his armies. He would change the plan of attack from before and add some Demons for added effectiveness. Demons made excellent killing machines, and helped frighten his Wraulls into attacking his enemies mercilessly, for fear of reprisal from the Demons. However, they cost Draskene a great deal of energy to bring into this place and in multiple numbers they could be hard to contain and keep on target. Then there was always the chance that they could be destroyed, as with Raydon.

That defeat had cost Draskene, as whenever a Demon he brought into this place of existence was destroyed, he lost a bit of his own power. And because of this, he wanted Duncan and his friends to pay dearly.

Gathering up his maps and battle plans, Draskene summoned Bin to him once again. Minutes later, the short, balding servant arrived, out of breath from hurrying.

"Yes, master?" he asked nervously. Bin was forever nervous around Draskene, always fearing he may be mercilessly disciplined for some unknown, or imagined dereliction of duty.

"Have your servants send these plans and maps to my Wraull generals in the Thunder Mountains. They are to attack and defeat the Dwarves at Calheller, two mornings from this upcoming morn. I will send a score of Demons to help them in their endeavor. We cannot afford to fail this time!"

Draskene turned his back to dismiss Bin, who shuddered inwardly at the thought of a score of Demons being unleashed on the lands. He hurried from Draskene's private quarters, the old Royal Chambers, to his faithful animal servants/messengers. They would have to hurry to get to the Wraulls on time. If they didn't he hated to think what his punishment would be.

◆   ◆   ◆

"Now!" shouted Martyl as he leapt out into the fire-lit street. The others followed close behind, spread out across the street, yelling at the tops of their lungs.

The eighteen Prime Guard stationed before the corral gates were shocked, but only for a moment, then they too leapt into action.

Ten Guards on horseback sprang forward, their war horses charging forward with a burst of speed. All ten Prime Guards lowered their pikes, aiming for the chests of their adversaries.

It took only seconds before the distance between the two groups dropped to about fifty feet. Martyl knew it was now or never.

He hurled the first oil flask into the forge just ahead of him on his left then the other into the forge just ahead on his right.

It was too late for the riders to slow or stop their mounts when they realized what Martyl had done. Almost immediately, the intense heat of the forges ignited the oil flasks, exploding their contents outwards. A burst of flame from the left and the right of the riders rushed out into the street, igniting man and horse.

Human and equine both screamed in agonizing pain as the burning oil landed on them, burning and searing flesh. Reyna fought back the tears as she listened to the screams of the horses, their painful torment making her wish she had listened to Martyl and stayed back. No animal deserved this, she thought, although the Prime Guard did.

How many Prime Guard and horses were caught in the inferno they couldn't tell. Martyl and the others knew that the noise and fire would bring the rest of the Prime Guard who were searching for them, down on them soon.

In no time, the fire burned itself down, the combustible oil consumed. Man and horses, in various stages of pre-death, writhed and screamed on the ground, the residual flames still burning at flesh and clothing.

Through the smokey haze, the remaining Prime Guards charged, after waiting what they thought was a safe time period. Jumping over their fallen comrades, four mounted Prime Guards headed straight toward Martyl and the eight guards on foot followed close behind.

"Circle!" yelled Martyl above the noise and confusion. The others rushed to him immediately, everyone standing back to back, weapons drawn.

The horsemen thundered even closer, their lowered pikes less than ten feet away. Martyl knew they had little chance on foot against armed soldiers on horseback and wondered if he had been brash one last time. Still, he was determined not to go down without a fight and he was sworn to protect Duncan at all costs.

Just as he thought the horses would be upon them, Rorn and Dirn broke from the circle, charging forward, yelling their battle cry, "Brey'la!" Their axes were slung across their backs as they sped forward on their stocky but powerful legs.

The mounted Prime Guard did not slow down or pay heed to the battle cry. They thundered forward, steering their horses towards the two crazed Dwarves, hoping to trample them underfoot.

That was precisely what the Dwarves were hoping for too and as the distance between them and the horses fell a few feet, they reached for their battle axes and swung.

Both horses and their riders toppled over into the street, the front legs of the horses severed near the chest. The riders had been so sure they would trample the Dwarves, they kept pikes focused on Martyl and Duncan, not expecting what was to happen.

Just as quickly, the Dwarves ran to the fallen Prime Guards and dispatched them with a neat axe blow to the neck, severing their heads. Their crippled mounts screamed in agony as they bled to death in the street.

Now fully unnerved, the last two mounted Prime Guards and the ten on foot slowed their pace and approached with caution. They had time and numbers on their side and new reinforcements would soon be on the way.

Martyl knew this as well and began advancing, desperate to get their horses and get out of here as soon as possible.

"Attack!" shouted Martyl over the screams of the fallen horses and their riders.

On Martyl's command, the small party broke formation and charged forward, each spreading out to find an opponent. The remaining two mounted Guards charged forward, followed by the eight on foot.

Faster than their comrades, the two cats were the first to meet the oncoming enemy. They each charged straight for one of the horses, hair raised and fangs barred. As the horses reared up to stomp on them, the cats sprang forward, in perfect unison. Their lithe, supple forms arced through the air and collided with the neck and chest of each horse. The horses nickered and screamed as they were clawed and bitten by the ferocious cats. Big Cat and Patches sunk their fangs into the horses' necks, their front claws wrapped around the back of the horses' necks and their powerful rear legs clawed mercilessly at the horses' chests.

Seconds later, the horses toppled over, with the cats springing clear at the last moment, only to circle back and attack the Prime Guards trapped beneath their fallen mounts.

Now with only eight Prime Guards, all on foot between them and the corral, Martyl thought they may actually have a chance if reinforcements didn't arrive too early. He raised his sword and swung at the first Prime Guard to reach him. The man parried his blow than thrust back, narrowly missing Martyl's body. Two more Prime Guards moved in to help the first, forcing Martyl back. He parried two more attacks from two different men and saw the third bringing his sword down for what would be a killing blow when suddenly Reyna was at his side.

She came in low, in almost a crouch and thrust her long knife into the thigh of Martyl's third attacker. With a scream he went down and she was on top on him immediately, plunging her knife into his throat without a moment's hesitation. Years of living on and beneath the streets had taught her to be brutally efficient.

Now Duncan was beside Martyl, on his left, pushed back by two Prime Guards. He was holding his own, as was Martyl, against a superior number of foes, but both knew it was only a matter of time before they tired out. It had already been a long day on them *before* this battle.

Both men were pushed back and separated from Reyna who was just rising to join them again. Martyl, worried for her safety, risked a glance over to where she was. Two Prime Guards were almost on her, swords raised to attack.

"Reyna!" he screamed, trying to warn her.

"Brey'la" he heard in reply as Dirn and Rorn charged through the carnage on the street towards her.

Duncan and Martyl fought side by side as now the last Prime Guard joined the other four in attacking them. It was now five on two and both men were doing all they could to keep from getting circled, which they surely knew would spell their doom.

From above they heard a screeching bird call then one, and immediately after another Prime Guard fell before them, an arrow sticking out of the back of each man's neck.

Now only three on two, Martyl and Duncan redoubled their efforts, pushing back against their attackers. Swords crashed and sparks flew, thrusting, parrying, attacking. Spurred on by the knowledge that his friend was indeed alive, Duncan attacked harder, pushing his adversary back.

Rorn and Dirn occupied the last two Prime Guards, rushing in between them and Reyna, axes swinging before them. The Prime Guard lunged forward, their swords clanging against the dwarves' axes. The dwarves held their ground and were immovable, their corded muscles bulging as they pushed back against the enemy with their axe handles locked with the swords.

Reyna rushed forward, rolling on the ground at the last second behind the Prime Guards. She slashed out at their ankles with her knife as she rolled past. Both men screamed and toppled over to the ground as their ankles gave out beneath them, only to be hacked apart by Dwarf battle axes.

Patches and Big Cat sprang from the fallen horses and their riders and rushed to Duncan's side. In a blur of motion, both cats knocked a man to the ground, claws raking at armor and flesh. Their teeth, however, found a soft throat and bit right through.

The last man standing began backing away quickly with Martyl giving chase, not able to afford to let anyone escape. Before he could attack, another arrow shot through the air and brought the Guard down.

With a loud flutter of wind, Ar'ye set down on the street amongst his comrades.

"I was beginning to think we may have lost you back there," said Duncan with a big grin.

"No such luck, I'm afraid," Ar'ye replied with a smile. "I hid on a rooftop for awhile after you went into the sewers. Then I went in search of some arrows. When I saw the street on fire, I knew it would be you."

"Glad to have you back, Ar'ye," cut in Martyl. "But right now we better get our horses and get out of here. There will be more Prime Guards here in no time. Reyna, can you get us some horses once we get into the corral? And quickly?"

"It shouldn't be a problem," she replied.

"Let's go then," commanded Martyl. "Everyone stay close. When we're all mounted, Reyna will lead the way out of the city. Understood?"

Everyone nodded in acknowledgment and headed for the corral. Martyl opened the gate cautiously then peered inside. There were scores of horses and ponies about, and no guards.

"Go," he commanded Reyna.

Immediately she entered the corral and whistled a tune. Several horses and ponies trotted up to her and she stroked their necks and whispered softly to each one.

"The tack is in that building over there," Reyna said to Martyl, pointing to a small structure in the corral.

"Rorn, Dirn," stated Martyl calmly.

Both dwarves immediately set off at a run for the building to retrieve the tack they would need, their stocky legs carrying them along as fast as possible.

Reyna walked the selected horses and two ponies out to the others and fitted each animal with a bridle and halter.

Martyl, ever anxious of more Prime Guards, kept a watchful eye on the street the entire time. It paid off as, in the fire-lit distance, he saw a number of men marching their way.

"Everyone mount up. Now!" he barked. "More guards are on the way. Reyna, lead the way out of here, but do not get ahead of me."

She smiled at him, knowing he was concerned for her safety and did not want to be too far away to help.

"Don't fear my safety," she told him with a smile. "There are none here who could keep up to me on horseback."

With a start, Reyna spurred her horse, Wind Dancer, forward. This was her chance now to pay the Prime Guard for all they had done to her family and people.

Martyl took a quick glance at the others to see if they were mounted yet then followed Reyna. Duncan and Ar'ye followed, astride horses of their own, followed by the cats and lastly the two dwarves on a pair of ponies Reyna had called over. Onward they charged, their steeds galloping through the body-littered street before the corral gate.

Reyna checked her mount's pace so the others could keep up, not having her experience and confidence on horseback. Ahead of them, shouts rang up from the remaining Prime Guard, over fifty strong, marching and riding up the street towards them.

"The only way out of town is through there!" Reyna shouted over the thundering hooves and sky, pointing straight ahead at the Prime Guard.

"We will have no chance against that many," Martyl shouted back. "Is there no other way?"

"None," replied Reyna, matter-of-factly. "But don't worry. I've come too far tonight to be stopped now. Follow me, keep low over the horse and keep moving!"

Before he could utter a protest, Reyna and Wind Dancer shot away from him and the others, straight into the Prime Guard. Martyl was not sure if she was incredibly brave, incredibly insane or a little of both!

The Prime Guard marching toward them were thinking the same thing. They saw a startlingly beautiful middle-age woman streaking through the rain towards them on horseback, her face set in bitter defiance. Startled, the men on foot scattered like leaves in the wind before her mighty steed. Several of the riders also side stepped out of her way, except for one.

A rider on the largest of the horses strode before Reyna, his sword out and pointed before him. She recognized him as the leader of the garrison stationed here in *her* town. She dug her heels into her steed's sides, her size a good deal below the Guard's stallion. Still, Reyna had no rival on horseback and wasn't about to back away.

The garrison leader was expecting Reyna and her smaller horse, when faced with his larger stallion and drawn sword, to stop or at the very least go around him. She and her horse did neither. Reyna directed her mare straight ahead. At the last second, she veered just slightly to her right. She literally vaulted from her mare's back onto the garrison leader's horse. Landing behind him, on the horse's rump, she startled the big stallion and he began bucking. Quick as a cat, her knife was out and then she slit his throat from behind. Wind Dancer had stopped as soon as she felt the loss of her rider. Reyna leapt back onto her and spurred her forward again. At this time, the Prime Guard were scattering about the street as the big stallion's rear legs flailed about, its rider already on the ground, his flowing blood turning the mud on the street a reddish, oozing mess.

"Follow Reyna!" shouted Martyl over a crash of thunder.

He lowered himself over his horse's neck as he had been told and sped after the fleeing woman who just saved their lives yet again that night.

The others did as they were told and dashed after Martyl who was already into the throng of Prime Guards. Martyl had his sword drawn and hacked at anyone who ventured too close to his speeding steed. A few Prime Guards lost their lives either to his sword or by being trampled beneath the fleeing horses but most had the sense to avoid the mini-stampede barreling down on them.

Duncan followed as close behind as he could, not having been on horseback since he was a very small boy. He clung to his steed's neck as tightly as he could, his legs trying vainly to hold onto the horse's slick sides. He dared not try to swing his sword like Martyl for fear of falling off. He feared being pulled from his mount or cornered but the horse had other ideas. He followed directly behind Martyl and Reyna, not hesitating to trample anything or anyone in his way.

Patches and Big Cat followed Duncan's horse, running as fast as they could to keep up. They snarled and spat as they passed through the panicking Prime Guard, adding to their fear.

Ar'ye and the Dwarves brought up the rear. Ar'ye too was not overly comfortable riding a horse and was doing his best just to hold on at this breakneck speed. The Dwarves, for their part, were fairly accomplished riders. The only reason they were in the rear was because their ponies were not as fast as the horses and partly because they chose to be rear guard. They both swung their battle axes viciously, wading through the Prime Guard and killing as many as they could.

After what seemed like hours to the beleaguered party but what was really only several minutes, they arrived at the town gates. All sentries were gone, the entire garrison, or what was left of it, back several blocks trying to put themselves back together.

Still, Martyl knew that their pursuit was not over yet.

"Very impressive, Reyna," he admitted. "You are indeed an accomplished rider. We must flee to somewhere with cover. The Prime Guard won't be long coming after us."

"There is a small forest to the south of the town," Reyna offered. "We could reach it in less than an hour."

"That's the wrong way for us," stated Rorn.

"We haven't much choice at the moment." It was Martyl again, a pained expression on his face. "The Prime Guard we left behind will only be a few more minutes getting themselves together and after us. Even if we managed to stay ahead of them, they'd follow us to the Iron Hills. We don't want that."

The others nodded in agreement. Except Reyna.

"You go on. I'll lead them away. The storm will wash away your tracks and you'll be long gone before they realize what happened."

"She's right," added Martyl. "Everyone go." He sidled his horse up next to Reyna's. "But you can't do it alone. Rorn, Dirn, watch over Duncan. We'll meet up with you as soon as we can. The Prime Guard, in confusion probably aren't sure how many of us there were. We'll lead them astray while you head for the river. Don't wait for us. Just keep going."

Duncan started to protest but Martyl stopped him. "You know this is how it has to be. Now go!"

He swatted Duncan's horse on the rump, spooking it into a run. He hoped that if he didn't make it back that Duncan would be alright with the Dwarves and Ar'ye. He hated to part with him but this was the best way to protect him in the current situation.

Rorn and Dirn gave Martyl and Reyna their Dwarven salute and Dirn added, with a smile, "See you on the other side, Royal Knight."

The Dwarves may have been taciturn and gruff toward Martyl and the others but they recognized bravery when they saw it. They were beginning to feel more than a little respect for the Royal Knight.

As Martyl watched his friends leave, he wondered if Dirn meant the other side of the river or the other side of life.

Chapter Twenty-One

As fast as they could, the four mounted figures galloped into the rainy darkness before them. Though only on ponies, the two Dwarves had no trouble keeping pace with Duncan and Ar'ye on horseback, as their horsemanship was not very good. Patches and Big Cat brought up the rear. Although they were large and powerful, the four on horseback knew the two cats couldn't keep this pace indefinitely.

No one said a word as they continued on, leaving the frequent thunder crashes to punctuate their silence. They all felt saddened and pained at leaving Martyl and Reyna behind to distract the Prime Guard from following. In just the few short hours they had known her, all of the small party from Calheller had quickly grown to respect her strong character. Even the stoic Dwarves were impressed with her strength and courage, especially the miraculous escape past all the Prime Guard blocking their exit!

Each one of them tried to think of other thoughts, to keep their minds off the probable loss of their two friends but it was no use. Every thought kept returning to the fact that they had mostly likely seen the last of Martyl and Reyna.

Despite his prowess with a sword, his hands, or any weapon for that matter, there was only so much one man could do. And against the thirty or so Prime Guards that still remained, as fatigued as they all were, they all knew what the outcome of the next clash would be.

Still, there was the chance that they could elude the Prime Guard that would be following them. Reyna was an exceptional horse rider, definitely the best any of them had ever seen. If anyone could get away, she could. But there again was the dilemma.

Martyl and Reyna did not want to just leave the Prime Guard behind. They had to be sure that they were spotted leaving Equilon to draw pursuit after them. Everyone knew that their reaching the Iron Hills and finding the lost sword Brach'dir was the most important thing. If some of them had to lose their lives along the way to ensure their objective, that was regrettable, but acceptable.

Duncan knew that was the way the Dwarves saw their mission. But he saw it differently. He had already lost his parents years ago to the Black Paladin and just a day ago he had lost Salena. He couldn't stand to lose anymore people close to him. He was still numb inside at the loss of his dearest friend, and love, and he didn't know if he could ever get over losing her. All he could do to keep going was to think about his eventual encounter with the Black Paladin and the revenge he would extract.

"Ar'ye, do you have any arrows left?" asked Dirn from behind him and Duncan.

"Yes, about two dozen," he replied, a little perplexed. "I retrieved as many as I could while separated from you."

"Maybe you could fly back and make sure we aren't being followed," said Dirn, with a wry grin.

"Yes," added Rorn, also looking a bit mischievous. "And you can make sure Martyl and Reyna can follow us to the river."

When the next bolt of lightning flashed, they all saw an empty horse where Ar'ye had once been mounted.

◆   ◆   ◆

"Get ready to ride," whispered Martyl. Reyna nodded silently in agreement. She knew very well that she and Martyl were most likely going to give their lives so that the others could escape and continue on their journey. Losing her life had not been on her agenda this evening, especially after surviving for so long on her own, but Reyna knew that it was for a good cause. If Martyl's friends succeeded, there was a chance, albeit a small one, but nonetheless a chance, that the Black Paladin would be defeated. If her giving her life to aid their escape could accomplish that, Reyna felt her life would not be lost in vain. Besides, she smiled to herself in the rain, I took care of that pompous Prime Guard battalion leader Graddig myself.

Reyna closed her eyes for a moment to indulge herself in the memory of what she had done. She hated all the Prime Guard, but especially Graddig, as he was this battalion's leader. He was also the man who had killed her father, right before her eyes, nearly fifteen years ago. Even back then, barely older then Martyl's friend Duncan now, she knew that one day she would get her revenge. In her mind's eye, she saw the look of surprise, then terror, in his eyes as she jumped onto his horse and slit his throat.

Before tonight, Reyna had never killed. She always managed to hide from danger in the past, and she knew that was what kept her hidden and alive all these years. It frightened her how easily it came to her tonight. She was killing right alongside these seasoned warriors as if she had been trained long ago to do so. A part of her realized that it was just a natural progression from her running and hiding—from pursued to pursuer. Now she was back to being the pursued.

Reyna glanced at Martyl in the torch-lit dankness. His handsome, weather worn features were covered by shadows and the rain streaking down his soaked hair onto his face. The water followed old lines long since worn into his skin. She saw him tense and place his right hand on his sword pommel as the voices of their pursuers reached them.

She knew he wouldn't be defeated without a big battle and she was determined to stand by his side, win or loose.

With a shout, the first of the Prime Guard on horseback was through the town gate, sword drawn. Six other riders emerged after him, followed by at least twenty on foot, as near as Martyl could tell.

"Ride!" he shouted to Reyna.

She kicked her mare, Wind Dancer, into motion, followed closely by Martyl. The Prime Guard were hot on their heels, shouting orders at them to stop and lay down their weapons. The Prime Guard on foot began to fan out into two different lines, leaving only the area north to the river open and south back to town. Three of the mounted Prime Guard spurred their horses ahead, splashing furiously through the water and muck on the ground. Soon they were in front of Martyl and Reyna who where trying to ride as circular a course they could to give Duncan and the others enough time to have their tracks rained out.

Martyl and Reyna reined their horses back as they saw the Prime Guard ahead of them. They wheeled their mounts around and headed east, only to be cut off by a fence of bristling swords and armor, the Prime Guard on foot marching towards them.

Martyl whirled his horse about and headed to the west, followed by Reyna. Before long, they encountered another line of armed Prime Guard, pushing towards them.

As another bolt of lightning lit up the stormy night sky, Martyl took a quick look at their situation. The Prime Guard had now encircled them, on horseback and foot, and was marching in, ever-tightening the noose.

Wind Dancer and Tarna, Martyl's steed, began to snort and paw at the spongy earth beneath them. They too sensed the impending doom about to befall them. They may not have understood the human element of the fight but they felt their riders' fear and knew something bad was about to happen.

The Prime Guard on foot stopped, forming a large circle, about sixty feet in diameter, as best Martyl could tell through the rain. All were armed with long swords, pikes and shields. The mounted Guards rode about the outer circumference of the circle, also armed with pikes, long swords and shields.

Martyl continued to watch, his horse Tarna slowly shifting about in a circular motion, trying to afford Martyl a complete view of their surroundings. Reyna had Wind Dancer counter their movement in the opposite direction so they could watch different sections of the circle at the same time.

The Prime Guards in front of Reyna broke formation and a mounted Guard raced through the opening, pike lowered and shield raised.

"Martyl!" yelled Reyna in alarm.

Martyl spun Tarna around and spurred him forward. The Prime Guard shifted his direction to come after Martyl and braced himself to impale him on his pike.

In what looked like a suicidal move to Reyna, Martyl raced ahead, sword still sheathed. At the last possible moment, he drew his sword and, in an upward swinging motion, brought the sword from his side. The Prime Guard had his pike leveled at Martyl, expecting him to possibly try and jump from his horse as Reyna had done earlier, so did not expect this sudden sword attack.

Martyl's sword sliced upward, cleaving the wooden handle of the pike in half. As the horses passed each other, Martyl swung his sword backwards at the mounted Prime Guard and succeeded in neatly severing his spinal column.

The Prime Guard, still almost thirty strong, were never-the-less becoming more and more disconcerted. They may have been trained warriors, but most of their battles had been against poorly armed civilians and local militias. It had been many years since they had been faced by the likes of someone like Martyl. To make matters worse, their captain had been slain earlier by a woman! They knew that the two before them and their escaped comrades were no mere Renegades or other such easily defeated opponents. The Prime Guard also knew that they had no choice—they must succeed in stopping these horse thieves at all costs or else payment to the Black Paladin would be with their lives.

This time the circle opened at two ends. A mounted Guard at each opening charged forth, pike lowered and ready to strike.

Reyna and Martyl exchanged knowing glances then trotted apart to meet their adversaries. They both knew they couldn't last much longer.

Reyna urged Wind Dancer into a gallop, steering her directly at her oncoming target. The Guard braced his pike as his horse closed in the distance. Just before his pike was in reach of striking her, Reyna slid off to the left of Wind Dancer, her arms wrapped tightly about the horse's strong neck. The pike passed harmlessly over Wind Dancer's neck. As her feet touched the ground, Reyna used her horse's forward momentum to propel her legs back up in the air. She arced them up over Wind Dancer's back and scissored them around the Prime Guard's outstretched arm.

The speed of the two horses, going in opposite directions and the force of the impact itself, drove both Reyna and the Prime Guard to the ground.

Over the galloping of his own horse in the mud, Martyl heard the crash of bodies behind him. He didn't turn to look. Inside, he felt a coldness in his heart as he realized what had most likely happened. In a blind rage, he pulled back hard on Tarna's reins and then pushed with all his weight and strength on the big horse's neck. Like a sack of wet flour, Tarna went down before the on-rushing Prime Guard.

Martyl quickly rolled free of Tarna, hoping the horse would roll the opposite way as him. Luckily for Martyl, Tarna did, his training expertly done. The Prime Guard was not so lucky.

Tarna went down too hard and fast for the Guard to avoid. His horse skittered to a halt in the slick, shallow mud, throwing him over his lowered head and onto the ground below.

Martyl was on him like a cat, one quick slice of his sword neatly decapitating the prone Guard. With his free hand, Martyl wiped the splattered blood and mud from his rain and sweat streaked face. He was incredibly sore, tired and wet to the bone but only one thing occupied his mind at the moment—Reyna's safety.

Slogging across the muddy field, Martyl saw two figures struggling on the ground. Both were nearly unrecognizable in the dark, covered as they were in mud and clumps of grass. A shriek rent the darkness, as loud as any of the thunder claps overhead. Through the rain, Martyl saw one figure on top of the other, a knife plunged into the chest of the one on the bottom.

A knot tightening in his throat as he rushed forward, Martyl reached the two figures on the ground. As he neared, he saw Reyna slowly removing her knife from the chest of the fallen Prime Guard.

"Get up, quickly," he barked to her as the sound of swords being drawn from scabbards could be heard.

Reyna got to her feet, knife poised and ready to attack. She and Martyl could both see the circle of Prime Guards moving in on them now, coming in for a mass attack, hoping they would be more vulnerable on foot than horseback. Wind Dancer and Tarna pranced about nervously, their keen senses alerting them to the approaching danger.

"Stay near me," Martyl commanded. Reyna nodded in assent, not taking her eyes off the ever-tightening circle.

Martyl and Reyna moved about the inside of the circle, making feints here and there, testing for weakness. The Prime Guard knew they had their quarry trapped and were in no hurry. They were being slow and methodical, leaving no room for error or escape.

At last, feeling desperate and trapped, Martyl lunged at the Prime Guard closest to him. His sword thrust was met with a block by his intended victim, sparks lighting up the darkness around them as the metal blades slid across each other. Again he thrust forward and again his attack was thwarted. Martyl was extremely fatigued and just couldn't put together a combination of moves to finish his opponent.

Now two more Guards moved in, breaking formation to assist their comrade. Martyl swung his sword wildly now, trying to hold back his attackers. He was pressed back further and further, his every move just barely keeping the Prime Guards' swords from slicing him open. Martyl was dimly aware of Reyna being separated from him at this point, hearing a scuffle behind him somewhere.

Suddenly a new sound filled the air. Like the cry of a huge bird of prey, Martyl heard, "Ra'ak, Ra'ak!" and the zing of arrows streaking through the night sky.

"Ar'ye!" shouted Martyl above the din. Two of the Prime Guard trying to circle him were laying at his feet, arrows protruding from their backs. With the last of his strength, Martyl charged his attacker, driving his sword into his body through the leather armor.

Martyl spun around, frantically searching for Reyna. He spied her only ten feet away, bleeding from a cut on her head and being hauled away by two Prime Guard. He knew that the Prime Guard would take her alive if possible, to use as entertainment after the battle.

Heedless of his own safety, Martyl rushed after them. Hatred and rage coursed through his veins, giving him the strength to press on. Prime Guard sprang into view on his path in various numbers and Martyl quickly cut them down. His arms felt like lead and he no longer felt the weight of his sword. He had one purpose left now—to save Reyna, no matter the cost to himself.

Moments later he reached her, slashing the legs of the Guard on his right. The man toppled over, screaming in agony as he lay bleeding to death, his right leg severed at the knee. Without the support of the Guard, Reyna toppled over, too tired and injured to support herself. The other Guard, caught off balance all-of-a-sudden, tumbled over with her.

Martyl was on him in an instant, his knee driving into the Guard's stomach, knocking the wind from him. Too tired to swing his sword, he drove the pommel into the Guard's temple, fracturing his skull. Martyl, barely able to move now, knelt beside Reyna, trying to shield her body with his.

All around them, shrieks of pain rang out as Prime Guards dropped, felled by Ar'ye who could see nearly as well as a cat in the dark. Several times, a Prime Guard came at them, sword drawn and ready to attack, only to be slain by an arrow.

After what seemed like hours to the beleaguered Martyl and Reyna, but in reality Martyl knew from his battle training to be only several minutes, the last of the Prime Guard were dispatched by Ar'ye.

He gently lowered to the ground beside Martyl and Reyna and said with a smile, "We couldn't leave you to fend them off alone."

Martyl was too weak to do anything other than smile and say, "Thanks. Help us to our horses, will you."

It was well into the late night/early morning by the time the battered and tired party arrived back at the river bank. Martyl and Reyna, along with Ar'ye's guidance, met Duncan and the Dwarves, with much fanfare.

Rorn was the lone guard and he greeted Martyl with a wry grin. "Welcome back, Martyl."

"Thanks," replied Martyl, "But we wouldn't have made it without Ar'ye's help and Reyna's strong will."

Rorn acknowledged the other two with the same grin then motioned for them to join Duncan and Dirn, already fitfully resting near the river bank.

"Rest while you can," he said, "It will be light in a few hours and we need to be underway. Besides, I have extra eyes and ears to help me."

Martyl looked to the edges of the sleeping area and saw two shadows moving about and realized that Patches and Big Cat were on constant vigil over them. Feeling tired beyond belief, Martyl acquiesced to Rorn and gratefully spread out on the cool ground with Reyna beside him, glad at last to have some rest.

When morning arrived, the sky was clear again, the rain having stopped during the night. The sun rose over the eastern sky, its warm, yellow rays sparkling on the rain soaked grass and swift running water of the river.

The small group awoke almost as one, each member standing and stretching, trying in vain to assume a position that would keep their wet clothes from touching skin as much as possible. It was a losing battle. Only the cats seemed to be able to dry themselves to any effective degree, their constant preening removing the unwanted, excess water from their fur.

No one spoke much, save for the usual good-mornings. Everyone was still tired and battle weary from the night before. They all shared a hearty meal of cheese, bread, dried meat and water. Their appetites were working in overdrive after the previous evening's activities. When everyone was finished eating, they packed up and mounted the horses.

"There is a ford back upstream," stated Dirn, once they were all on horseback. "We can cross there to the other side. From that point, we must ride north around the Dead Woods, to the southern tip of the Fire Wind Flats, then turn south again and head east to the Iron Hills. This is a longer route than traveling by water, but we no longer have that option."

"Why can we not simply ride through the Dead Woods?", asked Duncan, not caring to spend any longer than necessary to get to the Iron Hills. He had already came a long way and lost so much, he just wanted the journey to be over.

Ar'ye saw the impatient look in the Dwarves' eyes and answered before they could. "There are very dangerous things in the Dead Woods, Duncan. It is likely we would not all make it out. No one enters there lightly unless they are foolhardy. Very dangerous creatures live there. Some even say that creatures from the Black Magic Wars of old found refuge there when the Dwarves and Men banished the Demons from the land. It is best if we avoid there altogether."

"Listen to your friend, Duncan," added Dirn. "He is right. The Dead Woods are not for us. We have no choice but to go around them. And even then, our journey will not be easy. The Wraull homelands are on the Fire Wind Flats and extend into the Char'Nak Mountains. We will have to maintain constant vigilance for any of their patrols. Our best protection is the Dead Woods themselves as the Wraulls will not venture too close to them but as Ar'ye said, there are even greater dangers in the 'Woods. It will not be an easy journey, that much I know for sure."

"So be it," replied Martyl. "We have little choice in the matter. Let us be underway." With that he turned Tarna to the west, heading back upstream to the ford they missed in their haste in the dark two nights ago.

They rode in silence, only the horses making any sounds, snorting whenever one of the cats got too close. The horses were not easily spooked but cats this large could take one of them down and their natural instinct was to avoid predators at all costs. If one of the horses became too skittish, Reyna would ride up alongside and softly whisper in its ear, almost instantly calming it. Martyl could not help but notice the amazing rapport Reyna had with the horses. In face, she had the same bond with them as Duncan did with the cats. He smiled to himself and found his admiration and fondness for her growing even deeper.

In less than an hour they reached the river ford. Here a group of trees from the Dead Woods had been felled, whether by natural forces or something more sinister, none of them could tell, but all felt uneasy. Looking across the river at this point, they could easily see the dark, forbidding growth of old-wood forest. Very little light penetrated the foliage, adding to the dark, mysterious feel of the Dead Woods. Strange sounds emanated from the forest across from them. Blood-curdling shrieks and otherworldly howls permeated the thick woods and traveled across the river to greet them.

The horses began to prance, getting nervous, sensing the danger before them. Patches and Big Cat felt it too, their ears laying back against their heads and their fur beginning to bristle.

"The animals sense the danger and evil ahead." It was Rorn, trying to keep his pony still as it began pacing in circles at the river's edge. "We must remain vigilant at all times, especially at night. There are some creatures here that will venture beyond the confines of the 'Woods into the surrounding countryside in search of new victims." His face contorted to an even more grim visage than usual as he conveyed that last information.

"There are many tales from the past of our Dwarven colony in the Iron Hills being attacked by the horrors of the Dead Woods," added Dirn.

"My people also told us tales when we were young of the evils of this place," agreed Reyna.

"I've heard of them too," added Martyl, "when I was a Royal Knight, years ago. Still, we have no choice but to go this way. Let us begin crossing now, while it is still early."

Martyl dismounted, followed by the others, holding his horse's reins tightly to keep it from shying away any more. He rummaged in his pack and produced some rope. Handing one end of it to Ar'ye he said, "Take this end across the river and secure it. We can use it to help guide everyone across."

Ar'ye took the rope and with little effort, lifted up into the bright morning sky and flew across the river to the far side. Choosing a particularly stout tree trunk, he secured the rope about it and flew back to the others.

Pulling firmly on his horse's reins, Martyl headed toward the water. Duncan followed after him with Reyna closely behind. They made it across with little incidence, the trees damming up the water so it was only knee deep in that area. Rorn, Dirn and Ar'ye followed next, again leading their horses with little problem. Their initial reluctance at approaching the Dead Woods had subsided somewhat but the horses remained wary nonetheless. Their ears constantly swivelled in all directions, vainly attempting to pick up any sounds of danger. Lastly, Patches and Big Cat crossed, waiting as long as they could before venturing into the water, having had more than their fair share in the past few weeks. Luckily for them they were able to cross the fallen trees themselves, their superior balance and agility allowing them to bound from trunk to trunk with minimal contact with the water.

When they were all safely across, Martyl retrieved his rope and stowed it away. "Rorn, you may as well lead us around the Dead Woods to the Iron Hills. My knowledge of this area is not as up to date as yours. Dirn, bring up the rear and make sure no one lags behind. The rest of us will ride in the middle."

Everyone quickly rode into the given formation and Rorn set out, his pony eager to be moving. They kept a steady pace, keeping about a quarter of a mile between them and the forest. Any closer was not too wise but any further away and they risked being caught out in the open by Wraull patrols. After all the combat they had seen the past few days, none of them were too eager to face any more battles.

Chapter Twenty-Two

Thousands upon thousands strong they marched, from the northern Untamed Lands and the flat lands between the Sylvan and Thunder Rivers. Draskene's Wraull forces were vast and powerful. At the head of each of the two legions were the Demons he summoned to lead them, straight from the netherworlds.

These Demons were not as powerful as Raydon had been, for Draskene could not afford that kind of power loss and still maintain control over them. These Demons were merely the weaker type, his human minions who either willingly or by force, gave up their bodies to possession. It required much less power to open a gate to allow in a Demon's essence as opposed to its entire body and mind. However, the Demon also possessed less power this way. Still, these Demons would suffice for what Draskene had in mind—the leading of his Wraull troops into battle against the Dwarves of Calheller.

Both groups of Wraulls had been waiting for this order to attack for some time. They were a warring race to begin with and were natural enemies of the Dwarves. The two races had been fighting for thousands of years since the Black Magic Wars and the Wraulls saw this as their chance to strike a savage blow to their enemies.

They destroyed everything in their paths, vegetation and animal life alike. The Wraulls and Demons had voracious appetites for meat, and the land before them was ravaged.

Each of the two armies moved as a cohesive unit, the Wraull war drums beating a steady rhythm, the troops marching in rigid formation. Miles away the ground shook and vibrated with their incessant onward march. The Dwarves would know well in advance of the impending attack but it would make no difference to them—they had nowhere to run anyway. Their mountain fortress was already surrounded by thousands of Wraulls in the forests around the Thunder Mountains to the east and to the west. That area was already decimated from a previous attack. To escape that way would be suicide as the Dwarves would have no cover, protection or resources to live on and would be cut to pieces by the Black Paladin's human forces to the south and west.

The Wraulls knew they had superior numbers and with the help of the Demons and their magic, they hoped to rid themselves of their greatest enemies once and for all.

The bright, cheery morning sun soon gave way to a glowing yellow blistering sun that drew all the moisture from the air and their bodies. Tired from the previous night's activities, the small group from Equilon was becoming increasingly restless. Having decided by midday that they had put enough distance between themselves and the river, Martyl called a halt to their travels.

"We need to rest awhile," he said as he dismounted from Tarna. "We will need to be as alert as possible come nightfall as we travel this area. There are many dark things that live in the Dead Woods and the area surrounding them."

The Dwarves nodded their agreement as they too dismounted and began eating a mid-day meal of cheese and dried meat, washed down with water.

Ar'ye and Duncan slid wearily from their saddles and sat off from the others, sharing their lunch with Patches and Big Cat. Reyna, always putting her horses first, tended each of their mounts, first watering them by hand from the large flasks she carried on Wind Dancer, then checking their hooves for any signs of damage or abnormal wear.

Martyl offered to help but she declined, saying instead, "Maybe you should check on your young friend. He has been rather quiet and distant since I first met you last night. Or is that normal for him?"

"No, it is not," Martyl replied wearily. "He lost his friend Salena three days ago in a Wraull attack on the Thunder River."

"I would say from the look of him that she was more than just a friend," stated Reyna casually as she examined Tarna's hooves.

Martyl grinned in spite of himself, amazed at how perceptive Reyna was. "True," he corrected. "She was one day going to be his queen." Martyl glanced over at Duncan and Ar'ye feeding the cats and added, "I suppose you're right. I'll be back soon."

"May I sit down?" Martyl asked as he approached Duncan.

"Sure," the other replied non-enthusiastically.

"Duncan, I know you're in a great deal of pain right now," Martyl began, "but it will pass, believe me."

Duncan looked back at him with a carefully neutral expression.

"I'm not saying to forget her," Martyl continued. "She will always be there in your memories and heart. But you need to be careful right now, to make sure you don't endanger yourself or one of us by acting recklessly, thinking you have nothing less to loose. Salena came on this expedition with us because she believed in you and wanted to help. As long as you are alive to remember that, part of her will always live on. If you die needlessly, her death will have been for nothing. You don't want that, do you?"

Martyl left that last question to hang in the air between them for a moment, studying Duncan's face before he rose, placing his hand on Duncan's shoulder giving it a squeeze and adding, "I miss her too. I promise we'll make Draskene pay."

With that, Martyl turned and walked back to Reyna, hoping that Duncan would see the wisdom of his words.

"How did it go?" asked Reyna as Martyl approached.

"I don't know. He is still pretty quiet. Only time will tell but I fear we may run out of time."

"He seems strong," added Reyna, as she moved on to the Dwarves' ponies. "And he has you and his other friends for support. Time will heal his wounds."

Reyna looked away from him then, returning to her ministrations on the ponies and Martyl realized she was speaking from experience. Like Duncan and himself, she had lost not just her family but her people and her way of life. Reyna had survived against terrible odds and was there unexpectedly when they needed her to help them escape Equilon alive with horses. But she had a savage, ruthless dark side as well. Looking at her again, Martyl wondered how such a beautiful and caring woman could be such a brutal killer when the need arose. That is what he feared would happen with Duncan—that when faced with terrible odds he may decide to stay and fight to the death rather than retreat to live and fight another day with better odds.

"Do not worry, Martyl," Reyna said to him, seeming to read his very thoughts. "I was not about to give my life foolishly last night. We had no other choice for our actions and I believed in your cause, even having just heard about it. And I do not think your young friend will choose death either, given a choice. Surviving as I did all those years, I learned to read people quickly. It was a necessity living as myself and the others had to. Give him time. He will be okay."

Reyna reassured Martyl with a smile and added, "And don't worry so much about me either. I did okay before you came along."

Despite himself, Martyl grinned back and felt better inside then he had in days.

She came to slowly, groggily, fighting through layers of pain and fatigue, her muscles screaming their protest as she tried to move. Her eyes did not want to open, her body trying to keep her sleeping for awhile longer, needing the time to repair the damage.

"Water," she heard someone croak out. "I need water." For a moment she wondered who would be asking for water. The voice seemed so far off and distant and very tired. Then she realized it was her voice. It was so weak and hoarse she didn't even recognize the sound of her own voice!

Then someone was giving her something to drink. Instinctively, her parched lips parted to allow the life-sustaining liquid in.

Sputtering and coughing, Salena sat up with a start. Like the morning sun burning the fog off the ground, her memory cleared and came flooding back. She was being abducted by Henaach, leader of a slain Wraull patrol, and taken back to Draskene, the Black Paladin! As her eyes focused, she saw Henaach crouching before her, a flask in his hand. Salena knew it wasn't water she'd been given—it was the foul tasting Wraull drink that Henaach gave her occasionally to keep up her strength.

"It's about time you woke up," Henaach growled at her. His fetid breath and ghastly appearance made her wince with apathy towards him. "I forgot how weak the race of Man was," he goaded her. "Now get up. We need to be on our way."

Unceremoniously, Henaach hauled on the rope he had bound Selena with and got her standing before him.

"That way," he pointed north-east. "There we will meet up with more Wraulls and then with them we will head back to the Black Paladin."

Salena bit her tongue, a retort coming to her about Henaach being scared to take her back on his own past the Ogres that he believed were still following. She knew better than to invite his wrath, her head still sore from the last time he struck her. Besides, she told herself, the longer they stayed away from Arundel and the Black Paladin, the better it was for all of them. She had no misconceptions about why she would be wanted by Draskene. He was after information about Duncan's quest and if he didn't already wonder about her origins, he certainly would after seeing her in the flesh.

Salena had already come to terms with facing her death and was now not afraid to do so. She was not about to die foolishly or needlessly but she was not afraid to give her life if it meant protecting the others.

So on she marched, the Wraull drink burning through her veins and relieving the pain and discomfort she felt. Salena knew that sooner or later the drink and the forced marches would take their toll on her battered body. It was not being given the time to heal properly and naturally, but there was nothing she could do about it. She would face that time when it arrived.

As they walked in the glaring mid-day sun, Salena observed their geography as they went. She was anxious to take her mind off her situation, and to remember where she was should any chance to escape arise. The land was flat and fairly unremarkable save for a dark forest that loomed in the distance off to the east. Even from several miles away it looked dark and forbidding and Salena wondered if it was the dreaded Dead Woods that Martyl and the Dwarves had talked about. If it was, that meant that the Iron Hills were just on the other side of the forest and that's where Duncan and to the others would be! Unfortunately, she told herself, she had no way of knowing how large the Dead Woods were and how long it would take to get through or around them to the Iron Hills. For all she knew, the others were already there and on their way back.

Then another thought struck her—what if no one else survived the Wraull ambush set for them? Salena had never allowed herself to even consider that before, but now, as her mind wandered as she walked woodenly on, she considered it. What if the others in her boat weren't so lucky as she was? It was a very strong current and the falls weren't far away. What if they were swept over? What if the Wraulls killed them? What if she was the last one of the party from Calheller?

Sorrow and despair now began to eat away at Salena's will. Why hadn't the others found her by now? They wouldn't just give up on her, surely not Duncan and Martyl. And was she not still traveling towards the Dead Woods and the Iron Hills beyond? Wouldn't they have crossed paths by now if they were still alive?

The river, Salena thought to herself. The river, if they had stayed on it, would have carried them farther and faster than walking. That must be why they hadn't crossed her path. Salena hung onto that hope. The others must have made it. They had to!

"The time draws near, my Lord," stated Grendle dourly. "I have seen it in my scrying crystal. The Black Paladin has given word to his forces to attack us again. It will be at dawn on the morning after next."

King Balamir was not pleased by this news and his battle-hardened features showed it. Still, he knew this battle was inevitable. He had just hoped that the small party that had set out two days ago would have had more time to reach the Iron Hills and possibly the Rey'ak before the battle. Balamir knew that their chances for survival were not good. They were outnumbered by the Wraulls five to one and they had barely driven them back months ago when Draskene had first attempted to take Calheller. If the Rey'ak were to finally offer their assistance instead of flying idly by, they may have a chance. But that was wishful thinking on the part of the Dwarves and Balamir knew it. They had asked the Rey'ak before for help and had been turned down—the Rey'ak choosing to remain neutral in the conflict.

Except now they too faced a war and possible annihilation by the very forces as did the Dwarves. And, Ar'ye, the Rey'ak who had come here with Martyl and Duncan, had said that the Rey'ak wanted to help now. They had seen the error of their ways and realized that no one could remain neutral with an evil power as great as the Black Paladin. Yet why had they not arrived with any forces or even messengers that forces may be on their way?

"Sire," it was Grendle again, calling his thoughts back to the meeting in the war chambers. "There is more yet. I have seen Demons with the Wraull forces as well. As many as a dozen, possibly more. It seems that Draskene is trying harder yet to obtain Calheller."

"They will not have an easy time of it!" shouted Galani, the General of Defense for Calheller. "My forces are ready for mobilization. We await your command, my Lord."

"As are my forces, sire," added Belan, the General of Offense. "My patrols have been following the Wraulls in the forests about the Thunder Mountains and are ready to attack when the word is given."

"Thank you, Generals," said Balamir. "I know our people could not have better protection than what your forces offer. I only wish we did not need them but that is just an old man's wishful thinking. You are certain of the time of the attack, Grendle?"

"Yes, my Lord. The crystal has shown me when it will be."

"Very well then. We have less than two days to make final preparations. Deelan," the King spoke to the yellow-robed First Minister who had been sitting quietly at his side. "I want you to work with General Galani and evacuate the city into the mountain fortress. That will be our last bastion of defense.

"General Galani, I also need you to work on plans for defense of the outer city. We need to keep it from falling into Wraull hands as long as possible.

"General Belan, let your forces know that we have a time for the Wraull attack. We will attack at midnight before that day and try to take the Wraulls by surprise, using the night to their disadvantage.

"May the gods of the mountains be with us!"

The War council broke then, each member heading off to perform their duties, the Dwarves more solemn than ever.

Midnight of the second night came and Belan and his forces were ready. Silent as ghostly specters, they fanned out and infiltrated the Wraull camps in the forests surrounding Calheller. Dressed in green and grey forest clothes, their mighty battle-axes strapped to their backs, they slipped through the trees, even closer to their enemies.

They wore no armor, the element of surprise their protection. Belan knew his troops would suffer heavy damage if they were caught in a prolonged battle with no armor but they had a different plan. It was not to engage the Wraulls in open combat but to lure them into the many traps that served as the last line of defense for the city of Calheller. By foregoing armour of any sort, the Dwarf Patrols were able to move much more swiftly and, more importantly, much quieter to the Wraull camps.

The Wraull camps were stationed along ridge-lines overlooking the forest and city below. Sentries patrolled near brightly burning watch fires but the Wraulls could still only see as far as the firelight, their night vision being very poor. It was their sense of smell they relied upon to warn them of any unwanted guests and they went about sniffing the air like large two-legged dogs.

The sentries did not worry Belan. He had several bow-men with his forces and they could easily dispatch the sentries. It was the Demons, or lack thereof. None of his advance teams, upon reporting back to him, had made mention of seeing them. Belan had his two thousand troops spread out on both sides of the Thunder Mountains surrounding Calheller, no more than ten men per patrol to allow them to cover the most possible space. And still no mention of the Demons. He began to wonder if Grendle had seen wrong in his crystal and hoped so but knew in his heart that the Magic-User was rarely wrong. What Belan feared most was that the Demons had knowledge of the planned Dwarf attack and were lying in wait for them.

A series of short bird warbles cut the night stillness around him and Belan knew his troops were all in position. Cupping his fist to his mouth, he gave the requisite answer call and the attack began.

Like cats in the dark, the Dwarves left their places of concealment with graceful fluidness and attacked. From out of the dark forest, arrows flew straight into the Wraull sentries at each camp. With muffled cries, they fell where they stood, bearing mute witness to the Dwarves streaming out of the woods into their camps.

Howling like mad banshees, the Dwarves swept over the fallen sentries, axes drawn and ready. Unable to see well in the darkness, the Wraulls were taken by surprise as per the Dwarf plan. With their homeland at stake, the Dwarves fought bitterly and relentlessly, hacking away at their opponents who both out-sized and out-numbered them.

Screams rent the night air, both Dwarf and Wraull as combatants fell on both sides. Within a few minutes, the Wraulls recovered from the surprise attack and began to gain the upper hand.

Watch fires left unattended and scattered by the battle began to spread into the forest around them and greedily consumed the pine needle fuel all over the forest floor. New screams and cries for help sprang up as the fires spread, trapping unwary Dwarves and Wraulls alike. The smell of burnt flesh began to permeate the air as dead and dying bodies were consumed by the marching flames.

The extra light given off by the many blazes did not help the Dwarves either. Their advantage of fighting in the dark was virtually gone now and the Wraulls were able to see just how few their opponents were. The smoke from the fires thickened and intensified, burning the eyes and lungs of the Dwarves and Wraulls alike.

Belan knew that the first part of the battle was over. His patrols had done some damage, but how much was unknown. In the morning, if they survived, they would be able to judge the effectiveness of the raid. But now it was time for part two of the plan. Raising his battle horn to his mouth, Belan sounded out two blasts to signal the retreat. Now it was Galani's turn, he thought to himself as he raced through the burning forest to the mountain passes that would lead his troops and himself to temporary safety.

The Dwarves made no attempt to hide their retreat or to keep it quiet. In fact, they tried hard to make sure the Wraulls pursued them! Headlong they crashed through the trees and thick undergrowth. They jumped over fallen logs and scrabbled under the ones they could not jump. Branches whipped their faces and battered their bodies but they did not slow for anything. All hell was breaking loose in the mountains around Calheller and the Dwarves were in the center of it.

Soon their flight from the fires and the Wraulls led them back to prearranged checkpoints in the woods. As the Dwarf patrols passed with the Wraulls hot on their heels, Dwarves hidden in the brush leapt up. With torches already lit, they ignited the piles of dead wood, leaves and pine needles placed in strategic locations. The flames leapt to life immediately, hungrily consuming the fuel placed there for them. The Dwarves continued away in a hurry, the pursuing Wraulls caught in the fury of the flames. Their death screams followed after the Dwarves as they fled back to the mountain passes.

Other Wraulls were led into traps consisting of long, thin tree branches pulled back and fixed in place with rope vines. The branches had dozens of wooden spikes attached to them and as the Wraulls approached, the Dwarves released the holding vines and the spiked branches lashed out, impaling many Wraulls on them.

The Dwarves were efficient and ruthless, their cunning tactics making up for their lack of numbers and size.

But all did not go well for all of the Dwarves. Several Dwarf Patrols did not even make the retreat. They encountered heavy resistance at the Wraull camps and were cut down before the order to retreat was even given. Others that did not make as fast a retreat were caught in the fires set by their fellow Dwarves or were forced to take alternate routes to avoid the fires. This ultimately led them to face more Wraulls who were closing in the gaps from all sides. They did not give up easily, and each Dwarf cut off from the main retreating force stood his ground and fought until the death. Several of them were only taken down after they could no longer swing their mighty battle-axes, the bodies of slain Wraulls piled so deep about them that they could no longer attack or defend themselves.

Another Dwarf Patrol, on the south side of the Thunder Mountains, was waylaid by one of the large, bear-like Walusks that lived in and around the Thunder Mountains. The smell of blood, both Dwarf and Wraull, and the screams of agony assailed the senses of the massive beast and it came to investigate. Lumbering through the dense foliage, it burst forth into a pitched battle between a Dwarf Patrol and several dozen Wraulls. A Wraull spear missed its intended victim and instead hit the Walusk in the shoulder. Although only a small flesh wound to such a large creature, it nonetheless drove it into an enraged fury. The Walusk charged ahead, its huge fore-paws swinging and batting at anything in its path. Three Dwarves and at least a dozen

Wraulls went down before it. The rest prudently scattered to carry on their battle elsewhere.

High atop the rugged cliffs that overlooked the forests below, General Galani had his Dwarf Patrol stationed, ready to carry out the third phase of the plan. After General Belan's Dwarf Patrols were through the narrow passes that led into Calheller, General Galani's forces were to dislodge the rocks and boulders they had carefully positioned. It was hoped this would begin an avalanche as they cascaded down upon the pursuing Wraulls.

In patient silence they waited, their senses assaulted by the raging battles in the forest below. Thick, acrid smoke from the fires below billowed up to them. Many Dwarves began coughing, their eyes watering from the smoke but they held their positions. Being Dwarves, they did not shy from a good fight, especially against the vile and hated Wraulls. However, they did not like sitting and waiting while their fellow Dwarves fought and died all about them. Still, they knew their role was important and they were determined to see it through.

As the first of the Dwarf Patrols involved in the attacks on the Wraulls began to arrive at the passes, the Dwarves on the cliffs tensed for action. Split second timing would be required to prevent injuring or killing their comrades below while ensuring the maximum number of Wraulls were killed!

Suddenly, blood-curdling screams rent the air. They were not the sounds of dying Dwarves or Wraulls. They were the other-worldly sounds of Demons unleashed on this world. They leapt from hiding near the entrances to the passes to Calheller. The Demons had been scouting for the hidden passes for the morning's attack and had been cut off from their Wraull troops when the Dwarves launched their surprise attack. Unfortunately for Belan's patrols, they were now trapped between the Demons on one side and the Wraulls on the other.

They were, however, not completely unprepared. Before leaving for this hit and run mission, Grendle had imbued the axe of each patrol's captain with the magic necessary to face the Demons. He did not have the power to equip every axe so the members of each patrol knew that if their captain went down, his axe had to be retrieved.

Howling and screeching, the Demons sprang upon the unsuspecting Dwarves. With claws like iron they sliced through the forest cloaks of the Dwarves and ripped apart their bodies. The Dwarves on the cliffs watched in dismay yet there was nothing they could do. The Demons were out of reach of the trap they had hoped to snare the Wraulls in and if they gave away their hidden location, there would be no chance of setting off their trap.

When the initial shock of the surprise attack by the Demons wore off, the Dwarves regrouped and those with the magic-enhanced axes stepped to the fore.

The Demons were not full-blooded Demons like the one sent after Duncan weeks ago. These were lesser Demons, men whose bodies were inhabited by Demons brought to this world by Draskene. Although their powers and abilities were not great as a full Demon like Raydon, they were nonetheless formidable opponents. The bodies only vaguely resembled men, having grown misshapen and hideous by the Demon inside. Their strength was vastly multiplied and their eyes shone with an unnatural and ethereal light from deep within. Their mouths were open and wide, large, sharp fangs protruding from all angles and poisonous spittle dripped all about their mangled faces.

The Dwarves still remaining in each of the battered patrols fought valiantly to keep the Wraulls away from their captains so they could fight the Demons unhindered. Their only route to safety lay past them.

The Demons fought bitterly, hating all living things in the world, especially men and Dwarves, who drove them away after the Black Magic Wars. Those out of reach of their claws and fangs they spit at, and many Dwarves fell from the poison, writhing in agony for minutes until they finally lay still in death.

Eventually, all the Dwarves and the pursuing Wraulls were situated at four different points—the entrances to the passes leading to Calheller. The Demons, despite their strength and ferocity, were finally overcome, but at a great cost in lives for the Dwarves. As the last one guarding each pass was killed, the Dwarves swept into the trap area.

Galani's Dwarf Patrols on the cliffs no longer had a space between the fleeing Dwarves and enraged Wraulls. The two armies entered the passes as one, fighting each other all the way through. For the Dwarves this was bad news and Galani knew it. It was a great victory for the Dwarves to have felled so many of Draskene's Demons for that would definitely hurt him for the power it cost him to bring them into this plane of existence. However, the Demons' deaths had not been in vain. They had taken only a small amount of Dwarf lives in actual combat but the irreparable damage they had done was to hold the Dwarves long enough for the Wraulls to catch them and enter the passes. Now their trap could not be sprung as they had hoped.

Galani surveyed the situation one last time then made his decision. They would have to risk the loss of their own patrols to keep the Wraulls out. Already, hundreds of Wraulls were beyond the avalanche point and, once past the tired Dwarf Patrols in the passes, would be into Calheller itself. He could not allow their entire force to get that far.

Steeling himself against the inevitable loss of his fellow Dwarves, Galani gave his battle horn two short and three long blasts. The signal was given and the choice made.

Straining with the effort, the Dwarves up high levered and pushed boulders down the cliff faces. They bounced, jumped and rolled down, crashing into other rocks and boulders as they went. Within seconds, the Thunder Mountains reverberated with the sounds of cascading rock. When the sounds of crashing rock ended, the cries of crushed bodies screaming in agony could be heard.

Galani and his spotters could not see yet through the massive debris clouds that rose up from the edges of the forest floor. They had no idea how many Dwarves and Wraulls were caught up in the falling rocks but they knew that at least the Wraull advance would be stopped for a while. Their enemies would have to painstakingly clear the debris from the passes before they could get into Calheller.

Turning his attention back to the other side of the passes, Galani listened for signs of the battle below he knew would be going on as the Wraulls who made it through tried to get to Calheller below.

Screams and shouts rose up to him and his spotters but they were only the sounds of Wraulls. Galani was surprised by this, expecting to hear at least some cries from the Dwarves but they seemed to be silent. At last the dust began clearing and he thought he saw a winged shape coming toward him. Demons! he thought to himself—but then recognition of the form eased his fears.

The figure set down gently beside him and said in the same halting fashion as the previous Rey'ak he had met, "I am K'ier'ak of the Rey'ak. I am sorry we are late but we had a long flight. It is safe to enter your passes now. We have removed the last of the Wraulls."

Galani was speechless but took Kier'ak's proffered hand and vigorously shook it.

Chapter Twenty-Three

Two more days of dreary, pain-filled travel on Henaach's leash passed for Salena, her mind and body both numb from exhaustion and the terrible Wraull drinks she was given three times daily now to keep her on her feet.

Henaach relentlessly pushed on, north and west, vainly trying to reach another Wraull Patrol to return Salena back to Draskene with. The Ogres that had decimated his patrol days earlier were still on their trail. Henaach knew they would not stop pursuit until either himself and Salena were dead or the Ogres were. The feud between Ogres and Wraulls was as old and bitter as the hatred between Wraulls and Dwarves. Unfortunately for himself, Henaach thought, he was alone in the Untamed Lands and had to return back to his master through both of his enemies—Ogres and Dwarves.

Still, one did not rise to captain of a Wraull Patrol by being cowardly or stupid. As soon as he found more of his kind, Henaach would reverse his course and exact his revenge on the Ogres that still pursued him.

As he had hoped, the storm two days ago had washed away a great deal of his tracks. This had bought him some time but now the Ogres were on his trail again. Twice he had spotted them as he gained high ground to look about. From the top of a rock studded hill yesterday morning and again today, Henaach had seen the Ogres, eight of them, still doggedly pursuing him and his captive.

Again he looked at the feeble human woman marching along in front of him. How he longed to just kill her, taste her flesh then be gone. She was a hindrance to him and he feared that she may yet lead to his downfall. But if his Master ever found out, he would certainly face a death much longer and crueler than the Ogres would give him. Of that Henaach was sure and it was his fear of Draskene that kept Salena alive. Henaach also knew that Draskene would very likely reward him quite well for this prize and he was rather looking forward to that.

Caught up in his personal musings, Henaach was taken by surprise when Salena started with a gasp and actually began moving away from him, the rope holding her to him going taught as she pulled.

"Easy girl," growled Henaach, planting his feet firmly and coiling the rope in his meaty fist.

Salena stared back at him, wide eyed with fear and just said, "Wolf!"

Henaach looked behind him where Salena was staring and saw a great white wolf speeding across the plateau towards them. He was surprised that the human woman had seen it before him but then again she was probably on the lookout for an escape chance.

Baring his crooked, yellow fangs at her in imitation of a hideous grin, Henaach whistled shrilly and the wolf sped ahead towards them even faster, if that was at all possible. Minutes later it approached Henaach, sniffing him then sitting at his feet, not even winded from the run.

Salena marveled at the size of the beast. Standing, it's broad back reached to Henaach's waist, well over three feet tall. It's fur was white as snow and the eyes were red as blood and made her skin crawl whenever the wolf looked at her. She had the sensation it was sizing her up for a meal. Moments later, her foggy mind remembered the tales Martyl had told her and Duncan about the winter-wolves that the Black Paladin employed in his service. This must be one of them, she reasoned. Knowing what the wolf was and where it was from did nothing to calm her fears.

Henaach greeted the wolf with a low growling sound from deep in his throat. The wolf barked once back at him. Spotting the wooden tube in the wolf's collar, Henaach removed it and the message contained therein Again, the same message as sent to him by the birds that were killed in the Ogre attack.

Henaach glanced over at Salena who was now sitting on the ground, taking advantage of this time to rest.

"It seems you are indeed very valuable to the Black Paladin. He does not send his messages idly and never have I seen him repeat his message."

Salena paid him no heed and did not rise to the bait.

Turning back to the wolf, Henaach said, "We cannot turn back yet as an Ogre hunting party pursues us."

The wolf, Frost, stared back at Henaach but his eyes showed he understood.

"Go ahead into the Untamed Lands and bring back some of your kindred that we may then attack and feast on Ogre."

Frost barked his acknowledgment then sprang ahead to find the packs of winter-wolves that ranged the Untamed Lands.

Henaach smiled to himself. A pack of winter-wolves would make easy work of the Ogres that followed. Then he would have his revenge and be off to deliver the woman to his master.

Meanwhile, they needed to keep ahead of the Ogres until Frost and the other wolves returned. They were only a league or two from the Dead Woods but Henaach knew better than to seek refuge there alone. To the north he spied a small hill surrounded by trees. Pointing to it, he told Salena to get up and lead the way.

For two days the group from Equilon rode alongside the Dead Woods. They stayed within a quarter of a mile of its dark, leafy borders as Martyl suggested to give them some protection from the openness of the Untamed Lands. They were making excellent time and were now further ahead than if they were still on foot. The time lost going to Equilon in the first place was made up and besides the horses, they had gained another valuable ally in their quest.

By noon of the second day, the ground began to rise and the forest rose with it. The path they were following would now force them against the eaves of the Dead Woods themselves and possibly into its outer edges if they were to follow it still. This troubled Martyl as he knew they were at danger even this far from the deadly forest, let alone riding right up to it or in it. However, if they were to leave the path they were on, they would be forced to ride through a large gully that had been created in the past when one of the large creeks flowing in the Dead Woods had overflowed its banks in a flood and washed away the hillside.

Martyl did not like this course either as it meant riding through an area they could not easily defend themselves in, being trapped in a high-walled gully.

Calling a halt, he turned to the others to ask their counsel on the next step of their journey.

"We must decide now whether to turn off our current path and enter the gully to stay clear of the Dead Woods or continue on and risk getting closer, possibly entering the 'Woods."

"Either way is dangerous," cautioned Rorn. "If we enter the gully, we leave the high ground to any of our enemies. We could also be caught in a flash flood should one of the 'Woods creeks or rivers overflow in a storm such as the one we had a few nights back. The banks are too steep to climb quickly and choked with shrubs all around the top."

Martyl nodded his acknowledgment, having surmised that himself.

"The Dead Woods hold their own dangers too," added Dirn. "We are already dangerously close. We were lucky our first night that we had no unwelcome visitors but we have several more days travel before we leave their dark shadow. The odds are against our leaving here unscathed."

"I agree," added Ar'ye. "My people tell tales of the evil creatures that live here. Like the Demon Spawn."

"What are they?" asked Duncan, his curiosity as always piqued by the unknown.

"Descendants of the Demons from the Black Magic Wars," replied Dirn. His face was grimmer than usual as he continued. "Some of the greater Demons, their power still strong after the defeat of their brethren, hid in the Dead Woods. When the rest of their kind were banished from this plane, they remained hidden but their power, as the world changed, began to wane. The Demon Spawn are their descendants and are the most dangerous of the 'Woods denizens. They do not have the power or strength of the Demon you and your cat fought, being susceptible to normal weapons, but in numbers, they could very well prove to be our undoing."

"I agree, yes," broke in Martyl, "but if we are in the gully, there is still a good chance they may come down there for us. I feel if we stick to the highlands, we still have a straight line to run if need be or even the 'Woods themselves for shelter. We will have escape options."

"I am with Martyl," stated Rorn. "Both ways are dangerous, but here we have the high ground, and it may prove to be advantageous."

Duncan, as always, trusted Martyl's judgement and gave his vote for the highlands. Reyna too sided with Martyl and Rorn.

Dirn and Ar'ye were not going to go alone and also added their vote to the others.

"Then its settled," stated Martyl. "We will continue on the high path."

As they continued forward, Dirn rode his pony alongside Ar'ye and said, "Keep your sharp eyes open. I don't have a good feeling about this."

"Aye," replied Ar'ye, "neither do I."

As the day wore on everyone became increasingly agitated. The horses and ponies frequently whinnied and started at seemingly nothing. Both Patches and Big Cat, ever at Duncan's side, showed their uneasiness with low growls directed at the Dead Woods. On two different occasions Patches charged into the dense undergrowth of the

'Woods, chasing something only he and Big Cat could detect with their superior feline senses.

Ar'ye sat light in his saddle, ready to take flight with his hunting bow at the first sign of any danger. Dirn, riding just ahead of him reached back occasionally to finger the handle of his battle-axe strapped to his back.

The others in the party were a little more reserved in showing their discomfort with being so close to the Dead Woods. Duncan and Reyna felt reassured by Martyl's seemingly calm facade and Rorn remained as taciturn as ever. Still, they all rode as close to the gully edge of the path as was possible, leaving as much room as they could between themselves and the 'Woods.

As the sun made its way across the sky, passing to the west, the shadows of the Dead Woods began to grow and creep towards them, bringing more and more feelings of dread. When early evening had passed and dusk was settling on the land, Martyl called a halt for the day.

"We will rest here for the evening," he told the others. "With the wash on our west, it is too dangerous to go on in the dark. The horses could stumble and go down or become entangled in anything growing across our path."

Dirn was clearly not impressed by this but kept it too himself. He conceded secretly to himself that Martyl was right, it would be dangerous to go on in the dark.

Martyl, seeing the look on his face added for his benefit, "We will keep a fire and a watch, however. It may be dangerous to do otherwise at night near the Dead Woods."

As if to prove his point, a shriek rent the night air, causing everyone's hair to stand on end, including the cats.

The horses neighed their fear and discomfort and began pacing side to side, their eyes beginning to widen in fear. Wind Dancer was the only one to remain calm as Reyna stroked her neck and spoke softly in her ear.

"Demon Spawn," muttered Dirn as he un-slung his battle-axe, his powerful arms flexed to swing it at the first target he could find.

All eyes turned now towards the darkness of the Dead Woods. Many more cries now echoed out of the black wall of trees and dark shapes could be seen in the dense underbrush.

Suddenly, a dozen misshapen dark forms rushed from the trees. Some crawled, some walked, some bounded out. All were covered in scales and tough hide, horns, barbs and spikes protruded from their grotesque bodies. The foremost of the Demon Spawn leapt off a fallen log and came right at Duncan. His horse, Roper, reared up in fright and danced backwards on his rear legs. Being an inexperienced horseman, Duncan only held on for a few seconds before tumbling off the back of the horse.

Martyl spurred his horse Tarna forward, his sword drawn and raised to strike. Down he swung and nearly cleaved the hideous creature in two.

Now the other Demon Spawn erupted from the forest, fangs and claws tearing at the air as they came.

Roper, now riderless, bolted into the night in terror. Duncan raised himself up shakily, the breath just returning to his lungs as another of the Demon Spawn leapt at him. It saw an easy target with him kneeling on the ground and Martyl was now occupied by several other Demon Spawn.

Faster yet though were Big Cat and Patches. Big Cat leapt over the approaching Demon Spawn and landed between it and Duncan while Patches flanked it and began to attack. The Demon Spawn saw the cats and with reflexes almost a match for their own it checked its attack and leapt again, over Big Cat and caromed into Duncan.

In a tangle of flailing limbs, the two rolled down the side of the gully to the bottom, a large cloud of dust and the darkness obscuring them from sight of all but the two cats.

Knowing their human was in grave danger, both cats sprang down the embankment and onto the Demon Spawn. With enough strength to knock a man out, both cats rained blows down on the attacker, their razor sharp claws ripping chunks of black, oozing flesh from the Demon Spawn. Moments later it lay dead in the gully.

Ar'ye saw Duncan topple over into the gully but before he could fly to his rescue, he was dragged off the back of his horse Sky by two of the Demon Spawn. They came at him from behind as he turned to see where Duncan fell. He fought back as best he could, being taken unawares but was no match for the steely strength of his attackers.

Dirn was at his assistance immediately, his battle-axe chopping the muscular creature like firewood. Rorn had also left his pony and was now watching Dirn's back as he pulled Ar'ye to his feet.

Only Martyl and Reyna stayed on their horses. Being trained riders, they were able to keep their mounts under control and use them to their advantage. Both Wind Dancer and Tarna kicked and bit at any Demon Spawn that approached them. Sky and the two Dwarf ponies bolted after Roper.

Martyl and Reyna worked their horses towards Ar'ye and the Dwarves, trampling any Demon Spawn that got in their way. Even so, for every one they killed, three more joined the fray from the Dead Woods.

"We need to retreat from here," shouted Dirn, wiping black ichor off his face after his axe split apart a Demon Spawn. "Down the gully is our only hope. Away from this accursed forest!"

Martyl didn't like the idea of being trapped down there any better than he did on the top here but he also needed to get to Duncan. He knew he would be safe for the time being with Patches and Big Cat but he also knew they were all better off together, strength in numbers and all.

The ground beneath them began to rumble then and the Demon Spawn began to hold back, no longer pressing their attack. Everyone looked around in the gathering darkness but couldn't see anything. Martyl's warrior instincts began to bother him and he wheeled Tarna around to face the gully. Suddenly, the ground between them and the lip of the gully split apart and a huge, black worm-like creature rose up out of the ground.

Up it rose, at least twenty feet above their heads and an unknown length still hidden beneath the ground. It's scaly body oozed a foul smelling slime that was enough to cause everyone to fight back the feeling to retch.

Tarna and Wind Dancer, despite their rider's efforts, had had enough. Fear overtook them and they began to buck and kick like wild. Martyl was thrown to the ground while Reyna did an amazing aerial dismount and landed on her feet in a crouch. Both horses, now riderless, were gone after the others.

The initial shock worn off, Ar'ye fit an arrow to his bow and let it go. True it flew and pierced the armored hide of the Demon Spawn worm, but to little effort. Again he let another arrow fly and again the worm paid it no heed.

"It's too big for the amount of arrows you have!" shouted Dirn. "We must run, now!" He looked to Martyl pleadingly, hoping he would give the order for everyone to leave.

Again Martyl was faced with leaving behind one of their party, and this time it was Duncan! But, as before, he knew they had no choice. They could not stay in the open against an opponent this big. If they remained, or went down into the gully, it would most likely end in their demise by the great worm. And, there was a good chance that it didn't know Duncan and the cats were down there. If they fled that way, they may inadvertently lead it to him.

Yet if they fled to the forest itself, they would most certainly have more Demon Spawn to fight.

With a massive crash, the Demon Spawn worm hurled itself to the ground in an effort to smash them all. Everyone sprang clear and Martyl made his decision.

"Into the forest. It will be less likely to get us there." He wasn't entirely sure about that as the worm lived beneath the Dead Woods. Martyl just hoped it wouldn't be able to heave its bulk up into the thick trees of the forest floor.

The five of them ran as fast as possible into the Dead Woods. The smaller Demon Spawn had fled before the onslaught of the worm and were nowhere to be seen. Martyl led the way, his sword chopping at vines and branches that blocked their path. Reyna and Ar'ye followed with the Dwarves bringing up the rear.

At last they reached a gnarled old oak tree, its trunk so big around that the five of them could have joined hands and not circled it! A shallow depression was carved out of the ground on the east side of it and the giant tree's roots stuck out like monstrous limbs.

"We'll rest here for now," Martyl said. "The bole of this tree will provide us with some cover should the Demon Spawn come after us again."

The darkness of the Dead Woods at night was nearly impenetrable and all the company had trouble seeing except Ar'ye. So being, he offered to stand guard.

"I was hoping you could fly out and look for Duncan, actually," Martyl said to him.

"I am afraid I cannot at the moment," replied Ar'ye. "My wings were damaged when I was pulled from my horse. Not seriously, but enough I will need time to rest them. It is akin to you trying to run with a sprained ankle."

Martyl smiled tightly and gripped Ar'ye's shoulder in understanding. He knew that Ar'ye would not leave Duncan if he could help it at all.

When the dust had settled and his senses regained, Duncan took stock of his surroundings. He rose to his feet, shaky but unhurt and saw what was left of the Demon Spawn that had attacked him. It may have been a match for him, he had to admit, looking at its size and musculature, but it was no match for his two cats. Duncan smiled at them in the darkness, silently praising them for their diligence in protecting him. He knew that nothing would ever separate them from him, their bonds were that strong, transcending all boundaries. He would just as easily give his life for theirs if he had too.

As his wind and wits fully returned, Duncan decided it was time to try and get back up the side of the gully to join his friends. He could hear the shouting as they battled the Demon Spawn and he knew they needed his help.

Using roots and stones protruding from the gully walls, Duncan began hauling himself up the embankment. The sounds of the battle above were steadily growing louder when all of a sudden they stopped. Seconds later the ground began to rumble. Debris began to tumble down the slope of the gully side and Duncan was washed back down to the floor of the gully. Looking up, he saw a gigantic worm, already broken free of the earth and towering above the top of the gully. Duncan heard the twang of Ar'ye's bow and the sound of arrows penetrating flesh. His hopes were buoyed somewhat at the thought of knowing his friend was still alive but shortly turned to worrying about his own survival.

The worm crashed into the rise where the others last were, the ground shaking and more debris rained down on Duncan and the cats. The three of them began moving further along the gully to get out of the way when the ground rumbled anew. Big Cat and Patches sensed what was happening before Duncan and began moving away at a much faster pace, growling at him to follow. Duncan knew better than to second guess their feline instincts and trotted after them, just as the gully wall exploded in a shower of dirt, rocks and broken trees.

Risking a glance back in the near total darkness, Duncan could just make out the outline of the hideous worm's gaping maw. It was big enough to swallow him standing, with row upon row of dagger-like teeth coming right for them.

The Demon Spawn worm had given up on the others as they fled the ridge for the confines of the Dead Woods. It detected the vibrations of Duncan and the cats as they tried to climb out of the gully and decided to go after them instead. It heaved its massive black bulk out of the new tunnel it had just dug into the gully. Viscous slime oozed from its open mouth and down its gigantic body to lubricate its passage over the ground, helping to propel its tremendous bulk along.

Both cats fell back behind Duncan, putting themselves between him and the worm, the whole time growling threats at it. Glancing back again, Duncan saw that Martyl and Rorn were wrong about the gully being created by flash floods. It was the same size around as the worm and must have been created by it as it roamed the outskirts of the Dead Woods in search of prey! On he ran, his legs fueled by pure adrenaline at this point, his heart and lungs pumping blood and oxygen at a furious rate to help propel him to safety.

On ran Duncan and the cats and the worm lumbered along right behind them. With nowhere to run but straight ahead it was a race to see who could reach the end first. If I just knew where the 'end' was, Duncan thought to himself. Despite the situation, a part of himself found it ironically amusing that his life may depend on the outcome of a race with a gigantic, dagger-toothed worm! He smiled to himself in the growing darkness and plunged on ahead, a second wind giving him an extra boost of speed.

Suddenly, the ground before them dropped off sharply, almost like a cliff, but with a slight incline. It was the cliff that saved Duncan and the cats from the worm, and the incline, albeit small, saved them from a perishing fall. Down they went in a tangle of arms and legs, two cats and a man, tumbling head over heels. The worm reared up on its massive torso and bellowed at the sky, its prey lost. The worm was powerful in the Dead Woods and the nearby areas but to go down into the Untamed Lands it would be at the mercy of packs of winter-wolves, Wraulls and Ogres with its power and strength diminished. No one could challenge it in the Dead Woods. It could wait for other prey, even its own kind, other Demon Spawn would do. The worm dove back down and disappeared beneath the surface of the ground in a spray of dirt and stone.

"There was nothing more you could have done, Martyl," Reyna said, trying to console Martyl over the loss of Duncan, the cats and horses. "We all knew it would be risky," she continued, "and if we had of taken that gully, the worm would have had us for sure."

"I know," he replied, rising to his feet from the root he was sitting on. "It's just that I was his sworn protector and now I don't know what has become of Duncan. I guess now I know how he felt at losing Salena—the pure helplessness you feel at the situation, despite all your best laid plans."

"We can't stay here much longer," interjected Rorn. "The Demon Spawn are sure to come back anytime now. The noise from that worm is gone and the others aren't likely to remain in hiding from it much longer."

Inwardly Martyl grimaced at what that meant—the worm had most likely gone after Duncan and the cats down the gully path. Still, he knew Rorn was right and they couldn't afford to wait in the Dead Woods indefinitely. He was a hardened warrior and knew he had to take an opportunity to survive when presented with one, despite the losses that occurred to present it.

"We need to get our horses back. We'll never get beyond the Dead Woods without them. Is there any chance they will return to our last spot?" Martyl was asking Reyna but he already guessed at the answer.

"They may, but if they were frightened as badly as I fear, they will run for quite a while." Even in the darkness she could see the downcast look in Martyl's face. "Wind Dancer is my horse and well trained. If at all possible, she will return for me. When the fear of the Demon Spawn subsides, she at least will return. She will also bring back the others with her if they are nearby." Reyna took Martyl's hand in hers and added softly, "I know my horses like Duncan knows his cats. We have a bond. I know we'll find them and your friend."

Martyl smiled at her in the darkness, hitched up his sword and said, "Alright then, let's find our horses. Reyna, stay up front with me and Ar'ye follow behind the Dwarves—we need your keen sight to watch our backs in this mess."

The others fell in step behind Martyl immediately, anxious to be doing anything other than sitting and waiting for the Demon Spawn to return. Cautiously they left the protection of the tree, heading back as best they could the way they had come in single file.

All were tense, weapons drawn and ready, their senses on hyper-alert. Martyl picked his way carefully over fallen logs choked with vines and brush. Black shapes scurried about, some running from them, others towards, only to turn aside as Martyl's sword and the Dwarves' axes glinted in the starlight that filtered in through the canopy of leaves above.

Within a few minutes they reached the site of their battle with the Demon Spawn and the worm and without hesitation followed the trail of their fleeing horses. Martyl kept casting glances down the gully whenever he could afford to, anxious to maybe spy a view of Duncan or the cats. Without definitive proof of where he had fallen to, Martyl knew it would be too dangerous to risk the others in an attempt to look for him down there. As if to reaffirm his thoughts, a pack of Demon Spawn sprang from the 'Woods just behind them, howling as their prey tried to escape.

Ar'ye spun around and loosed a pair of arrows in a heartbeat. Two Demon Spawn fell, one pierced through the throat, its scream drowned out in its own blood as it poured forth from his throat. The other fell silently, the arrow piercing its eye and brain.

Rorn and Dirn were at his side instantly, their battle axes cleaving apart any Demon Spawn who ventured too close. Having repelled the initial attack, the Dwarves and Ar'ye sprang ahead to Martyl and Reyna, desperate to ensure they were not separated in the 'Woods.

Onward they rushed, spurred on by the fact that the Demon Spawn were again on their trail. Throaty growls and hideous shrieks assailed them from both sides of the trail they followed, the Demon Spawn eagerly pursuing their quarry. Again, Ar'ye let fly with a few arrows, his accuracy still uncanny even in the dark and on the fly. The Demon Spawn kept pace but did not break from their cover.

Luckily for Martyl, the path left by the fleeing horses was easy to follow, even at the pace they were keeping trying to stay ahead of their pursuers. The ground began to rise as they went on and a small stream meandered past them. Soon it expanded into a large, fast flowing river that cut right across their path. Martyl skidded to a halt at the near bank and in the darkness tried to judge the width of it.

"Ar'ye," he called, "we will need a guide to cross the river. It is too swift in the dark to traverse without one. Also, I think it may help slow the Demon Spawn on our trail."

"What do you have in mind?" he replied in between gasps of air.

"Can you fire an arrow across the river into a tree with a rope attached to it? We can then pull ourselves across with the rope."

"I'll try," replied Ar'ye.

While he knotted the rope about the arrow shaft, Rorn and Dirn took up guard positions around Ar'ye and kept watch for any Demon Spawn. Their dark, cumbersome shapes lumbered about the edges of their vision, keeping close but not daring to approach within weapons' range after seeing how easily their brethren were dispatched earlier. They had time, and they would wait and attack when the time was right.

A light whistle followed by a dull crack signaled that Ar'ye had fired his arrow into a tree across the river. His keen vision had no trouble spotting a target in the darkness.

Grabbing hold of the loose end of the rope, Martyl tested its secureness in the tree by tugging as hard as he could. Satisfied with its fastness, he turned to the others again, "I will go across first and make sure both the rope and river bank are secure. Next, Ar'ye will follow. When he is across, he will provide cover fire as Reyna and then the Dwarves come across."

Everyone nodded in ascent and Reyna risked a quick kiss on his cheek before he left.

Martyl smiled and held her hand briefly then turned and entered the water. It was swift and cold, biting into his flesh and pushing him along with it. Moments later he reached the other side, drawing his sword and dropping into a defensive crouch. He peered about quickly but could see no Demon Spawn. Turning back towards the others, Martyl signaled for Ar'ye to cross.

Sensing their quarry was about to slip away, the Demon Spawn came at the Dwarves and Reyna in a rush. Ar'ye was already half way across and Martyl urged him on. Three Demon Spawn leapt in after him but were quickly swept away downstream by the river.

Rorn and Dirn took up a defensive position, putting themselves between the Demon Spawn and Reyna and the river.

"Follow Ar'ye," shouted Rorn. "We'll try to hold them back as long as possible."

A dark shape hurtled through the air and bowled into Dirn. The two went down in a jumble of arms and legs. With a tremendous effort, Dirn heaved his attacker, nearly twice his size, off himself. Reyna, knife unsheathed, was cat-quick as she leapt onto the Demon Spawn before it could get up and deftly cut its throat.

"GO! Now!," shouted Dirn, picking up his axe to stand by Rorn's shoulder, stepping over the bodies of three more Demon Spawn he had just disemboweled with his mighty battle axe.

Reyna did as she was instructed and began crossing the river. Ar'ye was already on the other side at this point and with his excellent Rey'ak vision was dropping Demon Spawn as they left the cover of the woods for the riverbank. Again the Demon Spawn pulled back and at last both Dwarves made the crossing.

When everyone was across, Martyl quickly cut the rope free and bundled the rest up for future use. Looking across the river, the group saw the dark shapes milling about the river.

"It won't take long for them to find a way across," stated Martyl. "We had better get moving."

Swiftly they turned and fled into the surrounding trees. It took Martyl only a few moments to pick up the trail of their fleeing horses, the path left behind in their panic easy to follow. On they ran, eager to put as much distance between themselves and their pursuers as possible. No one risked a glance back, their sole intent to reach the end of the Dead Woods and their horses and get out of danger. From there, thought Martyl, they would have to try and find Duncan. He could not and would not leave him behind. The only thing that gave him any reassurance that he would be okay was that he had Patches and Big Cat with him. Their protection was as much as his would be.

At last they stumbled through the last of the Dead Woods and onto the Fire Wind Flats. "The Demon Spawn will not follow us out of the 'Woods," huffed Dirn between gulps of air, his massive chest heaving with the exertion of trying to keep up with the pace Martyl set. Even Rorn and Ar'ye were breathing hard. Only Reyna seemed non-winded, her years of working with horses having provided her with exceptional stamina.

"There are other things to be feared," replied Ar'ye. "The Fire Wind Flats are home to tribes of Wraulls and packs of winter-wolves. We would be well indeed if we found our horses soon."

As if to add credence to his statement, a wolf howl shattered the still night air, followed by several reply howls.

"I've found their tracks again," cut in Martyl, his voice showing no sign of the urgency he felt. "They are heading back east, across the 'Flats."

Reyna followed the direction he pointed in and added, "They are trained to return to their owners but if they are as badly frightened as I believe by the Demon Spawn, they will continue to flee until they feel safe. That light off to the east, could it be a camp-fire?"

"It could," joined Ar'ye, "But it is not likely to be friendly in these parts."

"Nonetheless," replied Reyna, "the horses, if they see it, will most likely head to it, looking for food, shelter and safety."

Martyl looked at Reyna, and even in the starlight he could read her features—that she fervently believed the horses would head that way. "How far away do you estimate the camp to be, Ar'ye?" he asked.

Ar'ye scanned the 'Flats with his keen hunter's eye before replying, "About three or four leagues. We could make it before dawn if we went quickly."

Martyl considered for a moment then said, "Very well, we will follow the horses' tracks to the camp or as far as they go. If they veer off before then, we will decide at that time whether to follow them or continue to the camp and see if there is anything of use for us there."

With that he hitched up his weapon and was off at a quick jog, the others falling into line behind him.

Chapter Twenty-Four

Draskene barely held his fury in check. He watched his Demon and Wraull troops launch their attack against the Dwarves at Calheller through his scrying crystal. There would be losses on his forces, that he knew and accepted. What he could not accept, or tolerate, was the total annihilation of the forces he sent into battle. Draskene had not foreseen the Rey'ak coming to the aid of the Dwarves. He believed that the enmity between the two races would keep them from joining forces against him. That he did not anticipate and prepare for this bothered Draskene but he would not let is stop his plans.

Draskene saw the fall of Calheller as inevitable. That it would take longer than he originally planned was of no consequence to him. He had thousands more Wraull troops in the Fire Wind Flats. When they were summoned and organized, they would march again on Calheller. Sooner or later, the Dwarves would fall. After them, he would take the Rey'ak and their lands.

And, he reminded himself with a wry smile, there was the possibility of finding the hidden ocean kingdom of legend. But even Draskene knew his powers had limits. After this second defeat of Calheller, he could not afford to spread his forces and resources too thin. Once he extracted the information he needed from the mysterious woman traveling with Duncan and Martyl, he would organize a sortie across the ocean in search of the hidden realm, after the Dwarves and Rey'ak were taken care of.

He also knew from Bin's animal spies in and around Calheller that Duncan was still after the mysterious sword lost in the Iron Hills. But for once, he was having doubts. His adversaries were proving much more resourceful than he anticipated and even he, with all his powers, had limits. Draskene knew he could not afford to lose anymore Demons—they cost him too much in lost power and energy but he had other minions that could aid his Wraull troops.

Duncan picked himself up off the ground, shaking the dirt and small stones free of his clothes and hair. Patches and Big Cat, a few feet off to his left were doing the same, removing the debris from their tumble down the cliff from their fur.

Duncan took a quick inventory of their wounds and found that, aside from a few scratches and skinned limbs, the three of them were actually quite well off, despite their recent ordeal. Looking about, he surmised their location to be somewhere on the Fire Wind Flats. He knew that without the others, he didn't stand a very good chance out here alone. His supplies were on his horse which was nowhere to be seen. All he had with him was his sword and hunting knife. Without his horse, Duncan knew he had a very little chance of catching up with the others.

He didn't despair, however, for he knew that eventually, once they could, the others would come looking for him. Duncan just hoped that they, like himself, had managed to escape the Demon Spawn and giant worm as he had. If they hadn't …

He refused to dwell on that. It was hard enough losing Salena. Duncan couldn't bear the thought of losing anymore of his friends, even the taciturn Dwarves were growing on him. He felt bad that they were all giving up so much for him and he hadn't done anything yet. Duncan promised himself then, that given the time and opportunity, he would repay them all. That of course meant defeating the Black Paladin, and to do that, he had to extricate himself from his current predicament and find the others.

Scanning the horizon east to west, he could only make out flat, barren land in the moonlit sky. To the north, maybe an hour away, as best as he could tell in the dark, Duncan saw a small camp-fire. If he was to have any chance finding the others, he would need supplies, at least some water. He also knew that the chances were good that it was a Wraull camp he saw, not friendly traders. Even so, he had no compunctions about killing a few more Wraulls after losing Salena.

Hitching up his sword and securing his knife, Duncan called the cats and they were off.

It was well into the night when Frost returned to Henaach, a pack of eight winter wolves following him. They were nearly the size of Frost himself, standing almost three feet tall at the shoulder, their thick, broad bodies covered in fur as white as snow. Their blood—red eyes shone in the moonlight, giving them an even more fearsome appearance.

Frost approached Henaach, growling softly in his throat.

"Good work, my friend," approved Henaach.

He tossed the wolf a piece of meat from the fire where he was roasting it. The wolf devoured it in a single bite, its white fangs flashing in the firelight. Despite herself, Salena shivered at the site. She had seen the cats on the Misty Isles eat before, and they were every bit as dangerous as these wolves but they just didn't frighten her as much.

As if he sensed her fear and discomfort, Henaach turned to Salena, who was still bound to him by the rope and said, "You are wise to fear these beasts. Packs have even been known to take down Walusks that stray from the woods of the Thunder Mountains."

He grinned wickedly at her and went back to feeding himself. The wolves paid her no due and took up positions ringing the small camp.

Salena ignored Henaach as best she could and tired to rest. She had long ago finished the meager portion of food she had been given and wanted now only to rest. Her body and mind was more tired now than ever before in her life after being forced to march endlessly day after day in the company of this dreaded Wraull.

She lay with her back to the fire and stared at Henaach's broad back. How she hated that form in front of her and how she desperately wanted to kill him, or at least maim him. Salena knew she didn't have the strength or weapons to kill him without getting herself killed in the process but she knew that, given the chance, she would see to it that she seriously hurt him. Her eyes bored into his back and with her hatred welling up inside her, she wished him a horrible, slow death.

A loud growl brought her attention back to her current situation. Salena sat bolt upright, her senses on full alert. Were the ogres upon them, she wondered? All the wolves, including Frost, were up and growling, moving to the southern side of the camp.

"Be still and quiet, girl," growled Henaach. "I warned you before, you will fare much worse with the Ogres than with me."

He flashed her his yellow, hideous fangs again in what she believed was his imitation of a smile. Hefting his massive battle-axe, Henaach stood and peered into the darkness after the wolves.

His night vision was not good enough for him to see beyond the edge of the camp illuminated by the fire but his sense of smell was exceptional. Like the wolves, Henaach tilted his head up and sniffed the air.

"Man," he declared with a growl, but he did not recognize the other scent he picked up. It was animal, he was sure of that, but not what type.

Then recognition flashed in his mind and he realized what was happening. Turning back to Salena, Henaach whispered to her in the dark, "I recognize the smell now, girl. It is one of your friends from the river with those monster cats come to try and rescue you. Well don't get any ideas because those wolves will finish them off!"

Hope, fear and dread all welled up in Salena at once then and burst forth like an overflowing dam. She knew that Duncan and the cats were powerful but she saw the wolves and their immense size and was terrified for them. Heedless of her safety, she shouted out in the dark, "Duncan, NO, it's not safe!"

Henaach snarled his outrage and screamed at her, "That was very stupid, girl!"

As he rose to strike her, all hell broke loose.

Duncan and the cats, upon approaching the outer edge of the camp fire, slunk as low to the ground as possible. He could make out two dark silhouettes against the firelight, one very large and one small. Judging by the size, Duncan knew the larger one was most likely a Wraull, but he was unsure about the smaller one. There were also several large bulky forms surrounding the campsite that he could not discern.

Patches and Big Cat both growled quietly but ominously beside him, their rear quarters bouncing up and down slowly and their tails flicking quickly side to side. They seemed overly anxious to get to the campsite and Duncan wondered why.

He knew that if it was a Wraull camp, which it most likely was out here, the advantage in the dark would be his unless the Wraull smelled him coming. In that case, his advantage was lost. Added to that, Duncan still didn't know who else was by the fire—another Wraull? Unlikely by the size. A captive? Possibly. And the dark shapes ringing the camp. Were they more Wraulls? He needed to be certain before he went charging in. Duncan smiled to himself in the dark as he realized that he was now thinking like Martyl and wondered if his friend and mentor would be proud of him for abandoning his headstrong ways.

Then he heard growls coming from the camp. They didn't sound like Wraulls to him, more canine. Winter-wolves! he thought to himself. Duncan's pulse raced faster as he realized what he may have gotten himself into when a shout erupted from the camp. It was a familiar female voice, yelling his name!

Acting purely on instinct and emotional overload, Duncan yelled back, "Salena!"

He realized then that the other, smaller figure was Salena. How or why she was there he didn't know or care. All he knew was that he had to save her. Failure was not an option. Having no time to formulate a plan, Duncan leapt to his feet, sword drawn and ran towards Salena.

Henaach snapped back to the darkness as he heard Duncan's yell, Salena forgotten for the moment.

"Kill," he shouted at Frost and the other winter-wolves. At once they sprang off into the night to intercept Duncan and the cats.

"No!", shrieked Salena at the top of her voice. All her rage, hatred and fear of Henaach rose to the surface and burst forth and she acted without even realizing what she was doing. All she knew was that she couldn't let Duncan die alone.

Before Henaach could turn back to her, Salena sprang from her crouch and landed on the seven foot tall Wraull's back. Quick as a cat, she coiled the very rope he had bound her to him with about his neck and jumped off his back.

The wolves bounded from the edges of the firelight into the darkness, towards Duncan and the cats. As Duncan rushed forward to meet them, he saw Salena locked in a deadly embrace with the Wraull by the fire. He knew he could never make it in time past the approaching wolves but he knew the cats could.

"Big Cat," he called, "Help Salena."

Immediately the huge orange and white cat took off, leaping over the winter-wolves as they approached, jaws snapping and teeth gnashing. As they drew near the wolves, Patches jumped before Duncan, placing himself between them and his human. Paws planted firmly, the great cat made his stand and let out an earsplitting growl.

Frost, bigger and faster than the other wolves, was the first to face the cat. He towered above Patches and was easily four times his weight but the growl stopped him dead in his tracks. Despite his size, Frost was afraid of the fearless cat and backed up a pace or two. Not wanting to face such daunting claws and fangs, Frost used his breath weapon. Opening his maw wide, he spewed forth a freezing vapor cloud that could freeze flesh solid and shatter steal.

With lightning quick reflexes, Patches puffed his fur up and the freezing vapor merely iced the tips of his fur. That was all it took though for the others to arrive. As they rushed in, one of the wolves barreled into Patches from the side, jaws snapping and down they went.

The wolves were upon Duncan now and he was furiously swinging his sword to keep them at bay. One leapt to him and he swung, cleaving its two front legs. Another nipped at his legs and he danced about trying to keep some distance between himself and his attacker.

Then two wolves came at him at once. Duncan parried their lunges with his sword and always tried to keep one of the wolves between himself and the others, hoping they would not release their freezing breath if they thought they might get one of their own. A third wolf came in from his left and he didn't see it and was knocked down as it crashed into him.

Sensing the distress Salena felt, Big Cat rushed to her aid. With another big leap, she cleared the camp's fire and landed right on Henaach's chest. He raised his right arm to protect his throat as she tried to sink her teeth into it. At the same time, Henaach was flailing his left arm about in an attempt to grab the rope from Salena.

Salena was on the ground now with the rope about Henaach's neck pulled taut. She dug her heels into the soft earth, pulling as hard as she could. Having no choice, Henaach staggered back to try and relieve the tension on the rope and to get away from the thirty pound cat tearing at his chest and face.

Big Cat swatted at his face with one paw while the other clung tenaciously to Henaach's leather armor. Her back feet were planted firmly on his stomach and she raked them repeatedly, trying to cut through his thick hide armor and disembowel him.

Salena coiled more of the rope about her hands. They were bleeding freely now, the rope cutting through her flesh as she and Henaach played tug-of-war for life. She pulled furiously on the rope, all the while screaming at Henaach and taunting him.

"I'm going to kill you, you bastard!" she shrieked at the top of her lungs. "How do you like being tied up!"

Henaach roared in fury, enraged now beyond all control. He no longer cared if the Black Paladin wanted this girl alive or not. He was going to kill her now and worry about the consequences later. He stopped fighting for the rope and instead use both hands to grab Big Cat and fling her from him. She hit the ground hard, rolled, and came up snarling. For the first time in his life, Henaach felt fear as he looked into those feline eyes.

Duncan lost his sword as the wolf took him down. Instinctively his arms went up to protect his face and neck. He felt excruciating pain as the wolf clamped down on his left forearm and he screamed out loud. As if in answer, he heard Patches growl somewhere nearby. A moment later he heard a yelp and then the crushing pressure on his arm abated. The wolf on top of him collapsed and Duncan hurriedly rolled out from beneath it. Rolling away into a defensive crouch, he pulled out Sliver and braced for the next attack. None came, but the spectacle before him made his heart catch in his throat.

Big Cat leapt at Henaach again, and crashed right into his mid-section. With his breath knocked from his lungs and Salena pulling on his neck from behind, he crashed to the ground like a sack of wet flour. With no more resistance on the rope, Salena toppled over as well but was on her feet instantly and running over to Big Cat and Henaach.

As a natural born killer and protector, Big Cat wasted no time and with one quick bite, she sank her formidable fangs into Henaach's exposed neck. His eyes were wide in shock as he felt his life-blood seeping from his body. He tried to fight the cat off but her powerful jaws were closing off the air passage to his empty lungs, crushing his windpipe. As his vision swam before him, the last thing Henaach saw was the puny human girl pulling his knife from his belt.

Duncan staggered to his feet and was astounded and shocked by what he saw. There were only four wolves left—one much larger who stayed behind the other three. Patches was between them and himself, his grey and white fur streaked with blood.

The wolves snarled and snapped but when Patches growled back, they shrank away and regrouped. In a rush, the four wolves came at him again. His mighty paws flashed out, razor sharp claws shredding the nearest wolf. Down it went, but the other three took the mighty cat down in the a tangle of legs and fur.

Duncan yelled and rushed to his aid but before he could get there, the wolves sprang again and Patches rose up to face them, his fur now unrecognizable it was so blood covered. There were only two wolves left now and they circled the injured cat, paying the dagger wielding human no heed as he hobbled closer.

Both wolves struck at once, one from behind and the other from the front. Duncan screamed out again, trying to get their attention, to come after him, to give Patches time. He knew he would never cover the last few feet in time otherwise. But, to his amazement, Patches rose again, clinging to the back of the largest of the winter-wolves, the only one still alive at this point.

Frost flung himself to the ground, desperately trying to dislodge the demonic cat attached to his back, but to no avail. Patches sunk his teeth deep into his neck, neatly severing Frost's spinal column and the wolf fell to the ground, dead.

Patches lay there on the wolf's broad back, his own wounds bleeding out onto Frost's snow white fur. He raised his head as Duncan reached him and quietly purred as Duncan stroked his head.

"I love you, Patches," Duncan choked out. "Thank you for saving my life." His eyes burned and his throat hurt as he looked at his fearless cat and stroked his massive head. Patches laid his head back down and didn't make another sound.

Salena plunged Henaach's knife into his chest repeatedly, his torso now a bloodied pulp of mangled flesh. Big Cat approached her mewing softly and tried to nudge her away.

Salena paid her no heed and kept screaming, "I'm going to kill you, you bastard!" over and over.

Duncan grabbed her wrist and said, "Enough, Salena. He's dead."

She froze for a moment and then reality came crashing back and Salena remembered who and where she was.

"Oh Duncan," she sobbed as she fell into his arms, tears streaming down her cheeks. "I thought I would never see you again."

He stroked her head as he held her to his chest, fighting back his own tears of joy and grief.

"It's okay," he reassured her. "I'm here. We'll rest a bit then find the others. Are you okay?"

"I think so. Big Cat saved my life Duncan, I don't think I could have done it without her. Where is she?" Salena asked, looking around for Big Cat.

Salena scanned the camp area and realized they were alone. Then her glance fell on Patches, just outside the camp, Big Cat sitting beside him quietly.

"Duncan!" she gasped, "Patches is …"

"I know," he replied woodenly. "He gave his life for me."

His voice began to crack and he went silent, trying to cover the emotion. Big Cat was at his side immediately, rubbing her head against his side, trying her best to soothe his pain.

"Help me bury him so that his body is not disturbed by carrion," he managed to get out without losing his facade of control.

With Big Cat keeping a silent but somber vigil, Duncan carried Patches away from the dead wolves and Henaach to a clear patch of grass beneath a lone tree a few hundred feet from the camp. His eyes burned with unshed tears and his throat ached with the lump that formed but he refused to break down. He had to be strong for both himself and Salena, to make sure they were okay. Together, over the course of the night, Duncan and Salena gathered rocks and stones and made a cairn above Patches to mark his grave. As they labored through the night, Duncan and Salena talked about Patches and told each other stories that came to mind of him. They vowed that night to never forget him and his sacrifice.

Duncan had faced the loss of his family years before but he had a special bond with his cats that could not be broken. That night he felt a terrible sorrow, as if a part of his very soul had been cut from him. It would be a long time before this wound would heal, if it ever would. He looked off to the west as Salena dozed, her head on his shoulder, and promised his beloved cat that Draskene would pay.

Chapter Twenty-Five

The sun was just beginning to rise in the east, its golden streamers of light illuminating the sky with a brilliant shine. Martyl, Ar'ye, Reyna and the Dwarves approached Duncan and Salena where they slept fitfully.

Ar'ye saw them first, his keen vision spying them before the others. He also saw the slain winter-wolves and lone Wraull and his heart began to quicken in anticipation.

"Martyl," he whispered, "I see Duncan, and I believe Salena, along with Big Cat ahead."

Martyl looked at him dumbfounded at first but quickly recovered from his shock.

"Is your wing better? Well enough to fly in and have a look?"

He too was leery of the situation, but desperate to make sure Duncan was okay and find out how Salena was there.

"I think so," replied Ar'ye.

Tentatively, he flapped his wings, his broad back and chest flexing and heaving with the effort as his feet left the ground. He rose to about one hundred feet and scanned the horizon for any sign of danger. Moments later, he set down and reported, "All is clear Martyl. And I saw our horses too, just beyond Duncan, feeding on a grassy patch."

Not wanting to waste anymore time, Martyl give his orders. "Ar'ye, take Reyna and Rorn with you to retrieve the horses. Dirn, you and I will check on Duncan and see what has happened here."

With that, they were all off at a run, eager to get their mounts back and their lost comrades.

As Martyl and Dirn approached Duncan and Salena, they marveled at the site of the carnage around them. They counted nine winter-wolves, most showing signs of trauma from bite and claws marks, and one butchered Wraull. Duncan and Salena both lay beside a rock cairn, unmoving except for the rise and fall of their chests as they breathed deeply, even in their sleep. Big Cat watched them approach and rose to greet them, stretching in the warm sunlight that now bathed the ground.

Seeing only Big Cat beside Duncan, Martyl feared what may have happened. Kneeling down, he gently shook Duncan who woke with a start, his hand reflexively reaching for his sword at his side.

"Easy, Duncan," whispered Martyl. "It's me, Martyl. You're okay."

Groggily, Duncan came to, his mind and body still cloudy from the previous night's battle.

"What happened here?" asked Martyl. Then, with more than a trace of delight in his voice, "And how did you find Salena?"

Salena awoke now and after rubbing the sleep from her eyes realized where she was again. Upon seeing Martyl, she leapt into his arms, hugging him and saying, "I'm so glad to see you again. And you too Dirn. I thought I was lost."

Then looking around she saw only them and her heart began to sink.

Sensing her fear, Martyl said, "Don't worry. Ar'ye and Rorn are here too, as is a new friend we found in Equilon, Reyna. They are retrieving our horses right now. Now maybe you two can fill us in on what we missed while we wait for the others."

Taking a deep breath to begin, his voice still betraying his emotions at the loss of Patches, Duncan filled Martyl and Dirn in on his encounter with the Demon Spawn worm and later the battle to save Salena.

When he finished, Martyl commended him and the cats on their bravery and combat skills and expressed his deepest sympathies for the loss of Patches.

By that time, Ar'ye, Reyna and Rorn returned with the horses. After Reyna and Salena were introduced, Salena told them her story about her capture by the Wraulls and her subsequent escape and rescue by Duncan and the cats. It was now well past noon and Martyl suggested that they begin their trek again to the Iron Hills before any more time was lost.

Duncan and Salena rode double on Roper, unwilling to be separated again after just finding each other, while each of the others had their own mounts back.

They rode in silence, the morning slowly slipping into afternoon before they stopped to eat and water the horses.

"I believe we should reach the Iron Hills in another day," stated Martyl to everyone as they sat in a circle, sharing their supplies.

"I agree," added Rorn. "The ground is already beginning to rise to meet the Fire Top Mountains."

"How will we know what we are looking for?" Duncan asked, looking at Martyl and the Dwarves.

Martyl and the Dwarves looked at each other before Martyl answered. "We won't, for sure."

Duncan and Salena stared blankly at him before he continued.

"The Black Magic Wars were very long ago and much has changed since. You remember what King Balamir told us—a Dwarf and human settlement was started here then wiped out by the Wraulls. That is when the sword was lost.

"There are ruins left, but they are not much more than rubble I am afraid. Wraulls and other obstacles are bound to be in our way I am sure. Even without any opposition, we will have no clear idea of where to begin looking."

The Dwarves echoed his sentiments with their usual gruffness, knowing all to well what was most likely waiting in store for them.

"We have lost many patrols over the years searching for other relics like the sword," stated Rorn in his matter-of-fact manner. "Our people gave up long ago trying to find them. There is more here than just Wraulls, or so legend tells. I still believe this to be a fool's errand, our last hopes resting on the shoulders of our rag-tag group and the chance of finding the Brach'dir."

Rorn went silent then, having said his piece, and stared at the ground where he was sitting.

"We have one thing with us they never did," replied Martyl, "and that hopefully will make the difference."

"You don't honestly believe in those old legends and folk tales, do you?" sneered Rorn.

"To some degree, yes, I do. Besides, your own king approved of this expedition and decided who would wield the sword."

"I know what was decided," Rorn sighed wearily, "and I like the boy, he has spunk for sure, but I just don't know what to believe anymore."

Duncan caught Rorn's glance at him and began wondering just what he and Martyl were discussing. Everyone else seemed a little puzzled as well, except Dirn who was remaining quiet as usual. Knowing he was being left out of something, Duncan asked Martyl, "What are you not telling me?"

Martyl looked at the two Dwarves and they just shrugged their shoulders. He turned back to Duncan and said, "There is more to the legend of the Brach'dir than you were told in Calheller. What you were told is common knowledge to most but there is more, which you may as well know now."

Duncan was taken aback and asked, "Why wasn't I told in the beginning?"

"For your safety," Martyl said. "I was afraid that if you knew all of the legend, you may have run off on your own again like you did to come to Arundel from the Misty Isles. It is my duty to protect you, from your enemies, and yourself."

Duncan looked away from Martyl, feeling embarrassed and ashamed, but Martyl continued.

"Do not blame yourself for your deeds. You did what you thought was right. Now let me tell you the rest about the Brach'dir.

"As the legends go, the sword was forged by the Dwarves to defeat the Demons in the Black Magic Wars. What isn't known to others is that the magic imbued in the sword came from a member of the Arundel Royal Family, a very distant relative of yours. The sword was a joint effort by the race of Dwarves and Man.

"When the Black Magic Wars were over, one of the members of the house of Arundel left to start a new settlement, joined by Dwarves from Calheller. It was to be a time of peace and prosperity but the Iron Hills held other dangers now that the Demons were gone.

"The settlement was decimated by a particularly brutal attack and the sword was lost. The reason why you were chosen out of the group to wield it, should we find it, is that only a member of the House of Arundel can wield it. That is due to the magic imbued in it upon its forging."

"I'm through with making foolish mistakes," said Duncan. "We'll get this sword and then see about Draskene."

"Good," replied Martyl, taking Duncan by the shoulder. "Let's get going."

As dawn broke over the Thunder Mountains, the sun's warm yellow rays peaked through the crags and fissures, casting shadows on an already eerie and grisly sight. Pillars of smoke rose from the dozens of separate blazes that had burned through the night, the acrid smoke assaulting the lungs of the Dwarves and Rey'ak who looked down from the passes above Calheller.

"Wait here, general Galani," said Kier'ak, signaling his men to take flight. "It is too dangerous to go back into the forest on foot just yet. Let us look for any survivors from either side from the air."

Galani wanted to have his own Dwarf Patrol search for Dwarf survivors but he conceded to Kier'ak's wisdom. It would be safer and easier from the air with all the fires raging below as well as possible Wraull troops on the loose.

The Rey'ak lifted off, at least two hundred strong by Galani's skilled count as he watched them wing their way over the forests of the Thunder Mountains. His initial shock at their arrival had worn off but he was still hesitant to believe after all this time the Rey'ak had decided to help the Dwarves.

What could have happened, he wondered, to make them commit to aiding the Dwarves against the Black Paladin? What did they want in return?

Kier'ak and his troops flew north over the Thunder Mountains, their keen eyes searching the thick, smoky forest below for any signs of life from the previous night's battle. Any Wraulls they spied, and there were few, were dispatched quickly and quietly, the Rey'ak aerial arches very efficient.

The Dwarves they met were an entirely different story. There were scores of them cut off from escape by the fires set the night before or by pockets of Wraulls still able to fight. Again, the Rey'ak took care of the Wraull situation, but many of the Dwarves were reticent to accept their help in getting back to the passes of Calheller. There was the issue of pride as well as trust, since the Dwarves trapped in the forest had no way of knowing the Rey'ak came to help.

As the morning wore on into the afternoon, the last of the Dwarves made it back to the passes leading into Calheller. To their dismay, they were still blocked with enough rubble to prevent them from easily getting through. Kier'ak, eager to get on with getting his message through to the king, offered Galani the use of the flyers to carry the Dwarves over the impassable obstacles.

At first his stubborn Dwarf pride would not let him accept on behalf of his troops but he soon realized that the sooner he got his Dwarf patrols back onto his side of the passes, the sooner they could begin setting up their next defenses.

Galani gave the order and his signals on the tops of the passes relayed his commands via smoke signals to his trapped troops below.

Moments later, like an aerial ferry service, the Rey'ak, one Dwarf carried between every two of them, slowly transferred the survivors of the previous night's battle into the safety of the Calheller passes.

When the last of the survivors was brought up, Galani called over two of his senior captains and gave them orders to have the passes cleared as soon as possible so the Dwarf Patrols could again enter the surrounding forest, but to ensure measures were taken that they could be sealed off again if the need arose.

After the captains had accepted their orders and set about organizing their troops, Galani at last turned to Kier'ak and said, "Come. We shall go to see King Balamir and you may give him the news of your arrival and your people's pledged allegiance."

"If I may," suggested Kier'ak. "My men could be of assistance here still, aiding in the clearing of your mountain passes and serving as aerial lookouts."

"By all means," replied Galani, feeling relief at knowing his overworked troops would have assistance.

Kier'ak conferred with his lieutenants for a few minutes, giving them their orders and wishing them safety and luck.

The Dwarves, hard workers and master of stone as they were, readily accepted the Rey'ak's offer, if only to have the added benefit of their airborne archery skills.

"May we begin?" asked Kier'ak as the last of the Rey'ak began helping the Dwarves. "My King has sent me with the utmost urgency to speak with your King. It is of great importance to both our peoples."

"I am sure it is," answered Galani. "I know King Balamir will be very pleased to hear of your assistance last night and into today. Let us be on our way."

Kier'ak fell into step beside Galani, his long legs keeping pace with Galani with ease, despite the brisk pace the Dwarf general kept. General Galani's personal bodyguards followed them, one on either side and two behind them as they walked, keeping a slight distance but close enough to react if needed.

Kier'ak paid them no heed, knowing that the Dwarves had been at war for a long time against the Wraulls and were not about to take any chances with anyone. He also knew that his people were openly disliked and if not for the fact that they arrived in time to help in the battle last night, he may well have not been given the chance to see the king now.

The Rey'ak were a proud and strong race, content to exist in their own and keep the outside world outside. But now things had changed. Draskene had a massive Wraull army amassed on their borders of the Firetop Mountains. They did not have the safety of a mountain fortress like the Dwarves to aid them in defense, nor did they have the numbers the Dwarves did.

Kier'ak's people preferred the open expanse of the mountain plateaus. From there they could soar on the thermals like the eagles and hawks and command great visions from the sky. The mountains provided an obstacle for the Wraulls, it was true, but once through the passes they would find the Rey'ak communities easy targets on the broad plateaus. The Rey'ak would be a brave and fierce foe, Kier'ak knew, but in the end, the sheer number of Wraulls would overwhelm them without help.

As they wound their way down the mountainside, the trees began to give way and become sparser and Kier'ak's keen ears began to hear the sounds of a city below. At last they broke through the woods and Kier'ak, as traveled as he was, was rendered breathless at his first sight of the Dwarf city of Calheller.

The sun was nearly done its descent in the western sky. They had spent nearly all afternoon to get to this point. It's reddish rays spilled through the crevasses in the mountain tops to illuminate the silver paved streets beneath them. As if lit by a magical fire, the streets glowed a warm white light as the silver reflected the sun's rays. Very few people were about, only the blacksmiths and shop keeps who could supply the army, the rest of the city evacuated against the Wraull attack.

Sadness filled Kier'ak's heart then, along with empathy for the Dwarves. For the first time he truly understood the beauty of the mountain city the Dwarves called home and hoped that they would endure the Wraull onslaught and may one day become true friends with the Rey'ak. He realized then just how wrong his people's way of isolationism was and was truly sorry for it.

"Coming?" asked Galani, looking back at Kier'ak.

"I'm sorry," he replied, "I was just caught up in the beauty of your city."

Galani smiled and said, "I shall see to it personally that you get a tour fit for a dignitary when all this war business is done, if you like."

Kier'ak smiled back and found himself liking Galani more and more.

"I would like that."

He found himself hoping that he and Galani would have time to get better acquainted in the future and visit each other's homes. It seemed like they may have more in common than he originally thought. He felt ashamed of his people's belief that they should remain isolated from the rest of the world. He had just met the Dwarven general and already he felt a strong kinship with him.

As they entered the city itself, Kier'ak found himself even more at awe as he took in the beauty around him. He marveled at the skill and art that went into every building, carved from stone, he was told by Galani, in a quarry in the south of the Thunder Mountains and then brought back here to Calheller and shaped and dressed and put in place.

The sun had completely set by now but no lamps lit the street. Instead, a thin layer of silver had been laid over the paving stones and it now shone dully in the early evening starlight. Kier'ak was greatly humbled by the skill possessed by the Dwarves in their mastery of stone and metals and said so to Galani.

"Perhaps, when this war with the Black Paladin is over, our peoples can share their ideas and technologies," Galani said in return.

They continued on in silence then, each lost to his own particular thoughts, Galani's four bodyguards an ever-present shadow just out of reach, keeping vigil.

At last they reached the Gardens of Life and Kier'ak was rendered speechless upon seeing their beauty, he and his people being fond admirers of natural works of art. Galani noticed Kier'ak's spellbound awe and with a smile, explained its significance and all that it represented. Despite his feelings of comradeship toward him, though, Galani did not tell Kier'ak that the garden's main purpose was to maintain the spell that kept the distance of the mountain fortress under an illusion of great distance. There were some things that were still necessary to keep secret until one was completely sure of their allies. Still, Galani slowed their pace just a bit, knowing that Kier'ak would enjoy the extra time to view the gardens.

At last they rounded the final bend in the garden and the majesty of the Thunder Mountains opened up before them. Kier'ak was startled by the sudden appearance of the mountains and the crashing waterfalls. He was silently curious as to why he didn't hear their presence much sooner. He knew the Dwarves must have some kind of illusion at work, but he knew better than to break protocol and ask. If he wanted to get aid for his people, he knew he could not offend the Dwarves and asking personal secrets of defense was a sure way to start.

Two Dwarf guards stepped forward to great them, saluting General Galani as they did so.

"Call down the transport," he commanded. "I have a guest to see the King."

The two guards eyed Kier'ak quickly then complied with Galani's orders. They knew better than to question his orders and besides, this was now the second Rey'ak to enter their city. Things were definitely getting stranger, they thought!

Kier'ak stood patiently with Galani and his four body guards as the pony drawn cart made its way down the mountainside. He paid no attention to the sideways glances he was given by the two guards who summoned the transport. He knew he would feel the same way if their situation had been reversed. He also knew, once word of the previous night's battle made its way back, he and his people would be accepted with a little more grace. Or so at least he hoped.

When the pony cart reached the bottom, Galani stepped forward and said to the driver, "My men and I will escort Kier'ak to the King. You may wait here with the guards."

The driver and the two guards were a little surprised at Galani's use of Kier'ak's name, but quickly realized that he must be important if Galani would refer to him so, instead of just 'the Rey'ak as had been the policy with their last Rey'ak visitor weeks before.

Galani climbed aboard and motioned for Kier'ak to sit next to him, while his body guards took the seats in the rear. It was a rough trip up the mountain, the cart bumping and jostling all the way and Kier'ak thought a couple of times it would have been easier and quicker for him to just fly up the path but he sat and endured the ride with his Dwarf hosts.

Upon reaching the peak of the trail, two more guards stepped forward to greet them. These, noted Kier'ak wore blue uniforms, with a crest of a blazing sun rising over the mountains on the chest. They saluted Galani and upon his command raised the portcullis to allow entrance into the Royal Halls themselves.

Kier'ak steeled himself and prepared to enter the mountains. Up to now, he had been fine with his lot, chosen by his king to be an emissary to the Dwarf King, but now he was faced with entering the mountain and traveling beneath it. Like Ar'ye and the rest of their race, they were fond of open spaces and did not care at all for small confined areas or underground.

Galani led the way in, followed closely by Kier'ak and his body guards. Kier'ak was mesmerized by the jewel encrusted walls that reflected and magnified the torch light to fully illuminate the cave before him. The boiling oil pots on ledges above him did not escape his keen observation either, and he repressed an involuntary shudder at the thought of their use.

As he followed Galani, the floor sloped gradually away and the small group traveled further underground until after a few minutes, the tunnel leveled out into a huge chamber with a small subterranean lake and a pair of large oak doors barring the way into another chamber.

"Please wait here with my men," asked Galani, "while I go forward to announce us to the king."

Kier'ak watched as Galani skirted the small lake and entered the massive, iron-bound oak doors. He waited patiently, Galani's guards keeping a silent, unobtrusive vigil. In his mind, he rehearsed what his king bade him to say to the Dwarf King in order to secure their help. He was heartened somewhat by General Galani's genuine warmth and friendship towards him but he also remembered the distrust and animosity he and the other Rey'ak had encountered from the Dwarves they rescued in the Thunder Mountains the previous night. The Dwarves were well known for their ability to hold a grudge. If they decided not to join forces with the Rey'ak, both races could be lost before the Black Paladin's massive forces.

After a few minutes, the doors reopened and General Galani emerged from the Conference Hall. He motioned for Kier'ak to approach and enter the Hall while the body guards remained outside the mighty doors upon their closing.

"King Balamir," Kier'ak said reverently as he bowed before the King at the head of a large rectangular table, "I am Kier'ak, cousin to King Ae'rik of the Rey'ak. I was sent here to request your aid in our most trying of times."

He rose from his bent knees and took the seat preferred to him by Galani. Across him and Galani sat two other wizened Dwarves, one dressed in a green robe and another in black. They stared at him with what seemed to be mixed looks of astonishment and apathy.

Kier'ak felt self-conscious in their stare, not having had any time to rest, clean or otherwise refresh himself since joining in the battle the previous night. He hoped that it would at least help confirm his sincerity and desperation.

King Balamir stared at Kier'ak long and hard for what seemed to Kier'ak as an eternity but was in fact only a few minutes before speaking.

"Many times in the past our people have asked yours for help and each time we were refused, the Rey'ak deciding it best to remain hidden and neutral. Now it seems that you are no longer hidden from this menace known as the Black Paladin, and you cannot remain neutral anymore. If we were to turn our backs on your people now, it would be a fitting reward for your refusal to help us in the past."

Kier'ak felt his hopes fall at that point, his stomach sinking into a deep pit. He had feared this, but still he had his orders. Even if the Dwarves refused to aid them, he and his men were to stay and fight alongside the Dwarves to the last Rey'ak, in the hopes that they may change their minds. He did not think that at this point it would make any difference.

Balamir let his words hang in the air for a moment, their icy content seeming to chill the very air in the room before he continued.

"But that would help neither of our people at this point. General Galani told me of your valiant effort in last night's battle. Without the help of you and your fellow Rey'ak many more of our troops would have been lost."

Kier'ak's eyes and hopes lit up like small stars at this—there was hope after all! The two Dwarves across from him seemed to look a little less severe as well, if that was at all possible.

"We must learn to forget past indifferences and to work towards a united future, one that will see an end to the menacing evil of the Black Paladin. You are not the first Rey'ak to come through our city in recent days. Just a few weeks ago, another of your kind came through here with three others and left again with them, along with two of our best Dwarf Patrol Captains on a desperate mission of utmost secrecy. He told us that the Rey'ak had been seeking our help for sometime but were unable to get to us because of the Wraulls. His name was Ar'ye. Do you know of him?"

"Alas I do not, but I can assure you, like all our people, he will do all in his power to help those he is with. It is our way with our allies."

"Tell us then, Kier'ak, our new allies, how desperate is your situation? You have seen our plight. If we are to join forces, we need a strategy. You have already met General Galani, and General Belan. Seated across from you are Grendle, our magic-user, in the black and Deelan, my first minister, in the green."

"As you know," began Kier'ak, addressing the entire table, "our people are secluded in the Fire Top Mountains. We were unknown to the races of Man and Wraull until about twenty years ago when the Black Paladin discovered us, through use of his black magic. We have had many border skirmishes with his Wraull troops over the years but they were always small in number and never a real threat.

"That has changed recently. The Wraulls have now amassed a massive army at the foot of a pass that leads into the Fire Top Mountains. They are waiting for something, someone, to lead them into the pass and overrun us. There is a dark force taking shape within the army and we fear once it matures, the attack will begin. We have no magic of our own and once through the pass, our lands are open plateau and will be easily overrun.

"It was difficult for my sortie to escape the noose the Wraulls have tightened around our homeland. They have archers all along the mountainsides and seek to shoot us down whenever we try to fly out. I lost nearly twenty men just trying to get out of the pass to get here."

Grendle spoke up as Kier'ak finished. "I do not doubt your claim that something dark is growing in the Wraull army. That is Draskene's way—to lead the battle with some dark creature of his own design. I shall endeavor to scry what is happening but the distance is far and Draskene's likely to be shielding his activities."

"From your report of last night's battle, General Galani," began Balamir again, "it will take Draskene some time to build and move another army here. His one remaining large force is the one centered at the Fire Top Mountains. Either he will attack the Rey'ak with it or he will move it here to assault us again. Either way, this is the most feasible target for our combined forces to attack."

"I agree," said General Galani. "We should take the battle to him for once instead of waiting here for it."

"The hunters I brought with me are prepared to stay and help defend your city as long as need be, King Balamir. We are still nearly two hundred strong."

"If I may, sire," cut in General Galani.

King Balamir nodded his head in assent. He was king and a brilliant tactician in his own right, but he respected the views of his generals.

"Kier'ak's hunters would provide excellent reconnaissance for our troops heading to the Fire Top Mountains. They could seek ahead for the easiest routes, take out small Wraull patrols, ensuring a quick march to the Fire Tops. If a few were to leave soon, once plans are solidified, they could reach the Rey'ak ahead of us, inform them of our arrival and have forces ready to join us."

"And yourself, General Galani?" asked King Balamir, looking at his Defensive General. "You will be staying behind with our reserve forces, to ensure our homeland is safe."

"Of course, sire," responded Galani, not the least bit enthused at the prospect of missing out on a battle. "I will inform General Belan of our plans as soon as he returns from the front."

"Good, then let's determine them now."

The next morning, General Belan was back in the city to report to the king and First Minister on the results of the attack two nights before. Along with him were scores of wounded Dwarf soldiers, in need of better medical aid than could be provided in the field.

He greeted Kier'ak warmly, as, like Galani, his prejudices towards the Rey'ak were washing away quickly in the light of their newfound alliance.

After his wounds from battle were properly cleaned, stitched and bandaged by the healers, General Belan was met by King Balamir and First Minister Deelan who informed him of his next campaign.

As with General Galani, Belan was delighted to be finally taking the fight to the Wraulls instead of sitting back and waiting for them to penetrate the Dwarf defenses. He also knew that the casualties to his Dwarf Patrols would be high but was heartened to know that Kier'ak and his hunters would be leading the way and providing aerial support.

Anxious to be on his way, and knowing time was of the essence if they were to aid the Rey'ak, General Belan announced, "I can have my Patrols ready to leave in two days. It will take us seven days to reach the Fire Top Mountains, providing the weather and other obstacles don't delay us.

"There is a pass, to the north of the Iron Hills near the Char'nak Mountains that opens into the plateau leading into the Fire Top Mountains. We will make for there, coming up behind the Wraulls and hopefully surprising them. If Kier'ak or another of his hunters flies ahead of us as we approach the pass and can get the Rey'ak hunters prepared on the other side, we should have a good chance."

Belan knew that there was a lot left to chance—the Dwarves getting to the pass in time, in strong enough numbers, and the Rey'ak getting the message to help in time. Still, they had no other options and it was their best chance so far.

"Get what supplies you need, General," said King Balamir, "and be on your way as soon as you can. General Galani, your Patrols will be on high alert and are to remain posted in the Thunder Mountains bordering Calheller, keeping an eye out for any further Wraull movements.

"May the gods of the mountains be with you, men."

For two days, the six from Calheller, along with Reyna, traveled on to the Iron Hills. All were much happier, having left the dismal Dead Woods behind and having found Salena, alive and well. She showed no outward signs of the ordeal she went through with Henaach to her friends, but at night she slept fitfully and would wake in cold sweats.

Duncan was quiet the first day out from Henaach's camp, still thinking about Patches and the battle the night before. Big Cat stayed at his side constantly and seemed to lend him some strength.

At last, as the Iron Hills drew near, the ground began to rise and become rocky. The horses picked their way more carefully and slowed their pace. Finally, Martyl called a halt near noon on the second day. As they all sat, sharing a lunch of cheese and fresh berries that Rorn and Dirn had picked from nearby bushes, Martyl stated his plan for the next day.

"Tomorrow we should reach the ancient ruins. Once there, we will search for clues as to the sword's whereabouts."

"What sort of clues?" asked Duncan.

Martyl was silent for a moment before answering, "I am not entirely sure. I will not lie to you all—our chances of finding the sword after so many generations have passed are extremely small. Countless others have tried and failed in the past. I am hoping that since we have an heir to Arundel that our chances may be better.

"Doubtless, there will be many dangers awaiting us. Some, like the Wraulls, we will be accustomed to. Others will no doubt be new and even more deadly, sent by the Black Paladin himself possibly, to way-lay us. We shall need to be alert and prepared at all times for the eventualities."

Duncan and the others did not seem overly heartened by Martyl's revelations but they did not show it, save for the downcast glances they all gave one another. They had all been through a lot up to this point and were not about to give up and turn back now, no matter how bleak their future may seem at this point in time.

When they finished eating and packing up their supplies, Martyl swung up on Tarna and said, "We travel on until sunset then set up camp for the night."

The others followed, mounting their horses, Duncan and Salena riding Roper together, right behind Martyl and Reyna who had the lead, side by side. Big Cat kept stride with Roper, careful to stay in the horse's line of sight so as not to spook him. The Dwarves followed on their ponies and Ar'ye brought up the rear on his horse. His keen eyes always scanned the horizon behind them for signs of pursuit.

The rest of the day and early evening went by quietly. They crested a large rise and Martyl called a halt. Everyone stared breathless at the sight before them. On the plateau beneath them lay the ruins of a small city, long ago broken and decimated. The skeletal remains of its outer defensive wall lay shattered and strewn like the bones of some long dead behemoth. What was left of buildings, shops and homes were scattered here and there, broken reminders of the lives that once lived here.

"There lies C'aleth Arn," stated Martyl reverently.

"The city of peace and hope," translated Rorn.

"It doesn't look like it had either," sighed Reyna. "It seems as though this place has seen more than its fair share of hard times."

No one else said a word as they all stared down at the ruined city before them. Each seemed to be overcome by a feeling fo despair and sorrow, thinking of the brutality that befell this place centuries ago, and the daunting task before them as they undertook the final leg of their journey to find the sword, Brach'dir.

"Let's set up camp for the night." It was Martyl who broke their reverie. "Tomorrow we begin our search and everyone needs to be as alert as possible."

Bin was nervous about approaching his master with the news he now had. Draskene had been in a foul mood for the past two days, ever since learning of his Wraull forces being decimated in the Thunder Mountains by the Dwarves and Rey'ak. Still, it was his duty to inform Draskene of all that his animal spies could tell him. To do otherwise, if he were to be found negligent in his duties, the penalties would be severe. Bin knew all too well just how severe. The image of the two Prime Guards from Frost Lake who had let the girl escape was burned forever in his mind. He could still hear the sound of their skulls being crushed beneath the Demon-horse's hooves every time he closed his eyes.

Yes, he would bear this ill fortuned news to Draskene. After all, his familiar's had worked hard to get to him in time for the information to still be relevant. It was not their fault (or his, he reminded himself) that the news was not to Draskene's liking.

As Bin traveled through the castle, he wondered to himself what this news would do to Draskene's plans. After all, this particular aspect had been high on his priority list. Now that they had failed, where would Draskene turn his attention next? He had a strangle hold on all the free lands except for the Dwarf city of Calheller and the Thunder Mountains. There were the Rey'ak also, who were now more than just a pain in his side. They had actually joined forces with the Dwarves! Bin knew that this had come as a surprise to his master. Could it be that his master was not as all powerful as he believed? Could they possibly lose Arundel to King Aramid's returned son?

The last thought bothered Bin and he told himself never to think of it again. At last he reached Draskene's quarters and as he neared the door, it swung open of its own account.

He heard Draskene bid, "Enter, Bin."

A shiver rose up his spine and in spite of his fear (or maybe because of it), he felt reassured again of Draskene's power. After all, he thought, if even I, his most trusted servant cannot approach undetected, how can a lost boy and his friends pose a threat?

"What news to you bring me from your animal friends, Bin?"

"Not good, I fear, my Lord," replied Bin, a little fearfully.

Draskene just stared at Bin, his eyes seeming to bore into his very soul, commanding him to speak.

"One of my falcons near the Thunder Mountains followed Frost and Henaach to bring back news of their progress. It seems that both were killed by Duncan and his cats, and the girl rescued."

Bin stared nervously at the floor, fearful that Draskene would vent his anger on him.

"Are you sure?" asked Draskene, the anger in his voice physically palpable.

"Yes, Master. He saw them, along with other winter-wolves, dead. Duncan, the girl and one cat still live."

"Leave me," commanded Draskene.

Bin did not hesitate. He quickly turned on his heel and vacated the room. The door closed behind him of its own accord. As he made his way down the hall, he heard a deafening boom and felt the very stone he tread upon rumble beneath him. He knew Draskene was not pleased with the turn of events and he hastened as far from the castle as he could. It was best to let his master work through his frustrations himself! Bin had seen these fits of rage in the past and although they weren't frequent, he knew all too well the destruction that would ensue!

Chapter Twenty-Six

The next morning, everyone was up at dawn, eager to be under way. The sun was a dull orange orb in the eastern sky, much of its light and warmth blocked by the shroud of mist that had settled over the Iron Hills during the night. What light that did spill through cast eerie shadows through the mist. Strange spectral shapes seemed to dance and flit about, toying with the eyes and imagination, making everyone see things that weren't really there.

The horses and Big Cat, their senses of smell and hearing much superior to the people they were with, were not so easily fooled by the shadows. They sensed that there was nothing really there and remained calm.

Martyl gathered everyone around for a quick breakfast while the horses were allowed to graze on what meager grass they could find.

"We shall split up to enable us to cover more area, faster," began Martyl, once the others were seated around to eat. "Rorn, you, Selena and Duncan search to the north. Dirn, you and Ar'ye search to the west while Reyna and I search to the east. We will all start and meet up at the southern edge of the ruins below us, here."

He pointed down the slope in the misty gloom to a spot they could barely make out—a crumbling tower, once part of the wall that surrounded the city.

"Do not separate from your partner and everyone be alert for danger. If anyone encounters trouble, call for help and we will all come as fast as we can. Since we do not know where the sword is located, we must travel slowly and observe everything. We will find a suitable location to keep the horses—we shall have to travel by foot to make sure we miss nothing. At dusk, we will meet back at our designated meeting place to rest for the night."

No one questioned Martyl or his choice of groups. They all knew very little of this place, having been abandoned by men and Dwarves alike for generations. As they were, each group was evenly matched to best face the hazards they may encounter.

When they finished eating, everyone packed their supplies on their horses and then set off down the rocky slope to the ghost-town below. The horses picked their way gingerly, an occasional misstep setting in motion minor rock slides and spooking both horse and rider alike. After a tense thirty minutes or so, the six horses and seven riders reached the plateau that the dead city of C'aleth Arn rested upon.

The sun rose higher in the early morning sky, its heat burning away some of the mist but around the city it still hung tightly, giving the ghostly illusion of a soul rising from a dead body.

Salena felt a shiver run down her spine. Whether it was from the cool damp mist or the eerie vision before her, she wasn't sure.

Martyl signaled everyone to stop when they reached the bottom then motioned for Rorn and Dirn to dismount and circle the half-remaining tower before them. Martyl himself walked his horse ahead slowly, as bait, to the tower entrance. Silently, the Dwarves crept around the rubble of the wall to the backside of the tower. Tarna walked forward, calm and sure of himself, his flared nostrils releasing jets of warm air in the cool mist around them.

Minutes later, Rorn and Dirn emerged from the tower, signaling all was clear. Martyl signaled for the others to approach and dismount.

"The horses will be fine here," stated Reyna as she quickly surveyed their surroundings. "There is water in that shallow depression near the tower and there is some grass they can graze on. They may wander in search of more but they will not go far. They have been trained to wait for their riders, going only as far as necessary for food and water, but they will always return. Even if frightened away, they will return."

"Very well," replied Martyl. "Take your weapons and a supply of food and water for the day. There is no telling what we may, or may not find inside the city remains. We will meet back here at dusk."

Duncan was anxious to be off to search the ruined city. At last he would find the weapon with which he could face Draskene and reclaim his kingdom, as well as exact his revenge. The past couple of weeks, the desire for revenge had fed and nurtured him, growing inside him like a living entity, threatening to burst forth and consume him at any time.

He was just a boy when his family and homeland had been taken away from him. It was Connor and Martyl who had raised him to one day reclaim his throne, to defeat Draskene. It had been their dream, as much as, if not more than, his. Duncan had been happy living in the Misty Isles, surrounded by the giant cats and Salena and her people. Still, he knew as heir to Arundel he had to try to end Draskene's evil reign.

It wasn't until he thought he had lost Salena and the loss of Patches right before his eyes that Duncan truly began to understand hate and the all-consuming fire of revenge. There was nothing he wanted more now that to make Draskene suffer, to feel the pain of loss that he did now.

Big Cat padded silently along at his side, between him and Salena, ready to aid either should they need her help. Her tail flicked minutely, side to side, the only outward sign she showed that she was uncomfortable with their surroundings.

Salena kept her left hand on Big Cat's powerful back, absently stroking her out of habit, her right hand resting on the hilt of her short sword. She was not about to be taken from her friends again.

Rorn crept through the rubble just ahead of them, searching for any dangers, hidden or otherwise. He was beginning to develop a grudging admiration for this young man and his companions and wanted to see him stop Draskene as well. Every fifty feet or so he would stop, motion Duncan and Salena to stay put and listen intently. Each time, he would crouch down, listening attentively. Big Cat seemed to be listening also, her whiskers and ears attuned to one direction, then another the next time.

Duncan and Salena waited patiently while Big Cat and Rorn tried to discern what they felt or heard and where it was coming from, but each time Rorn would shrug and continue on, motioning for them to follow.

As midday approached, the sun at last began to burn away the last remnants of the dismal mist that surrounded them. Visibility was greatly improved, but they still saw nothing that heartened them in their search. There were no buildings at all left standing. Time, the elements, and war had seen to that. Here and there, pieces of a wall remained, the corner of a foundation somewhere else. The streets themselves were virtually non-existent. Weeds, shrubs and even the odd small tree sprouted up through cracks in the stone.

Rorn set a steady pace, not too fast as they needed to explore wherever something caught their eye, someplace that looked like it may conceal the sword they were after.

Salena spied one such place and motioned for Duncan and Rorn to follow her. It was a low, squat building, nearly fully intact, obscured earlier from their view by large piles of rubble.

"This resembles a barracks used by Dwarf Patrols," commented Rorn as he approached. He was in an attack stance, battle-axe ready and in his gnarled hands.

"We must be cautious," he continued. "We have no idea what may be inside."

There was no door, the wood long ago rotted away. Some sunlight managed to penetrate the entryway and Rorn peered in cautiously. He was going to suggest that Duncan send Big Cat in first to determine if their was someone or something waiting for them but thought better of it. He knew Duncan would sooner go in himself than knowingly risk his feline companion.

"Light me a torch," he commanded and Duncan handed him one from their supplies, lighting it as he did so. "Follow close behind and do not separate."

Rorn led the way into the building, Duncan and Salena following close behind. Big Cat entered last, but once they entered the large room the doorway opened into, she walked to the center of it and scanned the area with her keen feline eyes.

The room was deathly quiet. Rorn moved ahead, emboldened by the fact that Big Cat did not seem to sense any danger. After a few moments, they had covered the perimeter of the room. Piles of debris were scattered throughout but nothing more of interest was found, except a rotten wooden door at the opposite end from where they entered.

"This is the drill hall," explained Rorn. "Through that door is the sleeping quarters. Maybe we will have more luck there."

They made their way to the door when Big Cat suddenly leapt to the fore and began pawing at the base of the door. Salena's heart leapt and she instinctively grabbed Duncan's hand. He squeezed back to reassure her while drawing his sword with his right hand. Rorn passed the torch back to Salena and motioned her off to the side of the door. With Duncan right behind him, he approached and with a well placed kick, shattered the door.

The element of surprise was on their side. A large black shadowy object scampered from the doorway and fled to the back of the room. Big Cat bounded through the shattered door, faster than Dwarf or man could ever hope to be.

There was a crash as she caught her quarry and the two tumbled across the floor. As Salena entered, torch in one hand and sword in the other, Duncan and Rorn were close enough to see the flash of a white paw as Big Cat rained down blow upon blow on their unseen enemy.

Her prey sufficiently stunned, Big Cat opened her large jaws and her teeth neatly severed its spinal cord. As she rose to her feet, a rat the size of a medium dog dangled limply from her mouth.

The tension now abated, Duncan, Rorn and Salena let out the collective breath they had unknowingly been holding and began laughing.

Martyl and Reyna covered ground fairly quickly. He had experience in stealthy exercises from his training as a Royal Knight and it came back to him readily. Reyna, for her part, had spent the better part of her adult life waging guerilla war on the Prime Guard that occupied her homeland. She was very adept at moving quickly and stealthily, even more so than Martyl. And, she was just as quick and deadly with a blade. Martyl was glad to have her at his side.

In the dim light of the early morning, fog shrouded sun, Martyl caught himself stealing the occasional side-long glance at Reyna. She was a kindred spirit, driven from her home by the same foe, not belonging anywhere except with her chosen family of friends.

In the silence of their search, his thoughts drifted back to the night she found them in Equilon. Her aid had been invaluable. In fact, without her help, they may not have made it out of the town alive. She risked her own life to help them, virtual strangers, knowing nothing about them except that they were in trouble. Reyna was a fierce fighter when roused, and a loyal friend.

He smiled then, not realizing in his reverie that he was looking at her as he did so. Reyna saw his smile and flashed him one back. Caught off guard and realizing what he had done, Martyl blushed and hoped she wouldn't see his reddening face in the misty gloom. He chastised himself inwardly for feeling like a boy. By not keeping his head clear, he was risking the lives of all those with him.

Reyna was much more in tune with her feelings, though and grasped Martyl's hand, saying, "Do not be embarrassed Martyl. I too feel the same way." She smiled at him, facing him now as they stopped walking.

"I know you cannot show any of your feeling right now for you fear they would jeopardize your quest. That is fine. I know you are a Royal Knight and you are sworn to protect the heir of Arundel, Duncan and can have no other life until that is fulfilled. I admire and understand that and wish to help as much as I can. I am content to know that when this is over, we will have all the time we need to fully get to know one another."

Martyl grasped her hands in his, looking directly into her eyes and said, "Thank you, Lady Reyna."

She smiled again at him, then, knowing how awkward it must be for him, pulled her hands free even though she enjoyed holding his, and began walking again.

"Tell me of this sword, we seek," she said, changing the subject. "Why this one in particular?"

Grateful for the new direction their conversation was taking, Martyl began.

"Centuries ago, during the Black Magic Wars, many magical weapons were created to combat the Demons and evil magic-users that threatened to destroy the Dwarves and Men of the world. One such weapon was this sword we seek—Brach'dir. It was created by the Dwarves of the Thunder Mountains—their magic was the strongest at the time—for the ruling King of Arundel, a distant relative of Duncan's. It's name means Mountain Light in our tongue.

"This sword was used successfully in many battles against the Demons and in later years against the Wraulls and other evil creatures still in the world. Then one day, the Dwarves and men decided to build a joint colony to expand their frontiers, here, at C'aleth Arn—the city of peace and hope. The heir of Arundel at that time came with the people of Arundel to settle here. The city prospered for many years until the Wraulls began to breed again and regroup. One day, without warning, thousands of them descended upon the city and everyone, human and Dwarf, man, woman and child, was slain. The sword was lost. Over time, the sword was forgotten and it became only a legend.

"I myself believed it to be only a legend until it's existence was confirmed by the Dwarves at Calheller while we were there. It's whereabouts are still unknown, but it is believed to still be in these ruins."

"What if someone else found it, long ago?" asked Reyna. She hated to seem so negative, but the question needed to be asked, for all their sakes.

"That may be a possibility," conceded Martyl, "but I need to believe otherwise. Besides, its magic can only be wielded by the heir to Arundel. It was forged with their blood."

"Despite knowing the legend and the Dwarves' confirmation, you still have no clear idea where to look?"

"I am afraid not."

They carried on in silence then, dutifully checking anything that looked like it might conceal a sword.

Ar'ye and Dirn spent the morning hours searching in silence. Neither felt compelled to speak to the other and they kept their distance.

In the fog enshrouded gloom about them, Dirn was constantly reminded of the battles his people had against Draskene and his Wraull forces. Everywhere he looked, there was destruction of epic proportions. This had once been a thriving community of Dwarves and men, a symbol of their triumph over the Demons in the Black Magic Wars. Now it was a symbol of the destruction that awaited them all, should they fail in their endeavor.

Dirn did not like it here. His mood grew sullen and dark, the devastation around him making him think of the destruction that may be befalling Calheller that very moment. He was committed to helping Martyl and Duncan find the sword as he knew that was their best hope. Yet he longed to be home, to defend his city from the ravages of the Wraulls. Surely they would be attacking anytime soon, if they had not already.

And the Rey'ak. Were they truly going to help now, as Ar'ye said, fearing war with Draskene one way or the other, no longer able to stay neutral?

He looked at Ar'ye casting him a sideways glance as they traveled down a rubble strewn street. Dirn thought about all the time Ar'ye had proven himself over the past weeks while they had traveled together. Maybe he owed him more than he had given him. Maybe his people had seen that to remain neutral in the danger of Draskene was an error and really would help the Dwarves.

Dirn called a halt to their search and rested himself on a low, flat section of wall that was still upright.

"Have a seat, Ar'ye," he said, patting the stone beside him. "We cannot search on empty stomachs all day." He handed Ar'ye a small loaf of bread and a large chunk of cheese from his pack.

Ar'ye took the proffered food and sat next to Dirn. They ate in quiet for several minutes before Dirn broke the silence.

"I am sorry for my hostility toward you these past weeks," began Dirn. Ar'ye was taken aback but continued looking ahead, eating, not wanting to interrupt the Dwarf, eager to see where this was heading.

"You have proven yourself to be a great ally in our search so far and you deserve better treatment, from myself and Rorn. Just because our peoples in general do not see eye to eye does not mean we cannot."

Dirn offered his hand then to Ar'ye, who, still a little surprised, took it in his own.

"Thank you, Dirn," replied Ar'ye. "That is good to know. Know you also that it is true what I said earlier. My people do wish to make amends for not aiding your people in your times of need in the past. We realize now that we cannot remain neutral in these times against the Black Paladin and his Wraulls and will do all we can to help."

"That is all we can ask," finished Dirn solemnly. He reached in his pack and drew out a flask that Ar'ye hadn't seen him with before. Dirn caught his look and smiled.

"This is my own private supply of ale for this trip," he half-whispered, as if afraid someone may hear and take it from him. "Have a sip with me before we begin our search again."

Ar'ye gladly accepted the flask and took a deep drink. He enjoyed a sip of ale now and again like most others, and had naught but water for sometime now. He took a mighty mouthful then spluttered as it went down. Wiping his face, he handed the flask back to the Dwarf who was smiling mischievously.

"My own personal blend," he laughed. "It takes a little getting used to!"

He slapped Ar'ye on the shoulder playfully then jumped down from the wall. Ar'ye followed him, a smile crossing his weathered features, and the two continued on their search.

At dusk, the seven members of the three groups met up at the tower, at the entrance to the city. True to Reyna's word, the four horses and two ponies were only a whistle away. All six trotted up to Reyna and she lovingly patted each one on the neck then set about checking their hooves for any obstructions.

Martyl started a small fire at the entrance to the tower. He was not too worried about it drawing any unwanted attention as their presence must surely be known by now. He had the Dwarves, Duncan and Ar'ye gather round and recount their versions of the day's events. All had nothing to report. What they had seen of the city so far was barren and virtually lifeless.

"What do you suggest now?" asked Duncan, who most of all felt the futility of searching such a vast area with no clues. The need to find the sword was weighing heavily on him.

Martyl poked at the burning fire with a long stick, watching the embers and coals shift about as air was exposed to fresh areas. A piece of wood popped in the heat, seeming to demand an answer of him also.

"I must admit, for the first time since coming on this quest, I am truly at a loss as to how to proceed."

That was clearly not the answer Duncan, or the others had hoped for, but they held their tongues, sensing he had more to say yet.

"I know only of the legend, that it was forged by the Dwarves for the rulers of Arundel at the time of the Black Magic Wars. It was said that the wielder of the sword fell in battle here, at C'aleth Arn and that none other than an heir of Arundel could wield it."

Martyl was silent then but the Dwarves knew of the legend also and knew he was keeping something back. Rorn caught his eye and Martyl gave an almost imperceptible shake of his head, as if to say, let it be.

Rorn decided that whatever Martyl had decided on the issue was best left alone. He had confidence in Martyl as their leader and as a man of honor and deferred to his judgement on the situation.

Changing subjects, he said, "I felt a presence today."

The others looked up from the fire and all eyes were on Rorn.

"I do not know what it was or where, but I could feel it in the air. I think the cat felt it too."

Big Cat, at Duncan's side as always, looked up and her gaze fell on Rorn as he talked about her. Rorn felt an involuntary shiver run down his spine. He wasn't used to animals knowing he was talking about them. He also wasn't used to being in the company of an animal that could kill a Demon or pack of winter-wolves. Rorn made a mental note to never say anything derogatory about the large cat in front of him.

As if in response, Big Cat gave a small meow of affirmation. Duncan interpreted for her to everyone else.

"Big Cat did sense it. I felt something a little odd at times also."

"Did anyone else?" asked Martyl.

The others all responded, "No."

"Then maybe it was only in the north section of the city," began Martyl. "Tomorrow, we will ride to your last location, leave the horses again, and continue from there. It's our best lead so far."

"I do not know if it was the sword I felt," interjected Rorn. "It was a dark presence, unsettling."

"It may be something guarding the location," Martyl put forth. "The magic of the sword can only be wielded by a member of the Arundel Royal Family but many would be drawn to its magic nonetheless. What else of interest would there be in this place?"

No-one had an answer for him, each trying to picture what lay in store for them tomorrow.

"Eat and rest," said Martyl, as he rose. "I will take first watch. Rorn, you will relieve me, followed by Duncan, Ar'ye and last Dirn."

Martyl stepped out into the growing darkness, the others talking softly back in the tower. Reyna approached him, having finished with the horses.

"I have left the horses to graze for the night," she said. "They will not go far and will be here before dawn."

Martyl did not doubt her on the horses, having seen their loyalty several times now.

"Join the others for food and rest," he said to her. "I am not sure what tomorrow will bring."

Reyna knew he was bothered by their failure to find the sword today but she also knew that he could not be consoled. Such was his dedication to the quest that he would accept nothing short of complete victory before he would rest comfortably. She smiled at him as she passed into the tower with the others, her heart heavy in sympathy.

Hours later, Duncan found himself on a hilltop, rubble and debris strewn all about him. He couldn't remember how he got there, just that he needed to be there. Skeletons by the hundreds were scattered everywhere, twisted and broken, lifeless like the city itself. He studied them more closely and discovered some to be human, some Dwarven and some, he presumed by the size and skulls with wolf-like features, to be Wraull.

In the distance he could hear war drums beating. He recognized the sound as being Wraull, remembering from his boat ride down the Thunder River.

The drums grew nearer, and the very earth began to tremble beneath his feet. Duncan looked about anxiously for his companions but they were nowhere in sight. Looming on the horizon like a great, ominous cloud, thousands of Wraulls marched towards the lone hilltop upon which he stood. Nearer they drew, drums crashing and swords clashing, the cacophony of noise threatening to overwhelm him.

From beneath the hill, another rumbling began. Duncan looked down and to his amazement, a concealed doorway began to slide open. In columns ten abreast, men and Dwarves issued forth to meet the Wraull onslaught, their footsteps and drums echoing into the still night air.

Duncan called to them but they paid no heed. They marched on, oblivious to his presence. He remained a mute witness to their upcoming struggle.

A flash of lightning lit the sky, followed by a raucous peel of thunder seconds later. It was as if this was the signal to begin.

Archers from both sides let loose, valleys of arrows, some tipped in poison, some tipped with flame, all deadly. Combatants on both sides dropped by the scores, the once still night air now rent with screams of agony and bouts of thunder.

Both sides continued forward relentlessly, closing the distance between them. Duncan heard the Dwarf battle horn blow followed by the shout, "Bray'la!"

Battle cries from both the men and Wraulls rang out also and Duncan thought he heard, "For Arundel!" shouted more than once. As if in a trance, he watched as both sides collided on the run.

Swords clashed and bodies fell. The coppery scent of blood assailed his nostrils as more and more men and Dwarves fell before the massive numbers of Wraulls.

At last the Wraulls broke through and rushed toward the hillside opening. Seeing what was about to happen, Duncan could stand by idly no more. Drawing his sword, he rushed to stop them, seeing only a handful of defenders at the opening.

As he reached the bottom, Duncan braced himself for what was to come. How he wished Martyl or Big Cat were here to help him. Where were his friends? What had become of them? Sword drawn, he was ready to battle the first Wraull that crossed his path.

He did not have to wait long. At least a dozen rushed towards him—and right through! Duncan stood dumbfounded for a moment, trying to fathom what had just happened. He turned to follow the Wraulls when more passed through him. And more. Before he realized it, he had been over-passed by more than a hundred Wraulls and they were still advancing.

In horror, he saw the Dwarves and men guarding the hillside entrance cut down and the Wraulls disappearing inside.

Sheathing his sword, Duncan set off at a run after them. As he passed into the hill, it opened into a large well-lit chamber and then broke into a downward passage.

He followed it down, torches in sconces on the walls lighting his way. Ahead of him he could hear the sounds of battle, and the screams of men, Dwarves and Wraulls, as they battled each other in this tomb.

Duncan's heart raced in fear and anticipation of what he would find below. At last he reached the end of the tunnel. It opened to reveal an underground complex, of obvious Dwarven design, filled with Wraulls and the dead bodies of scores of Dwarves and men. Along with the dead soldiers, Duncan could see the bodies of women and children, human and Dwarven, slain.

He cried out in despair and frustration but the Wraulls paid him no heed. Duncan cast about the room, something pulling inexorably at him to search it out. He staggered to the center of the room, numb inside from the destruction of life before him until he came to a stone sarcophagus. The Wraulls spied it also and were converging upon it, somehow still unaware of his presence.

Duncan searched for the sword Brach'dir, feeling it was there, when a voice in his mind screamed at him, "Flee!"

Without thinking, he did as he was bid and fled for the passageway up to the surface. As he passed the entranceway to the tunnel out, he saw two Dwarves, mortally wounded but still alive, pull on a pair of heavy ropes. With tremendous effort, they pulled down two key support beams and sprang their trap. The ceiling caved in, sealing everyone in the underground chamber in an earthen embrace with no escape.

With a start, Duncan sat bolt upright. His brow was beaded with sweat and his skin felt cold and clammy. Instantly his dream flooded back to him. He knew where the sword was! It was in the stone sarcophagus, buried beneath a hilltop! He had to tell Martyl!

He rose quietly, despite being overly anxious, knowing the others needed their sleep. Dirn was on watch now and he silently acknowledged Duncan's rising with a wave, then turned back to his duty. Big Cat raised her head up from her paws and after surmising everything was okay, went back to sleep.

Duncan knelt next to Martyl, who was sleeping close to the tower entrance, and gently shook him awake.

Martyl awoke at once, sword in his hand, his years of combat training always at the fore.

"What is it?" he whispered once he saw Duncan's face peering at him in the receding night. Dawn was not far off now.

"I know where the sword is," Duncan replied, barely able to contain himself.

Martyl eyed him warily then rose and pulled Duncan with him to the tower entrance to where Dirn kept watch.

"Is something wrong?" Dirn asked as they approached.

"Duncan may know where the sword is. The Dwarves know as much about this as I do so you may as well listen to his account and offer what input you can. Tell us Duncan. Where is the sword?"

"I had a dream," Duncan began, his eagerness beginning to dull somewhat now that he had an audience. Self-doubt began to creep in and he wondered if what he dreamt was really what he believed. Still, what did he have to lose by telling Martyl and Dirn? If his dream was only that, they were no worse off than before. In the end, he decided any idea was better than where they were currently and he defeated his self-recrimination.

"I saw a hill and from its peak I could see the people, Dwarves and men of C'aleth Arn battling thousands of Wraulls. The Wraulls were winning then pressed on into a tunnel that opened into a hillside. I followed them in and saw a stone sarcophagus. The Wraulls did too but before they could defile it, Dwarves pulled the ceiling down and buried everyone and everything."

Martyl was quiet for a moment, pondering this when Dirn said, "The part about the cave-in sounds like a Dwarf trap to prevent enemies from plundering our treasures. It is conceivable that the Dwarves here built such a place in a hill for defense and would have destroyed it before letting the Wraulls take it."

"I think you saw the resting place of the sword, Duncan," said Martyl at last. "Part of the legend I did not tell anyone was that an heir of Arundel would be sought out by the sword if they were close enough. I did not want you to generate your own visions from wanting to find the sword so badly. It was better you didn't know and to let the sword seek you. It now seems it has done so. The sword was most likely laid to rest with the person who wielded it, to be returned to Arundel with the body, but was buried when the Dwarves caused the cave-in."

"I agree," replied Dirn. "That sounds most plausible."

Duncan was positively beaming at this point, happy to at least be able to contribute something of unique value to their quest. For so long, the others had protected him, sheltered him. Now he had done something for them!

"Do you think you can recognize the hill?" asked Martyl.

"I think so," replied Duncan.

"Good. Awake the others. We will eat then be on our way."

They ate a quick breakfast of cheese and bread washed down with cold water. Everyone was quiet as they ate, lost in their own thoughts about where this would lead. The entire purpose of their journey had been to find a weapon to fight the Draskene with and now it was possibly within their grasp!

The excitement was a palpable entity in the air around them. Salena squeezed Duncan's hand as they finished eating, silently conveying her support and belief in him. He smiled back at her before rising and gearing up his horse. The others followed suit and soon the party was moving northwards through the ruins in search of the hill in Duncan's vision.

Duncan and Salena on Roper led the way. The horses traveled at a steady walk, everyone alert for any signs of a trap or the hill-top, uncertain exactly what they would find. The scenery around them did little to ease the feeling of uneasiness that followed them. Section after section that they passed was littered with destroyed buildings and piles of rubble. War and time had combined to ravage what was once a vibrant city and turned it into a ghost-town. Rorn and Dirn both felt uncomfortable as they rode on, images of their home of Calheller becoming like this haunting them.

They rode north through the ruined city for several hours, the progress slowed by rubble and debris, the roadway choked with branches and scrub-brush. For the first time since setting out on their quest, the way would have been quicker on foot as the horses were forced to walk slowly to check their footing among all the loose stones and debris across their path.

At last the ground before them began to rise. The sun was now out and near its zenith, the air still, the only sound was the buzzing of insects and the swish of the horses' tails as they swatted them away. Duncan's pulse quickened as he recognized the top of the rise. It was no longer a lone, solitary hill as in his dream. It had been worn down by time and weather, into a steadily rising knoll, ringed at the top by a bowl-shaped depression caused by the cave-in seen in his dream.

"There!" pointed Duncan excitedly. "That's where I saw the sword! Inside this hill!"

Martyl was about to warn him to be quiet. Despite the fact they had seen no-one in two days did not necessarily mean they were alone when he was cut off by a deafening screech from above.

As one, the whole group looked upward as the winged shadow passed over, blotting out the sun.

Chapter Twenty Seven

Five thousand Dwarves, mounted on war ponies, began the march to the Fire Top Mountains in an effort to aid the Rey'ak and possibly end the Wraull threat both nations faced.

They began the march the day after the failed Wraull attack on the Thunder Mountains. General Belan led half of the Dwarf force, along with the two hundred odd Rey'ak led by Kier'ak. Kier'ak had tried to argue to get the Dwarves to send more as even with their five thousand added to the Rey'ak force of ten thousand, they would still be outnumbered four to one. King Balamir steadfastly refused, wanting to keep forces behind. General Balamir commanded the remaining Dwarf forces that stayed in Calheller, just in case Draskene or the Wraulls had any further attacks planned.

Their march was quick and uneventful, the Untamed Lands denizens not wishing to engage such a large and obviously well-organized force. The Rey'ak provided aerial scouting and any possible threats could be easily skirted if the need arose. Even the ogres and winter-wolves that inhabited this region gave wide berth to the Dwarves. They had no seize engines, towers, catapults or other such devices of war. This was to be a quick strike against the Wraull forces amassed in the Fire Wind Flats, not a protracted engagement. Being heavily outnumbered, the Dwarves were relying on speed and stealth, the element of surprise to give them the advantage. Anything other than the supply wagons that went with them would just be too cumbersome and slow.

The terrain itself did little to hinder them either. The ground was relatively level and clear, with only the odd copse of trees dotting the landscape. There was no cover for the Dwarves to take refuge but they needed none. The mass of the Wraull forces had been concentrated in the two areas—the Thunder Mountains, which was now nearly Wraull-free, and the base of the Fire Top Mountains, to which they now headed.

The Dwarf army kept north and east across the Untamed Lands, passing the spot where Duncan and Salena fought Henaach and the winter-wolves by many miles. Even with an army this size, the Dwarves wary of straying too close to the Dead Woods. For two days they traveled, stopping every so often to water their ponies and check their hooves for damage. They were not moving at a hurried pace, but steady and constant, each day covering fifteen leagues. The Dwarves stayed well clear of the Dead Woods, knowing all too well what dangers lurked there. They had no desire to become embroiled in a battle with Demon Spawn before they reached the Wraulls. For much the same reason, they avoided the Iron Hills and C'aleth Arn, knowing there were many dangers in the ruined city also.

General Belan alone knew of the party that traveled to C'aleth Arn. The fewer who knew of the plan to recover the Brach'dir, the better. His thoughts and wishes for success traveled to his comrades Rorn and Dirn and the others with them, but he knew if this attack succeeded in slowing or halting the Wraull army, their homeland would be safe for sometime. He knew they would all never be truly free from danger until the Black Paladin's reign was ended once and for all. The quest for the sword was too intangible a dream for a warrior like him. Belan felt better knowing his forces were marching to a definitive goal, even if it meant heavy losses, possibly even his own life. Even in the night they advanced, eager to reach their destination and take the battle to their enemy for the first time.

By the middle of the third day, the Dwarves reached the edge of the Fire Wind Flats. They had journeyed nearly fifty leagues and were tired and sore, their mounts even more so. Kier'ak dispatched a dozen

Rey'ak scouts to check out the 'Flats so they could best determine their next course of action.

The Fire Winds Flats were the remnant of a long dead volcano that was part of the Fire Top Mountain chain, which still was home to several volcanoes, giving the chain its name. During the Black Magic Wars, the Demons had used their powers to cause this particular volcano to erupt, decimating an army of men and Dwarves who had assembled here to strike at the Wraulls of the Char'nak Mountains. In its place now was a broad expanse in the shape of a giant bowl, ringed by rocky debris. The Fire Wind Flats rose above the Untamed Lands, stretching to the bottom of the Char'nak and Fire Top Mountains, keeping the two chains separated. At the far eastern edge, the 'Flats narrowed into a defile that led upwards into the Fire Top Mountains. It was here that the Wraull army was amassed, waiting for the signal from Draskene to attack the Rey'ak.

The 'Flats got their unusual name because of the winds that blew down from the Fire Top Mountains. Hot, sulfurous volcanic air was swept from the lofty peaks of the Fire Top Mountains and funneled through the pass at the end of the Fire Wind Flats to sweep across the broad expanse. Very little grew in this hot, oppressive choking air covered area.

The first of the scouts reported back and the signal was given to ascend the rise to the Fire Wind Flats. There were no Wraulls to be seen within a few leagues at least so it was relatively safe for the Dwarves to set up camp. The ponies were unsaddled, walked to cool down then fed and watered. The camp cooks set up their fires and began the monumental task of feeding their forces. Sides of beef were roasted over open pits and huge iron kettles boiled vegetables. A perimeter guard was set up with two sentries every fifty feet.

Kier'ak's scouts returned at different points throughout the remainder of the early evening and into the night, all reporting the same thing—the Fire Wind Flats were clear of all Wraulls. Their forces gathered at the pass into the Fire Top Mountains.

Belan, a handful of his captains, Kier'ak and two of his top scouts, met in Belan's tent after the sun had set. Four burly Dwarves blocked the entrance, their eyes and ears alert, battle axes in their meaty, calloused hands.

"We have given you our best up-to-date information, General," began Kier'ak. "It will take us a day to cross the 'Flats to where the Wraulls are. Once there, our forces in the Fire Top Mountains will join us."

General Belan was quiet for a moment, thoughtfully studying the maps of the terrain they had to cross, laid out before him.

"I don't like crossing such a large open area," he began. "If the Wraulls learn of our approach, we could be cut down by archers before we even reach them."

"My scouts will see that that does not happen," replied Kier'ak. "They will be flying at least an hour ahead of us and any Wraulls they spot will be dispatched immediately. No Wraull sentries can spot a Rey'ak in the sky if we do not wish it."

Belan studied Kier'ak for a moment, his wizened eyes taking in the measure of the Rey'ak before him. Kier'ak and his hunters had made short work of the Wraulls in the Thunder Mountain passes a few days back. Maybe, he thought to himself, I should learn to trust Kier'ak and his hunters. They have proven themselves trustworthy and valuable allies.

"Very well," decided Belan at last. "We will place our trust, and lives, in your hands." With a stern unwavering look, he added, "Don't let us down."

Kier'ak was all too aware of the Dwarves' mistrust towards his people but he also knew what a big step in their interracial relations this was, so he simply replied, "We won't."

He then turned to his scouts and said, "Have a perimeter set up around the camp. Beyond that, I want two men stationed a quarter mile out from the perimeter at each of the compass points."

The Rey'ak slipped out through the tent wordlessly and were gone, seeing to their orders immediately.

"Let your men rest tonight, General," said Kier'ak. "We have superior night vision and are better suited for it."

General Belan was about to reply in the negative when he stopped himself. They were a combined army now, and as such, needed to work together. He quickly weighed their situation in his mind, his warrior training effortlessly sizing up their location and encampment. In the end, he saw no harm in letting the Rey'ak take watch tonight. After all, they were still a day's march from the Wraull forces and his men could be ready at a moment's notice.

"Very well," he replied finally. "The watch is yours."

"Thank you," replied Kier'ak. "Good night and good hunting." With a smile, he was gone into the night.

General Belan turned to his captains and said, "Tell your troops to rest tonight. We will take comfort in the Rey'ak keeping watch and be fresh for tomorrow's march."

The captains responded affirmatively and headed out into the night. They too had conflicting thoughts on the Rey'ak. On one hand, it would be nice to leave the guard duty to the Rey'ak and their keen vision but there was still the doubt of their conviction to help. Too many years of self-imposed neutrality were hard to overcome and the Dwarves were self-sufficient and stubborn to a fault. Still, if their forces were being granted a night's rest after three days of nonstop traveling, they would take it.

Bin was in his quarters, getting ready for bed, when he heard a loud insistent tapping at his window. He was in a room on the third floor of the castle so he knew it was not a person trying to get his attention. As he moved across the room to the window, he tried to think what it might be. None of his familiars in the stables were out but he did have many others who traveled the lands, living abroad, only to return to Arundel when they had important information for him. Once he received the information, it was up to him to determine if it needed to be relayed to Draskene or not. Often it did not, but the familiars were rewarded nonetheless.

As he neared the window, Bin could make out the silhouette of a large bird perched on the sill. He released the latch and opened the glass panes. The bird, a burnt orange colour and standing nearly two feet tall, cawed to him once and waited for him to lean in.

Bin could smell the brimstone and sulfur odour about the bird. He recognized it as one of the Fire Hawks from the Fire Wind Flats. Not much going on these days, he thought to himself, except for the Wraull army waiting to advance on the Rey'ak. Still, he knew he should hear his familiar out, just in case.

The bird spoke to him in its own tongue, known to very few men except Bin and others like him. It told him what it had seen, a large Dwarf force, accompanied by Rey'ak, heading to the Fire Wind Flats, one day ago.

Together with the information Bin had gathered about the Wraull defeat at the hands of the Dwarves and Rey'ak in the Thunder Mountains, he knew this could only mean one thing—they were taking the initiative, joining forces and going after the Wraulls. He thanked the bird, fed it some dried meat he kept in his room and bade it wait for him to return.

Again, Bin had to bear bad news to his master. Just a few days back he had confirmed the Wraull defeat in the Thunder Mountains. Now he had to tell him that the Dwarves, once almost beaten, were on the offensive now, with help from the Rey'ak no less! Draskene had never once lashed out at Bin, but Bin still feared him. He had seen many times what happened to those who failed in their service to the Black Paladin. Their screams of horror and pain were always present in his recessed thoughts, just beyond everyday thoughts, but close enough to the surface to make his blood chill at times like this.

His stomach knotted, Bin passed through the stone halls of the castle. There were few people here now, compared to when King Aramid ruled. Draskene preferred to keep the palace empty, save for his most trusted and valuable servants, like Bin. The grounds themselves, and their buildings, housed the forces that guarded Arundel and Draskene from the outside world.

It was late now, and he carried a lit oil lamp with him to light his way. Since the fall of his Wraull forces and Demon familiars, Draskene was resting. His magic was strong and gave him great power, but he was not omnipotent. After large expenditures like calling up Demons, he needed rest to recover. Only Bin, Draskene's most trusted servant, knew where he rested, or was allowed to approach him. Even so, Bin did not do so lightly. He knew this was important and the punishment for not informing him would be much worse.

He took many dark, back passageways, known only to himself and Draskene, and possibly those of Arundel's royal family, but they were long gone. Bin stepped through a secret door, down a flight of stairs, rested briefly on the landing, then continued down again. He passed through another secret door and down a small winding corridor until at last he came to Draskene's resting place. The door, as always, was closed and warded with protective spells. Bin knew the words to cancel the wards and spoke them. The door swung silently in.

"What is it, Bin?" asked Draskene. He sat cross-legged on the floor, hands folded in his lap in meditation. His body levitated effortlessly about six inches off the ground.

"I have important news for you, my lord," the smaller man replied quickly. "A Fire Hawk from the Fire Wind Flats has spied a Dwarf army, along with Rey'ak, marching towards the Wraulls forces at the Fire Top Mountains."

Draskene looked up, his eyes smouldering. He did not have the power to spare to call up his Demon familiars to help. Nor would they arrive in time at the Fire Top Mountains. Things were not going his way. It had been a long time since he had this kind of difficulty with his plans. Still, he had seen them through in the past and he would again. He was secure in his power.

"Send the bird back, Bin," began Draskene. "Have it gather as many of its kind as it can to assist the Wraulls and inform them of what is happening. After that, the Wraulls will have to fend for themselves. The Dwarves cannot hope to win without heavy losses. This will just prolong the inevitable. We will be victorious eventually."

"Yes, my Lord."

"And Bin, what of your wolf? Has it returned yet with news of Henaach and the girl?"

Bin swallowed then replied, "No. I have not heard anything."

"I see," replied Draskene and his face grew dark.

Bin hurried from Draskene, back to his quarters and informed the Fire Hawk of what to do. The bird leapt off the ledge and disappeared into the night sky. Bin secretly began to wonder if his master had possibly overreached himself at last. Things were not going so well any longer. The return of Duncan and Martyl, along with the mysterious girl and big cats had caused a great deal of havoc for his master. Still, it was his duty to serve his master Draskene, to keep him informed to the best of his and his animal familiars' abilities. He had no desire to see the heir of Arundel return and he would do his best to see he did not.

He watched the Fire Hawk wing its way east, over the parapets and outer wall of the castle until it disappeared into the blackness of the night. Bin had lost several of his familiars as of late but the Fire Hawk was not one to be taken lightly. It was fully twice the size of the two hawks he had sent to Henaach, with a wingspan of nearly seven feet and talons strong enough to tear through leather armour. But its size was not its only forte. The Fire Hawk also had the ability to breathe fire, like a dragon, but much less powerful. Still, they could badly burn a foe, even armoured. If enough of them joined the Wraulls, it may make enough of a difference.

Bin closed the window, smiling wickedly to himself as he pictured scores of fire hawks incinerating the Dwarf army and their Rey'ak allies. He put out his oil lamp and crawled into bed to sleep.

Dawn broke over the eastern horizon, golden rays of light slipping between the peaks of the Fire Top Mountains and spilling onto the plain of the Fire Wind Flats below. Where the streamers of light touched, the fog shrouding the 'Flats dissipated. The Dwarves were up and packing their things already, the war machine on the move.

Kier'ak's scouts came in, reporting only a few Wraull sentries ahead for the next ten leagues, and these were dispatched quickly and quietly by the bowmen. The Rey'ak and their keen night vision were no match for the Wraulls and now the Dwarves had a clear path all the way to the base of the Fire Top Mountains where the bulk of the Wraull army waited.

General Belan was delighted to hear this and already began forming a renewed opinion of Kier'ak and the other Rey'ak—one much more fitting of a close ally. Still, he had a difficult decision to make. It would take them all day to travel the ten leagues across the 'Flats. No matter how careful they tried to be, the Wraulls would hear their advance when they were a few miles away. This did not bode well for the Dwarves as the Wraulls would be prepared for them, or worse yet, mount an attack while the Dwarves were still tired from travel. What they needed was a way to draw the Wraulls out, to come to the Dwarves and meet them in the open, where they could use their cavalry to an advantage.

He discussed his concerns with Kier'ak while the captains readied their men. At last, Belan and Kier'ak settled upon a plan that they both thought was reasonable and had a good chance of success. They Rey'ak would fly ahead of the mounted Dwarves until they reached the Wraull forces. Then, the main body of Kier'ak's scouts would attack the Wraulls from the air, harry them, anger them enough that they would be drawn out and pursue the Rey'ak. The Rey'ak would then fall back, making sure they did so slowly enough to keep the Wraulls interested in the pursuit. There was a large cluster of boulders and other volcanic debris scattered across the far end of the 'Flats, about two leagues from the Fire Top Mountains that the Dwarves would wait at, hidden as best they could, until the Rey'ak drew the Wraulls to them.

Meanwhile, twenty or so Rey'ak scouts would fly above and around the Wraulls back to the Rey'ak forces in the Fire Top Mountains and inform them of the situation. They would then lead the scouts back and join in the fray.

Belan shook Kier'ak's hand and wished him luck. Kier'ak returned the gesture and with a flourish of his wings, was off with his comrades, flying towards the mountains and their destiny.

General Belan gave the order and his forces moved out also. They traveled slower today, both to conserve their energy and strength and to give the Rey'ak time to accomplish their goal.

With five thousand armoured Dwarves on horseback, there was no chance of them sneaking up on the Wraulls unawares. For a force that size, they did move surprisingly quietly but the creaking of leather saddles and traces and the clinking of metal armours could not be reduced entirely and when magnified by their numbers, the sound was quite loud.

The sun had now risen high overhead in the late morning sky. Its glare was fierce and penetrating, heating the air to almost an unbearable degree. The only wind that blew was down from the Fire Top Mountains. It swept across the flat plain of the Fire Wind Flats and carried with it the heat and sulfurous smell of the volcanoes leagues ahead.

The Dwarves knew full well what the terrain ahead had in store for them. The Fire Wind Flats had earned their name because of their fiery, volcano heated air that swept across them. The ground was sere and hard packed, very little vegetation growing on it. The grass was brown and stunted and the cavalry's ponies were forced to rely on the grain and hay brought with them.

Water was also a problem here, and two wagons laden with kegs were brought along to water the ponies and the troops alike. The Dwarves were prepared to engage in a quick strike, not a prolonged battle. They had supplies enough to last them a week to ten days, no more, with most of that being used for travel. Their engagement with the Wraulls was to be brief, but no doubt brutal. This was not the terrain they wished to be engaged upon in battle for an extended period of time. Their mission was to attack the Wraulls, harry them, disorganize them, hopefully drive them back to the Char'nak Mountains. This would then in turn allow the Dwarves and Rey'ak to travel openly between one another's realms and open relations between the estranged races.

By noon, the Dwarves had reached the prearranged spot to await the Rey'ak and, hopefully, the Wraulls. Many Wraull sentries lay dead, scattered about the rocks and craters of the volcanic wasteland. Arrows protruded from throats and eyes, attesting to the precision of the Rey'ak archers.

So far, so good, thought Belan as he observed the dead Wraulls strewn about. His confidence in Kier'ak and his scouts went up another couple of notches. Still, he dispatched several of his captains and their Dwarf Patrols to scour the area for any Wraull activity. While they were gone, each rider saw to his mount, walking, watering and feeding them. The ponies were the Dwarves lifeline in this battle, and in getting home again, so they valued each one as much as their own lives.

Thirty minutes later, the Patrols returned, bearing no reports of Wraull activity anywhere in the vicinity. Even more Wraull bodies were found further east, all dead from arrow wounds, almost exclusively to the head and neck.

When the Patrols had finished checking their mounts, General Belan called his captains together for one last counsel before the battle.

Plans were drawn up and traps set in place for their foe. Large swaths of the plateau were doused in flammable oil and Dwarf archers were busy digging pits, staggered at different intervals. The pits were lined with pikes and spears, some with oil, some with both. When the pits were finished, they were covered with tarps and a light covering of dirt to help conceal them.

By the Rey'ak's estimate, the Dwarves would be outnumbered nearly three to one, but they had the element of surprise on their side, as well as the excellent marksmanship of their aerial allies. Still, they knew this would be a decisive battle in their war against Draskene. Scouts were sent ahead, on foot and unarmoured to ensure their stealth. They returned at early evening reporting to General Belan and his counsel. The news was not good, but then the Dwarves already knew they were seriously outnumbered. By their best estimate, the scouts believed there were ten to twelve thousand Wraulls amassed at the pass into the Fire Top Mountains. There were no machines of war, siege engines, towers, or catapults of the like as the geography of the land pretty much limited their use. The Wraulls also possessed no cavalry, all of their soldiers on foot only. This would work to the Dwarves advantage as the Wraulls left the mountain pass and headed across the 'Flats. They would be able to stage a mounted attack against the Wraulls' superior numbers, giving them a slight advantage.

The sun was beginning its slow descent into the western sky by now. The Dwarves ate their meals cold, no fires being lit this close to the Wraulls as they didn't want their presence known just yet. There was nothing left for them to do now but wait, and hope that their plan succeeded.

With the fall of night came the cries of battle. General Belan was at the head of the main body of the Dwarf army nearly three thousand strong. They were positioned in the open, on the right side of a massive outcropping of rock. There they would hold until the Wraulls that escaped the pits and oil drenched fields reach them, riding into them and cutting them down.

Captain Graik was in charge of the archers, one thousand strong, spread across the center of the Fire Wind Flats. Burning pits of pitch were scattered amongst them, the archers waiting for the signal to light the 'Flats up with their own fire.

Captain Kean was in charge of another one thousand Dwarves—heavy armour and weapons. They stood in front of the archers, one to a man, lances and pikes lowered and braced, prepared to hold back any Wraull attack from reaching their comrades as they fired upon the enemy.

Several hundred Dwarves remained back half a mile with the unused ponies. They served as a rear guard in case any Wraulls managed to skirt the Dwarves and their traps. They were also there to ensure the ponies were ready and available should the archers and heavy infantry require a hasty retreat.

Screams of the mortally wounded carried across the still night air as the Dwarves tensely waited. The sharp twang of hundreds of bows could be heard, followed by the sickening sounds of arrows penetrating flesh.

General Belan started as he heard the flutter of wings near him and Kier'ak seemingly materialized out of the dark sky before him.

"It has begun," he quickly rasped to Belan, his superb physique showing sings of extreme exertion. "We have flown non-stop for several hours now with the Wraulls in pursuit."

"Drink this," offered Belan as he handed Kier'ak a flask containing Tirnal. "It will help restore some strength temporarily."

He did not bother to tell Kier'ak that it would exact a toll on his body later, requiring him to rest more than usual. It they were successful tonight, Kier'ak, his people, and the Dwarves could rest peacefully for many years. If they failed, it wouldn't really matter.

"Thank you," replied Kier'ak as he greedily swallowed from the proffered flask. "We are leading the Wraulls this very minute to your positions. Behind us follow nearly one thousand more Rey'ak. I must go now to aid my people. Farewell, General and may we meet when this is over."

General Belan gave Kier'ak his best Dwarf military salute and wished him luck. As quickly and mysteriously as he arrived, Kier'ak was gone into the night.

Like thunder rolling over the 'Flats, the Wraulls ran, heedless in their fury of the attack by the Rey'ak to think they may be headed into a trap. Numbering in the thousands, the ground began to shake as their armoured feet pounded the ground. The Dwarves held fast, everyone of them committed to seeing this battle through, at last a chance to take the fight to their enemy and possibly put an end to their menace once and for all.

Judging the distance of the Wraulls from their noise, Captain Graik commanded the archers to fire. One thousand arrows, dipped in burning tar, were launched into the black night sky. Like a stream of miniature comets, they blazed upwards in a long arc, then whistled back down to earth.

Some arrows found their mark and pierced a Wraull throat or eye, but the Dwarves were not the marksmen the Rey'ak were and most bounced harmlessly off the heavily armoured Wraulls. Before the Wraulls could react, however, to the threat before them, the ground beneath their feet roared to life and they were caught in a blazing inferno as the oil soaked ground ignited.

Ear piercing screams rang out into the night as the Wraulls were engulfed in flames. Those in leather armour were burned outright by the oil fires but those in chain and plate mail were roasted alive by the heat. Their skin began to boil and blister from the heat and their metal armor seared their flesh. The smell was unbearable and thick black smoke covered the 'Flats, making the darkness practically impenetrable, even to the Rey'ak.

Realizing they were in a trap, the Wraull commanders signaled their troops to split off, south and north, to try and skirt the oil-fed fires. No sooner had they left the smouldering oil fires when new screams of pain and agony rang out. In moving around the fires, the Wraulls walked right into the second trap set for them by the Dwarves.

The coverings on the pits gave way and scores of Wraulls crashed heedlessly into the spears and pikes at their bottoms. Dwarf pike-men ran up to the pit edges and furiously stabbed at any Wraull who tried to climb back out. More Dwarves rolled boulders or threw rocks into the pits, trying to crush whatever life remained out of the trapped enemy.

The Wraulls were hammered mercilessly by the Dwarves and the Rey'ak archers were doing their best at eliminating any Wraulls outside the pits who tried to attack the Dwarves. The smoke from the oil drenched 'Flats and burning bodies was not so thick here yet, giving the Rey'ak an excellent opportunity to continue their sharpshooting.

The Wraulls had by this point had enough, despite being angered into a killing frenzy. They knew now that it was not just the Rey'ak they fought, but Dwarves as well, who it seemed had managed to booby-trap the Fire Wind Flats. This was very disconcerting to them as they had believed the Dwarves all but beaten up to now and never would have suspected a counter-attack in their own backyard.

Signal horns bellowed and the Wraulls began to retreat. The oil fires had died down now, most of the volatile fuel expended. Several thousand Wraulls lay dead or dying across a broad expanse of the 'Flats and thick, reeking black smoke hung like a funeral pall over the bodies. The retreating Wraulls did not linger, but pressed on double-time, walking on and over the dead and almost dead with no sign of remorse.

General Belan heard the horns and knew a retreat was being called, even though he couldn't see it yet. The fires and pits were nearly half a mile away but the sound of armoured Wraulls on the retreat was unmistakable. He gave his own orders and one thousand of his nearly three thousand man force left under Captain Buren to slow or halt the retreat. The Wraulls could not be allowed to regroup with those still entrenched in the pass to the Fire Top Mountains. If that were to happen, the Dwarves would not stand a chance against a fully pre-pared, properly defended larger force. They had to win tonight, and with a minimal loss of their own forces.

Captain Buren's cavalry swept into the midst of the Wraulls, com-ing at them from the west, materializing out of the haze like wraiths. Long spears lowered, the Dwarves skewered their enemies, and tram-pled those who avoided being speared. A wide swath was cut through to the fleeing Wraulls' ranks and they were split into two forces as the Dwarves drove a wedge through them.

The Dwarves wheeled their small but sturdy steeds about and raked the smaller force they had separated. Wraulls fell by the hun-dreds but they still came on. Now that the element of surprise had worn off, the Wraulls had formed ranks and were mounting a coun-terattack.

The Wraulls that had been separated from the larger force split apart and reformed, changing direction and now the Dwarves and Captain Buren found themselves pinned between the two Wraull forces. Captain Buren raised his horn to signal for help from General Belan but before he could wind it, a Wraull launched a large stone from a sling at him. In the haze and confusion he did not see it and it struck him on the side of his armoured head.

Buren crashed to the ground and the Wraulls roared in defiance while clashing with the Dwarves. Huge maces and flails, wielded by the Wraulls inhuman strength smashed down on the smaller Dwarves. Bones shattered and skulls caved. The ponies were not safe either, the Wraulls savagely attacking the Dwarves' mounts, their weapons breaking equine bones as easily as Dwarf bones.

Trapped, the Dwarves under Buren fought back just as savagely. Even though they weren't defending Calheller or the Thunder Mountains directly at the moment, every one of them knew that the continued safety of their homeland depended on what happened here. Their mighty battles axes swinging, the Dwarves hewed their way through the Wraulls. The closest to Captain Buren tried to set up a perimeter about their fallen captain while one of his standard bearers jumped down to pick him up.

His head was a wet, sticky mess as blood continued to ooze from the head wound. His helmet lay off to the side, cracked nearly in two. The standard bearer knew that it was a good sign that Captain Buren was bleeding freely—it meant he was still alive.

The Wraulls pressed in tighter, eager to make sure the Dwarves did not rescue their fallen captain. Despite being nearly two feet taller and over one hundred pounds heavier, the Wraulls were not a match for Dwarven tenacity. They fought back viciously and they held their ground allowing Captain Buren to be laid upon the back of his mount who had courageously stood over his master's body and repelled several Wraulls on his own. The pony's hooves were blood stained and his eyes were wild with fear and rage.

General Belan could not see the specifics of the battle in the smoke covered darkness but he could hear the change in the Wraulls. No longer did they sound panicked and disorganized. Now he heard the sounds of battle, weapons clashing and Dwarves screaming in pain. He had a messenger ride back to Captains Graik and Kean to have them advance upon the Wraulls from the rear. Kean and his heavy infantry would try to drive the Wraulls eastward into Belan's cavalry. Graik and his archer would provide cover fire and also ensure that any Wraulls who tried to break free of the cavalry were dispatched.

Spurring his mount on, General Belan led the remaining two thousand mounted Dwarves forward to rescue their brethren. They hammered the outer edges of the Wraulls and pushed their way towards Captain Buren's beleaguered command. The trapped Dwarves rallied as they saw their general coming for them and with a last valiant effort, surged through the Wraulls.

Like a well-oiled machine, General Belan and his men split apart so that a path formed, hemmed on both sides by mounted Dwarves. The injured, from Captain Buren's party, including Buren himself, rode safely through the column to the rear lines.

From the air above, a hail of arrows rained down on the Wraulls closest to the Dwarves. They were felled by the hundreds as the Rey'ak rejoined the fight, having flown back from the pits and fires, leading Captain Kean's forces safely through. General Belan and his forces drove into the Wraulls, forcing them back against the pikes of Captain Kean's forces to the rear. The Rey'ak continued to send their deadly missiles into the midst of the Wraulls, stopping each counter-attack before it could grow to become a danger.

The Dwarves and Rey'ak, hopelessly outnumbered in the begin-ning, were now finally starting to seriously cut down the Wraull num-bers. Dead bodies, Wraull, Dwarf and Rey'ak alike, lay scattered across the Fire Wind Flats as one of the largest and bloodiest battles since the days of the Black Magic Wars raged on.

Suddenly, streaks of fire lit the night sky, and with them followed the shrill shrieks of Fire Hawks. They tore through the sky and descended upon the Rey'ak, talons tearing and fire spraying from their beaks like miniature dragons.

Taken off guard by an enemy every bit as stealthy and acrobatic in the air as them, the Rey'ak suffered severe losses in a short time. As with any flying creature, their wings were their key to survival in the air. The Fire Hawks, with razor sharp talons and their fiery breath, shredded and scorched many Rey'ak wings. Unable to fly, the Rey'ak plummeted to the ground. Those that did not die from the fall were quickly set upon by the Wraulls, frustrated no more by their inability to attack their assailants while in the air.

The Fire Hawks wheeled about the sky over the battle below. Some now broke off the attack with the Rey'ak and began strafing the Dwarves below. Their incendiary breath ignited small blazes all over the battlefield as dead bodies and the wooden axe and mace handles caught fire.

Now it was the Wraulls turn to press the attack and they did so with a vengeance. Thousands of them lay dead all around them but they still had at least as many able-bodied fighters left as the Dwarves. The Dwarves tried to hold their lines as best they could. With Captain Buren still down, a young lieutenant named Carda took command on his remaining forces. He led the small company of mounted Dwarves away from the battle then wheeled them back around. With a running start, they charged headlong into the Wraulls with as much force as they could muster. The front line of the Wraull assault was broken under the onslaught and as General Belan watched amazed, he ordered another mounted platform to follow.

The Rey'ak were unable to provide aerial support at this point, their primary task now was to put an end to the Fire Hawk threat. Although the hawks were smaller and faster, the Rey'ak still had the use of their long bows. Kier'ak gave the command and the remaining Rey'ak retreated to a safe distance. Hovering several hundred feet away, they took aim at the hawks and fired.

Like tiny flaming stars they plummeted to the ground. The remaining hawks screeched in anger and went after the Rey'ak.

The Dwarf archers, unable to fire their deadly missiles into the melee on the ground for fear of hitting their own brethren, now had perfect targets, lit up against the night sky. A storm of arrows was launched skyward as the Fire Hawks pursued the Rey'ak. While the Dwarves may not have been as accurate as the Rey'ak, they did have their superior numbers and were attacking from the rear.

Nearly half the remaining Fire Hawks fell from the sky, their blazing bodies igniting more infernos amongst the combatants on the ground. The Rey'ak turned and fired again, decimating their numbers further. The remaining handful of Fire Hawks had enough and began retreating to the Fire Top Mountains. Kier'ak could not risk them bringing back more of their kindred or warning the Wraulls still there so he dispatched twenty of his best marksmen to ensure they never made it back.

The Dwarf heavy infantry had by now skirted the pits and fires separating them from the battle and engaged the Wraulls from the rear. Their attack was swift and unexpected, the Wraull's attention on the Dwarf cavalry and the aerial attacks by the Rey'ak.

With pikes lowered, they marched into the heart of the Wraull forces and skewered all they could. When the Wraulls realized they were beset upon from the back, before they could turn to attack, the Rey'ak were back and again began to cut down the Wraulls.

With his keen eyes, Kier'ak got an excellent overhead view of the battlefield and saw that the Wraulls were on the verge of being routed. Their numbers were badly reduced and it was time for the final blow. He found General Belan and informed him of the situation. Now it was time for the archers to finish things.

Belan gave the command for all the Dwarves to fall back, infantry and cavalry. A second command was sent out to Captain Graik to have his archers begin strafing the battlefield. Kier'ak and his archers did the same from above.

Screams from the dying and wounded continued to ring out, but now they belonged solely to the Wraulls. Under the constant volley of arrows, the last of them fell. Kier'ak gave the signal for a cease-fire and the Rey'ak cris-crossed the battlefield from the air, searching for any survivors from either side.

As dawn broke, the sun's warm rays spilled across the Fire Wind Flats and the remaining Dwarves and Rey'ak stared in awe at the carnage before them. Bodies, by the thousands, lay strewn across the great plain before them. Fires still smouldered, smoke rising into the clear morning sky like spirits leaving the earth for the heavens. Moans and coughs of pain still echoed from the bodies before them, not all of them yet dead.

As the wind blew across the 'Flats the smell of burnt bodies and death assailed those still alive. As battle hardened as they were, many of the Dwarves and most of the Rey'ak could not bear to look at the carnal house scene before them. But there was still work to be done, and General Belan knew the sooner it was done, the better.

He called for the reserve troops left behind to guard the rear during the night. It was their job this day to seek out any Dwarves or Rey'ak who were still alive and able to be helped and bring them back to the camp and the healers.

It was a most unpleasant duty, but one that needed to be done. The Dwarves knew this and set about their business as stoically as ever. It was a long process and covered the better part of the entire day. They found Dwarves and Rey'ak both, some so badly injured with missing limbs, destroyed bodies, crushed bones that they best they could do for them was end their misery there. They were dispatched quickly and efficiently, the Dwarves powerful arms having no problem snapping the necks of their comrades. Those that could be helped were placed on litters and hauled back to the camp for the healers to try their best and save them.

Wraulls were also encountered that still lived. They were shown no mercy, save a quick death by decapitation with a battle-axe. Those still alive in the pits were summarily buried alive with rocks, the Dwarves unwilling to spend any arrows on them as their archers were dangerously low on the precious ammunition.

Finally, as night rolled in, the last of the search parties came in. A perimeter was set up about the camp, watched by both Dwarves and Rey'ak. Despite their nearness to the Wraulls still in the Fire Top Mountains, everyone not on watch slept like the dead, exhausted from the previous night's battle.

Chapter Twenty-Eight

The wyvern was so large that it blotted out the sun as it glided effortlessly through the still afternoon air. Large leather wings, easily fifty feet across cast an intimidating shadow on the ground below. It's eyes, sharp as any hawk's, spied the party on horseback beneath and bellowed out its fury.

The horses, as brave and as trained as they were, had no experience with anything like this. They reared up in fear and bolted. Everyone but Reyna, just like a few nights before in the Dead Woods, was thrown. She managed to hang on for a few moments before doing an aerial dismount and landing on her feet, dagger drawn and ready. Crouching low to present as little a target as possible to this new threat, she quickly scanned the area to see where the horses were bolting to so as to make it easier to find them later.

"What is that?" gasped Selena as she scrambled to her feet.

"A wyvern," replied Dirn shakily as he too got to his feet with everyone else. "That must be what Rorn and Big Cat sensed yesterday. It must have been watching us, waiting until we got close to the sword!"

"Everyone, take cover!" commanded Martyl as he grabbed Duncan and Salena each by the arm and propelled them under the cover of a broken but still standing partial building.

The wyvern circled above them, swooping down for a closer look. As it neared the ground, its reddish-brown leathery skin blended in with the destroyed buildings around them. A rush of fowl smelling air swept over the huddled group and they all fought back the reflex to gag.

"If it wasn't for its putrid stench, you'd never know it was there," grumbled Rorn as he tried to flatten himself further against the wall.

"That's why we never saw it before," stated Martyl. "It is camouflaged to live in these ruins and kill whoever gets close to the sword. It must be attracted to the magic even though it cannot use it. It's like a beacon, calling it here!"

The wyvern had come around for a second pass now and tried to get its head beneath the overhang of the wall. Ar'ye let an arrow loose and it bounced off the wyvern's thick scaly hide as if it had hit a mortar wall. Rorn pulled a throwing axe from his belt and flung it as hard as he could as the wyvern swept past. The axe had better luck, being heavier, and managed to cut into the side of the wyvern. It was only a flesh wound, but it elicited a shriek from the flying behemoth that caused everyone to cover their ears in pain.

The wyvern wheeled away from the wall and slashed its tail in defiance. The end of its tail was like a gigantic mace, with a large ball of bone at the end and four long spikes protruding from it.

Martyl dropped instinctively, pulling Duncan and Salena down with him. Dirn pulled Reyna down as a shower of stone and broken brick rained around them. Ar'ye and Big Cat, with their superior reflexes, were both well out of the way but Rorn was not so lucky. Still standing, preparing to throw his other axe, the wyvern's tail spikes struck him. There was a thud followed by a sickening crunching sound. As the wyvern flew past, it flicked its tail again and Rorn's body, crushed and bloodied, was flung against the wall they sheltered beneath.

The wall, already weakened from time and exposure to the elements, began to crumble as Rorn's lifeless body caromed into it. The overhang, barely hanging on as it was, broke away and began to cascade down on the survivors.

"Everyone move!" shouted Martyl. He had to grab Dirn and drag him with him as he stared in shock and disbelief at his friend.

"Split up!" Martyl shouted again. "Don't give it an easy target. Stay low and find cover!"

Martyl stood his ground where he was, watching to see that his order was followed, that everyone found cover. The wyvern saw everyone scatter except him and dove in. It screeched in rage again as it saw its prey scatter but it went for the one who was standing still. Talons half the size of a man opened to snatch its prey where it stood.

Martyl could feel the air rush past him as he dove headlong into a shallow ditch to this left. The fetid reek of the wyvern made him gag again but he held it in check with a supreme effort and got up to run. Martyl had only moments before the wyvern circled again to come back and he knew he wouldn't be that lucky again.

Scrambling along, trying to move as fast as possible while hunched down, Martyl was already thinking of a plan. He knew the wyvern's hide would be too tough for a single archer with limited arrows to kill but if they could keep the beast on the ground, their swords and axes could hack away at it. It would be dangerous, and gruesome, but they had very little choice.

Reaching the crumbling remnants of another building, Martyl dove head-first behind it. The sound of the wyvern rushing past filled his ears and dust filled his nose and mouth.

Spitting out the dust, Martyl looked hurriedly about him for the others. He saw Dirn and Ar'ye crouched in the mouth of what use to be a tunnel leading into the sewers. It was caved in now, with just a small circular opening running out of an embankment. He looked again quickly, didn't see the wyvern, and made a mad dash for the other two.

Dirn and Ar'ye, mindful not to make too much noise lest they draw unwanted attention to Martyl and themselves, quietly but urgently waved him on as they watchfully scanned the sky for the return of the wyvern. Seconds later, Martyl was crouching in the sewer pipe with them, peering intently up at the sky for their antagonist.

"I have a plan," he gasped out to them. "Do either of you have any rope?"

"I do, in my pack," replied Dirn. His voice betrayed the anger he felt at the loss of his friend.

"Good. Now this is what we're going to do. Dirn, you and Ar'ye will position yourselves up there," Martyl said, pointing to part of a building that still stood, complete with a section of roof and chimney. "As the wyvern chases me, I will lead it past you and you will snare it with the rope, hopefully causing it to fall to the ground. At that point, we will all attack and try to dispatch it as quickly as possible."

"It's suicide!" growled Dirn, careful to keep his voice down. "You'll never make it. We don't want to lose you, either."

Martyl was touched by Dirn's concern but there was no other option, and he told him. "We've come too far to turn back now. The sword is near and we don't have much time left before Draskene mounts another attack against Calheller, if he hasn't already. Besides, I don't intend to let it get me, just chase me." He tried to smile, but it was forced and Dirn and Ar'ye both knew it. Still, Martyl was their leader and if this was his plan, they'd see it through.

"Now," he continued, "did you see where the others went?"

"There," pointed Ar'ye across what used to be a street.

The paving stones were broken and choked with weeds and splotches of bright red blood dotted it where the wyvern had bled after Rorn's axe attack. Martyl followed his finger and saw the rest fo their party crouched behind a large pile of debris.

Another terrifying screech rent the air and the wyvern streaked down towards them, its prey spotted. Ar'ye stepped out of the culvert and released three arrows in rapid succession. This time he did not aim at the armoured body but at the huge, leather skinned wings. They pierced them easily and the wyvern let out a piercing wail and wheeled about.

Quickly Ar'ye got back into the culvert as the wyvern roared past. Martyl took this moment of confusion to run to the others to inform them of the plan. He signaled Ar'ye and Dirn to get in place and be ready.

Martyl was quite winded by the time he dashed across the broken ground to where the others hid. He slid into them, behind the rubble and hastily explained his plan. Their part, he told them, was to wait here, hidden as best as possible, until the wyvern was down, then they were to join in the frenzy and kill it as quickly as possible.

"Be careful," Reyna said as she hugged him. Salena gave him a quick hug too and Duncan stepped forward to clasp Martyl's arm in luck and farewell. No further words were spoken as Martyl stepped out from concealment. A quick glance to the rooftop and he spied Ar'ye and Dirn, rope in hand, patiently waiting beside a still solid looking chimney.

Sprinting, he crossed the shattered old roadway and stood near the partially collapsed building where Dirn and Ar'ye were positioned. Seeing the movement, the wyvern was on him in seconds. It screamed its challenge and swept down from the sky, streaking towards this puny man who dared challenge it.

Martyl did not have his sword out, knowing that a single stroke, no matter how lucky, would not kill the beast. His best defense was speed and agility, and he did not know if he had enough of either to survive. He held his ground until the last second, then rolled to his left towards the remains of the building.

Ar'ye saw the wyvern coming and had the rope ready. One end was tied into a noose that he hoped to throw over the wyvern's head and around its neck and the other was looped about the chimney to hold it in place once they roped it. Dirn was ready with his throwing axes and his battle axe was slung over his back.

As the wyvern sped past, Ar'ye flung the rope out. It was his job as he had the keener eyesight and if he fell, he would not get hurt as he could fly back up. He had been cautious of flying anywhere near the wyvern thus far, not wanting to face the creature in the air.

The rope flew outwards towards the wyvern but its speed was greater than Ar'ye had anticipated and he missed his mark. Instead of its head or neck, he snagged its right foot. The rope pulled taut and then everything crashed!

The speed and weight of the wyvern were strong enough that when the rope tightened, two things happened. The chimney was so old and weak that the bricks gave way and it sheared right off, moments after the rope caught the wyvern. The wyvern itself, being held one instant then released the next, could not compensate in flight for the differing stresses placed upon it. Like a lead weight, it dropped gracelessly from the sky.

Not waiting for the dust to clear, Dirn threw his two axes into the cloud of dust on the ground, eager to exact revenge for the death of his friend. Duncan, Salena, Reyna and Big Cat leapt from their cover and went running towards the confusion.

The wyvern was dazed from its fall but was already struggling to its feet. Duncan was the first one in, sword swinging. He brought his sword down in a sweeping arc and struck the wyvern's neck. It screamed in pain as his sword cut the flesh and a geyser of blood sprayed forth.

It was far from a killing blow however, and it turned its head to snap at him. Big Cat ran in and leapt atop the massive creature's back and sank her teeth in. The wyvern shook its body trying to unseat this new attack but could not do so, Big Cat's claws firmly fastening her to it.

Salena and Reyna both joined in, there daggers plunging into the neck of the wyvern over and over. Dirn was down from the roof now and approaching from the rear, running as fast as his stocky legs would carry him.

Ar'ye hovered above and took his time, getting a good shot in with his bow. On his fourth try, he pierced the wyvern's right eye. It released a bloodcurdling shriek and began thrashing about wildly. Duncan, Salena and Reyna abandoned their attack for fear of being crushed as the wyvern thrashed and screamed in pain.

With a cry of "Bray'la!" Dirn strode up to the wyvern, his face a mask of rage and swung his battle axe in a maddened frenzy. He paid no heed to his own safety, swinging his axe like a berserker. The ground beneath his feet was muddy and sodden with the blood of his opponent. He was still hewing away with his axe when he heard someone calling his name. It was Ar'ye, hovering safely behind him.

Dirn finally came back, and before him lay the wyvern's still, lifeless body, headless and butchered.

"It's over," said Ar'ye quietly. "Help us find Martyl."

Dirn shouldered his axe, belted his throwing axes after retrieving them then joined the search for Martyl.

He was found a short distance from the carnage, lying in a shallow depression beside the old road, cut and bruised but otherwise okay. He missed the final battle having been knocked senseless as the wyvern crashed into him but was now up and eager to resume the search for the sword.

"We must bury Rorn first," said Dirn. It was a statement of fact and no one argued. They gathered rocks and masonry which were abundant and made a cairn over his body, his battle-axe laid upon his chest in the Dwarven style of burying their dead. Each of them to a moment of silence to pay their respects to their fallen comrade.

They commenced digging for the sword that afternoon. Salena and Reyna took watch at the top of the hill, constantly scanning the horizon for any further signs of danger. Martyl did not believe there would be any for awhile as they wyvern, even if it was sent by Draskene, would have been alone. Its nature was too wild and untamable for even someone like Draskene to keep it from attacking anything that came near, like Wraulls.

Big Cat lay resting peacefully between the two women, her head on her paws, still observant, however, as her sense of smell and hearing were far greater than the humans with her. If anything did approach, she would most likely sense it long before they did, even while resting. Just having her there beside them made Salena feel much safer.

The horses and ponies, recovered by Reyna shortly after Rorn's burial, grazed peacefully now, atop the hill as well. They showed no outward signs of the morning's ordeal affecting them, much different than their human counterparts.

Down below, Duncan had wandered about the base of the hill until he found the spot he thought he saw in his dream. It looked no different than any other part of the hill but no one else had a better idea so they began digging. They all had small shovels brought with them from Calheller and in less than an hour, they had cleared away enough dirt to discover square stone blocks, some big, some small, most broken and cracked, lying in a jumble.

Dirn looked up from his digging and said to the others, "This looks like the remains of a collapsed tunnel ceiling. Definitely a Dwarf trap, set to seal off the entrance to an underground tunnel."

There was a renewed effort now as the four began digging in earnest, the possibility of their goal being within reach driving them on. Dirn, his experience with Dwarf traps a definite asset, directed the others where to dig and what to watch out for so as to not cause further collapse. The Dwarves were masters at underground living and defense and always had ways around their traps, even when set off, to get into the sealed off areas. To those unwary enough to just dig, they were liable to set off further cave-ins.

Finally, with hands raw and blistered, enough dirt was cleared away to begin the next task. Under Dirn's careful instruction, they began to move the stone blocks that would allow them entrance to the tunnel without causing further collapses. Many of the blocks were so large that it required the effort of all four men to move them. Some few were small enough that any one of them was capable of moving them. All the blocks, big or small, were hastily cast aside as they delved deeper into the tunnel.

After what felt like days to Martyl, Duncan and Ar'ye, unaccustomed to intensive labour such as this, but was in reality only a few hours, they had cleared the wreckage. They shored up the opening and were now staring down into the inky blackness that was, they hoped, the final resting place of the Brach'dir.

Excited as the rest, but ever cautious, Martyl asked Dirn, "Are there any other dangers we should be expecting after we enter?"

"This was built long ago," replied Dirn, "so I cannot say for certain. But, I would think that the collapsing tunnel was a final safeguard against unwanted intrusion. Still, I will lead the way in and watch for any possible further dangers."

"Wait a moment before we begin. Duncan, Ar'ye, get some torches from our supplies and have Reyna and Salena come down here. I want to scout the area myself one last time before we enter."

With that, Martyl was off into the ruined city, slinking through the rubble, looking for any further signs of enemies. He did not want to be trapped down an ancient subterranean refuge with little hope of escape. At last, satisfied that they were still alone in the ruins, he returned to the others nearly an hour later.

Everyone was gathered round the mouth of the tunnel, excitedly talking about what they would find and that at last their quest was at a turning point. Duncan handed Martyl a torch and lit it with his own, eager to get underway.

"Reyna, you and Salena wait here for us, with Big Cat. If anyone or anything approaches, call for us immediately."

Both women nodded their assent to Martyl who then turned to Dirn and said, "After you."

Dirn entered the dark opening, torch thrust out before him, scanning the walls, floor and ceiling for any hidden traps as he went.

The passageway had been built by Dwarves to be used by them and men, but after the forced collapse, and the centuries of disuse, the others were forced to crouch as they walked. It was not lit with light shafts and sparkling gems like the tunnels in Calheller. This was a bunker, used as a last resort to retreat to in case of a losing war, which was the case here. It sloped downward gently and went on for about one hundred feet. Then it leveled out and opened into a vast chamber, far enough across that the light from their torches did not reach the far walls.

The air was dry and stale, having been trapped in here with the dead for many centuries. The room itself was dry, a testament to the Dwarf engineers who built it all those long years ago.

"Stay close," cautioned Martyl as they began to enter the chamber.

"Its this way," Duncan said, "I can feel its presence, calling me."

He began to walk apart from the others, drawn inexorably to a large stone sarcophagus in a far corner. The others followed close behind, making sure they were there to come to his aid should he need it.

When he stood before the stone sarcophagus, Duncan said, "This is it. The sword is in here."

Martyl stood beside him and looked at the inscription chiseled in the stone.

Πρινχε Καραμ

Σον οφ Κινγ Ρετηορν
Σλαιν βψ Ωραυλλσ ιν βαττλε

He motioned Dirn to come up beside him and said, "Inspect this and make sure it's not trapped."

The Dwarf scoured every square inch of the sarcophagus, probing here, picking there, even tapping his axe handle on it in various places.

"It's free of traps, as far as I can tell," he said at last.

"Very well," replied Martyl, looking at the other three. Even in the torchlight, he could see the eager expectation on their faces. "Everyone push together on the lid and we'll shove it off."

Torches laid down at the corners, the four began to push against the stone lid. It was heavy and sealed tight with age, but eventually it began to give way. With a grating screech, the lid slid back then crashed to the ground.

Martyl was the first to pick up his torch and peer inside. The body of a long dead prince of Arundel lay before him, withered and desiccated with the passage of time. Laid on his chest, hands still grasping the pommel, was a beautiful, shining long sword, untouched by age. Martyl knew this had to be the Brach'dir, forged by the Dwarves with the help of the magic from the King of Arundel. Only a magic sword could remain unblemished for thousands of years.

Respectfully, he moved the dead hands away from the sword, inwardly wincing as the brittle bones snapped with the movement. He removed the sword then turned to Duncan and presented it to him.

"Here is the Brach'dir. Lost to your family generations ago, it is now returned. Let us hope it will help return you to your rightful throne."

Duncan, overwhelmed with emotion, accepted the sword. Conflicting feelings raged inside him as he stared at the flawless blade before him. Part of him was ecstatic at finally being given the weapon to reclaim his throne but fear and uncertainty also warred within him. What if he wasn't strong enough to wield it, now that he had it? Everyone was counting on him and now the time to prove himself was here. Could he do it?

His reverie over his internal conflicts was broken by an exclamation from Dirn. He had gone off on his own while Duncan stared at his new sword and had apparently found something of interest to himself.

The others went to him while Martyl asked, "What is it?"

"I found another lost relic!" he exclaimed. In his hands was a large war mace with an inscription in Dwarvenish on the handle.

"This is the Dran'spe—Skull Crusher in your tongue. There are legends of Dwarf heros through the ages using this war mace in battle against the Demons. It is very powerful indeed!"

A quick search by the others turned up nothing else of value. Human and Dwarf skeletons littered the floor, along with a few Wraull skeletons—those that made it down before the tunnel collapsed.

Dirn led the way back out, still cautious of the route, carefully checking for any traps or signs of collapse in the ancient tunnel. Minutes later, they emerged from the depths of the ground and entered the daylight.

Salena watched for Duncan as he exited and a large smile spread across her pretty face. "You found it, didn't you!" she exclaimed excitedly as she saw the glimmering steel blade in his hands.

"Yes, and now its time to take back what is rightfully mine, to defeat Draskene," Duncan replied somberly.

"Don't go rushing off yet," cautioned Martyl, resting his hand on Duncan's shoulder. "The Black Paladin has many spies, and no doubt knows we have the Brach'dir, or he will very soon. He knows it is the only weapon capable of harming him and he is not about to let us walk right up and openly challenge him. He will have Arundel surrounded by his minions, human and otherwise, and will be preparing to stop us."

"That's all the more reason why we need to attack as soon as possible," argued Duncan.

"I admire your determination, Duncan," began Dirn, "but listen to Martyl. He's right. We need to return to Calheller first, let them know we have the sword. We can possibly get a force of Dwarves to go with us to Arundel."

"And we can assemble the Renegade forces in Gullhaven as well," added Martyl. "That may still not be enough but we stand a much better chance than just the six of us and Big Cat."

"As usual, you're right," replied Duncan somberly. "I was just caught up in the excitement of finding the sword and seeing the end of this journey in sight. We've been so far, through so much, I just want it to be over."

"I know," finished Martyl. "We all want it to be over. It will be, soon enough."

Just then, Big Cat, ever watchful, looked skyward and let a low growl escape. The others, fearful of another wyvern, looked upwards worriedly, afraid of what they might find.

"It's okay," said Ar'ye, moments later. "It is a fellow Rey'ak." He let out a series of whistles which their unseen aerial visitor returned before swooping down from the sky to land next to Ar'ye.

"Hello, my name is Rav'vik. It is odd times indeed that one finds a Rey'ak, Dwarf and men traveling together."

"We are on an errand for King Balamir," replied Martyl, careful not to give away too much of their situation just yet.

"As am I and my fellow Rey'ak," replied Rav'vik. Seeing their confused looks, he elaborated. "Our people have realized their mistake in trying to remain neutral. We have joined forces with the Dwarves and attacked the Wraulls who were amassed on the Fire Wind Flats. That was yesterday. We were victorious and now march on to the Fire Top Mountains to route the last of them. I, and others, are doing aerial reconnaissance to make sure no Wraulls have escaped."

Dirn was standing, mouth agape, staring at Rav'vik. When he recovered enough to think straight, he was full of questions.

"What news do you have of Calheller? Have the Wraulls attacked again? How many did King Balamir send with you?"

Rav'vik was accustomed by now to the Dwarves being shocked at the Rey'ak involvement in this conflict but he was also pleased that much of the earlier hostility had dissipated.

"The Wraulls in the mountains and forests surrounding Calheller are no more. Our combined forces were triumphant. As for troops, five thousand were sent east to the 'Flats, under the command of General Belan. There were heavy losses yesterday but he still commands and at this moment is heading to the Fire Top Mountains. If any of you would like to join us, I will be happy to escort you to our troops."

He looked expectantly at Dirn and Ar'ye but both spoke at once, "Thank you, but our friends still need our help."

"Very well. Safe journey to you all."

With a flurry of feathers, Rav'vik lifted off and was gone. Ar'ye and Dirn both looked considerably happier than they had in a long time after hearing that their people were working together to defeat the Wraulls.

The others were pleased as well to hear the news and Martyl said, "Let's get going then. It looks like we may have a safe journey back to Calheller after all."

Reyna whistled for the horses and minutes later they were saddled and riding west to Calheller.

Chapter Twenty-Nine

Dawn broke for the second morning after the furious and bloody battle between the Dwarves and Rey'ak and the Wraulls on the Fire Wind Flats. The sun's orange rays spilled through the gaps in the mountain peaks as it crested the Fire Top Mountains. The snow on their peaks was bathed in the sunlight, turning them a brilliant orange, giving the illusion they were aflame.

This gorgeous spectacle was not wasted on the Dwarves or Rey'ak, both making their homes on or in the mountains. General Belan and Kier'ak let their combined forces admire the spectacle before them for a few minutes before barking out the day's orders.

Troops began forming ranks and soon a procession of mounted Dwarves were following a flying vanguard of Rey'ak toward the last Wraull stronghold in the Fire Top Mountains. All were eager to leave the death and destruction of the previous battle behind them. The smell of death still lingered in the air and they knew it wouldn't be long before winter-wolves and other carrion arrived to feast on the dead.

The Dwarves and Rey'ak had done their best to bury their dead and erect a small stone monument on the battlefield to commemorate their sacrifices. When their battle with the Black Paladin was finished, once and for all, they would return and see to it that a proper monument was built.

They were en route no more than an hour when scouts sent out the previous day began returning. One by one they told the same tale—the Wraulls had been thoroughly defeated and all stragglers were killed. Rey'ak from the Fire Top Mountains arrived and reported that the last of the Wraulls there had been slain as well, even those trying to retreat. No quarter had been given, not even to the ones who fled.

General Belan was quite happy to hear this last news. He and his Dwarves were thanked profusely for their aid and were offered an escort back to Calheller. Kier'ak himself offered to lead it and General Belan gratefully accepted. The order was given and the Dwarves turned back westward for home.

Several hours later, a lone Rey'ak scout flew towards the homeward bound Dwarves and their escorts. It was Rav'vik, the last of the scouts to return. He gave his report to Kier'ak and General Belan, the latter extremely eager for more information.

"Where are they now? It is important I see them," demanded General Belan.

He was careful not to give away the purpose of their mission, seeing the same need for caution that Martyl did. It was not that they didn't trust the Rey'ak, after all they had done to help, but the fewer who knew about the sword the better. The Black Paladin always had ways of finding out about the most secret of plans.

Rav'vik offered to lead the way and General Belan gave the order to follow. If the boy found the sword, he thought to himself, I will see to it that he gets back to Calheller safe with it.

The company of six rode along in silence, each wrapped up in thoughts of their own. Duncan was envisioning his encounter-to-be with Draskene and how that would turn out. Self-doubt still gnawed at his mind but he was determined to see this through to the end, whatever that may be.

He had been primed his whole life for this moment and now it was almost upon him. He had the Brach'dir, the sword with the power to defeat the Black Paladin. Duncan just feared that maybe he didn't have the strength required to wield it properly. After all, what did he know about magic, besides his dagger Sliver that he carried? From all accounts, the Black Paladin was a dark, ominous force feared by all. Who was he to think he could defeat him.

From the corner of his eye, he saw Salena watching him. She smiled when he looked her way and he returned it, feeling again the love for her he kept locked inside. That was his motivation now, not a promise made long ago when he was a boy. He still wanted revenge, he admitted to himself, but he was older now, and much more mature after this journey. What mattered most to him now was having a kingdom to call his own, to have Salena by his side as his queen.

Astride Sky, Ar'ye rode up alongside Martyl and said, "I hear hoofbeats, many of them, approaching from behind."

Martyl called a halt and everyone reined in their horses. He didn't think it was Wraulls as they didn't travel by horse, more often just as likely to eat them.

"Take a look," Ar'ye," he ordered. He was not about to take any chances now that they were this close to the end of their quest.

Ar'ye flexed his powerful chest and back muscles and his wings began to beat. Moments later he was aloft and winging his way towards the source of the horse sounds. A few minutes later he returned, setting down on his horse's back just as smoothly as he left.

"It is a Dwarven army, a few thousand strong by the looks, and a host of Rey'ak flying in guard formation. They appear to be headed this way."

Martyl mulled over the possibilities quickly. It appeared that Rav'vik had reported their location to General Belan who, knowing about their quest, was probably most eager to see if they had found the Brach'dir and to make sure they made it safely back to Calheller.

Again, they seemed to run into a streak of good luck.

"Ar'ye," he began, "fly out to them and bring them this way. It seems our trip back may be easier than we expected."

The others waited patiently until, after a few hours, Ar'ye and a flock of Rey'ak appeared in the midday sky overhead. They set down and by the time the introductions were over, General Belan and the first of the Dwarves had arrived.

"Greetings, Martyl, Royal Knight," Belan said as he strode forward to grasp Martyl's arm. "Was your journey a success?"

"Yes," replied Martyl, "but at a cost. We lost Rorn and Patches, one of the cats. Both died bravely, defending us."

"I am truly sorry," Belan admitted. "It has been a time of loss for us all. But, now let us hope it is our turn to inflict loss upon the Black Paladin!"

Cheers rose from the army of Dwarves and Rey'ak now milling about.

"If you would," continued General Belan, "let us escort you at least as far as Calheller. There you can rest safely until we determine how next to proceed."

"Thank you," replied Martyl gratefully. "We would appreciate that."

◆   ◆   ◆

Draskene was beside himself in anger. His Wraull forces in the Fire Top Mountains were decimated and the Dwarves, along with their Rey'ak allies, were headed back to Calheller.

Even more disturbing, there was a shift in the field of magic all around him. Like a spider in its web, he could feel the treading of another into his magical domain. A great magic had been awakened and he feared he knew what it was. Duncan must have found the Brach'dir. Still, he was just a boy and would not know how to wield it to its full potential. Just like a spider, Draskene would lie in wait in his web and when his prey was mired in its strands, he would attack.

There were preparations to be made before he faced this young upstart. He had the help of the Dwarves and they had the help of the Rey'ak. Duncan would most likely be coming for him with armies from both races, now that the Wraulls were defeated. And there was the mysterious girl with him as well. If she was truly from a hidden island kingdom, would they be sending forces as well?

Draskene wished he had more information on that possibility but things had not worked out that way for him. All his efforts now would have to be focused on defending Arundel. When that was done, he would see to making all those involved pay. Yes, he smiled to himself, they would pay dearly.

Turning to his castle's defense, Draskene summoned Bin. Within moments, his faithful servant arrived, entering Draskene's private quarters.

"Yes, master?" he asked.

"We need to marshall our forces in defense of the castle," began Draskene. Bin was visibly taken aback by this. He knew things were not going as well as hoped but he never imagined that his master, the Black Paladin, could actually be faced with defending his own castle.

Draskene saw his look of worry but did not deign to acknowledge it. This was only a minor setback. They would be victorious. How could they not?

"Send word to the Prime Guard in Gullhaven and all outlying areas. They are to return immediately and begin preparing for battle. Have your familiars send word to their brethren, their help will be needed also."

"Yes, my lord," replied Bin as he hastened from Draskene's quarters. Things must be worse than he thought, if the Prime Guard were being recalled and his familiars brought in. Of the former, there were several thousand. Of the latter, that could be reached in time, there were only a few hundred that would be of use in battle—the winter-wolves and fire hawks. Still, he would do as his master commanded. Any less could prove disastrous.

Two days passed by, quiet and uneventful as the battered group that set out from Calheller weeks earlier made their way back in the company of the combined forces of General Belan and Captain Kier'ak.

Duncan's mind was focused solely on one thing—his inevitable confrontation with Draskene. In his mind, he played out dozens of scenarios, envisioning how each one would start. The end was always the same—his victory over Draskene and the reclaiming of his family's kingdom.

Salena rode alongside him, as ever watchful as Big Cat over Duncan. She would watch him surreptitiously as they rode back to Calheller, careful not to let him see her doing so. She worried about him, knowing that the final confrontation with Draskene was approaching. Salena knew how badly Duncan wanted to confront the Black Paladin, to reclaim his kingdom, avenge his family and prove to her father he was worthy of marrying her. So much of his future depended on the outcome of this encounter. Even his very life. She would love him no matter what. She wanted to tell him several times during their ride back that it didn't matter to her, that they could just go back to the Misty Isles but she knew he could never let go of this quest. His entire life had been devoted to it and he would not rest until he saw it through to its conclusion—no matter what they may be. That was another part of him she loved and had to admit she didn't want changed either—his dogged determination to see things through to the end.

In the end, Salena decided to continue to keep an eye on Duncan and if he seemed to change drastically or otherwise appear to act in a fashion that may get himself hurt, she would let Martyl know immediately and together they would confront him and do something about it. Or at least try. She knew Duncan was too determined to be easily swayed.

Martyl rode alongside General Belan and Captain Kier'ak, the three battered leaders discussing their journeys over the past weeks. Martyl and Belan both decided that Kier'ak could be trusted with the news of the Brach'dir and the fact that Duncan was going to wield it against the Black Paladin. The Rey'ak knew little of the legend of the sword or the lost colony in the Iron Hills and Kier'ak listened raptly as he was filled in. He and his hunters had pledged their allegiance to the Dwarf cause so Martyl and Belan had no qualms telling him of the sword's supposed power from its forging during the Black Magic Wars.

Reyna traveled silently by Martyl's side, seemingly happy just to be riding and no longer on the run, while Ar'ye spent the time conversing with his fellow Rey'ak.

During the second day of their travels, the army passed within a few hours ride of where Duncan had buried Patches after the battle with Henaach and the winter-wolves to rescue Salena. Martyl watched him closely now, knowing what the cat had meant to Duncan and wondering what he would do. He didn't have to wait long to find out.

Without a word to anyone, Duncan spurred Roper ahead and veered off the path everyone else was following.

"Keep going," Martyl said to General Belan. "I'll get him back."

With that, Martyl and Tarna were gone and with Martyl being a far more experienced horseman than Duncan, caught up to him in no time. He wheeled Tarna about so that Duncan and Roper had to stop short.

"Where do you think you're going?" asked Martyl, even though he was pretty sure of the answer already.

Duncan stared at him stonily for a moment and Martyl saw Big Cat come out from behind Roper to sit beside Duncan, facing Martyl. He wasn't completely alone, thought Martyl. Of course the cat would be at his side.

"I'm not leaving Patches buried alone out here. He gave his life for me and deserves better than that. He's going back to Arundel with me."

"We don't have time for this," replied Martyl. "This area is still dangerous and we have to get back to Calheller."

"Go on without me then," continued Duncan. "I'll catch up. I'm not leaving him behind, alone."

Martyl turned as he heard horses coming up behind him.

"He won't be alone, Martyl," said Dirn as pulled alongside on his pony. "I'll go with him."

"And us," chimed in Ar'ye and Salena, strolling up on their horses.

"Let him go," added Reyna, looking more at home atop Windancer then any of them could even hope to. "A few hours more won't matter. We have all lost so much. If he feels better doing this then let him. We don't mean to go against your wishes as our leader, but can't you see he feels this is necessary?"

Martyl stared at them for a moment, all that remained of the group that left Calheller all those weeks gone past. They had been through a lot together and had grown immeasurably since then so that none would recognize their former selves. Still, they were the same inside, where it counted, and he knew that Reyna was speaking from the heart. In the end, he gave in, saying, "We'll all go. Besides, Duncan, you'll need help bringing him back."

Duncan looked at each of his friends briefly, and dipped his head to them in silent thanks. Without a word, he was off again to where he had lain Patches to rest.

Reyna, being the fastest and best rider among them, was sent back to General Belan to tell him what they were doing. He was not happy in the least, fearing that the sword may be lost yet again before they had a chance to wield it.

Captain Kier'ak calmed him by sending a party of ten Rey'ak scouts along with Reyna to provide aerial support if it was needed. General Belan was still not happy but he was a little more at ease. Knowing there was little else he could do, he continued with his troops on towards Calheller.

In just under two hours, Duncan and the others reached the cairn built to protect Patches from scavengers. They quickly removed the rocks and revertly placed his lifeless body in clean linen sheets that were used to wrap him. When finished, they placed him on a travois Reyna had borrowed from the Dwarf army and attached it to Duncan's horse, as he would not allow anyone else to haul Patches.

Big Cat walked solemnly beside her fellow cat, occasionally rubbing up against the travois and meowing softly as if to pay her respects also.

The Rey'ak scouts kept their distance, flying ahead of the others on horseback to make sure the way was clear. They did not understand what drove Duncan and the others to do this for a fallen animal but they did not ask, either, leaving the others to their sorrows.

A few hours later, they regrouped with the returning armies and fell into place. Martyl went back up to the front with General Belan and when questioned about what happened, merely replied, "Duncan has a bond with these cats that is hard to describe. It transcends anything I have ever seen between a man and his pets. Even in death, it is still there."

Belan thought to question him further but the look Martyl gave him made him think better of it.

As night fell across the Untamed Lands, the bulk of the Dwarf army set up camp, looking after the ponies and wagons and feeding the troops. The Rey'ak sent out scouts to watch the perimeter but the night remained uneventful. They were close now to Calheller and the Thunder Mountains. The crash of the Thunder River over the Dwarven Falls could be heard as a loud roar in the distance. The mountains themselves loomed up as giant behemoths, beckoning them on, urging them home.

It was a clear night, the moon full and bright and the stars shining brightly. A warm breeze blew across the land, carrying the scents of late summer mixed with the cooking fires to everyone.

Duncan and Salena sat alone with Big Cat. Martyl and Dirn were discussing the next course of action to be taken and Ar'ye, after inviting Duncan and Salena to come with him to meet the Rey'ak, went off to find some of his old friends.

The body of Patches, wrapped in the linens the Dwarves used for burial, lay near them and Duncan repeatedly stole glances at it, as if by force of will alone he could bring back his feline friend.

"I know you didn't want to leave him," Salena began tentatively, "But he is gone now. He will still live on in our memories and in our hearts. As long as we are alive to remember him."

She was looking at him as she said it but Duncan did not see her. His mind was filled with thoughts of how he would defeat Draskene. Since finding the sword days ago, that was all he thought about. It was a fire that burned inside him and threatened to consume him. Salena knew this and was frightened about how this would ultimately affect Duncan. She was about to say more when Reyna returned from checking on the horses. She sat next to Salena and as always, seemed to know intuitively just what she was thinking.

"I know you are worried for him, Salena," she said softly, just loud enough for Salena to hear. "But it has to be worked out, on its own, over time. I too have lost people and horses just as near to me as people and felt as he does now. In time it will pass. Some of that anger and hatred is needed to see us through hard times, to give us the determination to drive on against the odds. Give him a little more time. The wounds are still fresh."

Salena smiled at Reyna, silently thanking her for the support. She felt a little better but she knew deep down inside that she couldn't stop worrying until the matter with Draskene was finished.

Soon sleep overtook them. Big Cat slept watchfully at their side, the ever vigilant cat keeping watch over her humans even in the safety of the Dwarf encampment. Sometime during the night, Martyl, Dirn and Ar'ye returned as well, laying their bedrolls down with the others of their small company from Calheller. Even now, with their own peoples about them, Dirn and Ar'ye felt more at ease with Martyl, Duncan, Salena and Reyna. They had formed a bond of friendship and mutual respect for one another that was not easy to sever.

The night was uneventful and the entire camp slept peacefully. In the morning, they awakened to the smell of breakfast cooking over open flames in the center of the camp. A light mist covered the ground but it quickly evaporated as the sun cleared the Fire Top Mountains in the east and its golden rays spread their warmth across the Untamed Lands.

The camp was alive with movement, Dwarf soldiers going about their business, eating in shifts and seeing to the loading of their ponies. Within an hour of rising at dawn, they were underway again. As the day wore on, the Dwarves became louder and more joyous, happy to be returning home with a victory over their sworn enemies. The mood was infectious and the Rey'ak too joined in the singing of the Dwarf songs.

The group from Calheller, along with Reyna, stayed together, near the front of the army, but removed in spirit from the festive mood. They had seen a lot of battle and had all lost someone close to them over the past few weeks and knew that there was more bloodshed and loss in store for them yet. Duncan and Martyl would ultimately be facing Draskene himself and neither was foolish enough to believe Salena and Reyna would stay behind. They knew also that Ar'ye and Dirn would follow them, both as representatives from the Rey'ak and Dwarves, but also as their friends. And of course, Big Cat would be there, never leaving Duncan's side. For these seven, there would be no rejoicing until Draskene himself fell before Duncan's blade.

By late afternoon, they began the ascent into the Thunder Mountains. The vanguard of the army had barely made it into the foothills when several Dwarf Patrols appeared out of the rocky hillside. General Belan rode forward and the Patrol Captains saluted in recognition. Runners were sent off ahead to inform King Balamir and General Galani of General Belan's victorious return.

As they rode through the forested mountain passes, Dirn was shocked to see the devastation caused by the Wraull attack while he was gone. His mood lightened when he heard of the total defeat of the Wraulls and their Demon leaders at the hands of his Dwarven comrades and their new Rey'ak allies. Several of the Rey'ak accompanying the Dwarf army home gladly filled Dirn in on the events he had missed, relating tales of Dwarf and Rey'ak heroism alike. Dirn felt a sense of shame hover over him as he thought again about how he and Rorn had treated Ar'ye at the beginning of their journey. He vowed never again to think ill of him or his people, thankful for the help they had given his own people in their time of greatest need.

As the sun began its descent in the west, the armies marched down out of the Thunder Mountains and into the city of Calheller. Dirn's heart, along with all the other Dwarves returning, swelled with pride as their city shone before them in all its grandeur. The sun lit up the silver lined streets with a breathtaking brilliance that had no equal in the kingdoms of man or Rey'ak.

Townsfolk and merchants alike lined the streets to great the victorious army as it made its way to the Fountain of Life and the mountainside palace of King Balamir. The Dwarves lining the streets rushed out to meet their returning loved ones and showered them with cheers of joy. For the first time in countless years, the threat of a Wraull invasion was quashed, if even only for a short time. The Dwarven people at last felt hope and a possible end to the Black Paladin.

Not only had news of the army's victory traveled ahead of it, but it seemed rumors of a great weapon to be used against Draskene had been found. The Dwarves had seen Duncan and the others leave weeks before and now they returned escorted by the combined forces of the Dwarves and Rey'ak! What could they have possibly found? Although every effort had been taken to keep their quest secret, wild speculation ran rampant through the streets and many people remembered tales of old of great magics lost after the Black Magic Wars.

At last the throngs of Dwarves cleared out and the procession reached the Fountain of Life. Duncan recalled how on his last visit here an illusion obscured the nearness of the mountains and the Royal Palace. The illusion was still present and as they passed to the far side of the gardens about the fountain, the mountains suddenly reared up before them again.

General Galani was there waiting for them and he greeted General Belan, Captain Kier'ak and Martyl heartily. Belan and Kier'ak dismissed their troops, the Rey'ak following the Dwarves to the army's quarters of the city for rest and meals. Dirn and Ar'ye said farewell to their military comrades and stood with Duncan, Salena and Reyna, awaiting whatever came next.

General Galani motioned them ahead where they boarded two pony drawn wagons and began the ascent back up into the mountains to the Royal Palace.

General Galani eagerly listened as General Belan and Captain Kier'ak filled him in on the victorious battle over the Wraulls on the Fire Wind Flats. Martyl rode with them, listening quietly, learning what he could.

In the second wagon, the other five, along with Big Cat, rode in silence, content to take in the serene beauty of the majestic mountainside.

Upon reaching the entrance to the mountain and the Royal Palace, the occupants of both wagons were hurried inside and ushered to the King's chamber. Duncan reflected sadly to himself how the last time he was here he was accompanied by both his cats. He absently stroked Big Cat's head as they walked, thankful to at least still have her at his side. He was thankful too that his friends had survived the journey intact as well. Despite his gruff demeanor, Duncan realized that he missed Rorn more than he thought. He knew that his cat and Rorn had both given their lives freely to make sure he would have the chance to face Draskene. He just hoped he wouldn't let their memories down. The time was fast approaching when he would be facing Draskene.

Chapter Thirty

Dawn arrived and the remaining numbers of the party that originally set out from Calheller all those weeks go rose and joined one another to see Martyl off. Dirn had volunteered to go with Martyl, to see him safely through the forests to the west of the Thunder Mountains and the areas surrounding Frost Lake. Martyl agreed, even though Duncan had asked to go with him but was denied, as the Dwarf knew the land between Calheller and Gull Haven well. Besides, it would be wise to have a second pair of eyes and ears alert for whatever traps the Black Paladin may have left for them.

To ease Duncan's protestations, Martyl had told him, just before setting off, that both he and Dirn were expendable. If they did not return within a week, Duncan was to set off with the Dwarf and Rey'ak armies and defeat Draskene when they took Arundel back from his forces.

"I don't know if I can do it," admitted Duncan quietly, to no one but Martyl. "At least not without you at my side. You have been with me all the way. I won't know what to do when the time comes."

"You will be fine," assured Martyl, grasping Duncan by the shoulders. "You have been through more at your age already than I had. You have defeated a Demon, Wraulls and a wyvern. You rescued Salena without me. I believe in you, Duncan. You will do fine, even without me. Still, do not despair. I have no plans to let Draskene or his minions stop me when we are so close to his defeat. I will return, I promise."

Martyl shook Duncan's hand in the warrior tradition, grabbing his foreman and clasping it for a moment. Next Dirn grasped him the same and said loud enough for all to hear, "Don't worry, Duncan, I'll keep him safe." With a smile and a wink, the normally taciturn Dwarf stepped back, to be greeted by Ar'ye.

The Dwarf and Rey'ak, at first at odds with each other, now faced each other as friends. "Be sure to return safely, Dirn," Ar'ye said at last, "I would be honoured to fight at your side."

"No," stated Dirn, "the honour would be mine. Look after each other. We'll be back soon."

Salena and Reyna both gave Martyl and Dirn quick hugs and wished them a safe journey. Even Big Cat rubbed her head against each of them, as if leaving some of her scent behind to ward off potential enemies.

Hitching their provisions onto their horses, Martyl and Dirn set off from Calheller at a trot, eager to get underway. As they climbed the mountain trail out of the city proper, Martyl looked back one last time to see their friends standing silently below, watching them ride off. He hoped that that would not be his last memory of them.

They talked little as they rode on, man and Dwarf both lost in their own private thoughts. The day wore on, cool and breezy, the mountain air crisp and refreshing. The trail they followed wound its way through the Thunder Mountains and down into the forest below. At first there was only desolation—broken and burned patches of forest where Draskene's Wraull forces years earlier had tried to assault the Dwarves in the Thunder Mountains. Even though they were defeated, much of the forest had been razed and very little grew here. It would take many more years and a concentrated effort on part of the Dwarves to reclaim this land and cleanse it of the foul destruction wrought by the Wraulls.

Martyl was particularly taken aback by what he saw. He had been through this forest years ago when he was a Royal Knight under Duncan's father, King Aramid. It had been lush and green and filled with wildlife. Now it was desolate and barren and he was filled with sadness. He had been unconscious when Duncan and Salena had brought him through here weeks ago and he wished now he didn't have to see this wanton destruction.

He looked at Dirn and saw the pain he felt mirrored in the Dwarf's countenance. However much this pained himself, he knew it was even worse for the Dwarf as this was his homeland.

For the first time since leaving the Misty Isles, Martyl found himself wondering what they may find when they finally reached Arundel. He had been so preoccupied with getting the help and weapons they would need to defeat Draskene, he never actually gave any thought to what they may find in Arundel when they got there. Just seeing the destroyed forest around him made Martyl sick.

Finally, by late afternoon, they reached the edge of the woods and the shore of Frost Lake.

"There's a Dwarf Patrol fort nearby," stated Dirn, breaking the quiet. "We should be able to secure a boat to take us and our horses across Frost Lake. Once across, it will only be a day's ride to Gull Haven."

"Very well," replied Martyl. "The sooner we get there, the sooner we can try to procure more troops."

Dirn cupped his hands and brought them to his mouth, making bird noises as he blew into them. He waited a moment until similar bird noises responded.

"This way," he motioned to Martyl.

They traveled quietly through the thinning woods until they spotted a wooden fortification before them and a dock on the water.

Six burly Dwarves stepped out of the concealment of the trees and introduced themselves. Dirn introduced himself and Martyl and said that they were on an urgent mission for King Balamir.

"Yes," began the Patrol leader, a Dwarf named Browmer. "Word of your arrival at Calheller with the heir of Arundel and a magic sword to defeat Draskene has already reached us. How may we assist you?"

Martyl stepped forward, taking charge of the situation from Dirn before he cold speak, his need for haste urgent. "Then you must also know of our need for secrecy and haste. We need a boat, large enough to carry our horses across Frost Lake."

Browmer and the other Dwarves regarded Martyl for a moment then shrugged, saying, "Follow us."

Martyl and Dirn followed the six Dwarves a short way through the thick woods, picking their way cautiously over fallen logs and brambles until they entered a clearing that led to the shore of Frost Lake. There, moored to a wooden dock were several boats of Dwarvish construction.

Browmer led them to a small barge-like boat and said, "Take this one, Royal Knight, and may your journey be a success."

"Thank you, Browmer," replied Martyl. "I hope it is as well, for all our sakes."

The Dwarves murmured their assent to Martyl then helped him and Dirn push off from the dock. The wind blew steadily and soon the shore and the watching Dwarf Patrol faded into the distance.

Once they were well underway, Martyl fed and watered the horses then prepared a meal of cold meat, cheese and ale for himself and Dirn. They ate in silence until Dirn finally asked, "Do you believe the Renegades in Gull Haven will join us?"

"Yes. When I was with them a few weeks ago, they were eager to strike out against Draskene. I believe they will join us with very little persuading."

"I hope so," answered Dirn. "But are they a disciplined and seasoned force? The Prime Guard are no mere band of brigades. Numbers alone will not be enough to win this war. We will need skilled fighters."

"That my friend, I do not know. They may very well be town and farm folk opposed to the Black Paladin's rule, with nothing left to lose. Draskene has stolen their lands and their hopes and dreams. A man with nothing left to lose can be a very dangerous opponent."

"I suppose," was Dirn's unenthusiastic response.

He had been trained as a Dwarf Patroller and was Captain of his own Patrol for many years. He had seen countless skirmishes with the Wraulls during his hard life and did not see how a bunch of disgruntled towns folk and farmers could hope to do battle against one of the finest armies in the land. But still, help was help and they needed it desperately. Even though the Wraulls were effectively eliminated for the time being, if Draskene was not defeated now, he would build up his armies of Wraulls and Demons again and again until no one stood in his way of total domination.

When they finished their meal, darkness was beginning to settle over the lake. Martyl put away their supplies then lit two oil lamps at the bow of the boat. Their orange flame gave off enough light that they could see by and the clear night sky offered bright stars by which they could navigate.

Martyl offered to take the first watch letting Dirn sleep while he steered the boat. A cool night breeze filled the sails and the barge continued on its way to the western shore.

Unlike his first trip across the lake weeks earlier, Martyl was now conscious and able to enjoy the beauty of the scenery. The full, bright moon shone on the placid waters, turning the surface a silvery, frosty colour, giving the lake its tell-tale name. The weather remained calm this time around, no storms raged to harry the trip. At midnight, Dirn woke and relieved Martyl. The two spoke briefly, commenting on the beauty of the evening before Martyl retired until morning.

When dawn came, the sun rose and its warm golden ray's spilled through the gaps in the peaks of the Thunder Mountains to wash over the barge. The shoreline was in visual range and shortly after they finished their breakfast, the barge was on shore.

Martyl and Dirn mounted their horses and were off. They were less than a day's ride from Gull Haven but they were also dangerously close to the borders of Arundel. This was the reason Martyl wanted to go alone, or with only one other. A larger party would be suspicious and easily spotted traveling the open country between Frost Lake and

Gull Haven. This was land tightly controlled by the Black Paladin and armed groups did not ride about it unchallenged!

It was another clear, beautiful day, the sky a soft blue and the sun was shining warmly above. Martyl kept Tarna at a slow trot so that Dirn's pony could easily keep pace. In the forests, the pony was much more nimble and could set the pace, but out on the open grasslands the pace had to be reduced so it could keep up.

The two riders talked amiably, joking with each other, enjoying the fine weather. Despite the seriousness of their mission and the impending war, they were not about to let their spirits be dampened this day. They stopped for lunch and watered their horses on the banks of the Gull River near midday.

Martyl's horse Tarna looked up from grazing the river weeds, ears canted forward, eyes searching. Martyl saw him and he turned to follow Tarna's eyes. Off in the distance to the west, leaving the direction of Gull Haven, was a platoon of Prime Guards. Their black uniforms were easily discernible against the blue horizon as they rode southward toward Arundel.

Martyl motioned to Dirn and together they lay as low as possible against the riverbank, hoping they would not be spotted. It bothered both men to hide from the Prime Guard but they had no other choice. The two of them had very little chance against an entire platoon, and besides, their mission depended entirely upon stealth.

They waited the better part of an hour until the Prime Guard had passed well out of sight. At their closest, they were only three hundred yards away, yet Martyl and Dirn managed to stay hidden, along with their mounts. When Martyl deemed it safe to resume travel, they did so.

"Draskene must be calling his troops back to Arundel in preparation of an attack," stated Martyl matter-of-factly. "Yet how can he know what we are about?"

"The Black Paladin has many eyes and ears across the land, Martyl," replied Dirn. "I am sure he knows we have the sword and now that his Wraulls are defeated in the Fire Wind Flats, he will gather what forces he has left in a desperate bid to defeat whatever we bring against him. He knows the Dwarves will attack now, trying to crush him once and for all before he can rebuild his forces."

"Then we must hurry. We need to secure the help of the Renegades and then join our friends before the assault on Arundel. This will be our only chance."

Refreshed from their unexpected afternoon break, Martyl and Dirn rode on and by early evening arrived at the city of Gull Haven. The gates stood closed and barred and a squad of Prime Guard patrolled menacingly.

"What now?" asked Dirn as they surveyed the scene before them from the cover of a copse of trees several hundred yards away.

"It looks as if Draskene has ordered the city locked down. No one will be allowed in or out without proper authorization. He knows about the Renegades yet has been unable to find them. Even though their numbers are small, there are enough of them to cause trouble for the reduced number of soldiers here now that the rest are off to Arundel."

"And how does that help us?" rumbled Dirn irritably.

"It has made getting into the city harder but once in, we should be able to move about much more freely as there will be less Prime Guard about."

"How are we going to get in? We cannot just walk up to the gate and ask. Dwarves are the sworn enemy of the Black Paladin and the Prime Guard will attack the moment they see me. Not that I'd mind," Dirn smiled wickedly, fingering the blade of his battle axe.

"Can you swim?" Martyl replied with a grin of his own.

They waited for a few more hours until nightfall then made their way down to the riverbank. Martyl did not want to leave the horses unattended while they were gone but there was no other option. They removed their bridles and saddles so that the horses could roam freely and not become entangled, stored their provisions beneath a washed up tree trunk then entered the river. When Dirn protested leaving the horses untethered, Martyl reminded him that they were trained by Reyna's people to come when called.

"Remember how Reyna called them back before," reminded Martyl.

"Yes, but that woman had a special way with horses like no one else I've ever seen. It may be different for you and I."

Martyl just shrugged, choosing not to reply since he secretly felt the same as Dirn. His thoughts went to Reyna then and for a moment he allowed himself to imagine what his life may be like with her when all this was over. Then he waded into the river, his sword strapped tightly to his back and they were off.

The current was swift and the water cool as they coursed towards the city of Gull Haven. The sky was slightly overcast so no stars or moon shone down on them, making it less likely they would be spotted. In about five minutes they were approaching the outer bridge that spanned the Gull River, joining both halves of the wall guarding the city.

The rushing water sped them past the outer bridge and the sentries on top of it paid them no notice, thinking they were just pieces of river debris being swept out to sea in the dark.

A few minutes later, Martyl and Dirn were carried past the central bridge that spanned the river, joining the city at its center. Martyl thought back to the last time he was in this river a few weeks earlier and how he and Patches had jumped in at very nearly this exact spot to escape a patrol of Prime Guard intent on their capture. It was time they got out, he thought to himself and he began kicking for the south bank. Dirn followed, his short but immensely powerful limbs propelling him easily through the racing water.

Moments later, they pulled themselves up the riverbank and huddled in the shadows of an abandoned building.

"Nice trick, Martyl," Dirn complimented. "It seems the Prime Guard is expecting a large assault from the outside, not a small one under its own nose!"

"Yes, well now we must make our way to the Nag's Tale without being seen. It was there that I made contact with the Renegades and hopefully can again. Are you ready?"

Dirn checked his person for his two throwing axes and battle axe. All were present and he nodded his affirmation.

"Very well," began Martyl. "Stay close and out of sight. We don't want to draw any attention to ourselves."

Leaving their concealment of the shadows, the two men slipped quietly out into the street. It was dark and deserted, the city under curfew. Martyl and Dirn walked swiftly, yet cautiously for several blocks, Martyl leading the way. Martyl suddenly pulled Dirn back into a darkened doorway. With his finger to his lips, Martyl looked past Dirn and towards the corner. His eyes had not fooled him. Just ahead, two lights bobbed up and down, coming closer. Martyl edged back into the doorway and mouthed silently to Dirn, "Prime Guard."

Moments later, two Prime Guard walked within twenty feet of them, both carrying torches and talking loudly. As they passed, Martyl motioned to Dirn and the two sprinted down the street the Prime Guard had just come from. They stopped several hundred yards later in a darkened alcove while Martyl checked for pursuit. There was none and he whispered to Dirn, "We are almost there but we need to remain vigilant. There will be more patrols to make sure the curfew is enforced."

Dirn nodded his understanding and the two set off again. Despite Martyl's fears, they encountered no one else and they found the Nag's Tale. Cautiously, the two made their way across the street and up to the door. Martyl tried it but, as he suspected, it was locked.

"Keep a sharp eye for any patrols, Dirn, while I try to get the attention of the tavern's owner."

Dirn moved into a place of concealment across from the tavern that afforded him an excellent view of the street and tavern together. Like an owl at hunt, his head turned one way then the other, his eyes peering into the dark, constantly scanning for Prime Guard.

Martyl knocked several times, fearing that the noise would attract unwanted attention before the barkeep he knew as Bron answered the door. He waited several minutes, his heart racing and his blood pounding in his ears. He glanced across the street many times at Dirn who watched and waited also. He was not an easily frightened man but Martyl fully realized the danger to himself and Dirn if they were spotted by the Prime Guard on curfew patrol.

At last Martyl saw a light inside through the window. A middle-aged woman bearing a candle came to the door but did not open it.

"Who is it?" she demanded through the wood.

"A friend of Bron's," replied Martyl, his voice cool and neutral, despite the adrenaline coursing through his veins, unsure just how much information he should divulge at this point.

"He's not here," came the sharp retort. "Now go away. It is curfew now."

"It is urgent I speak with him," stated Martyl, growing desperate.

This was not going well. If they didn't get off this street soon, they would be spotted. There was no response and he saw the candle beginning to retreat away from the door. Deciding he had no other option, unless they gave up on having the Renegades assist them in defeating Draskene, Martyl made his choice.

Loud enough for the woman to hear, he said, "I am a friend. I am a Royal Knight, come back to aid in the defeat of the Black Paladin."

The candle was snuffed out and all was silent inside the closed tavern. Martyl suddenly feared he had said too much and was about to leave when the door opened and the woman said, "Inside. Hurry now!"

With a wave, he motioned Dirn back to him and the two entered the dark tavern. The woman peered out the door one last time, checking to see if they were spotted, then closed and latched it behind her.

"I am Kala," the woman said, introducing herself to Martyl and Dirn. "I am sorry about that but the Prime Guard have instituted a curfew and no one is to be out after nightfall. I was afraid you were sent to trick me."

As his vision became accustomed to the room's dark interior, Martyl could see the woman watching him intently. In the silence, he could hear someone walking purposefully down the street outside. Kala's glance turned to the window and then back to Martyl and Dirn as the footsteps receded into the night.

"I am Martyl, and this is my companion Dirn, from Calheller. We seek Bron on a matter of utmost importance. Can you tell us where we may find him?"

Again, she studied them, scrutinizing their trustworthiness, as if she could determine if they meant to deceive her by force of will alone, before answering. Like Martyl, she concluded it was best to just lay it all out at this point.

"Bron is my husband. Several days ago, he and many others were arrested by the Prime Guard and placed in the stockade. That same day, many of the Prime Guard that were stationed here began leaving the city, heading southward. Only a handful remain, watching the city and keeping us under curfew."

Martyl and Dirn exchanged knowing glances—the withdrawal of troops south to Arundel would coincide with their discovery of the Brach'dir. It would seem, without doubt now, that Draskene knew they were coming and he was doing everything in his power to prevent them from reaching him!

"Will you help him escape?" asked Kala, her face a mask of worry. "Bron told me of your encounter weeks ago. He mentioned that a Royal Knight had returned to defeat the Black Paladin and that the Renegades would help. It was because of this he was arrested. Bron was gathering more recruits and someone turned him in. Please help him. He is the leader of the movement and without him you will not gain the support of the Renegades."

She looked at them beseechingly and Martyl felt pity for her. So many lives had been ruined by Draskene and he had been able to do nothing about it. Now he had a chance to make amends, to perform his duty as a Royal Knight and help the weak and oppressed.

He looked at Dirn who merely shrugged and said, "Why not. We came here to get their help. There's no point in leaving here empty handed if we can help it."

"All right then," replied Martyl. "What can you tell us about the stockade?

"It is guarded by a half dozen Prime Guard at all times. It is also their barracks so at shift changes it is quite busy."

"When are the shift changes?" interrupted Martyl.

"Sunrise and sunset."

"Great. We've only got a few hours then, if we wish to do it tonight," muttered Dirn.

"We have to. We need to get back to Calheller as soon as possible. I need to be at Duncan's side when we begin."

Kala looked at them quizzically, trying to piece together what they were talking about but neither Martyl nor Dirn offered an explanation. The less who knew about the Dwarf assault on Arundel, the better.

"How many Prime Guard are still in the city?" asked Martyl.

"Over one hundred," replied Kala. "Half will be on curfew patrol while the other half are asleep in the barracks, which is at the other end of the stockade compound."

"This just keeps getting better," grunted Dirn, already not pleased with the direction things were heading.

"There's no point bemoaning the situation. I may be partially responsible for Bron's imprisonment—if it wasn't for our chance encounter, he may not have upped his recruitment policy and got caught. Besides, we need him to gather the Renegades to our cause. Are you with me?"

Dirn looked at him with a slight frown and said, "You should know me better than that by now Martyl. We've been through too much at this point to not go. Besides, do you think I'm going to let you have all the fun against the Prime Guard?" A smile flashed across his bearded face and was gone seconds later.

Martyl smiled back then said, "We need to go now. Kala, we'll need you to guide us to the stockade, then you are to return here at once. Is that understood?"

"Yes," she replied soberly.

"Very well, lead the way."

Quietly, the three crept out the door of the tavern and were down the nearest alley. They waited until a patrol passed by then they were off again. Kala led the way, her sense of direction unerring as she guided them down back-alleys and deserted streets, all the while deftly avoiding patrols of Prime Guard. At last, after an hour of skulking about, the three rounded a corner and drew up short in front of the stockade. It was well lit by many torches and, as Kala had said, six Prime Guard stood watch over the gate.

Martyl pulled them back into an alley and said, "Remember what we agreed, Kala. Leave the rescue attempt to Dirn and myself. Go back to your tavern where it is safe. We do not need to be concerned about your safety as well as ours as we attempt this. I promise, we will return your husband to you tonight."

Kala looked at him, worry etched in her already lined face, judging his sincerity before saying, "Thank you Martyl, Dirn. Be safe."

They watched her leave until she faded into the darkness of the night. Satisfied she was safely off, the two men turned back to the stockade and their next problem—how to gain entry.

Patiently they waited, watching the guards and the street, studying the area and the behavior and movement of the guards. Nearly half an hour passed when Dirn, growing impatient, said, "We need to act now. Time is running short and it will be sunrise shortly."

"I know," replied Martyl. "I was just hoping an idea would come to me."

"I may have one."

Martyl turned to look at Dirn, hunched down in the darkness of the alley. "Go on."

"It is only a rudimentary plan," began Dirn, anxious to be doing anything other than sitting in the dark alley. "Since the Black Paladin has been at war with the Dwarves now for several years and Gull Haven has been under his control, Dwarves do not venture here for fear of capture by the Prime Guard. Now, if you, a concerned citizen were to deliver me to the stockade under arrest …"

"Yes," agreed Martyl, seeing where this was going. "You would be my prisoner. I would be taking you to the stockade. That would get us close enough to the gate to attack the guards. We would have to be quick—if even one of them sets off an alarm, the entire barracks will be upon us!"

"I didn't say it was foolproof," grinned Dirn. "But it will let us get in close and give us the element of surprise."

"Very well then. Let us get ready."

Both men concealed their weapons. Their plan would not work if they were seen to be armed, an ordinary citizen and a Dwarf prisoner. Martyl adjusted his sword on his back so it ran the length of his spine, beneath his cloak and his dagger was slipped in his boot. Dirn adjusted his battle axe across his back so it too was unseen and kept his throwing axes at his sides covered by his cloak. They slipped away from their concealment and entered the street, Dirn walking with this head down and hands clasped before him, a loose cord of rope about his wrists. Martyl walked a pace behind him, head high. As they neared the stockade, Martyl waved to the guards and called out, "I have a prisoner. A Dwarf I found hiding in my shop!"

The guards sprang to attention, six pairs of eyes riveted on the strangers in the street. Two men detached themselves from the guard post and approached Martyl and Dirn. They were more than a little surprised to see a Dwarf and a man, apparently his captor, out after curfew.

"What are you doing out past curfew?" one of the two guards asked. "And what is a Dwarf doing in the city?"

They were only ten feet away from Martyl and Dirn at this point, their hands on their sword hilts already.

Just a little closer thought Martyl. Out loud, he replied, "I caught him hiding in the back of my shop. I was hoping for a reward if I brought him here."

"Your reward will be no punishment for breaking curfew. As for the Dwarf, he shall be executed at dawn as a traitor."

Martyl could see their grins in the torchlight as they approached and reached for Dirn. In a blur of motion, cat-quick, Martyl leapt on the two guards. Dirn flung the ropes from his wrist, grabbed his throwing axes and cast them at the guards remaining at the gate. Two dropped instantly and he was running towards the last two.

Martyl rained blows down on the two guards he tackled and they lay unconscious in moments. Rising, he pulled his dagger from his boot and he raced after Dirn. One of the remaining guards raced to the guard house to ring the alarm bell in the tower. On the run, Martyl hurled his dagger with deadly aim, striking the running man in the back, dropping him like a sack of flour.

The last remaining guard opened his mouth to yell, knowing full well he couldn't reach the alarm bell in time but before he could let loose, Dirn crashed into him full tilt. The two went down in a tangle of arms and legs but Dirn managed to come out on top. His iron hard fists pummeled the other man mercilessly and his face was soon cut and bloodied. Having sufficiently subdued him, Dirn bound and gagged the man then assisted Martyl in binding the other two men and hiding all five bodies.

Minutes later they were done and Dirn hauled their beaten but still conscious captor to his feet with one powerful arm. In his other hand, he held one of his bloody throwing axes and brandished it in the other's face. Martyl stepped forward and roughly removed his gag.

"Where is the man named Bron being held?" he asked, none to civilly.

Feared flashed in the guard's eyes but he still didn't speak.

"I'll ask one more time. If you don't answer, my friend here with the axe will hold his own execution, and it won't be quick."

To emphasize Martyl's point, Dirn pressed his axe firmly into the man's side until it cut his through his uniform and skin and blood began to trickle over the axe blade.

"If I show you, you'll let me and the others live?"

"Yes," replied Martyl. "You have my word." He looked him directly in the eye, letting the other take his measure of truth from that.

"All right," he stammered after a moment's consideration. "Follow me."

Dirn kept a firm grip on the man with one hand and his axe pressed tightly into his back with the other. Martyl followed closely behind the two of them, sword drawn, eyes searching. His pulse raced as they slunk through the corridors, waiting any minute for the Prime Guards in the barracks to come out and spy them. None did, however, their captive leading them straight to the stockade as they commanded, apparently afraid enough for his life to do as they bid with no tricks.

They entered the stockade and passed several locked cells until they came to one set alone from the rest.

"This is it," their captive said, a hint of fear in his voice.

"Open it," commanded Martyl.

The guard opened the door then was pulled back by Dirn. Martyl stepped to the doorway and called, "Bron, are you there? It is Martyl. I've come to help."

There was shuffling in the darkness of the cell then a man came into the light. For a moment, Martyl did not recognize the barkeep and owner of the tavern, he was so badly covered in bruises, dried blood and filth.

As his eyes adjusted to the light, Bron recognized Martyl and he grasped his hand in welcome.

"I had hoped you would come back," he said at last, entering the hallway.

"We must leave here quickly," said Martyl, not wasting time in pleasantries. "We have very little time. Follow me."

Martyl turned to lead the way and as he passed Dirn, he nodded to the Dwarf. Dirn struck the guard hard on the back of the head with his axe handle, knocking him to the floor unconscious. He had given his word to let the man live, but said nothing about letting him stay conscious while they were still there!

"We must release the others before we leave," Bron urged. "They are members of my Renegade teams and I will require their assistance in rounding up the others."

Martyl looked at Dirn who just shrugged and said, "We came here to get their help. We may as well do as he asks."

"Very well," replied Martyl, beginning to like this less and less. They were spending far too much time in here for his liking.

Dirn removed the keys from the prime guard and together the three men set about releasing the dozen captives in the stockade. In minutes, all were free and rushing as quietly as possible to the exit gate. As they snuck into a darkened alley, everyone dispersed and went separate ways, except for Bron, who after being quickly introduced to Dirn, led Martyl and Dirn to an old abandoned tool shed.

Bron searched around the bushes lining one wall until he found what he was looking for, an old key. He unlocked the door and led the others inside. Wordlessly, he shoved some crates in the middle of the shed off to one side, released a hidden catch, then opened a trap door in the floor.

"Thank you, Martyl, and Dirn," began Bron. "I will assemble our forces over the next few days and will meet your troops at the place of your choosing. You had better go now. It will only be a few minutes before the barracks rise and prepare for the shift change and our escape will be noticed. Go down these stairs then follow the tunnel. It will lead you outside the city to the Gull River." He handed them a torch from a bracket set in the wall near the stairs and lit it with flint.

"Farewell until we meet again," said Martyl, shaking the other man's hand. "In a fortnight we will be amassed on the southern shore of Frost Lake, preparing for our assault on Arundel and the Black Paladin. Your help will be greatly appreciated."

Martyl took the torch from Bron and headed down the stairs. Dirn and Bron shook hands briefly before Dirn followed Martyl down. As they neared the bottom of the steps, they heard the trap door close above them and then the distant sound of alarm bells.

They knew the barracks were up and the escape discovered. All they could hope was that Bron and his men stayed free this time.

For days now, Prime Guard from Gull Haven and the lands between there and the Thunder Mountains came pouring into Arundel. Several thousand had arrived and several thousand more were yet to arrive. The castle grounds were far too small to house so many so they bivouacked on the plains surrounding the fortress.

Thousands of tents were erected and camp fires burned day and night. It looked like a city had sprung up from the earth itself overnight. Angry and noisy, its denizens fought practice battles and honed weapons in anticipation of the battle to come.

The Rey'ak Hunters patrolled high above the soldiers below, their wings stretched out, soaring on the thermals that rose from below, like great birds of prey. Their keen eyesight scanned Arundel and the surrounding lands for all signs of their intended enemy. It was important they gain as much intelligence on Draskene's forces as possible before they and the Dwarves marched into battle.

Besides the Prime Guard encampment, the Rey'ak also spotted an enormous number of Wraulls marching to Arundel from the north, most likely the remnants of the tribes who were not in the battle on the Fire Wind Flats. The Rey'ak estimated their numbers to be at least two thousand, added to the five or six thousand Prime Guard already at Arundel or on their way.

To make matters worse, scores of packs of winter-wolves were prowling the lands between Arundel and the Gull River, making their way steadily to Arundel to join the human and Wraull force.

Though desperate to see what was going on in the castle itself, the Rey'ak had been warned by Grendle, the Dwarves' magic-user not to stray too close to Draskene's stronghold. His magic, it was feared, would detect them and put their covert mission in jeopardy. Even if they were to fly overhead, they would not detect what was going on deep in the bowels of the castle itself.

Far beneath the battlements and halls and quarters of the castle, in a chamber far beneath the ground itself, its single door protected by warding glyphs, Draskene stood in the center of a single, circular room. Manacled to the walls were four prisoners, Renegades from Gull Haven. Their beaten and broken forms hung limp from the iron bonds, their life slipping away as the ravages of torture consumed their fragile bodies. Their torturers had no more use for them after they gave up the names of the leaders of the Renegade movement but Draskene had one last use for them.

After they were transported under heavy guard from Gull Haven to Arundel, Draskene had seen to their imprisonment on his own, not trusting the location of his summoning chamber to anyone else. He left them secured to the chamber walls for several days to weaken them further, to facilitate the transference he was attempting now.

In a low voice, he began chanting in an ancient language. A low rumble began to sound from beneath the chamber and dirt and mortar began to fall from cracks in the walls and ceiling. The poor souls chained to the chamber itself shook with it, moans escaping from their battered bodies.

Other sounds began emanating from the room, from all directions. Unearthly moans, wails and screams rent the air and a sickly green mist rose from the floor. Like fingers reaching out, trailers of the green mist twisted and turned, groping for the men fastened to the walls. Slithering about their feet, the mist snaked its way up their bodies and entered their noses and mouths. As it worked its way through their broken bodies, the mist began remaking them. They shook and jerked, new life invading their dying forms, making them over into something far from human.

Bones broke and reformed, skin stretched and spikes bristled through tough growths of hair. Fingers crooked into talons, nails grew long and sharp. Teeth grew enormous and twisted, splitting their jaws and dripping spittle. When it was over, the four prisoners were no longer men. They had been remade, transformed into Demons by the Black Paladin.

His power and energy temporarily spent, Draskene left his new creations where they were to rest. The transition from the Demons' realm to this one was taxing for not just him. He left the summoning chamber and returned to his quarters. He would have preferred full Demons to these transformed Demons but a great deal of his power had been used in previous summons and these were all he could summon at present. They would have to do, he told himself.

Chapter Thirty-One

Four days after their departure, Martyl and Dirn returned to Calheller. They were weary and sore from the exhausting trip but they had a mission to accomplish and wanted to see it through.

As they entered Calheller, late the fourth afternoon, they were greeted by the Dwarven army as it began preparations for the march to Arundel. Nearly the whole of the Dwarves' forces were going to Arundel, six thousand strong, along with about one thousand Rey'ak. A small force of a few thousand Dwarves would remain behind in case any Wraulls from the Charnak's came down. Other than that, all their resources, and those that their new allies the Rey'ak could spare, would be sent to Arundel to try and crush Draskene once and for all.

It was a big gamble, but one the Dwarves and Rey'ak were willing to take. For many years now, they had been victims of the Black Paladin and his minions, always on the defensive. But now, hope had come to them with Duncan and the finding of the Brach'dir. Most of the Wraulls of the Fire Wind Flats had been destroyed and Draskene himself was showing fear as he fortified his position in Arundel and called all of his forces home.

Martyl just hoped their goals were not in vain. It was not that he didn't believe in Duncan, because he did, especially after all he had been through and survived on this journey to find the sword, but rather he knew a lot of things stood between Duncan and his actual confrontation with Draskene. Thousands would die before they even got close to the castle and then there would be the traps Draskene would have set for them. Martyl did not allow himself to believe that things would go easy for him and Duncan. He could not afford to.

Absently he waved at the Dwarf and Rey'ak captains as they greeted Dirn and himself on their way back to meet the others. At last they reached the quarters where the others of the small party awaited them.

Martyl was surprised to see Salena and Reyna training alongside Duncan and Ar'ye with several Dwarf weapon experts. All four were busy thrusting and parrying, slicing and blocking with swords, to see him and Dirn approach. Tired from their journey, the two warriors sat down on a bench and watched. Both were impressed with the sword-play they saw, even though it pained Martyl to see Salena and Reyna doing this. He did not believe they should be going with the army to Arundel, but rather they stay in Calheller where it was safer. However, he knew it was pointless to suggest otherwise to them. They were determined to see this quest through to the end, like the rest of them, no matter what that end may be. At least, he thought to himself, they are capable of defending themselves.

At last, as the sun began its evening descent behind the mountains, the Dwarf trainers called an end to the training session. They said their good-byes to their students then Martyl and Dirn, and were on their way.

"You're back!" exclaimed Duncan upon seeing his two friends. "How did it go?"

"As well as could be hoped," replied Martyl. "The Renegades, if all goes well, will be joining us in less than a fortnight now."

"It's really going to happen then, isn't it," said Duncan flatly, the full realization of the upcoming battle finally settling down upon him.

"Yes, it is," replied Martyl. "We still have a week to go and I suggest you use the time as you have been, by continuing to train and prepare for it."

Duncan nodded absently, his mind racing with thoughts. His whole life he had waited for this and now that the time was upon him, he suddenly felt unsure. Everything leading up to now had just happened as they were on their journey. He never had time to think about anything and let indecision and fear worm their way into his thoughts. But now, he had a week to ponder the battle he was about to walk into. So much rested on him, so many were willing to give their lives to see that he faced and ultimately destroyed the Black Paladin.

What if he let them down? What if he failed? What if his friends were lost along the way? Would he be able to wield the Brach'dir successfully? He had so many doubts now that he was beginning to feel sick to his stomach.

Martyl saw his look of consternation and, grasping him by the shoulder so Duncan had to look at him said, "Fear not. We will all be by your side. You are strong and you will succeed. It's natural to feel overwhelmed before a battle. Even I'm afraid."

Duncan looked at his oldest friend and mentor and smiled. "Thanks," he returned.

Martyl smiled back then said, "Now, turn in for the evening and tomorrow we shall take up some more training. I will ensure that we are all ready to go to Arundel."

The next morning saw the six of them up with the sun. They all ate a full breakfast of cheese and grain cereal washed down with cold milk. When breakfast was over, Martyl and Dirn led the other four out to continue their training.

They sparred with swords and quarter-staffs and practiced bone crushing swings with maces and limb severing chops with battle-axes. Target practice with the bow and arrow was given, every weapon of war covered, if only briefly, to ensure they would be able to fight with whatever weapon they found on the battlefield.

Of course Duncan would be wielding the Brach'dir and Reyna and Salena both had selected short swords they were comfortable with. Ar'ye had his bow, but Martyl and Dirn both felt it important that they be able to use other weapons in case theirs were damaged or lost.

For the next week, under the blistering hot sun, the four were put through their paces relentlessly. Martyl and Dirn were grueling taskmasters, making sure that the others had the defensive moves down as well as the offensive. Each day, Big Cat lay in the sun watching them through half-open eyes, her feline reflexes needing no honing, only rest, until the day came.

After their sixth day of intense training, Marty bade them all get some much needed rest. "You have done well," he addressed them. "I have no fears you will be capable of defending yourselves ably. Rest well tonight and tomorrow, for the day after we leave with the army to meet the Renegades."

The following day, Salena, Reyna, Ar'ye and Duncan sat in a small park near the army barracks while Dirn and Martyl were off discussing battle plans with the army. As usual, Big Cat lay at Duncan's side, purring contentedly while he absently stroked her soft fur.

They sat in silence, the four of them, their minds filled with what may happen the next few days. Each of them was worried for themselves, and each other, the fear and reality of what was to come fully settling on them.

Reyna was the least worried, having spent years alone in her town, hiding amongst the Prime Guard who occupied it. She was no stranger to death and destruction but she did not wish for it either, if it could be avoided.

Ar'ye had had some experience with death, his people having faced the Wraulls in several skirmishes the past few years in the Fire Top Mountains. Still, he too wished to avoid it if possible.

Duncan and Salena, on the other hand, had never faced the hardships the others had, having grown up in the secluded Misty Isles. Until recently, they had been unaware of the level of death and hardship wrought by Draskene. But in the last few weeks, both had endured great difficulties and loss and had proven their strength to the others, even though it was never truly doubted.

At one time, not too long ago, all Duncan could think about was avenging his family and defeating Draskene, to take back his father's kingdom and undo all the evil wrought by the Black Paladin. Now, after losing Patches and Rorn, he realized that there would be a price to pay if he was to be victorious and he was worried that it may prove to be too high. He could not bear losing Salena or Big Cat and even though he had only known Ar'ye, Reyna and Dirn a short while, he did not want to lost them either. And then there was Martyl. His oldest and closest friend, who was like an older brother to him. Duncan knew that Martyl would do whatever was needed to see that he succeeded and that scared him. He knew Martyl would not hesitate to give his life for him if need be. He did not want that on his conscience.

As if sensing each others thoughts, the four looked at one another and Duncan said, "Thank you all for your help and support. I couldn't have got this far without all of you. I just hope we are successful."

"Do not fear, my friend," replied Ar'ye. "We will succeed. We are not alone this time. We have the Dwarf army and the Rey'ak with us."

Duncan smiled at his friend, but it was tight and forced, his mind still dark with his personal fears.

That night the army headed out of Calheller on its long march to Arundel. Six thousand Dwarves, five thousand on foot and one thousand on horseback along with one thousand Rey'ak filed out of Calheller. The Dwarves were dressed in forest cloaks colored green and brown to camouflage them in the woods. Even in the open spaces around Arundel they would offer some limited concealment, especially to the Wraulls with their poor eyesight.

They were led by Belan and Galani, along with various captains and lieutenants. Captain Kier'ak led the Rey'ak and Martyl was present as well, his knowledge of Arundel an important asset in the upcoming assault. Like a gigantic beast lumbering through the forest, the army, in formation, snaked its way through the forests south of the Thunder Mountains towards the Thunder River.

Several patrols of Rey'ak flew ahead of the main body of the army, scouting for hidden enemies or other dangers, choosing the quickest, most direct path. It was important that the Dwarves meet up with the Renegades from Gull Haven on time as they were only a small force and if left exposed in the open by Frost Lake, they would be an easy target for the forces at Arundel to dispatch.

Every possible advantage was needed by the Dwarves and Rey'ak if there were to succeed. They were going up against a larger force and a fortified castle. Because the Dwarves had to travel through thick forest and cross two rivers to reach Arundel in a matter of days, they could not manage to bring any siege equipment with them. That meant no catapults, siege towers or other such devices to help breach the castle walls. What they did have on their side, however, was the ability to wage an aerial assault with the Rey'ak. Even though their numbers were small, in comparison, they could fly over their enemy and attack from above or even behind.

By early morning, just before dawn, the army had forded the Thunder River and now rested briefly on the small island between the Thunder River and the Sylvan River. Miles away, to the south east, the sky was lit with an eerie orange glow. It was not the sun beginning its daily trek across the sky as it rose for only a small area was lit up. Rey'ak scouts returned from that direction and landed to confer with the army's leaders, Generals Belan and Galani, Captain Kier'ak and Martyl.

From their position in the formation, a few rows back from the front, Duncan, Salena, Reyna, Ar'ye and Dirn watched curiously as they sky continued to glow in that one spot.

Reyna watched for only a moment before turning away and sitting down away from the others, her head in her hands. Salena noticed her and went to sit next to her.

"What's wrong?" she asked, sending something was amiss.

"That is where my home is. Was. Equilon. It seems the Prime Guard have burned it." Before she could look away, Salena noticed the tears running down Reyna's cheeks. Impulsively, she hugged the older woman who was becoming more like a mother to her every day.

"I'm so sorry," she whispered, not knowing what else to say.

"It seems the Prime Guard are being recalled from all their postings," stated Martyl after hearing the reports. "They will all be used in defense of Arundel. And, unfortunately for others, they are burning everything they leave behind."

He looked over towards his friends and saw Salena comforting Reyna. She knows already, he thought to himself.

There is nothing we can do for that city or any other, at this point until after Draskene is defeated." Everyone nodded in agreement as General Belan continued. "We have rested long enough. We need to be across the Sylvan River before noon."

He issued his orders and runners were dispatched to send them out to the troops. Like a giant leviathan come awake, the army rose and lumbered on.

Reyna cast one last glance back toward her home then woodenly followed the others.

By noon, they had crossed the Sylvan River and then turned west and north to stay close to the southern shore of Frost Lake. Everyone was extra vigilant now, the armies of Draskene only two days' march south. They pushed on, the pace brisk but not hard to keep. It was important to reach the Renegades on time but it was just as important that the army stay strong and rested, not worn out from a forced march.

They rested for the night, no fires of any sort allowed for fear the Black Paladin's forces would learn their location. Everyone ate cold meals then quickly feel asleep. Everyone, that is, except for the sentries who kept watch through the night, both Dwarf and Rey'ak, silent forms that watched from the darkness, eyes and ears alert for any sign of danger.

Martyl and Dirn did not sleep right away either. They strayed from their friends for a short while, quietly discussing plans and strategies to get themselves, and Duncan, into Arundel. If they could force a confrontation with Draskene, thousands would be saved and not die fighting if he was defeated.

At last, unable to come up with anything solid, they joined the others, rolled themselves up in their travel cloaks and went to sleep.

Dawn broke the second day, the sky an angry red as the sun's light scattered across the clouds that had swept in overnight. The army cooks were busy in the hours before, preparing a cold breakfast for the troops. They ate and drank quickly, tended to the horses and supply wagons then set out again.

The march was uneventful and by early evening of the second day they arrived at the shores of Frost Lake. They halted while once again the Rey'ak scouts reported back, this time telling of hundreds of men concealed in the reeds and bushes along the shores of the lake.

Martyl and Dirn, along with a handful of heavily armed Dwarves and Rey'ak, left the main company and traveled alone for nearly a mile. With their exceptionally keen eyesight, the Rey'ak pointed out the men where they hid.

"Bron," called out Martyl, "It's Dirn and Martyl. We've arrived with the Dwarven army."

There was some shuffling in the reeds off to his right and then Bron emerged from his hiding place. As he approached Martyl and Dirn, his expression turned to awe and disbelief.

"I see the legends of old are true. There truly are bird-men!"

"These are the Rey'ak," responded Martyl, his arm sweeping out to indicate the Rey'ak standing near him. "They have pledged their support in our battle against Draskene as well. It was they who spotted your men despite their concealment and led us here to meet you."

"That is good news indeed!" exclaimed Bron, shaking both Martyl and Dirn's hands. "I am glad to see you made it back safely."

"And you," replied Martyl.

"It was not easy. The alarm was sounded just as you left and I had a difficult time finding a safe-house to hole up in. But, I managed, as did the others. Then, just five days ago, we regrouped and after a long and fierce struggle, we managed to retake our city!"

"That is wonderful news!"

"Yes, we are happy, but we lost many men in the battle. We number only five hundred now but we are here, every last one, to aid in the fight against the Black Paladin. We are placing all our hope on you, Martyl, Royal Knight, and defender of the people. We still remember the days of King Aramid and what his Royal Knights stood for."

Bron grasped Martyl's shoulder, a gesture in brotherhood then whistled three times. The area about Frost Lake came alive as five hundred tattered, bruised and cut Renegades left their concealment and formed up behind their leader.

"We are ready Martyl. If you would take us to your camp, we will join your forces."

Martyl nodded and gave Bron a tight smile. He felt a little uncomfortable after hearing Bron's admission, but there was not much he could do about it. An army needed a leader, someone the men could look to in a crisis and rally about. If he was to be that man for the Renegades, then so be it. Who was he to misplace their faith in him. He had a job to do regardless and he would see it done.

"Do not fear, Martyl," began Bron, walking beside Martyl as they headed back to the Dwarf encampment. "No matter what happens, we will not hold you to blame. For too long we have lived under the yolk of the Black Paladin. You have brought us hope and even if we lose, we will have lived and died as free men again. That is what matters to us most."

"Thank you," replied Martyl. "That is all any of us can hope for in the end, to be free. But I promise you this, as long as I have breath in my lungs, I will fight to see the rightful heir of Arundel back on the throne."

"And that is why we will follow you, Martyl, because of your determination and honour."

Once back at the main camp, the Renegades were welcomed warmly by both the Dwarves and Rey'ak. The men of Gull Haven and the surrounding areas were awestruck as they watched the Rey'ak scouts flying patrols around the encampment. They had all heard legends of the Rey'ak but none, until now, believed them. Just seeing these "bird-men" of legend gave them a feeling that if their legends were true, then just possibly they could defeat the Black Paladin!

While the men of the three armies intermingled during meal time, their leaders were busy planning the next move they would make. Duncan and the others were included this time at Martyl's request. While Ar'ye and Reyna may have had some limited exposure to the types of fighting they were about to encounter, Duncan and Salena had none, and Martyl wanted to be sure all four of them were aware of what was likely to be happening.

They all sat about a large wooden table in the center of a massive tent that was erected to serve as the army's headquarters. On one side sat Duncan, Salena, Reyna and Ar'ye while across from them sat Generals Belan and Galani, Kier'ak and Bron. Martyl stood at the head and Big Cat slept peacefully at Duncan's side.

"I have little doubt Draskene knows we are here by now," began Martyl. "His forces will be firmly entrenched in Arundel and will have many traps set for us. We will endeavor to do our best to avoid these and for the ones we can't, we shall try to spring as many as possible before we attack."

"Now, according to the scouting reports from Captain Kier'ak, there are Wraull and Prime Guard forces amassed here," Martyl pointed to several places on a map spread out on the table. "There are also winter-wolves ranging across the open spaces around Arundel. There is no mention of what is behind the walls of the castle itself, but I'm sure it will be heavily fortified and there will be worse things yet inside."

Martyl, followed by the other leaders, went on for several more hours, discussing plans, contingency plans and contingency plans for the contingencies that failed. At last, as the four guests were starting to nod off, Martyl concluded the meeting, saying, "Remember above all else, no matter what happens on the battlefield, even if the Black Paladin's forces are utterly decimated, he must be defeated himself or he will return again. To do this, we must ensure that Duncan has a chance to face him. He is the only one who can wield the Brach'dir."

Duncan felt his face redden as all eyes turned toward him. He knew how much rested on his shoulders and felt uncomfortable being reminded of it. He was suddenly conscious of the sword strapped to his side and wondered again if he would be able to invoke it's magic—magic that was only activated when faced with a hostile magic so he as of yet had not chance to see if it even worked! Again self-doubt wormed its way through his thoughts, but with great determination he pushed them aside and rose to his feet, addressing the others, "Do not fear. I will see that Draskene pays for the evil he has wrought."

As he turned to follow the others out, he just hoped he could back up his big words with equally big action.

When morning came, the sky was leaden and overcast. The Dwarves and their allies began the march south to the beat of thunder in the sky. Flashes of lightning punctuated the dark sky in brilliant flares of white and blue. The rain had not yet started to fall, but it was only a matter of time.

Duncan's stomach and nerves were as tumultuous as the sky above. This was it, he thought to himself. This was really it. Today the battle would begin and shortly thereafter he would be facing Draskene. All his life he had thought about and trained for this day and now that it was before him, he no longer felt as brave as he once did. Even the reassuring weight of the Brach'dir sword strapped to his side did little to comfort him.

But his friends did. At his side, as always, were Big Cat and Salena. Ar'ye was there too and just ahead of him rode Martyl and Reyna. Surrounding all of them were thousands of battle hardened Dwarves and several hundred Renegades and Rey'ak. He would do his best, he told himself, to earn the faith so many had in him. He would not let his personal frailties overcome him. Too much depended on him to be strong and see this out. He could do it. He must!

At last the advancing army came within sight of Arundel and the juggernaut that was Draskene's army. Spread out across the plain between the castle and the Dwarves, thousands of soldiers, Wraull and man, stood in formation watching with undisguised hatred as the Dwarves and their allies halted just outside of the range of long bows.

Without waiting, the Dwarf captains began issuing their orders. Like industrious ants, the Dwarves began building a series of trenches and bulwarks, their sturdy, heavily muscled bodies easily digging through the earth and constructing makeshift, albeit sturdy shelters.

Many of the Wraulls, still enraged over their defeat at the hands of the Dwarves a few weeks ago, let loose a volley of arrows. All fell short of their intended targets and the Dwarves never even paused in their efforts to look. This further enraged the Wraulls and several hundred screamed their rage and frustration and rushed the Dwarves, hoping to start the battle now.

Before they got within three hundred yards, a hundred Rey'ak rose up from concealment in the Dwarf ranks and raked the advancing Wraulls with arrows. Within moments, the deadly hail of arrows stopped and the Wraulls lay dead in the no-man's land between the two opposing forces.

Roars of outrage rose up from the Wraulls and Prime Guard but this time no one left their ranks. It was very apparent what would happen if they were to rush the Dwarves. Besides, they had several traps laid out for their adversaries and they were firmly secured in their location. All they had to do was wait for the Dwarves and their allies to come to them. Sooner or later, they would have to. They could not stay out in the open, exposed on the flats for long. Their supplies would not last and eventually they would be flanked and surrounded by Prime Guards and Wraulls.

The Dwarves knew this too and planned to attack, but first they needed a secure position to fall back on in case a retreat was necessary. Several hours later, they were done. They had dug a vast ditch, nearly five feet deep and four feet wide that ran east to west for about a quarter of a mile. Every fifty feet saw ramp-ways that led out to either side of the ditch—south towards the enemy and north away from them. This provided them some protection from any stray arrows that may make it this far as well as hiding their movements from the enemy.

When they finished, the Rey'ak implemented the second part of their pre-battle strategy. As the leaders had talked the previous night, they knew that Draskene's forces had had plenty of time to fortify the area surrounding the castle with many traps. Now, before they advanced further, was the time to spring them.

Up they flew, over the Dwarven defenses and across the plain separating them from their enemy. Five hundred Rey'ak, half their force, filled the already dark sky, their winged forms blocking even more light. Each carried with him a rock or log or any other object they could drop. They rose up out of the bow shot, too far up to hit specific targets accurately like people but that was not their plan. Before they even reached their enemy, their loads were released. Like a hail storm, rocks and pieces of wood plummeted earthward with blinding speed. Many hit solid ground, striking with enough force to leave minor impost craters, sending up plumes of dirt and dust. Many others did not, and that is what the Rey'ak and Dwarves hoped for.

Draskene's forces had dug many pit falls in the area between themselves and the land the Dwarves would have to cross to get to them. The debris rained down on their camouflaged coverings and smashed through, exposing the gaping, spike filled holes beneath.

Their work done, the Rey'ak wheeled about overhead and flew back to camp. As they arrived, the second wave, containing the other five hundred Rey'ak took flight. Up they went as well, well out of range of enemy attack. This group went armed with their bows and flaming arrows. Once in place over the empty land between the two opposing forces, they released their fiery missiles.

Against the storm darkened sky they resembled miniature meteorites plummeting to earth.

As the arrows hit, the ground below erupted in a giant conflagration. Flames leapt up towards the sky as the oil drenched ground ignited. The heat was so intense that men on both sides of the impending conflict pulled back a little further. Black smoke filled the sky, blocking out even more of the sun. Once again, the Rey'ak, having successfully completed their mission, returned to the others.

Minutes after the huge conflagration began, it burned itself out, the oil that had been spread over the ground burned away, along with any vegetation that had been there. The earth was blackened and scorched, looking even more desolate beneath the dark-clouded sky.

The Dwarves did not rest, however. Now that their enemy expected them to wait in their trenches and come up with a battle plan after successfully diffusing two of the traps laid out for them, they were going to strike now. They had the initiative and needed to surprise their adversaries as they were outnumbered nearly two to one.

A horn sounded and out of the trenches and up the ramps rode two hundred Dwarves mounted on their sturdy battle ponies. They raced toward the Wraulls and Prime Guard, the thick billowing smoke helping to hide their approach. A safe path was laid out before them now that the pit falls had been exposed and the oil ignited.

As the iron shod mounts of the Dwarves thundered across the open grassland, the Wraull archers began letting loose volleys of arrows. They could not yet see their foe through the heavy wall of smoke but they could hear them. The Prime Guard joined in as well with bows and slings. A deadly barrage of arrows and stones flew through the smoke, seeking unseen targets.

The Dwarves rode on, heedless of the deadly missiles sent their way. Riders and mounts were toppled here and there, the endless hail of arrows and stones finding targets despite the cover of the smoke. With lances and pikes lowered, they emerged from the billowing smoke in a massive wall of armour and weapons and struck at the exposed flank of their enemies.

Scores of Wraulls and Prime Guard fell as the Dwarves cut a swath through them. They drove deep into the enemy's defenses then wheeled about and charged away.

The Wraulls, easily incensed and less disciplined then the Prime Guard, roared in outrage and gave chase, their large powerful legs almost capable of keeping pace with the armoured ponies. They pursued the retreating Dwarves, determined to overtake their quarry before they could reach the safety of their trenches. The distance between them was steadily decreasing as the battle ponies became fatigued, carrying armoured Dwarves for so long.

With the Wraulls nearly within striking distance of the rearmost Dwarves, the pursued and their pursuers broke through the smoke to the other side. As they did so, the Dwarves reined in their mounts and spun around in unison to face the Wraulls. Before the Wraulls could register this change, they were running straight into a wall of bristling spears. The foremost were unable to stop in time, and driven on by their brethren behind them, were skewered by the Dwarves.

Amid the shouts and clamoring, the pounding of hoof-beats and the jangling of armor and weapons could be heard. Slicing across the rear of the Wraull attackers, another unit of the Dwarf cavalry struck. Now caught in the middle of two mounted units and cut off from their comrades, the Wraulls were cut to pieces.

Through the smoky haze that now barely covered the land, the remaining Wraulls and Prime Guard now saw the trap the Dwarves had sprung. They rushed to their aid but before they could reach them, Rey'ak archers from high above rained down hundreds of arrows on them. Hundreds fell in the first few moments until at last they sought shelter behind their shields or beneath bulwarks.

In minutes, the Dwarves had cut down the last of the Wraulls that they had lured into their trap. Under cover of the Rey'ak, they returned to the main army, bringing their fallen back with them. They had inflicted serious losses on the Wraulls, killing nearly three hundred of them, but the Dwarves had lost fifty riders themselves.

For the remainder of the day, both sides glared at each other across the bloodied and fire-blackened battlefield. The occasional volley of arrows was bandied back and forth but no other attempts at engagement were tried that day. Rey'ak scouts reported in at regular intervals, giving the Generals Belan and Galani up to date reports on the enemies activities. Early that evening one of the scouts returned with some distressing news for the Dwarves. Catapults had been spotted at the rear of the enemy lines and were now being brought up to the fore.

"We cannot let those catapults reach us," stated Martyl matter-of-factly. "They will hammer our defenses until we are left broken and exposed and then we will be overrun by their superior numbers."

"What do you propose to do to stop them?" asked General Belan, his penetrating gaze fixing on Martyl.

"I will lead a small team on a raid tonight, after midnight. The catapults will be nearly within striking distance of us by then and Prime Guard will be preparing to set them up. They will be busy and not expecting an attack so deep in their ranks. We will strike fast, burning or disabling the catapults then disappear back into the night."

Or so he hoped. Martyl held no self-illusions of his own mortality and knew that this was in all likelihood a suicide mission but he could not ask anyone else to do it nor could they afford to let the catapults be used against them.

General Belan was intrigued but he too knew the risks all too well. "How do you propose to get across their lines undetected? And better yet, how do you plan to return once they have discovered what has been done? Their entire camp will be up in arms!"

"I'll take a small group of volunteers, no more than a half dozen men. We'll leave as soon as its dark, skirt well around their main camp, dispatch any sentries we find quietly then slip into the camp itself. Cloaked and hooded, we should appear like them and they would not expect the enemy to be within their midst. We will rely on stealth and surprise."

"It is extremely dangerous," cut in General Galani, "but I fear we have very little choice in the matter. Unless a patrol of Rey'ak could destroy it with fire arrows?"

"My scouts report that the catapults are heavily armoured," replied Captain Kier'ak. "They would not be able to inflict severe enough damage."

"Could a patrol not fly in and land and destroy them?" asked General Belan.

"They would be spotted as they tried to land. The area around the catapults is well lit. As Martyl has already said, they will not be expecting an attack from within."

"Very well then," acquiesced General Belan reluctantly. "Best of luck to you and your volunteers, Martyl."

"Thank you, General," replied Martyl as he left to find his volunteers. Duncan was at his side immediately, having been nearby during the meeting.

"I'll go with you," he said, not at all surprising Martyl.

"I admire your courage, Duncan," replied Martyl with a smile, "but now is not your time. You must remain protected until it is time to face Draskene. We just cannot risk losing you before then."

He saw the look of hurt cross Duncan's young face and he added, "Too much relies on you, my young friend. I know you don't like others risking so much for you but it has to be so right now."

"And its alright for you to risk yours for the sake of me?"

"It has to be this way."

"Then take this at least," said Duncan, handing Martyl his short magic dagger Sliver. "It's served me well but now I have the Brach'dir. Take it tonight. You may have need of it."

"Very well," replied Martyl with a smile. "But now I must be off. Stay with the others and keep each other safe. I will see you before the dawn."

He turned and left Duncan then, strapping Sliver to his waist and went looking for his volunteers. As he suspected, he did not have to look far. Dirn was there, battle-axe strapped to his back and his face blackened with coal.

"Not thinking of leaving without me, are you?" he said gruffly, a wry smile on his face.

"Never," replied Martyl as Dirn fell in step beside him.

"Two other Dwarves wish to accompany us," began Dirn. "They are good men, both Patrol leaders and veterans of many skirmishes with the Wraulls, and experts at not being seen."

Almost as if on cue, two Dwarves detached themselves from the shadows in the trench and approached Martyl and Dirn. Like Dirn, they were stocky yet powerfully built, their arms and chests knotted with muscles. They wore dark forest cloaks and their faces and hands were colored black with charcoal and grease. Battle-axes were strapped to their broad backs and throwing axes hung from their belts.

"Meet Brawer and Celen."

Martyl shook each Dwarf's rough calloused hand and thanked them for joining him and Dirn. As they talked quietly, two Rey'ak approached and greeted Martyl.

"Captain Kier'ak tells us you require volunteers for a dangerous assignment. May we offer our services? I am R'ev and this is Thel'ove."

Both Rey'ak wore the same dark forest cloaks as the Dwarves, their covered wings giving them the look of misshapen, hunched creatures similar to Wraulls. Their faces and hands too were blackened and their great bows were slung over their shoulders.

"Pleased to meet you," replied Martyl who then introduced the Dwarves. "Well then, if our introductions are complete, we should be under way. We need to disable or better yet, destroy the catapults before they are within firing range."

"Let us lead the way," said R'ev. "I have seen them from the air and our eyesight is better to lead in the dark."

Silently the six slipped away from the Dwarf trenches, heading east for an hour and a half, covering over four miles. At this point they were sufficiently far away from both armies and they turned south towards Arundel.

R'ev and Thel'ove led the way, their keen night vision allowing them to see as if it were dusk, not a cloud covered night. Three different times they came upon Prime Guard sentries, patrolling the area surrounding the army's main encampment. With silent, practiced ease, they snuck up on the unsuspecting guards and quick as cats, slit their throats with their daggers before leading the others on again.

After another hour of sneaking through the shadows and dodging larger patrols of Prime Guards and Wraulls, the small party at last was only a few hundred yards from the enemy's camp. They could see the shadowy forms of their adversaries moving about the tents and camp fires as they scanned for any sign of the catapults.

At last Thel'ove spotted them. "There," he pointed towards the sprawling camp before them. "About a quarter of a mile in from the edge of the camp. They are being rigged for firing now and will be used as soon as it is light out."

"Lead us in," stated Martyl, his voice sure and confident, despite the daunting task that lay before them.

Again the Rey'ak took point as the six crawled slowly across the ground, keeping as low as possible to avoid detection. They were well south of the front line now and the sentries were few and far between, the enemy not expecting to be attacked this deep in its own territory.

The minutes dragged slowly by as they inched forward, ever mindful of being discovered deep in enemy terrain. A loud boom echoed through the still night air and all six froze instantly. Moments later a second boom sounded, followed by the far off flash of lightning. R'ev motioned them forward again as the rain started to fall, realizing it was just thunder.

Soon they were within the boundaries of the camp and they huddled behind a tent, water cascading off their hooded forest cloaks.

"Now," began Martyl, "we need to be quick about this. The rain will aid us in keeping our disguises as everyone will be hooded and cloaked or in their tents to stay dry. We'll split into two teams, one for each catapult, Dirn, R'ev and myself will take the western one while Thel'ove, Brawer and Celen will take the eastern one."

The others nodded their assent as Martyl continued. "We need to destroy the catapults—fire would be best and it is easily accessible with all the camp fires about. If for some reason we can't burn them down, we'll have to disable them as best as possible. When finished, make your way out of the camp as silently and quickly as you can and we will meet up outside. I'm sure R'ev and Thel'ove can find us in the dark. Now best of luck."

The two groups separated and went their own way, snaking through the tents and soldiers, trying to stay away from the fires or anything else that may reveal who they were.

Despite the rain and cool night air, they found themselves sweating with fear and anticipation, adrenaline running high in their veins.

Martyl's group reached their catapult first and they scanned the area quickly. Watch fires burned brightly but all the guards were huddled in their tents, trying to escape the rain. Quick hand signals sent Dirn and R'ev in search of fire wood. Martyl produced four flasks of oil from beneath his cloak and began pouring them about the catapult. Dirn and R'ev appeared again, each carrying a firebrand which they promptly used to set fire to the catapult.

Despite the pouring rain, the oil covered wood and ropes ignited at once and flames leapt up to the sky. Before they could run for cover, a dark form hurtled out of the darkness and crashed into Dirn.

A blood-curdling screech shattered the quiet and at once Martyl knew what it was and why the catapult had no Wraull or Prime Guard sentries. It was a Demon, brought from the netherworld by the Black Paladin. Even the Black Paladin's own troops had no desire to be near such foul creatures.

"Run," commanded Martyl, not looking to see if R'ev listened, his focus solely on the Demon. "Warn the others before its too late. You can't help here." In one quick, fluid motion, he drew Sliver, thankful he had accepted it from Duncan and advanced on the Demon.

The Demon could sense the magic in the blade Martyl wielded and knew he was the more immediate threat. Springing off Dirn with otherworldly quickness, who had dropped his magic mace Dran'spe, it came towards him, misshapen limbs clawing at the air, eerie sounds escaping its gaping maw.

Martyl watched it approach, a thing of the night, like a nightmare come to life. He could tell it had been human once, now made over into something vile and disgusting. The skin was black and oozed an even darker inky substance and hair grew in small, spiky patches. Long crooked claws existed where there were once fingers and long fangs protruded at odd angles from the foaming mouth.

It gathered its muscular legs beneath itself then launched at Martyl, screaming its rage and hatred at him. Martyl waited until the last second then threw himself to the side. He could smell the Demon's foul scent as it hurtled past him and crashed into the ground.

Rolling to its feet, the Demon was up again almost instantly but not before Martyl closed with it. Knowing he had very little time before the rest of the camp was on them, he had to act fast. He threw himself on the Demon, his right hand sweeping out in a vicious slice. The Demon was caught off guard and tried to block the attack with its hands. Sliver easily sliced both off cleanly at the wrist.

Enraged with pain, it screamed its fury at him and rushed again, black ichor oozing from the stumps of its wrists. Before it reached Martyl, two axes flew through the fire-lit night and lodged themselves in its chest.

"Now Martyl!" howled Dirn, back on his feet and joining the fray. "It's stunned, but not for long."

Martyl lunged at the Demon, burying Sliver to the hilt in the Demon's chest. Black ichor spewed from the wound as it sagged to the ground, lifeless.

"We must go!" urged Martyl. "Can you make it?"

"I think so," grunted Dirn, picking up Dran'spe.

They started off towards the other catapult when Prime Guard began running towards them.

"Intruders set the catapult afire!" shouted Martyl as they neared. "We slew one and are pursuing the others. You must put out that fire!"

Thinking they were one of their own, the Prime Guard rushed past them without any questions, eager to stop the raging inferno.

Martyl looked ahead with an eye to the other catapult and saw that it was not burning. "There must have been a Demon there, too," he whispered to Dirn. "Can you make it outside the camp on your own? I'm going to try to disable the other catapult."

"Don't be mad!" exclaimed Dirn.

"I have to. You know that. We can't advance on this position until it is destroyed."

Dirn looked at him for a moment as if to judge his chances of success then said, "Very well. But just see to it you return. I don't want to have to tell Duncan why you didn't make it back with me."

They shook hands and then Dirn limped off while Martyl threaded his way through the dark parts of the camp to the remaining catapult. He moved quickly and silently, Sliver held tightly in his hand in anticipation of what he knew awaited him. All around him, men were shouting in alarm and rushing to the catapult he had already set ablaze.

As Martyl neared his objective, he looked about cautiously. Again, no one guarded this catapult either, at least not openly. Yet he knew another of Draskene's Demons lurked nearby. Peering into the fire-lit darkness, he spied the bodies of Thel'ove, Brawer and Celen, or what was left of them.

They had been ripped to pieces by something entirely inhuman, their blood spilled across the ground and their limbs torn from their bodies. Martyl looked away, his face betraying the utter hatred he felt towards the thing that did this.

Quickly he rushed to his fallen comrades and searched their bodies for the oil they brought with them to incinerate the catapult. Martyl found what he was looking for and began dousing the wood and ropes with it. As he moved about the other side of the catapult, he caught site of a scene that nearly froze the blood in his veins.

Crouched before him was the Demon, holding the arm of one of the Dwarves and gnawing on the bone, the flesh already consumed. Remnants of skin and flesh dangled from the spiky protrusions around its mouth and its maw was coated in blood.

Upon seeing Martyl approach, the hideous creature dropped its meal, fiery red eyes flashing hatred at the man before it. From its crouch, it sprang at Martyl, its jaws opening wide to reveal the razor sharp fangs that had once been human teeth.

As quick as it was, Martyl was quicker, having spent his life honing his fighting skill so that he could one day help Duncan reclaim his throne. The Demon flew through the air at him but just as it was about to reach him, Martyl grabbed its outstretched arms and fell backwards, letting the Demon's momentum propel itself over and past him.

It landed with a crash and as it rolled back to its feet, Martyl leapt onto the back of the Demon. The smell from the creature was fetid and made him want to retch but he kept his bile down long enough to slit its throat from behind with Sliver.

The magic imbued in the blade easily sliced through the muscles and tendons, the Demon's black, putrid blood spilling out. Martyl sprang back instantly. He watched for only a moment to be sure it was dead before grabbing a torch from a nearby fire then using it to set ablaze the catapult.

Without looking back, he ran, mindful now that his escape was not very likely. From out of the darkness, a knot of Wraulls appeared, blocking his path. Martyl had sheathed Sliver now in favor of his broadsword which he had drawn, ready to fight to his death.

The Wraulls growled in response to seeing him and came at him in a rush. Before the first one was ten feet away, it dropped dead, an arrow protruding from its throat. "Run!" cried R'ev from above Martyl.

At this point, all pretext of secrecy was over and it was a mad flight for the safety of the wilderness outside the camp. R'ev was now aloft, his exceptional night vision giving him the aim he needed to clear a path for Martyl.

At last they broke from the camp and into the darkness of the open country. Confusion ran amok in the enemy's camp thanks to R'ev attacking from different areas and they were not pursued.

Slowly now they made their way back, encountering the limping Dirn along the way. His wounds from the Demon were not life-threatening and he assured his friends he would be able to fight again the next day. Determined to make it back to the Dwarf battlements before morning, the three warriors hurried on. Shortly before dawn, the three haggard warriors made it back to the Dwarf camp.

Chapter Thirty-Two

Draskene was absolutely livid with rage and frustration as he watched his catapults and their Demon escorts be destroyed. The scrying crystal crackled with elemental energy as the Black Paladin's anger coursed through him unchecked.

Wrenching his hands free, he screamed his hatred at Martyl, the last of the Royal Knights. His anger still coursed through his veins, causing his magic to rise in ever increasing waves until at last he channeled it together and thrust it from himself. The anger induced magic flew from his hands as a bolt of white-hot energy and crashed into the wall of the scrying chamber. Chunks of stone and mortar blew outwards in the explosion and a great reverberating boom resounded throughout that part of the castle.

With slow, deep breaths, Draskene calmed and composed himself. It would do no good to lose his temper and focus now, he told himself. He needed to focus on what he had left, not what he had lost.

The Dwarves and their allies had been very resourceful the past day but they were still badly outnumbered. And he still had the winter-wolves waiting to be summoned into action. If only he had more Demons at his disposal, though. It bothered Draskene greatly that his Demon familiars, once the bane of all the lands, were now being dispatched almost routinely by Martyl and Duncan and their allies. They possessed only meager magic, but somehow they managed to thwart his plans time and again.

And now that boy, grown to a young man, the last of the line of kings and princes from Arundel, had found the fabled Brach'dir after it had been lost all these centuries.

The closer he came to Arundel, the stronger Draskene could feel its intrusion on his magic. He knew it had the power to destroy him, if it's wielder was strong enough in mind and spirit to master it. And that was the unknown—did Duncan possess the strength required to successfully wield the Brach'dir?

As his army continued to take losses, he wondered if he would indeed come face to face with Duncan and the sword. It he did, he would make that boy rue the day he was born for daring to face him!

Gathering his robes about himself and drawing them tight, Draskene stalked from his scrying chamber and went in search of his most trusted and valued aid.

He found Bin where he was most often, in his stables with his animal familiars. Bin sensed his master's arrival, and mood, before he even heard him and was at the door to greet him.

"Yes master?" he asked, head bowed.

"Ready the winter-wolves. They are to be used today. Send word to the army commanders of how and when they are to be deployed." He slipped Bin the orders written on a piece of paper rolled into a carrying tube.

"As you wish," replied Bin.

As quickly and silently as he arrived, Draskene was gone again, not needing to wait around to see if his orders were understood or carried out. Bin knew almost instinctively what was to be done and did it. He attached the tube to the collar of a winter wolf in the stable, whispered words of encouragement in its ear then watched as it streaked away with the coming dawn.

◆   ◆   ◆

The sky was still dark with the arrival of morning. Storm clouds hung like giant black birds, drifting lazily over the land. All through the trenches the Dwarves scurried like busy ants, preparing for the battle that was soon to arrive.

"Duncan, its time to get up,"

Martyl, having only rested a few hours himself after returning from last night's raid was already prepared and was now trying to awaken Duncan to do the same. At his side, as always, slept Big Cat, who lifted her head to watch him approach.

"You made it back safely!" replied Duncan, a wide smile spreading across his youthful face upon seeing his old friend safely returned.

"Yes, and with no small thanks from your blade Sliver. It saved me from two Demons."

Duncan looked at Martyl in surprise as the older man continued.

"I'm sure there will be more waiting as we approach the castle. Today is the day, my young friend. All we have trained and fought for will be put to the test."

"I'm ready," replied Duncan as he strapped Brach'dir to his side and pulled on a chain mail shirt.

The others of their small group were up now, eating quickly and donning their short swords and armour, except Ar'ye. Like the other Rey'ak, he eschewed heavy, confining armour in favor of keeping his wings free to allow him to fly which was his best defense.

"Reyna, Salena," began Martyl as he saw them approach, both wearing chain mail shirts, shields and swords.

"Don't bother, Martyl," cut in Reyna. "I don't want to hear it. We are as much a part of this fight as you and the others. I know you have sworn oaths to protect the weak and innocent but Salena and I are not weak." She was holding Salena's hand in hers, standing just in front of her, protectively as a mother would her child. "We've been training with the Dwarves and we're prepared. We will not be left behind. Our fates are as yours."

Martyl watched as Reyna stared at him, daring him to say otherwise, to refuse their request to join them in battle. Instead, he closed his eyes slowly, as if in sadness and when he reopened them a moment later he said, "Very well. Your place will be with us."

Addressing everyone this time he said, "Today we launch an assault on the Black Paladin's forces. It must be done now, before more Wraulls arrive from the north east and cut off our retreat or before more siege weapons can be brought out of Arundel to assail us. The six of us will remain together on horseback and follow after the main assault. Our goal is to reach the castle and confront Draskene. Only with his defeat can victory be truly achieved."

The other five nodded their understanding, fear and uncertainty showing on everyone's face except Dirn who was a seasoned warrior.

"Very well," concluded Martyl. "Mount up. Wait for my signal then follow me, staying together."

Dwarf runners scurried up and down the length of the trenches, carrying their commanders' orders, informing the troops of their plans. At that predetermined time, the signal was given. The entire attack force of the Dwarves and their allies sprang forth and launched their final offensive.

Like a great dark cloud rising from the ground, the Rey'ak, one thousand strong, rose aloft as one. Their exceptionally keen eyesight and long bows were ready to clear a path for those on the ground. The beat of their wings echoed in the stormy sky like distant thunder. Their battle cry, "Ra'ak" was even louder.

On the ground below, the Dwarven cavalry was out of the trenches first, a little over eight hundred after losing men and ponies the day before. Their battle standards, white-capped mountains with a bright orange sun emblazoned on a blue background, fluttered in the wind as they galloped forward.

Behind them followed the foot soldiers, all five thousand Dwarves and five hundred renegades. Their battle cry, "Bray'la" could be heard easily by the enemy as they chanted during their march.

Bringing up the rear, and not happy in the least to be doing so, were Duncan and Martyl and the others of their small company. All were astride the horses they had brought from Equilon, except Salena who had been given a roan named Sprite by the Dwarves. Even Ar'ye was mounted, preferring to save his strength until it was needed.

Duncan again did not like the fact that others were putting themselves in danger for his sake but he knew that Martyl was right. No one else could wield the Brach'dir and face Draskene but him. It was up to himself to see that he did so and succeeded.

The Rey'ak archers opened fire and a hail of deadly missiles rained down on the Wraulls and Prime Guard below. They ducked beneath their shields and whatever other cover they could find. Still they fell by the scores, some dead, some wounded, their cries of pain and anger filling the morning air.

From under cover of the deadly barrage the Dwarven cavalry struck. Eight hundred strong, they barreled into the enemy before them. Sweeping across their eastern flank, they raked the Wraulls and Prime Guard with lance and pike, skewering hundreds. Down the line of soldiers they tore, trampling any who did not fall to the weapons. The Dwarf captains signaled the cavalry to turn and reform and begin a second strike.

Draskene's forces had recovered from the shock of the initial attack and had now formed up ranks, heavy pike-men braced for the rush at the fore. Archers took up positions behind the front line and readied their bows. As the Dwarves came on in a rush, a hail of arrows sped through the early morning sky seeking their targets.

Dwarves and ponies fell by the dozens but on they raced, lances and pikes lowered. The Rey'ak were now targeting the Black Paladin's archers, trying to keep the Dwarves from getting cut to pieces. The second rush of the Dwarven cavalry hit the line of defenders and pushed through, the sturdy ponies brushing past the Wraulls and Prime Guard before them.

Like a monstrous beast ripping at the flesh of its prey, the Dwarf cavalry bit into the Black Paladin's army as it withdrew, then turned and drew a large number of defenders after it. The enraged Wraulls pursued the fleeing cavalry away from the main body of the army until it was several hundred yards away. The Dwarves drew their mounts into a tight circle, effectively closing off the Wraulls from their allies. A hundred Rey'ak flew overhead and released volley after volley of arrows until not a single Wraull was left alive.

By now the main force of the Dwarven army was nearing the battle-field. The cavalry had gone out first to weaken Draskene's forces and now the foot soldiers would join the fray. Still on the minds of the commanders was the fact that the Black Paladin's cavalry had not yet been spied. They knew it to be large and formidable and fully expected it to be in effect by now. The fact that it wasn't had them feeling uneasy but there was no help for it.

Covered in heavy chain mail from head to foot and armed with battle-axes and large maces, the Dwarves marched on, covering the distance between the two armies relatively quickly, despite their encumbrances. The Renegades from Gull Haven marched side by side with them, their forces integrated as one. As their battle cry, "Bray'la" rang out over the clash of weapons and armor, another sound emerged. A distant horn blew followed by the echoing thunder of thousands of hooves.

From the forests south of the battlefield, thousands of the Black Paladin's cavalry burst forth to the cheers of the Wraulls and Prime Guard under attack. They had remained hidden beneath the cover of the thick foliage for weeks now in anticipation of a Dwarf attack. Once Draskene had become aware of the Dwarves and Rey'ak joining forces, he was cognizant of the fact that an aerial assault by the Rey'ak would be devastating to his cavalry, so he had his commanders sequester the cavalry in the forest weeks in advance to keep them hidden from Rey'ak scouts and protected until called upon, which was now.

Like a black tidal wave, the Black Paladin's cavalry spread across the plain, forming into tight units that raced towards the Dwarves on foot. The Rey'ak gave warning and began raking the advancing horsemen with a blinding hail of arrows. Several hundred horses and riders fell, their screams of agony adding to those already injured and maimed on the battlefield.

The Dwarven cavalry turned to meet this new menace, abandoning the Wraulls and Prime Guard on foot to go to the aid of their own foot soldiers. They galloped towards the Black Paladin's cavalry, lances and spears leveled to meet the rush. Moments later, the two mounted forces struck head-on.

Weapons clashed and men and horses alike screamed in pain as steel skewered flesh. The Dwarves and their ponies, as stout as they were, were no match for the Black Paladin's war horses. Their immense size and weight carried them right through the Dwarves and their ponies, brushing them aside like bothersome gnats. Badly outnumbered and outsized, the order was given and the Dwarves fell back to form up ranks near their own soldiers.

They turned to retreat but their ponies were just not fast enough and the war horses chased them down with ease, their riders attacking the Dwarves from behind.

Seeing their allies being systematically hunted down, a unit of Rey'ak staged a daring rescue. They fired the last of their arrows in a deadly barrage at the foremost of Draskene's horsemen. Dozens fell but the massive war horses still came, their riders determined to be rid of the Dwarves ability to harry their soldiers from horseback.

A single cry split through the noise and tumult on the ground as Captain Kier'ak dove at the leading horseman. Out of arrows, he had two large, wickedly curved daggers drawn as he swept down upon the rider like a giant bird of prey. His fellow Rey'ak also out of arrows, followed his lead and began diving from the sky at the mounted soldiers, daggers slicing and cutting.

The Prime Guard fought back but they could not effectively watch the sky and the ground beneath them at the same time. Scores of riders and mounts fell before the order was given to abandon pursuit of the Dwarves.

As the Prime Guard wheeled off in the opposite direction, the Rey'ak left them to escort the Dwarves back to their own forces.

With the Dwarf cavalry attacking the eastern flank of Draskene's forces and the army attacking from the north, Martyl led his small band to the west, hoping to avoid any major engagements. The six riders and one cat raced out of the trenches once the foot soldiers were away and drawing attention away from themselves.

As they were only six and moving away from the battle, no one paid them any attention as they galloped across the plains towards Arundel. In the distance to the south the castle rose up above the forest that surrounded it like a gigantic monument. The stone-gray blocks and mortar looked cold and forbidding in the overcast light of the day. Martyl led them away from the forces at war on the plains and towards the forest. They kept close to the eaves of the wood, staying in the shadows to minimize their chances of being seen. At his side rode Reyna, followed by Duncan and Selena while Dirn and Ar'ye brought up the rear. Big Cat kept pace with the horses and stayed at Duncan's side, keeping close watch on her human.

They traveled unchecked for nearly a league before they encountered trouble. From out of the underbrush rushed ten winter-wolves, teeth gnashing in anticipation as they spied the small group. Draskene knew that Martyl would not endanger Duncan in the main battle but would instead try to sneak into Arundel with him. To prevent this, he had the wolves patrolling the forests, waiting.

As they leapt from the cover of the trees, Big Cat was there at once to meet them, her feline senses preventing any kind of surprise attack. With teeth and claws bared, she struck the first wolf to appear. They went down in a tangle of fur and teeth, snarls and yelps.

Duncan wheeled his horse about, heedless of any danger to himself, anxious to save his cat. By the time he reached her, only moments later, two of the huge winter-wolves lay dead, crimson blood streaked across their snow white fur.

As enraged as they were, the wolves were wary of Big Cat after seeing two of their pack cut down with such ease. They circled her, feinting attacks, looking for an opening in her lightening quick feline defenses.

Duncan screamed at the winter-wolves in rage and defiance as he saw them circling his beloved cat. Two broke from the circle but were felled in their tracks as Ar'ye let loose his arrows from just behind Duncan. Big Cat leapt at the wolf that moved in to close the gap created by his dead pack members, sinking her teeth into his large neck. A geyser of red shot forth as she tore out its throat.

With half of their pack now dead, the wolves howled in frustration and came after Duncan and Big Cat. From out of nowhere, Dirn, astride his pony, caromed into the wolves, scattering them.

"Go!" he shouted at Duncan, wheeling his mount around to face the wolves yet again. "You must reach the castle and Draskene! Go!"

He was swinging his new found mace, Dran'spe, wildly, keeping the snapping jaws of the wolves at bay.

"He's right Duncan. We have to go!" It was Martyl urging him on now, with Selena and Reyna with him. Martyl grabbed his arm and spurred his horse on, forcing Duncan to follow.

"We all knew the price that may be exacted this day," said Martyl sternly as they galloped on. "Don't let Dirn's sacrifice be in vain."

◆   ◆   ◆

The Dwarf cavalry, recovered from their rout by the Prime Guard, reformed when they reached their own forces. The Dwarf numbers, both cavalry and foot soldier, were drastically cut, the battle and subsequent retreat having claimed nearly a thousand lives at this point.

General Belan called his commanders to his side and issued his next orders for attack while the Rey'ak archers kept the Black Paladin's forces from rushing them. The cavalry was to form up into a wedge shape with the foot soldiers behind and inside the wall of horses. They would surge forward into the wall of Wraulls and Prime Guard, splitting their enemy's forces apart, allowing the Dwarf soldiers to emerge from the cover of the cavalry and strike at their disoriented enemy. The Rey'ak would provide cover fire for the advancing cavalry then join in the hand to hand battle once their ordnance was exhausted.

This was to be a final, massive assault aimed at breaking Draskene's forces. They had still not heard from Martyl or Duncan of their success or failure but they had to press on and see that they got the chance to face Draskene. Both sides were taking heavy losses but the battle would never truly be over as long as Draskene himself still lived.

The signal was given and the cavalry burst forth, pikes, lances and spears held tight, pointing straight at the enemy. A wave of blue clad riders surged across the battlefield, the thunder of their ponies iron shod hooves echoing in the damp morning air.

They closed the gap between themselves and the Black Paladin's forces, all the while the Rey'ak kept their enemy pinned down with a barrage of arrows from above. Like waves crashing on a sandy beach, the Dwarves washed over the Wraulls and Prime Guard before them, trampling and skewering any opposition. The armoured, barrel-chested war ponies knocked aside enemy soldiers while the riders hewed with their battle axes.

After the initial assault, the cavalry turned to its right and headed away from the main battle forces, drawing with it the mass of enemy soldiers that were separated from the main army. Quickly, the mounted Dwarves formed a closed circle about their enemy, effectively cutting them off from retreat or help. As their battle cry "Bray' la" rang out, the Dwarves drew their circle tighter and began eliminating their foes within.

The Dwarf foot soldiers were now deep into the battle, having been left in place while the cavalry lured off a large section of the enemy's forces. Many of the Rey'ak were now at their side, short swords and long knives drawn, their arrows long since expended.

Wraull and human bodies littered the ground in the thousands, as well as Dwarf and Rey'ak bodies. The battle was fierce and bloody, both sides determined to see an end to their enemies and this feud once and for all. The sounds of steel striking steel rang out as weapons clashed but louder yet were the cries of injured and dying soldiers as they screamed in pain.

Despite being outnumbered, the Dwarves and Rey'ak were actually holding their own and even beginning to overtake their enemies in some pockets of the battlefield until the Prime Guard's cavalry rejoined the fray.

From out of the rear ranks of Draskene's army, the cavalry issued forth, horns blaring as they galloped to the fore. They swept past the outer edge of the battle, striking at the exposed flanks of the Dwarves and Rey'ak, raking them with their lances. The Dwarven cavalry, finished decimating the Wraulls and Prime Guard they had severed from the main army, turned to face the Prime Guard cavalry again.

As valiant and determined as they were the Dwarves and their ponies were no match for the Prime Guard and their horses. Their lines were broken and scattered and they were systematically hunted down in groups and alone.

The Wraull and Prime Guard soldiers, seeing this, gained a new measure of strength and fought back with renewed determination against the Dwarves and Rey'ak. Sensing the rout that was about to take place, Captain Kier'ak called as many Rey'ak to himself as he could and took flight.

Their enemies cheered in delight as they watched the several hundred bird men flee. They surged forward, pressing in on the Dwarves who were forced to fall back into a defensive position. Unknown to the enemy, however, was the fact that the Dwarves and Rey'ak had planned for the Prime Guard cavalry to return and this was their contingency plan for that moment.

Like a deadly black cloud, the Rey'ak swept out of the sky and into the startled cavalry, wickedly serrated long knives slicing unprotected throats. Although vastly outnumbered, the Rey'ak had the element of surprise and the advantage of the air. The Dwarven riders, no longer being chased and harried by the larger war horses, turned, regrouped and charged into their enemy. Screams from men and horses rent the air as both sides collided.

The five riders and one cat raced towards the castle, its gray stone and mortar walls looming up out of the overcast day to greet them. As they neared, the iron gates barring their entrance swung open and out rode a dozen Prime Guard, none other than Draskene's personal body guards.

Like a dark cloud issuing forth, the black and scarlet clad riders spurred their ebony stallions on towards the small party.

Martyl saw them coming and felt his heart sink. They had come so far but twelve of Draskene's best horsemen were approaching and he didn't think the five of them would get through unscathed. Still, if at least Duncan made it to face Draskene it would all have been worth it. Glancing to his left where Duncan rode alongside him, Martyl yelled above the wind rushing past them, "Fall back, Duncan. We cannot afford to lose you now, we are too close."

Duncan's face relayed his response before the words could form on his tongue and Martyl continued, "Do not argue. If you cannot face Draskene, all of this is for not. Now do as I ask—you know I'm right."

Duncan felt his throat tighten as he realized the sacrifice his oldest friend was about to give. He hated that the others were risking their lives for him but he knew as well that it had to be so. More than just their lives depended on his facing and defeating the Black Paladin. The entire races of the Dwarves and Rey'ak and men would be defeated and enslaved if Draskene was not defeated. Again he felt the burden he carried like a massive weight about to suffocate him.

"You know he's right, Duncan." He turned to see Salena, tears running down her beautiful face. "You have to do this, for everyone. I'll be alright with Martyl. Go."

Ar'ye gave him a quick, tight smile before turning away while Reyna said, "Your family would be proud of you, just as your friends are. Now go, you must do as Martyl asks."

He took a deep, steadying breath before wheeling his horse away from the others, grateful none of them looked back to see the sheen of moisture that covered his eyes.

Ever faithful, Big Cat immediately left the others to stay by Duncan's side as the remaining four riders spurred their mounts on to face the Prime Guard, outnumbered three to one. Unable to look away, Duncan watched his friends ride to their doom as he circled around to avoid the Prime Guard.

Reyna was the first to reach the enemy, easily outdistancing Martyl, Salena and Ar'ye. She rode fearlessly towards the foremost rider who already had his spear at the ready, preparing to skewer her as she approached.

Just before she was within striking range, Reyna ducked low and slid over the opposite side of Wind Dancer, her arms wrapped tightly about her neck. The Prime Guard's spear pierced nothing but air as he rushed past. At the same time, Reyna was already back in the saddle and reining Wind Dancer about.

There was no rider alive who could match her prowess on horseback and she showed it now, coming up on her attacker before he could turn his mount and with one sure slice of her short sword severed his spine in one stroke.

Ar'ye had his bow out now and loosed a hail of arrows into the approaching riders. Three riders dropped but the other eight still came on and his quiver was now empty.

Like a man possessed, Martyl rode into the oncoming enemy, sword raised, yelling, "Arundel!" Reyna and Salena flanked him and Ar'ye covered his back as the four rode in diamond formation.

Even at a distance, Duncan could hear Martyl and he was proud to have been friends with someone so noble and brave. Unable to bear anymore, he looked away as he heard the clash of weapons and saw his friends surrounded. Cries of anger and fear and screams of pain assaulted his ears as he spurred his horse towards his destiny.

They waited in the darkened shadows, red eyes slitted to hide their gleam as they awaited their prey. Their misshapen limbs, corded with muscle, and covered in black, bristling hair, tensed in anticipation. This is what their master created them for—perfect killing machines that would stop Duncan before he reached Draskene.

With blood-curdling screams, they leapt from their places of concealment as Duncan rode up to the castle gates. The Demons worked in unison, both going for the horse itself, knocking it down, ensuring Duncan would have to stay and fight.

Roper went down with barely a sound, the Demons striking hard and fast, teeth and claws tearing away his throat. The big roan lay on the wet earth, legs twitching feebly as his life blood seeped into the ground.

Duncan lay pinned beneath Roper, his left leg trapped beneath the horse's bulk. Luckily the ground was soft enough from the rain that no bones were broken and he was able to wiggle about. Within a few moments he should be able to pull himself free, he thought, but overwhelming fear gripped him as he saw the two man-shaped Demons rise from the ground and approach him.

Duncan struggled furiously now, intent on getting himself extricated before the Demons reached him, when an earsplitting growl sounded from behind him.

It was Big Cat, her orange, black and white fur bristling in anger, her ears back in warning. The Demons paused for a moment, instinctively knowing that the large cat would be a formidable opponent but their master had commanded them to kill Duncan and his friends and they would do just that.

They crept closer, their once human bodies bent, twisted and broken into a sad parody of humanity. Without warning, Big Cat leapt at the closest of the two, knocking the Demon to the ground, teeth and claws ripping through the tough skin and coarse hair as if they were paper.

Adrenaline surged through Duncan as he watched helplessly as Big Cat was about to give her life to save him, just as Patches had done weeks ago on the Fire Wind Flats. He struggled furiously to get free of Roper, the horse's dead body keeping him from joining his cat.

Snarls and screams shattered the air about him as Big Cat fought the two Demons. Duncan had seen Patches defeat Raydon months ago but here it was two against one and she was tired from keeping pace with the horses and battling winter-wolves up to this point. He feared that this time may prove to be too much for his beloved feline, knowing she would not give up until either she or the Demons were dead, that Big Cat would defend him to the death.

With a final push with his free leg, Duncan rolled free of Roper and staggered wearily to his feet.

The Demons paid him no attention, caught up in their fight with Big Cat. All three combatants were bloodied and battered, but despite being tired and outnumbered, Big Cat was getting the better of them, her need to protect her human stronger than their desire to kill him.

Fearing for Big Cat, Duncan rushed to help her, Brach'dir raised before him, heedless of his own safety.

Sensing more than seeing him, the Demons broke off their attack on Big Cat and went after their intended quarry.

Still on the run, Duncan did not slow at their approach, but instead kept running. At the last moment, he swung his sword at the approaching Demons, striking the one nearest him.

This was the first time Duncan had tested the magic of the sword. He did not have to think about how he would call its power forth or what it would even do. He just acted, purely on instinct, desperate to save Big Cat and himself.

The Brach'dir answered his silent plea and as it had countless times in the past for his forebearers, the sword flared to life in Duncan's hands. It pulsed as if a thing of flesh and blood and began forming a symbiosis with him, drawing from his strength the power it needed to battle the Demons.

The sword penetrated the Demon's tough, leathery hide with ease, the blade razor sharp still, after more than a millennia had passed, its magic still strong. A moment later, the Demon lay cleaved in half at

Duncan's feet, its black blood soaking into the ground, its foul stench filling the air.

Still possessed of the sword's magic, Duncan ran on to the second Demon, only to find it too dead, its throat jagged and torn and Big Cat standing over its lifeless body.

Draskene was in his personal stables when he first felt the stirring of the sword's magic. Just as he knew when the sword had been found, he could feel its use, and this time it was much stronger.

"So the boy had used the sword at last," he said to his giant steed Night as he saddled him. "We shall see if he has what it takes to face me, the true master of this kingdom, and not just a couple of feeble Demons I summoned forth!"

Jets of red-hot steam punctuated the cool stable air as Night snorted his agreement. Draskene vaulted atop his hell-horse and charged forth from his stable. They tore across the castle courtyard, no one in their way as all the troops were now engaged in the battle with the Dwarves and Rey'ak. Only Bin remained to look after the castle. This was how Draskene wanted it, to face Aramid's son alone, and crush the last of the line of rulers once and for all. For months now this young upstart and his band of misfits had caused Draskene considerable grief. Now he would get his revenge.

Moments later, he saw his intended quarry, sword raised and staring straight at him. Foolish boy, thought Draskene as he barreled towards Duncan, he's going to make this easier than I thought. He spurred Night on, fully intending to run Duncan into the ground. Sparks and small flames leapt from the big horse's hooves and smoke rolled from his nostrils. The hell-horse had his head down and was set to charge right into Duncan when Big Cat leapt from out of the shadows and caromed into Night.

With a bone-jarring crunch, Big Cat crashed into the side of Night. Thirty pounds of hissing, snarling, clawing enraged cat driving into it at top speed was more than enough to shock even a hell-horse.

Night was driven off course and Duncan was able to roll aside and avoid being trampled.

Sensing Duncan's agitation, fear and excitement, Big Cat knew this was the fight they had come looking for and she was not about to let her human down. She launched herself a second time at the massive horse, landing on the side of his gigantic neck. She locked her front claws around the horse's neck and began raking furiously with her rear legs. Opening her jaws wide, she sank them deep into Night's throat, locking onto his windpipe and squeezing as hard as she could.

Draskene knew his Demon steed was in trouble but he had problems of his own, now that Duncan was back on his feet and advancing on him. As much as he hated to lose such a fine steed from the netherworld, he knew he could always summon another, once Duncan was dealt with.

With practiced ease, he vaulted from atop Night and landed only yards from Duncan.

"You shouldn't have come back, boy," taunted Draskene, raising his hands to attack.

Anger flashed across Duncan's face but before he could reply, bolts of red fire lanced from Draskene's fingertips towards him. Acting purely on instinct, he raised the Brach'dir. The bolts of magic fire were attracted to the sword and it dissipated them into the air around Duncan but Draskene kept hammering at him and it was all he could do to hold his ground.

"I'm going to enjoy killing you," continued Draskene, closing the distance between them, the fire coming faster and harder now, driving Duncan to his knees, the Brach'dir held before him like a talisman, trying to ward off evil. The sword was trying to draw the power it required from Duncan but he was not giving into it fully. Part of him was still reticent and unsure, putting up barriers inside himself, preventing the sword from allowing the two of them to reach their combined potential.

"You've caused me a great deal of grief in a short period of time and now you're going to pay dearly for it."

Duncan's strength was failing, Draskene's command of his own magic too much for him to withstand. He struggled to get back to his feet and mount some kind of defense but he couldn't. It was all he could do to keep his sword up and ward off Draskene's attack. Draskene poured on his assault with his left hand and reached for Aramid's sword with his right. He felt it would serve this young upstart fine to die by his father's sword!

When he was about to succumb at last, it was Big Cat who saved him one last time. She hurtled into Draskene, having finally dispatched his hell-horse and caught him off guard. She drew first blood, ripping open his side from his shoulder to his waist but it wasn't enough to stop him. With an angry roar, Draskene turned his attention from Duncan long enough to launch an attack on Big Cat.

The red fire bolts caught her in mid-air as she was making another leap. Big Cat went down without a sound, her fur smoking and burned.

When Duncan saw that, something inside him snapped, like a barrier giving way beneath too much weight. Draskene had been responsible for the deaths of his family and friends and all he had left was Big Cat and now he had killed her, right before his eyes! A fury like he had never known before burst forth and consumed him. The sword drew on the new wave of power it was fed from Duncan and came to life.

"NO!" he screamed as he saw Big Cat's still body smoldering in the cool mid-morning air. "I'll kill you!" he cried out at Draskene, the rage he was feeling now propelling him to his feet. All sense of self-preservation and even who he was and what he as supposed to do vanished as Duncan was filled overwhelming hatred for Draskene.

Draskene saw the look in Duncan's eye at that moment and realized that quite possibly he may have underestimated his young adversary. He continued to shoot fire bolts at Duncan but he no longer had him pinned down. In fact, Duncan was advancing towards him, sword held forth and ready to attack. With one last effort, Draskene poured the last of his strength into his magic, hoping to get past Duncan's defenses.

It was not enough. Duncan approached to within a foot of Draskene, the fire radiating about the two of them as the sword dispersed it away from Duncan.

"You've taken everything from me, you bastard," spat Duncan, staring his life-long adversary in the eye with cold hatred. "Now reap your reward!"

With all his strength and years of pent-up hatred, Duncan swung the mighty Brach'dir at his opponent. The sword, fueled by Duncan's raging emotions, ripped through Draskene's protective magic. With a scream, Draskene fell to the ground, his life-blood quickly pooling on the ground around him. His magic sputtered and flared then dried out as he at last died.

Duncan stood there a moment, dumbfounded, at a loss for what to do, as the realization that his life-long enemy was dead. So many had given their lives for him to get here, now what did he do? He had planned only so far as the defeat of Draskene. He never gave any thought to what he would after that time. Then he remembered Big Cat. Quickly he ran to where she had fallen and knelt beside her. He knew that Martyl, Salena, Reyna and Ar'ye were most likely dead, having given their lives for him to get past the last of the Prime Guard and he was heartsick over that but he had seen Big Cat killed right before his eyes. That was harder to take.

Gingerly, he stroked her head, his eyes filling with tears. He fought to hold them back, even though no one was around to see, determined to be strong no matter what.

Tired from his battle, Duncan sat on the ground and cradled Big Cat's head in his lap, still stroking her fur when he was startled to hear purring!

"You're alive!" exclaimed Duncan, unable to hide his emotion. Big Cat continued to purr and slowly got to her feet and began cleaning her wounds when she looked back out towards the castle gates.

Fearing that the Prime Guard had returned, Duncan wearily rose to his feet and turned to face them, sword at the ready. What he saw brought the biggest smile of his life to his face.

Although bloodied and battered, his friends were all there, Martyl, Salena, Reyna, Ar'ye and even Dirn, survivors to the end like himself. Salena was off her horse first and running to greet him, her arms wide open.

They embraced and kissed quickly before the others dismounted and congratulated Duncan.

"Your father would be proud, Duncan," said Martyl, hugging him close. "As am I. You will make a fine ruler of Arundel."

"Thank you," replied Duncan, before he sat back down, exhaustion now taking hold of him.

As they all gathered round and listened to Duncan relate his final battle, no one saw the dark-robed figure slip from the castle and into the surrounding countryside.

◆　　◆　　◆

When Draskene had been killed, his control over his soldiers vanished and most surrendered on the spot. Those who did not, continued to fight but were soon defeated by the Dwarves and Rey'ak. The Wraulls, seeing that the Prime Guard had either given up fighting or were being systematically eliminated, broke ranks and raced back to the Fire Wind Flats, harried all the way by the Dwarves and Rey'ak.

In the days following, the dead bodies were buried or burnt on giant funeral pyres to prevent the scavengers from desecrating them. For days a thick smoke hovered over the battle field and the stench of burning flesh could be smelled for miles around.

When the battle field was cleared and the surrounding countryside checked for straggling Wraulls a week later, Duncan had his coronation ceremony. Salena's father, King Kestewan came from the Misty Isles to give his blessings to Duncan and Salena and to open trade negotiations between Arundel and the Misty Isles. Both the Dwarves and Rey'ak sent emissaries to relate their respective King's best wishes and pacts of allegiance.

Ar'ye and Dirn stayed for weeks afterwards as emissaries of their peoples but after Duncan and Salena's wedding, they too returned home. Reyna and Martyl stayed as Royal advisors and married a few weeks later.

Months later, when all matters of the state were looked after, Duncan saw to the completion of a memorial for his parents. Their bodies were never found but a memorial garden was created in their honour. Next to the monument for his parents was a special memorial built for Patches.

With Big Cat and Salena as his side, Duncan watched the sun set over the garden and the headstones placed there in his parents' honour. For the first time since he was a boy, a tear rolled freely down his cheek.

978-0-595-46057-
0-595-46057-7

Lightning Source UK Ltd.
Milton Keynes UK
UKHW040614111119
353299UK00004B/38/P